SMOKE

AN IQ NOVEL

SMOKE

JOE IDE

THORNDIKE PRESS
A part of Gale, a Cengage Company

Copyright © 2021 by Joe Ide.
Thorndike Press, a part of Gale, a Cengage Company.

LIBRARY OF CONGRESS CIP DATA ON FILE.
CATALOGUING IN PUBLICATION FOR THIS BOOK
IS AVAILABLE FROM THE LIBRARY OF CONGRESS.

ISBN-13: 978-1-4328-9263-0 (hardcover alk. paper)

Published in 2021 by arrangement with Little, Brown and Company

Printed in Mexico
Print Number: 01   Print Year: 2022

To Thierno Diallo
for rescuing me from myself

I to my perils
Of cheat and charmer
Came clad in armor
By stars benign
Hope lies to mortals
And most believe her
But Man's deceiver
Was never mine.

The thoughts of others
Were light and fleeting,
Of lovers' meeting
Or luck or fame.
But mine were of trouble,
And mine were steady,
So I was ready
When trouble came.

                    A. E. Housman

PROLOGUE

Land Park was an upscale neighborhood in Sacramento. It was a serene area, lush, mature trees, green spaces and a jewel of a lake. The houses were expensive, with wide lawns, manicured gardens, luxury cars in the driveways. Nobody was at home at 344 Laurel Drive, a charming two-story traditional. The owner of the house, Dr. Greg Crocker, was an MD who'd made a career out of writing Oxy, fentanyl and Dilaudid prescriptions to anyone who claimed to have pain. Crocker and several cooperating pharmacists illegally dispensed thousands of pills. They were busted in a sting operation. Crocker served sixty months of a seventy-two-month sentence and was currently on parole. At the moment, he was doing his community service time at the free clinic over in Placer. His wife, Lulu, who wore her Fendi tobacco and black 100 percent mink coat whenever the temperature dropped below sixty degrees, was reduced to hawking overpriced makeup at Macy's. The house was up for sale.

Harrison Pearce had informed Crowe about all this and much more. Pearce had been there several times on unannounced visits. He knew the layout of the house and the alarm code, and he'd given Crowe a key to the back door. As part of his restitution, Crocker paid the state a high seven-figure fine, lost most of his possessions, and had to sell the house. But hidden away were Lu-lu's Fendi, a real Chagall, a seven-hundred-year-old samurai sword, a 1919 D Walking Liberty half-dollar worth nearly two hundred grand and a stamp collection worth double that. Crowe found them all, he was good at that. He wouldn't tell Pearce about the haul. This time he'd keep everything. He kicked the door down from the outside, setting off the alarm and left.

The California Department of Probation and Parole was housed in a beige, feature-less office building near the Capitol State Building. Crowe sat in reception, thinking, this is the last time. Crowe was on parole, not probation. People got the two mixed up. Probation was part of a sentence, an alternative to jail time. Serving, say, ninety days of supervised freedom for a first-time

B&E instead of thirty days in jail. Parole was early release, a privilege that came with conditions because you were still the property of the California Department of Corrections. Things like regular meetings, urine tests, mandatory employment, an ankle monitor, restricted movement, no intoxicants or guns, and no hanging around with your fellow felons. Break the conditions, and you served out the rest of your sentence plus a little extra for being stupid.

Harrison Pearce was a devious, pockmarked, midlife asshole who wore short-sleeve white shirts and cheap ties. He had a creepy, self-satisfied smirk, like he'd peeked through a hole and saw you boning your aunt. That Crowe was a suspected serial killer amused him.

"I've seen all types of criminals," Pearce said. Whenever he talked to Crowe he leaned back in his chair with his hands behind his head, his feet up on the desk. "And you're not the type."

"Then what type am I?" Crowe asked.

"An ordinary thug. AMSAK is smart, clever, thinks ahead, and that's definitely not you." Pearce gave Crowe info about rich parolees like the Crockers. Crowe would break in and steal the valuables. Pearce would sell the loot and give Crowe a commission, never more than a few hundred dollars. If Crowe didn't play along, he'd go back to the joint.

"The Crocker job is done," Crowe said as he sat down.

"Good. I want to talk about the next job. Should be a good one."

"Hold on. I want to talk about something else."

Pearce huffed. "Sorry, my friend. I set the agenda here and I said we're going to talk about —" It took a moment for Pearce to recognize his own voice. Crowe had his phone out and was playing a taped conversation.

"I'm running the show, okay?" Pearce said on the recording. "You get what I pay you and nothing more, is that understood?" There were more clips of Pearce specifying names and dates and giving instructions about who to rob, how and when. Pearce put his feet down and cleared his throat. He shook his head sympathetically, like this was a big mistake.

"That was not a smart thing to do, my friend. I've dealt with a lot of jokers like you who think they can —"

"Shut up," Crowe growled. "And if you call me friend again, I'll tie you to that chair and beat you to death." Pearce was the color of cornstarch.

"You're the one who committed the robberies," Pearce said, his voice rising. "Turn me in and you'll get charged with all of them."

"I was under duress. You weren't. You're a trusted employee of the government. If this comes out your whole life will turn to shit. Do I have to tell you about what happens to assholes like you in the joint?"

Pearce started to push back but deflated. "No, I guess you don't." Circles of sweat had appeared under his armpits. His tie looked too tight and his shirt looked too big.

Crowe said, "To the outside world, we're exactly the way we are. Case officer and parolee. The terms of parole are the same on paper but now on I do what I want. As for the robberies? Starting today, you're doing them."

"What?" Pearce said. He looked like he'd swallowed a spider or a spoiled egg.

"I'll sell the loot myself to the people I know," Crowe went on. "You might get a cut. It depends on how I feel." Crowe stood, put his arms in a Y and stretched. "I'm going out of town for a few days, and if for some reason somebody calls about me, you're going to say what?"

13

"That you're a model citizen," Pearce said, staring off. "The best parolee ever."

Crowe moved to the door.

"Come to my house and take this monitor off me — my *friend*. And do it fucking today."

CHAPTER ONE:
RUSH CREEK

Isaiah drove north on Interstate 5, out of LA, through the brown, brushy foothills of Southern California, housing developments on either side, their Spanish tile roofs like a field of umber Lego. Flocks of people moved out here despite the two-hour commute to LA. Nothing like affordable housing for 650 grand, but your own home was one of the few freedoms left in modern life. Twenty-five-hundred square feet to do anything you wanted.

Isaiah turned off the eight-lane 5 onto the two-lane 395, the towns smaller and farther apart, the foothills flattening into scrubby, monotonous desert. He'd been chased out of LA by a multitude of gangs and there was a bounty on his head. There were other reasons he'd fled too. He was exhausted, mentally and physically. His soul was bleeding. He didn't want to be IQ anymore. He didn't want to see any more suffering,

15

injustice and cruelty. He didn't want to hear any more victims sobbing and grieving or be around any more gangsters, killers, sociopaths and lunatics. He didn't want to be someone who sought out the cesspool, swam in it, made a living from it and nearly drowned in the shit and stink and filth of it. He was done. There had to be something else for him somewhere. He got text messages and voice mails from Dodson, Deronda, TK, Mrs. Marquez, a number of ex-clients but not the one he wanted. He'd get back to them at some point. He also got threats from Manzo, Hugo, Ponlok and a variety of other haters and would-be bounty hunters.

The 395 gradually ascended, through Lone Pine, Independence, Big Pine and Bishop. Grace's car performed well. The '68 Mustang GT was over forty years old, but she'd lovingly restored it in memory of her dad. This would be the last car he'd ever own. He got another call from Dodson, and this time he picked up.

"Where the fuck are you, son?" Dodson demanded. "You got every G'd-up mutha-fucka in America lookin' for your ass. You better be hidin' up on Jupiter 'cuz there ain't no place around here where you won't get your damn throat cut. Are you listening to me?" Before Isaiah could answer Dodson went on. "And you know what else? Manzo knows me and you is tight so I got mutha-fuckas following my ass around. I hope them goddamn Cambodians don't remember me. That's all I need, buncha' crazy niggas from TEC on my trail. You fuckin' up my future, Isaiah. What if I want to go to Cambodia someday? You ever think of that? I'd have to get off the goddamn tour bus and walk my ass to the Philippines."

"The Philippines are islands," Isaiah said. He knew this was Dodson's way of caring about him.

"You don't think I know that? I can read a goddamn map and by the —"

"Would you shut up for a second? I'm on the road now, somewhere between Bishop and Lake Crowley."

"That's smart. Not too many gangstas are into fresh air. Where're you going?"

"I don't know. I'm making it up as I go along."

"You gonna do the PI thing?"

"Not in this lifetime. I'm done with it," Isaiah said. "Too much evil. Too much death."

"I hear you," Dodson said. "I was wondering when you was gonna get tired of dealing with criminals every day. You got potential,

17

son. All kinds of other shit you could do that don't involve getting killed going to the supermarket."

"Have you heard from Grace?"

"No. Want me to reach out?" Dodson said. Isaiah thought a moment. Dodson could relay news to him, but news would be nothing but chest pain.

"No, that's okay."

"You coming back?" Dodson asked.

"I don't know."

"Ease on down the road, Q."

"I'll try."

He drove on, climbing into the Sierra Nevadas. There were pine forests, spectacular views and cool, sweet-smelling air. It was a revelation. There were actually places in the world that weren't all dirty streets, traffic noise and tall, ugly buildings. He could see blue sky and the chop on Lake Crowley and green ranchland dotted with cows and horses and sheep. He thought about Grace all the time. It went beyond missing her into some other category of loss and pain. They'd parted by mutual heart-wrenching consent. If they were together, she'd be risking her life, and she wasn't going to live on the road. She was an artist. She needed a place where she could paint in peace and privacy.

Isaiah took a detour off the highway and around the June Lake Loop. He stopped at the roadside and walked down to Rush Creek. He was astounded. It was the kind of thing you see on postcards. Fresh, clear water flowing and riffling over mossy stones, sunlight shimmering off reeded pools and shadowed with overhanging trees, birds darting through the branches. A weathered picnic bench listed on the bank, inviting you to sit, read, fish or do nothing at all. He chose the latter. He sat down and did nothing. Isaiah. Did nothing. There was no one around, not even a passing car. The quiet and utter peace were dumbfounding.

For the first few minutes, he was tense, waiting for a guy with headphones to appear and tell him he was in the middle of a movie set. It didn't happen. He watched water spiders skate in the shallows, swallows skimming and spiraling through a scattering of golden dust motes. After a while, he felt funny — well, not funny exactly. He felt — relaxed. He'd almost forgotten the word. He tested it, sitting there a long time, but the feeling persisted. His shoulders eased, his neck and back uncoiled. And then, with no warning or premeditation, he smiled, big and wide with a laugh behind it.

"I'll be," he said.

He got a room at the Aspen Lodge, a gradual feeling of dread bearing down on him as he walked through the door. He'd been okay until now, distracted by the newness of things. The flashbacks came in rapid succession, like a slideshow created just to terrorize him. He remembered Chinese gangsters beating him to the ground and Clarence Novelle hugging his dead girlfriend. He remembered the screams of the dying in the industrial zone and a white nationalist named Jenn shooting her boyfriend with an assault rifle. He remembered Flaco, a ten-year-old with a bullet hole in his skull, and a girl named Bridgette who'd been whipped by her pimp and his brother's murderer, Seb Habimana, slashing at him with a cane made from a human tibia. He saw his brother, lying broken on the asphalt. He saw himself hung in a stress position wearing a hood soaked in hot sauce and knowing he was going to die. He saw himself hog-tied by the Starks and a Cambodian gangster named Guda, pushing his head underwater, and Gahigi, a refugee from the Rwanda genocide, aiming a gun at him and the giant pit bull named Goliath with its jaws at his throat — and knowing he was going to die.

He had PTSD. It had changed him, distorted him like a funhouse mirror, but nothing about it was fun. He was alternately depressed and anxious, he couldn't take frustration, his temper was a land mine. He'd always told people who had the condition that they should seek help, that they couldn't get through it alone. Yet here he was, going through it alone.

He was groggy but hit the road anyway, continuing on 395 to Indian Hills, climbing a windy mountain road to South Lake Tahoe, a ski village and gambling mecca. Randomly, he took the 185 north into Pumas County, drove for a few hours, he wasn't keeping track. He reached a bridge that went over the Coronado River into Coronado Springs. It was a quaint, charming town. A main street of shops and brick office buildings, a Spanish-style city hall with a fountain and a courtyard. That seemed a good enough reason to stop, rest up, experiment with this relaxation thing. He got a clean, pleasant room with a kitchen at the Woodside Motor Lodge. He did his laundry, bought some groceries and scouted around.

Trim, nicely kept neighborhoods radiated from the town's center, dwindling to scruffy houses, trailers and isolated commercial buildings, a lone shopping mall at its edge.

Coronado Springs was neither big nor small, affluent nor depressed, with just enough traffic to know you were in the twenty-first century. The great outdoors was a short walk away. Everyone had a forest in their backyard.

Isaiah had four thousand dollars in a rainy-day account, a few hundred in cash and a credit card in his wallet. He phoned Tudor and told him to sell the house. He'd take less for cash and a quick sale. Tudor made it easy and bought the house himself. He always had an eye for a bargain. Isaiah didn't worry about having too little money. He worried about not having cash when he needed it. He kept an emergency fund in his shoe. Under the left sole, there were three damp one-hundred-dollar bills.

He established a routine. Rising early, eating breakfast at the Coronado Springs Family Diner and reading e-books on the banks of the river. He never had the time or the interest to read fiction but he surprised himself. Toni Morrison, Cormac McCarthy, Isabel Allende, Kazuo Ishiguro, Colson Whitehead and others. He drank the stories like water from Rush Creek and they quenched a thirst he didn't know he had. He stayed away from crime novels.

By nature, Isaiah was brooding, worrisome

and withdrawn. The PTSD brought these qualities to new levels. His mind was a cauldron of self-reproach, self-doubt and dread. He was convinced something bad was going to happen, but it had no shape or voice, nothing to tell him what it was or when it would strike. He kicked and punched himself for a thousand things he'd done or done badly or shouldn't have done at all. He avoided mirrors, even when he was brushing his teeth. He inadvertently caught his reflection in a store window. What struck him was his face, beset with worry and uncertainty. He looked lost, afraid to be found.

And beneath it all was anger, bubbling like boiling tar. He was angry at himself for standing in front of an unstoppable tide of evil and being pretentious enough to think evil would even notice him. He was angry at himself for leaving Grace. The love of his life. Sometimes, when the demons were still and his eyes were closed, he saw himself onstage at the Hollywood Bowl, blowing Dizzy's horn, tender and plaintive, and looking up at him from every seat was Grace.

Isaiah explored. He found hiking trails, bike trails, deer paths and logging roads, memorizing where they were and where they led. He did the same with the town. After two weeks, he knew the layout in detail and the name of nearly every street. The walking and hiking did wonders for his cardio; he worked out at the local gym too. Despite his mood and weight loss, he was in the best shape of his life.

There were gang tags near the outskirts of town. PN 14, or Pumas Nortenos 14. N is the fourteenth letter of the alphabet, a sign of allegiance to Nuestra Familia, the infamous prison gang. The gangs that chased Isaiah out of LA were Sureños, fierce enemies of the Nortenos. They had to be separated in the joint.

He rented a guest house in a quiet, threadbare neighborhood. It was a small one-bedroom, clean and minimally furnished. It was set back from the main house and surrounded by shadowy woods. His landlords, Mr. and Mrs. Ortega, were a warm and friendly couple with two young daughters. Mr. Ortega was a plumber. Mrs. Ortega worked at a bakery.

It was eleven o'clock in the morning. He went to the 24-hour laundromat and paid the attendant to do his laundry. A small luxury. He'd come back for it tomorrow. He walked through town and into an upscale neighborhood called Ridge Tree Heights.

He was trying to reach the national park and this was the closest route. A police car pulled over in front of him. An officer got out in that slow, deliberate way cops have. He could feel the cop's eyes behind the aviators, examining every aspect of the newcomer. The officer was six foot, the same height as Isaiah but thicker. A two-by-four to Isaiah's two-inch dowel. His khaki uniform was crisp and taut, his tactical belt shining like a polished shoe, the holstered Glock mute and ominous.

"Good morning, sir," the cop said. "Could I see some ID?" Isaiah knew better than to ask why. He handed it over. "It's Isaiah Kintay-bee?" the cop asked.

"Quintabe."

"Any warrants for your arrest, Mr. Quintabe?"

"No."

"If I call that in, will it check out?"

"Yes, it will."

The officer wore a sheriff's badge. His name tag said R CANNON. He breathed a deep sigh and looked around at the mountains as if he owned them. "What are you doing here, Mr. Quintabe?"

"Just walking."

"Just walking. To where?"

"The national park."

"It's a long walk."

"That was my intention."

Isaiah said nothing more. People with something to hide talk too much, give a lot of details or a complicated narrative. Cannon looked at the license again. "You live in Long Beach, California, is that right? What are you doing here?"

What am I doing here? Isaiah thought. You mean what is a nigger doing here. "Road trip. Thought I'd stop for a while."

"Where are you staying?"

"A guest house on Kenmore Street."

"Who does it belong to?" Cannon asked. Isaiah wondered if this asshole asked everyone who their landlords were.

"Mr. and Mrs. Ortega."

"I know Ortega," Cannon said, like he knew everybody. "He's a plumber, came out to the house a couple of times."

Cannon sounded puzzled, like why would nice people like the Ortegas have a tenant like this? Weren't there any other ethnicities available? The sheriff nodded as if there was much to be considered. There was a long moment of quiet. He's waiting for me to say something more, Isaiah thought. Let him wait. Cannon huffed as if somehow he was conceding something. He handed back the license. "All right, you can go. Some advice, Mr. Quintabe?" Isaiah knew what was coming. Most black folks did. "Walk somewhere else." Isaiah held his temper in check. It was banging against the bars of its cage.

Cannon drove away. What an idiot, Isaiah thought. He was glad he hadn't started anything. Would Cannon have listened to him, recognized his own prejudices and apologized? Never mind, Isaiah told himself. You're here for rest. You're here for peace. He walked on.

CHAPTER TWO:
BROKE WILL BE GOOD FOR YOU

Dodson was at the breakfast table, contentedly eating a bowl of Cocoa Puffs. He was thinking what a fine morning it was and how a big fat joint would be great right about now. Maybe he'd walk over to the park or shoot some pool or stay home and watch Judge Judy. Hard to believe she got the big bucks for being a crabby old bitch. They should give Cherise's mother, Gloria, a show. If they ever had a confrontation, Judy would throw her gavel away, give her robe to the Goodwill and get the fuck out of town.

Dodson was thinking nothing but good thoughts until Cherise came in. Unfortunately, she had one of her familiar faces. The one that said, *You and I are going to have a serious talk and it's not about me.* Dodson knew what the topic would be. His recurrent lack of employment. Isaiah had left him some money before he left town.

Twenty-five K. That was running out or maybe it already had. Cherise handled the finances. She'd never explicitly said, I don't trust you with money, Juanell, but that was implied and not unwise of her. She was hardly ever unwise.

He thought he could coast on the money at least six months but Cherise claimed a good chunk of it for Micah's college fund. The boy better become a hedge fund manager for what it was costing his daddy. He knew Cherise was going to demand he go back working for Deronda. There were no other realistic choices; Dodson had nothing but criminal activity on his résumé.

Cherise surprised him. The first words she said were, "I got you an internship."

"I beg your pardon?"

"Laurie Singer was my best friend in college," Cherise explained. "She's a creative director at Apex Advertising. I told her about your situation and she offered you an internship. The company grants them to people who've been disadvantaged in the job market, and if that's not you, I don't know who is."

"I don't see what good that does," Dodson said. "Far as I know, interns don't get paid."

"That's not important right now. You need

to get your foot in the door, Juanell. Any door. Maybe they'll keep you on as a trainee or give you an assistant's job. The point is, you can build on it. You're a husband and a father, in case you've forgotten. You are obligated to contribute to the financial welfare of this family. It's always been minimal and that has to change."

"Like I said, you can't force me to —" Cherise slammed her hand down on the table, the silverware jumped, milk sloshed out of the cereal bowl. It scared him.

"I am not fucking around, Juanell!" she shouted. He couldn't remember the last time he heard her swear. She was really pissed. Extra pissed. He should have noticed that before. "I love you, Juanell," she went on, a quiver in her voice, "and I'm going to say this because I love you."

"Uh-oh," he mumbled.

"If you don't take this internship, stick with it and not mess up on purpose, you'll have to move out." It was like something heavy and solid had smashed into Dodson's face. A wrecking ball or city bus.

"Move out?" The possibility had never occurred to him. He felt a single drop of sweat slide down his temple. The idea of leaving his home terrified him. *Get your shit together, son. Fight back.* "What's this advertising "company like?" he asked.

"What's it like?" Cherise said. "It's like any other business. You show up at nine, do your work, and go home at five."

"What about the people?"

"The people? What kind of question is that? They're like responsible adults everywhere."

Dodson smiled inside. His argument was coming together. "Most of 'em is white and been to college, right?"

"What are you talking about?" Cherise said, exasperated.

"I'm talking about me being street. How's somebody like me supposed to work in a place like that? Let me ask you. How many of them folks spent they whole lives in the hood? How many of 'em was a crack dealer and rolled with Crip Violators and ran a Ponzi scheme and sold counterfeit Gucci bags out the trunk of they cars? How many of them was locked up in Vacaville? I don't belong in a place like that. I'll stick out like Lil Wayne at Sean Hannity's birthday party."

Cherise sighed. "The cultural differences aren't as big as you say they are, and believe me, you'll learn."

"Learn? Learn what? How to be white? You know that shit ain't happenin'."

"Nobody's talking about you learning to

be white. And for starters, stop swearing."

"Stop swearing?" Dodson said, his voice rising a controlled octave. "Fuck, mutha-fucka, shit, nigga, bitch, and goddammit are like vowels to me. I'll have to pretend I lost my vocal cords. Fact of the matter is this. You can take the brutha out the hood, but you can't take the hood out the brutha."

"This brutha takes the hood out of herself every day," Cherise said.

Good point, he thought. Time to pivot. "All I'm trying to do here is save you some embarrassment."

"Embarrassment? What do I have to be embarrassed about?"

"Me showing up in an office full of white people as my natural self. I'm a nigga from the old school, hustler to the bone, and down for my hood. I'll make both of us look the fool. You think Laurie Singer's gonna appreciate you sending an uneducated ex-thug with no résumé and a criminal record to her place of business?"

"Yes, there are cultural issues, but like I said, you'll learn," Cherise said.

"From who?" He nearly laughed. She'd taken the bait. Time to end this and go back to your Cocoa Puffs. "Lemme see now, who would be my teacher? Not you, you're busy. TK, maybe? He sees a few white people at the wrecking yard — oh, wait, I should have thought of this before. Deronda! Maybe she can teach me a few things while she's twerkin' and selling fried chicken." Cherise had her arms folded over her chest, her mouth in a straight line. He went on, shaking his head. "No, that won't work. She hates my ass — say, do you remember Antoine's girlfriend, Felicia? That hooker who gave us a box of rainbow condoms for a wedding present and half of 'em was gone already? She's white. Maybe I could ask her."

Cherise's face lit up. "Grace. She'd be happy to help." Dodson was so ready for this he almost got up and danced.

"I don't know if you heard, but she got her own art show in Ojai. She's working round the clock. Call her if you want." Cherise's whole body went slack. He thought he heard her willpower break. Dodson couldn't believe she'd even attempt something like this. What gave her the idea she could bully the hustler's hustler? She must have bumped her head or taken too many allergy pills.

His mother-in-law, Gloria, came in. "Have you seen Micah's brown sweater? I can't find it any —" She saw Dodson, sighed disgustedly, and said, "Oh, it's you."

"Why is that always a surprise?" he replied. "I live here. You the one that's trespassin'."

"I'll find him something else." She harrumphed and left the room.

Dodson reached for the Cocoa Puffs and noticed Cherise looking at him, a slight smile curling the ends of her mouth.

In a pleasant voice, she said, "Did you know my mother was vice principal at Carver Middle School for twenty-five years? And when she wasn't doing that, she was teaching English. She dealt with white students, white teachers, white parents and white bureaucrats all the time." Something terrible began nibbling at Dodson's gut, like those parasites that eat you from the inside out. Cherise went on, smiling nostalgically and shaking her head. "Mama was something. Everybody was afraid of her, students and teachers alike. She was a stickler for — what did she call it? Oh, yes, *proper behavior.*" Cherise chuckled. "Mama had so many do's and don'ts, they wouldn't fit on the notice board."

Dodson was horrified. He nearly fell to his knees. "Please, no, baby."

"You said you needed somebody to teach you. Well, you got your wish."

"She'll break me," he said quietly.

"Broke will be good for you," Cherise said. "It'll let in the sunshine."

Chapter Three:
Queen Booty Booty

Deronda's father moved to Huntington Beach to be with his girlfriend. He left Deronda the house. She loved the extra room. It seemed to make the world bigger and Janeel's ruckus farther away. Grace was living in Isaiah's house. Tudor, the mortgage broker, told her the house had been sold and she had a week to move out. Typically, Grace hadn't said anything about being homeless. It was just like her not to impose, not to be pushy; if the situation was reversed, Deronda would have showed up on her doorstep with suitcases and a lawn chair.

They were at the Coffee Cup in their usual booth. "Aren't you gonna ask me?" Deronda said.

"Ask you what?" Grace said.

"Whether you can move into my place."

"I wasn't." She shrugged. "Maybe you don't want a roomie and I know you don't want a dog."

Deronda scowled, annoyed. "I don't know if you remember, girl, but last time I checked, we was friends, and as long as that dog is house-trained and don't eat little kids I'm cool with it."

"This is a little awkward," Grace said, "but, um — what would the rent be?"

"Rent? I'm mad at you now," Deronda said. "Maybe you didn't notice but I got bucks, and what are you gonna cost me? Four dollars on the electricity bill?"

"I don't know what to say."

"Say thank you and let's go pack your shit."

It was great having Grace around. She cleaned up after herself, did most of the chores, didn't play her music loud, had one or two friends drop in and that was it. She also knew when Deronda needed company and when she didn't. Ruffin turned out to be a good thing. The dog was a pussycat but nobody knew that except the two roomies. Everybody else saw a big-ass pit bull sitting on the steps.

A gallery in Ojai gave Grace her own show. She was out-of-her-mind thrilled. Deronda could relate, remembering her first food truck, how it felt to be in charge of your own fate, to be completely reliant on

37

your own skills and intelligence. Scary too. The world would decide whether your fate was worth caring about.

Grace set up her easel in the backyard and painted whenever she had "the right light," whatever that meant. Deronda didn't understand her paintings. Most of them looked like a box of melted crayons thrown up in the air. Grace broke down a few times, not because of the work, but because Isaiah wasn't there. He wouldn't see the show. He wouldn't see the best of her. Deronda would look out of the window and see Grace standing in front of a canvas, her face in her hands, weeping. Grace and Janeel got along great. They did puzzles and finger-painted. They went for walks and played games and sat on the back stoop singing Motown songs.

Deronda's business was thriving. She'd added two more trucks for a total of eight. Her fan base was growing fast. The caps and T-shirts sold well, she was invited to speak to aspiring food truckers, and she was working with a company to develop her own line of hot sauce. The only thing that fizzled was her advice blog, "Deronda Knows What Your Mama Didn't Tell You."

Dear Deronda,
My fiancé overspends. He's maxed out my credit cards on clothes and shoes and partying. Collection agents are calling and I can barely make the rent. I love him. What should I do?

Down to My Last Dime

Dear Last Dime,
I hear you, I truly do. Once I bought myself a pair of Jimmy Choos I couldn't afford and ended up trading them for food stamps. You want some advice? Get your ass a new fiancé. You can't eat love, spend love or drive it to work. Grow yourself a backbone, bitch. Throw the bum out or you're as useless as he is.

Dear Deronda,
My girlfriend likes sex more than I do. She's constantly nagging me to, as she puts, "give her the hard one," but half the time I'm not interested. What should I do?

Low T

Dear Low T,
The fuck is wrong with you, boy? You ever heard the expression, "use them or lose them"? You keep on like this and

your balls will get rusty and the next time you ejaculate, your dick will cough. The best thing you can do is break up with her. Let the poor girl have a life, you selfish motherfucker.

Janeel was still the engine of her life. He was in a private kindergarten and at the top of his class. At least that's what Deronda thought. He was the best-looking by far. By comparison, the other kids looked like Beanie Babies or apple head dolls. Janeel definitely had the most style. A low fade, Kendrick Lamar T-shirt, neon-green Nike 720s, size 2C, and Armani Junior distressed jeans. Deronda believed he was the smartest kid there but it was hard to tell when the class was playing with alphabet blocks. The teacher didn't appreciate Janeel singing "Let's Get It On," while the other kids were singing "I'm a Little Teapot." Let her complain, Deronda thought. She'd get hip to it sooner or later.

Janeel was also Deronda's biggest problem. She was driving home from work one night and got a call from a stranger named Bobby James. Years back, when she was president of the American Hoes for Freedom Association, she'd had sex with him in a bathroom stall at an underground club in

Compton. She might never have heard from him again. But then an article about her and the food truck business appeared in *LA Magazine.* There was a photo of her and Janeel. Bobby said they looked like twins. He also knew a lot of details about that night in the bathroom stall. He claimed to be Janeel's father, but worse than that? He wanted custody.

When she ended the call, she nearly drove into a fire hydrant. This bitch-ass, no-conscience motherfucker wants custody? Of her *baby*? He had no idea of the trouble he'd started or the trouble he was in. She'd burn up the food trucks and move to Zimbabwe before she'd let that happen. Her first thought was having Bobby killed.

Deronda had recently made friends with Michael Stokeley, former enforcer of the Crip Violators and the scariest muthafucka in the hood. Stokeley's weapon of choice was a sawed-off Mossberg riot gun. Dodson said you could point that thing up at the sky and still hit the nigga you was aiming at. Stokeley's aunt, Odeal Woodson, had fallen into a depression after her husband died. She had been a lively, capable woman who was always cheerful and ready to help. She was active in the church, volunteered at the food bank and was a docent at the hospital. Now she was wasting away in an old folks' home. Reverend Arnall visited Odeal, saw her situation and called Deronda. Deronda gave Odeal a job at one of the food trucks. At the time, she had no idea Odeal and Stokeley were related. Almost overnight, the seventy-five-year-old dispirited senior citizen became a happy clam. Doing something useful and getting a paycheck did wonders for her health and spirit. She was one of Deronda's best workers.

One afternoon, Stokeley stopped Deronda on the street. He didn't have a shirt on. He looked like Popeye's forearms had taken over the rest of his body, assuming Popeye had four or five bullet wounds and jailhouse tats everywhere but the bottom of his feet. Deronda started fumbling in her bag for money, but Stokeley said, "Naw, naw, it ain't about that. Y'all helped my auntie out. She was the only one in my life that treated me good. You need something, you need *anything,* hit me up." Maybe she'd ask Stokeley to fire the Mossberg into Bobby's forehead and that sorry motherfucker could take custody of his tombstone. She seriously considered the idea for an hour or so until she stopped at a bar, had a double Royal Crown Reserve, no ice.

When she got home, Grace said Janeel was asleep. Deronda looked at the little miracle for a long time and thanked him like she did every day. If it wasn't for him, she wouldn't have worked so hard, fought so hard and *struggled so hard* to elevate herself from Miss Ho of the Universe to a successful businesswoman. Bobby James, she decided, wasn't gonna get shit.

Deronda was sitting in a booth at the Coffee Cup, waiting for him. Bobby was fifteen minutes late. He was trying to make her sweat, but that wasn't happening. She could just see him. One more street thug with his baggy shorts, white T-shirt, a cap with a C on it, a gold chain or two and DMX's attitude. Yes, muthafucka, let's get up in front of a judge and see what's what. You can explain how you got your GED in San Quentin makin' twenty cents an hour stamping out license plates, and I'll drive my fleet of food trucks through the courtroom and show him my bank statements. The judge ain't giving you custody of an apple pie.

There was almost nothing about Bobby on the internet except some old stuff from high school and family pictures. No social media either. A wise move, Deronda thought. What was he going to post? Pictures of his bong collection? Cellblock D's ten-year reunion? An instructional video on how to make a shank out of a plastic cup? Bring it to me, homeboy. Deronda's got something for you.

A man sat down across from her and smiled. "Who are you?" she said.

"I'm Bobby James."

"You are?"

Bobby was wearing a dark gray business suit, a white shirt and a red tie. His hair was short, his nails were clean, and he looked a little like Drake. If Deronda didn't have a boyfriend, she might have let Bobby buy her a drink. He had some game; cool, confident, relaxed, his arm draped along the top of the booth.

"Are you surprised?" he said.

"Nigga, please," Deronda scoffed. "You couldn't surprise me if you had a gun, a roll of duct tape and the key to my house." But she was surprised. Very surprised.

"I've cleaned myself up since the last time I saw you. I have a degree in finance, I work at Wells Fargo and by the way? I don't have a criminal record."

"Well good for you. Now what the fuck do you want?"

"I want joint custody."

"Joint custody, my big brown ass,"

Deronda said with a snort. "You can't show up after all this time and ask for custody."

"That's because I lost track of you," Bobby replied. "I barely knew your name and after that night, I never saw you again. What was I supposed to do? Go back to that bathroom and wait for you? I had no idea I had a son until I saw that article in *LA Magazine.*"

"How do you know he's your son? You can't tell no resemblance with a four-year-old child. You better have some DNA in your wallet."

Bobby yawned and covered his mouth with his hand. "I'm taking you to court. I'm Janeel's natural father, and a paternity test will prove that. My brother-in-law is an attorney and we'll be serving you with papers very soon."

"Serve 'em on up," Deronda retorted. "I hope those papers are as soft as Charmin." Something was wrong, she thought, something was underneath. Bobby had no idea Janeel was his son. This wasn't his main play. He had a hole card. Deronda sighed wearily. "Look, I'm busy. Could we cut to the chase? What is it you want, Bobby James?"

"I told you what I want. Joint custody."

"You said that. But what do you *want*?"

She met his smug gaze with a steely one.

"Half the business," he said.

"Only half?" She laughed. "You have lost your fucked-up mind, Bobby James. I'm not giving you half a baloney sandwich let alone half of a business you had nothing to do with."

"If we go to court, things will come out that could ruin your reputation." Bobby went into his briefcase and found a thick file folder. He brought out two photographs. The first was an ad for a chain of hamburger restaurants. The centerpiece was a giant triple-decker burger dripping burger juice. Deronda was standing next to it looking back over her shoulder. She was grinning seductively, her world-famous behind gleaming and split down the middle by a Day-Glo-pink bikini. The caption said:

THE BIG MEATY BURGER
LA's Juiciest
You Know You Want Some

Before Deronda could reply, Bobby shoved another photo at her. It was an ad for a strip joint called the Kandy Kane. It said QUEEN BOOTY BOOTY APPEARING THIS WEEKEND! The picture showed her wearing a thong with her hands over her tits, eager men throwing dollar bills at her.

Deronda waved her hand dismissively. "Ain't no judge gonna care about shit that happened ten or twelve years ago. Ruin my reputation with who? People who eat fried chicken?"

Bobby's gaze got steely too. "No. I mean ruin your reputation with Janeel." Deronda went still. She felt like a drain had opened and emptied out her insides. "Want to see more?" he said. He gave her more photos. Snapshots, freeze frames and old social media. Deronda, posing with some gangstas, everybody wearing colors and throwing up signs. Deronda in a tiny dress, bleary-eyed, holding a joint in one hand and a bottle of Chivas in the other. Deronda passed out on the floor, her dress hiked up to her panties, I'M A WHORE and GOOD PUSSY HERE written on her face with a Sharpie. A shot of her fighting with another girl, wild-eyed and snarling, throwing a haymaker, her blouse torn. Deronda naked from the waist up, two handguns held across her chest like she was pledging allegiance to the NRA. On her twenty-first birthday she'd been arrested for DUI. Her mugshot was pitiful, like she'd been caught sleeping in a landfill. There were more but Deronda stopped looking.

"Be hard on a kid," Bobby said with mock sadness. "Learning these kinds of things about his mother. It might permanently damage the relationship, maybe even cause a break." He made a frown that was actually a smile. "I just had a terrible thought. What if things like this were circulated around the neighborhood? I don't even like to think about it. Kids can be so cruel. The poor boy would never hear the end of it." Bobby picked up the Kandy Kane ad, looked at it and sighed. "Queen Booty Booty. They'd stick this on his lunchbox, his locker, your front door and probably on the food trucks too. Sometimes you wish there was no such thing as Facebook. This will follow him forever and could even ruin his life. What a shame. What a tragedy."

A sudden calm had come over Deronda. An acceptance. War had been declared so stop fussing and arm yourself.

"Aren't you going to say anything?" he said.

In a quiet, even voice, Deronda said, "I'm gonna fuck you up, Bobby James."

He raised his eyebrows and smirked. "Are you threatening me with bodily harm?"

In the same voice, she said, "I'm gonna come down on you so hard they'll have to go frackin' just to find your ass. You go public with any of this, and I won't do nothin' with my food trucks except run your ass over."

"Is that so?" he said, stifling a yawn.

"You think you know me but you don't," she said in a casual way. "I will fight for my son in ways a scalawag like you can't even imagine." Her eyes narrowed into razor blades, her voice got low and ugly. "Here's my lifetime guarantee, muthafucka. If my shit comes apart, I'll pop you like a tick on a broke-dick dog. You'll have a dedicated enemy forever. Are you hearing me, Bobby James? I'm talkin' *forever.* You won't go nowhere, do anything or be with somebody without these eyes in your rearview mirror. I'd think on that if I was you." A spark of fear flashed across Bobby's face but he covered it with a smile.

He slid the file over to her. "You can keep this. See you in court."

CHAPTER FOUR:
BLUE HILL

Magnus Vestergard, aka Skip Hanson, had just been released from the Solano State Correctional Facility for Men, located in the nowhere town of Vacaville, California. He'd been sentenced to six years for assault with a deadly weapon. "Good conduct" knocked it down to five years and 1.2 months. As he took his first steps outside the prison walls, he didn't revel in his freedom, lust for a Quarter Pounder or even a woman. The anger he'd been holding back made his blood congeal and his head spin with hate.

The prison bus took him to Sacramento. From there he took the train to Union Station in LA. Then another bus to Bus Stop G in Long Beach. He got off, hefted on his backpack and walked to the Crest Motel on Long Beach Boulevard, stopping once for beer, Cheez-Its and Neapolitan ice cream. The room reminded him of his prison cell except it smelled of Lysol and roach powder instead of bleach and human stink. He took a shower and lay on the bed naked, content with being clean. He ate his snacks, watched TV and rested until the next day. He bought a junker from an old man at a wrecking yard. A Nissan Rogue with a bashed-in side, a missing fender and a bent frame. The old man said it ran fine, just keep your hand on the steering wheel.

Skip took interconnecting freeways through Downey, Rancho Cucamonga, Hesperia and Victorville. He was in the desert now, everything familiar. The brown brush, brown foothills and billboards for strip clubs. He opened the window and breathed in the smells of dirt and sage. He was starting to get excited but it didn't offset the dread. He reached Fergus. A one-block town with two gas stations, a motel and a diner. He was afraid it wouldn't be there, the dirt road and the sign that said MUNICIPAL LANDFILL 6 MILES. He drove slowly, gravel clattering against the undercarriage, dust clouding the windshield. He wanted to hurry. At the same time, he hoped he'd never get there.

He came around a bend and there it was. The wooden sign nailed to a dead tree, partially hidden by a layer of crud. BLUE

HILL PIT BULLS in dripping white letters. Skip couldn't pay the property taxes and the state had claimed the place. But the state had no interest in a rectangle of dried-out acreage no different than the desert around it. Time, weather, and vandals had beaten the house into a ruin. The front door was missing, all the windows busted out.

Skip got out of the car and went inside. Everything was either broken, smashed or missing. Skip wondered if cobwebs could be used for something useful, knitted into scarves or fermented into alcohol. He bypassed the other rooms and went through the hall to the back door.

He stood on the stoop and looked at what had once been his private world, his kingdom. The pit bulls he'd bred here were his disciples, his children, and the only things he'd ever loved that loved him back. There was the exercise yard with a high chain-link fence he'd built himself. One side was flopped over, nearly touching the ground, the other three leaning in different directions. He remembered the dogs playing, sleeping, scrapping, digging holes, mewling and yapping, eager for his company. For his touch.

He went into the barn. He ducked his way through a jungle of cobwebs and looked up at the hole in the roof. The shelves were broken, wallboards missing, the floor a mess of stagnant water and muck. The kennels were wrecked, gates missing, the wood full of termites and stained with water damage. He'd made these himself too. He walked past them, remembering the dogs who had lived in them. Atilla, Butch, Reaper, Warrior, fifteen in all, counting Goliath.

Goliath's kennel was at the end and twice as big as the others. Goliath. His champion. Skip's monument to himself. It took years of breeding to create him, a pit bull as big as a Shetland pony and vicious enough to eat the pony and still be hungry. He loved that dog most of all. It was the only thing that could make him cry.

Skip saw a gleam of something under the dirt and dried dog shit. It was Goliath's spiked collar, rusted and oxidized. He wrapped it around his neck and left the barn. He walked north into the desert. It was cooling off, the smells gaining density, the air crisper. The sun was going down, the light changing the brown hills blue. Skip had hunted here with his dogs, moving through the brush like fanged commandos scaring up birds and critters, Skip blasting them to shit with an assault rifle, the dogs fighting over the remains.

Skip arrived at the boulder shaped like a turtle. He went left and saw the flat rocks he used as stepping-stones so he wouldn't leave footprints. For old times' sake, he hopped from one to the other until he reached the special pile of boulders. There was no reason for anyone to have moved them, but he was surprised they were still there. The tangle of thorny acacia branches that guarded the hollow were gone.

Risking a rattlesnake bite, Skip got down on his belly, put his hand in the hollow and reached as far as he could. He grabbed the waterproof trunk by a side handle and dragged it out. Nobody but the dogs knew anything about his arsenal. He opened the trunk and laughed. There were guns wrapped in heavy plastic and metal boxes that held ammo, everything as before. Underneath the sniper rifle was seven thousand dollars in a Ziploc bag. Money he'd saved from his hitman jobs. He chose his favorite firearm. The Colt Delta Elite. It shot a 10mm FBI load that had a flatter trajectory and longer range than a 9mm. That's all he needed for now.

He went back to his car, got in and sat there a moment. It was dark now, the house held in the headlight beams. With the door missing and the windows gone, it looked hollow and bleached, like a skull left in the sand. The wind whipped Skip's anger into a dust devil that swirled and hissed through the dry brush. He'd come back here one day. He'd come back and rebuild the place and get new dogs and everything would be the same.

He returned to the motel, put the gun in the wastebasket and covered it with fast-food wrappers. They didn't clean the rooms here until you left. He scrubbed the dog collar with a toilet brush until it was shiny again. He put the collar on and looked at himself in the mirror. He'd always looked boyish but not anymore. Like loss, prison sped up your birthdays. He hated that too. One day you wake up and everything you'd ever done in your life was right there on your face. All your fuckups, hard times and humiliation, drawn in lines and creases and the light that was no longer in your eyes.

Skip knew he wouldn't live to old age. It was one of the reasons he was always anxious, always antsy, always in a hurry to get it done before death did him in. The dog collar was like a necklace of Goliath's teeth. Skip ran his fingers over the tips and thought about Isaiah. He'd lost five years of his life because of Q Fuck. He'd kill that bastard slowly and look at him while he did it. He'd leave the collar around his head like Jesus and his crown of thorns, hung limp and bleeding on the cross.

CHAPTER FIVE:
EYES LIKE A KOMODO DRAGON

"What would you do first?" Dickie asked.

"If I got released?" Billy said. "I'd get back to my investigation. Who knows what's happened by now?"

"I don't know what I'd do," Dickie said ruefully. "It's a nightmare out there."

Billy, Dickie and Nathan were in the main hallway on level D at the Feller Neuropsychiatric Institute. It was part of the county hospital known to the patients, law enforcement, and the community at large as "Schizo Central." The Fellers were rich. Their daughter thought she was an angel and jumped off the Coronado Bridge during the dry season.

Billy had been locked in here for a month. That in itself was humiliating, and hanging around with Dickie and Nathan did nothing for your self-esteem. They were eccentric, to say the least. Everybody else wore their street clothes, but Dickie preferred his stained, washed-out gray bathrobe and smashed corduroy slippers. His age, forty, coupled with his roundness, premature baldness and permanently puzzled face reminded Billy of Danny DeVito in *One Flew over the Cuckoo's Nest.*

"Another ridiculous day," Nathan said. "Hmm, I wonder. Should I stand in line for my cocktail of mind-numbing meds or play chess with Billy and beat him nine times in a row?"

Nathan was a primitive stick figure, all arms and legs with knots in unexpected places. His long, pinched, pimpled face only had two expressions. Impatience and contempt.

Dickie groaned. "My mom is coming today. I wish she wouldn't. She gets on my case for every little thing."

Nathan snorted. "It's not every little thing, dickless. You do inane shit." Dickie hacked into his dad's office calendar and added things like EAT DINNER WITH PUTIN and BUILD CAGE FOR THE WOLVERINE and BUY MORE LUBE. He hacked into the Mount Laughlin Observatory and put the rings of Saturn around Mars, deleted one of Neptune's moons and changed the Big Dipper into a woman with big boobs. He hated a nurse named Olga. He got into her

Amazon account and ordered three hundred pounds of kitty litter, a stainless-steel refrigerator, three lawn tractors and fifty pairs of G-string panties.

"Why do you keep calling it an investigation, Billy?" Nathan said. "You're not talking about that serial killer thing, are you? What a bunch of paranoid bullshit."

"It's not paranoid and it's not bullshit," Billy said. "William Crowe is AMSAK. He's murdered seventeen women, maybe more."

Nathan scoffed, his favorite thing to do. "I see. You know this Crowe person is guilty but no one else does? The police are clueless? You've solved the case while you're locked up in the loony bin?"

That last remark stung. Billy didn't belong in a goddamn hospital with a bunch of nonfunctional crazy people. His mom, Gretta, told him repeatedly that he had to face reality, but whose reality? What's to say her reality was any more valid than yours or anybody else's? You're paranoid, Billy. She'd been telling him that since he was in grade school. Why was it paranoid to prepare for bad shit in advance when you knew that sooner or later bad shit was going to happen? Maybe you don't see the hurricane, but you know damn well it's coming. So what if it's summertime? Fill your sandbags

59

and put up your storm shutters while you have the chance.

Billy's interest in serial killers began when he read several articles by Thomas Hargrove, a retired investigative reporter who founded the nonprofit Murder Accountability Project. The Project compiled and analyzed data on homicides. Hargrove examined FBI databases and discovered thousands of unsolved murders were linked to at least one other case by DNA. Using an algorithm developed by the Project, he concluded there were approximately 2,100 serial murderers at large at any given time. Michael Arntfield, a retired police detective, wrote a dozen books about serial killers. He estimated there were three to four thousand. Billy believed the higher number. It fit with his worldview. There was danger everywhere and everyone was capable of evil.

Billy was big on home security, one of many things his mom rolled her eyes at. He'd hidden weapons around the house. A nunchaku in the den, darts in the medicine cabinet, a hunting slingshot in the hallway closet and a Crosman air gun under the couch cushions in the living room. Billy felt most secure in the basement. His room and the bathroom were finished. The rest was a vast graveyard for cardboard boxes filled with junk. He'd installed a booby trap. A length of piano wire stretched across the basement stairs about ankle height. As a reminder to himself and his family, he'd put a sign up marking the hazardous stair: DEER CROSSING.

The thing that worried Billy was that there were no other exits except the stairs. If he couldn't hide from an intruder, he'd be vulnerable. His interest in camouflage and deception led him to the art of trompe l'oeil paintings. They were so realistic they tricked the eye. Like gates, stairs or doors painted with such detailed accuracy, people mistakenly tried to use them, sometimes with injurious results. Billy made a trade with an art student named Raffi. He would do all Raffi's term papers, and in return Raffi would paint a wooden stairway on a concrete wall. It looked absolutely real. Run into that, asshole.

One of the hospital rules drove Billy crazy. Patients on level D were not allowed to use electronic devices. There was some rationale about protecting patients' privacy. Like you'd take pictures of — what exactly? Mrs. Longfield talking to Gary Cooper? Dickie eating a hot dog sideways? Nathan digging in his ear with a pencil? Billy was cut off from the world. He really missed his sister,

Irene. She came to see him on weekends. She was a junior at Palomino High. She got excellent grades and was the All State catcher on the girls' softball team. Irene was pipestem skinny and her arms were unusually long. Her percentage of throwing out base stealers was higher than J. T. Realmuto of the Phillies, who led the major leagues. Irene acted like he was normal. Or what was normal for Billy. She was honest, said what she thought, gave him good advice and didn't take any shit. Her love was assumed.

His mother came to see him three times in three weeks. Gretta had nothing to say and neither did he. For ten awful, teeth-grinding minutes, they sat there, Gretta desperately trying to make small talk. At long, long last, she would glance at her watch, smile anemically and say she had to get back to court. She was so transparent it was laughable. Why didn't she just say it? *I have to get the fuck out of here.* Come to think of it, why didn't he? *You look like a sitting chair made of plutonium, Mom. Why don't you just go?*

Foremost in Billy's mind was Ava. He urgently needed to talk to her. She was all he could think about. She was the only person other than himself who knew Crowe was AMSAK. Crowe had killed Ava's twin sister, Hannah. They knew where he lived and worked. They had the killer's complete record. They'd been tracking him for weeks. The problem was how to nail him. Billy hadn't talked to Ava in five days. She must be going crazy, he thought. Maybe she had new evidence. Maybe she'd given up the chase. Maybe she'd forgotten him.

Nathan had somehow secreted a cell phone into the unit. Now it was the only connection to anything beyond the hospital walls. But Nathan was a prick. He rationed phone use like the last morsels of gull meat on a lifeboat lost in the Aegean. Billy thought about waiting for the right moment, but there was no right moment with Nathan. He was a round-the-clock asshole. Might as well go for it.

"Nathan, I need to use your phone," Billy said.

"*My* phone?" Nathan said, like everybody had one. "I'm sorry, but I'm afraid you've used up your allotted minutes."

"What allotted minutes?" He'd never heard this one before.

"The minutes I've allotted you."

"You've never said anything about allotments."

"Try again, oh, say, Monday afternoon after five."

"Come on, Nathan, it's important."

Nathan sneered. "What is it this time, Chicken Little? The neo-Nazis are planning to attack Hawaii? There was something in your aftershave that gave you syphilis? The Deep State is trying to silence you with a poison suppository?" Billy stopped himself from replying. Nathan was making his I'm-not-going-to-talk-about-this-anymore face. Pushing him was futile. He'd get angry and restrict your phone usage even more.

At Dickie's insistence, they were walking in tandem. It was never explained. "Dickie, could we for once walk side by side?" Billy said. "We look like a string of pack mules." Dickie stopped, scowled and folded his arms across his chest. Billy bumped into him and Nathan bumped into Billy. "Never mind," Billy said.

They went into the restroom together. A mistake. There was nothing weird going on, but Dickie and Nathan were so embarrassing. Nathan washed his hands before he took a piss. Ask him why and he'd say, "It depends on what you want to keep clean." Dickie always stood at the urinal with his pants down to his ankles. It was uncomfortable, shoulder to shoulder with a full-grown man, naked down to his gym socks with more hair on his butt cheeks than Bigfoot.

"Could you not do that?" Billy said, nodding at Dickie's pants.

"I have to," Dickie said. "You know very well I have extra sweat glands under my scro —"

"Forget it." Billy moved down a couple of urinals.

"Aww, man, something's wrong with my zipper!" Nathan exclaimed. He had tucked "Sergeant Pepper" back into his pants prematurely, leaving a large, delta-like stain around the crotch of his cargo shorts. Billy and Dickie howled with laughter.

"What a moron!" Dickie said, delighted. "What are you gonna do when we go to group? You don't have time to change!"

Nathan was easily embarrassed. His face was flushed, his acne flashing bright red. "Oh, my God, what am I going to do?" he bawled. Dickie kept laughing. Nathan was nearly in tears, furiously dabbing at himself with a wad of paper towels, his voice strangled. "I'm so stupid! I'm so stupid! Somebody help me!"

"Calm down, I can fix it," Billy said. "Come here. Stand close to the sink."

"What are you going to do?" Nathan said warily.

"This I've gotta see," Dickie said.

Billy turned on the faucet on high, cupped

65

his hand under the water and splashed three quick handfuls on Nathan. Nathan sputtered, backing away with his hands up, the front of his pants were soaked. Dickie was in hysterics.

"What the hell did you do?" Nathan shouted. "How could you do this to me, Billy? You'll never use my phone again. Never!"

"Shut up and do what I tell you," Billy said.

They went to the common room, other patients milling around, drinking lousy coffee and waiting for the group to start. Nathan looked like he'd been thrown overboard.

"What happened to you?" someone said.

"Can you believe it?" Nathan said. "The whole faucet blew up on me!" Everybody laughed, but they bought it.

"That was really cool," Dickie whispered. Billy looked pointedly at Nathan.

He shrugged. "Fine. Use the phone already."

Billy found the phone hidden in the fire extinguisher box behind the hose. He went to his room and stood behind the open door.

"Where've you been?" Ava said. "I've called you and called you. Who's Nathan, by the way?"

"Sorry, it's a long story. What's happening?"

"Crowe's on the move. He's left Sacramento. He's broken his parole."

Billy was flabbergasted. "What? When?"

"A couple of hours ago. He comes out of the house, okay? He's carrying a duffel bag and he's not wearing his ankle monitor."

"That's incredible. Why do you think —"

"Will you let me finish?" she said impatiently. "Then his wife, Shareen, comes out, and she's pissed, right? She wants to go with him, but he doesn't want her to. They argued, like a real yelling match, and then she gets in the backseat and won't get out. Right now, Crowe's heading south on 185."

Billy was alarmed. "You're following them?"

"Gotta go," she said. The call ended.

Billy stood behind the door thinking. Crowe had broken parole and not in a smart way. If he removed the anklet, the monitoring system would pick it up and his parole officer would be notified. Then law enforcement would be alerted and every cop in the area would be looking for him. A serial killer is obsessive. They go to extremes. They risk everything. That's what Crowe was doing, Billy thought. He wouldn't be taking a

67

chance like this if it wasn't for the irresistible urge to kill another victim. He didn't want to do it on his home ground so he was going hunting someplace else.

Billy was puzzled. If Ava knew Crowe had broken parole, why didn't she call the police? The realization floored him. Ava didn't want Crowe getting busted for a parole violation, she wanted to catch him in the act or worse yet, kill him. Frantically, Billy began dialing her back when the door swung wide. It was Rutger, supposedly "staff" but he was really a security guy. He looked like Mr. Clean with hair.

"I'm disappointed in you, Billy. Hand it over."

"Not yet, please, just one more call," Billy pleaded. Rutger didn't answer. He stuck out a hand that was more like a catcher's mitt. There was no way to resist. Billy gave him the phone and Rutger left. "Damn it to hell!" Billy shouted. What if Crowe caught Ava? What would happen then? He'd kill her, that's what would happen. Billy stepped out into the hall. He looked right and left. He had to escape. The only question was how.

He talked it over with Dickie and Nathan but all they came up with were a bunch of bullshit movie ideas. No, they couldn't make a disguise out of art supplies, there were no staff uniforms to steal, there were no loose ceiling tiles or air-conditioning ducts and no way to make a ladder out of bedsheets or break one of the windows embedded with wire mesh.

"The only way out is the front door," Billy said.

Nathan scoffed. "Good luck with that."

To get to the front door, you went down the main hallway to the nursing station. At least two nurses were there all the time, and one of them had to buzz you in or out. Strong-arming was not an option. Billy couldn't strong-arm anyone even if he wanted to. His body was like a stalk of steamed asparagus. Anyway, the nurses were behind Plexiglas and inaccessible. All they had to do was touch the alarm and Rutger would come running.

But okay, let's say you somehow got past all that and reached the sliding glass door. A nurse would sound an alarm. It was loud, like something you'd hear from an earthquake sensor in Japan. But even if you managed to get through the door, you'd only be in the lobby. There was a reception desk with a uniformed guard behind it. The guard also had an alarm so by the time you got out of the building, multiple alarms would be screaming, *The Asshole has escaped! Be on the lookout. The Asshole has escaped!* The entire security team would show up before you got off the hospital grounds.

"You're sunk," Nathan said. "Forget about the whole thing."

Billy thought a moment. "Dickie, when did you say your mom's coming?"

"At three," Dickie said dolefully.

"What's she like?"

"She's seventy-two. She uses a walker and she has eyes like a Komodo dragon."

"I met her. She's a very frightening person," Nathan said.

"Is she usually on time?" Billy asked.

"Right down to the second," Dickie said. "Even with the walker."

"Tell me more."

Three minutes to three. Billy, Nathan and Dickie were in the main hallway, trying to look nonchalant. The nursing station was forty feet away. Nurse Olga gave Dickie a dirty look and went back to her computer. Dickie was whistling, rocking on his heels with his hands behind his back.

"Why don't you play the tuba, Dickie?" Nathan said. "That way you can be more inconspicuous." He turned to Billy. "This is a terrible idea. It's laughable. You'll never make it!"

"Shut up, Nathan."

"Oh, by the way. How are you going to pay me for my phone?"

They heard a buzz, the sliding door opened, and there was Dickie's mom as described. She stumped in, the walker ahead of her, a mean, vengeful look on her face. She caught Dickie's eye and grimaced.

"Here I go," Billy whispered. He took off, sprinting past the nursing station, brushing Dickie's mom aside.

"Where are you going, buster?" she shouted.

Billy sprinted past the security guard at the front desk. "Hey!" the guard yelled. Billy kept going, across the endless lobby and through double doors to freedom. It startled him, breathing real air, feeling the sun on his face. For a moment, he couldn't remember where the parking lot was, but he got his bearings and took off again. As he turned a corner, he glanced back. Rutger and the security guard racing after him. Billy was in terrible shape. Playing chess and standing in line for your meds was not good exercise. By the time he got to the parking lot, he was sweating, wheezing and holding his side, a stitch stabbing him in the kidney.

Now all he had to do was find Dickie's mom's car, which Dickie described as a "Chevy or Ford, a pukey green color and so old it still has a radio antenna." The parking lot wasn't full, but there were still a lot of cars. Rutger and the guard were coming. Billy ran and rubbernecked. *Come on, let me get lucky, where the hell is it?* His lungs were burning up. He stopped and crouched behind a car.

"Billy," Rutger called out. "Come on back now, before you get into real trouble." He and the guard were walking along the different aisles. "Come on, kiddo. This is nuts." Billy was done in. He couldn't go on. "Come on, Billy, I'm starting to get pissed!" Rutger said. Billy thought about Ava and how she might be in danger and how she might need his help right now, right this minute. *Damn it, Billy, think of something!* And then he did. Dickie's mom was using a walker. She'd have parked in one of the handicapped spaces. He must have run right by them. Billy took a couple of heaving breaths, hunched down and duck-walked until his back couldn't take it anymore. Then he stood up and started running.

"Over there!" Rutger hollered. Billy saw the pukey green car with a radio antenna. He got there, looked underneath the right wheel well and found the small magnetic box right where Dickie said it would be. He fumbled to get it open. "Come on, goddammit!"

Rutger left the guard behind and was coming on fast, pumping his arms, his sneakers whacking the pavement. "Billy, don't do it!" he yelled. Billy got in the car, stuck the key in the ignition, the engine sputtering to life just as Rutger grabbed the door handle and swung it open. His big paw clamped on Billy's shoulder. Billy slammed the shifter in reverse and backed up fast, tearing himself loose from Rutgers's grasp, wheeling around and driving away. He drove frantically for five blocks, made several random turns and stopped.

His heart was pounding so hard he couldn't hear himself panting. *What now, Billy?* He had no money, no credit card, no phone, and he was driving a stolen car. He was hungry too. He'd skipped breakfast and lunch out of nervousness. Ava had probably called ten times by now or maybe Crowe had strangled her and left her body in a dumpster. Billy pulled over into a grove of trees. He didn't know what to do. How would he ever find Ava? The feeling of helplessness was overwhelming. He started to cry.

CHAPTER SIX:
ARE YOU MY DOG?

Isaiah was on the front stoop, reading the classifieds. He wanted a dog. It would be nice, having something around that liked him and didn't talk. The Ortegas' daughters were playing in the yard. Alicia was six years old and Juana was eight. They were outlandishly cute, funny and sweet. Isaiah was a little awed by them. He'd never had such close contact with children before. They seemed to be from a faraway land where toys came alive at midnight and mischievous elves put acorns in your shoes.

Tentatively, Juana came over and asked if he'd like to play with them. He surprised himself and said yes. They played a game that consisted of the girls running around randomly and shrieking with laughter while he chased them and made boogeyman noises. They collapsed on the lawn with hilarity.

Tired now, they sat on the back steps and

drank lemonade Alicia had made. It was so sweet Isaiah nearly spit it out. Juana had to go to the bathroom and as soon as she left, Alicia started crying in little hiccups, copious tears spilling out of her eyes. Isaiah had no idea what to do. This was an entirely new situation for him. She kept crying and crying, her tiny face scrunched up. Isaiah thought she'd wind down, but her sobbing got louder and more intense. It began to sound forced, but she didn't relent. Isaiah had a sudden epiphany. He realized she was asking him to comfort her. Having no moves of his own, he did what he'd seen parents do on TV. He edged over and put his arm around her. Instantly, she leaned into him and cried even louder. He was in a near panic. He was the only adult around. It was his responsibility to soothe her. *Say something, dummy!*

"What's wrong, Alicia?"

"I don't know," she said. Great, Isaiah thought. She wants me to dig it out of her.

"It's okay, you can tell me," he said, cringing inside. He sounded like Mr. Rogers except stupid.

Alicia shook her head, sniffling, more tears cascading down her cheeks, mixing with the mucus streaming out of her nose, the shiny goo running over her mouth and dripping

75

off her chin. She didn't seem to mind, but Isaiah couldn't stand it. He had no tissues, so with great reluctance, he offered her the sleeve of his brand-new T-shirt. "Here," he said. Without a moment's reservation, Alicia took the sleeve, scrubbed her face with it and blew her nose. It looked like a colony of snails had exploded.

"Alicia, please tell me what's wrong."

"The lemonade. It tastes bad."

"No, it doesn't," he said radiantly. "It tastes great! You did a good job!"

"How come you didn't drink more?"

He paused. He'd taken two and a half sips. "I'm not thirsty. I'll have some later."

"No! Have some now!" she insisted. She looked at him with hurt, sad eyes. He suspected she was neither.

"Okay! Can't wait!" He picked up the ridiculously tall glass, took a gulp and immediately felt his molars dissolve. His tongue was trying to crawl into his esophagus. "Good! Really good!"

"Drink more!" she said. He drank more. Every time he paused, she shouted, "Drink more!" The sweetness was so sweet it ached, throbbed, coated his organs with caramel and made him sweat. When he finally finished the glass, the sugar rush put on track shoes and ran circles around the yard. He thought he'd lose consciousness.

Alicia seemed satisfied but not at all grateful. "I'm going to watch SpongeBob," she said, and she went inside. He sat there a moment, trying to uncross his eyes.

"Are you all right?" Mrs. Ortega said. He turned around. She'd been watching through the screen.

He coughed. "Yes, I'm fine."

She smiled at him, warm and affectionate. "Thank you. Alicia is very sensitive."

After the sugar rush had subsided and he'd brushed his teeth three times, he sat at his tiny breakfast table and resumed his search for a dog. It was a meager compensation for his recent losses, a penny dropped into an empty well of needs.

One ad said: *Black lab, obedient, 6 yrs., all shots. Free to good home.* He called the number.

"Hello?" A woman's voice, hoarse and wary.

"Hi. I'm calling about the dog." She didn't say anything. "I'd like to come and see it," he added.

The address was twenty miles from town, a sketchy, hardscrabble area. The houses were far apart, stretches of thick woods between them, no borrowing a cup of sugar around here. There were lopsided trailers on cinder blocks, laundry on clotheslines, broken toys scattered in uneven yards. Isaiah parked the Mustang in front of the address. An abandoned car was parked next to the house, vines and skinny branches growing out of its eyes and ears. The house was in bad shape. Roof shingles missing, cardboard covering a dormer window, the plank siding gray and warped. But there was no trash around, the porch was swept clean, the footpath bordered with white rocks. A man and a dog came out.

"Hi, I'm Isaiah."

"Ned," the man said. He looked down at the dog. "Well, there he is. Go see if you like him, Duke."

Isaiah kneeled down and put his hand out, fingers down. Something Grace had taught him. Let him sniff you first, check you out.

"Hey, Duke, how are you?" Isaiah said. The dog trotted over, his mouth open, panting, pink tongue hanging to the side. He looked like he was smiling. Duke gave him the sniff test, and apparently he passed. Isaiah scratched him behind his ears, and the dog nearly swooned. Isaiah wished he could be that happy getting his ears scratched.

"Named him Duke because we thought he looked a little regal," Ned said.

"Yeah, he does."

Isaiah expected Ned to come forward and shake hands, but he sat down on the porch steps. He was wearing old jeans and a flannel shirt with the sleeves cut off. His chest and arms were thickets of tattoos. They covered his bald head too. From this distance, they looked like a really close, really bad haircut. Maybe Ned was forty, maybe he was sixty. He wasn't friendly or unfriendly, just doing what he had to do.

"Helluvah car," he said.

"Thanks," Isaiah said. "A friend loaned it to me."

"Some friend."

A woman came out of the house. She wore a faded Led Zeppelin T-shirt and cutoffs. She was younger than Ned, in her thirties. There were tats on her bald head too. Hers were larger and more distinct than Ned's, lots of curls and curves and swoopy lines.

"My wife, Cherry," Ned said, like he was admitting to a burglary.

"Hello," Isaiah said. "I think we talked on the phone." Cherry stood with her head tilted to one side and her arms folded across her chest. She gave a slight nod but that was all.

Isaiah tried not to stare. Ned and Cherry were a striking pair, like a Watusi couple in full native costume, strange and startling but obviously human beings. He took Duke for a walk. He was easy on the leash; alert and he didn't bark when he saw another dog. He was calm in traffic. Isaiah kneeled down and looked him in the eye. "Are you my dog?" he asked.

"I'm sorry," Isaiah said when he got back. "He's a great dog, but not the one for me." He didn't have a reason really except he felt no connection. Cherry was staring at him. Her light blue eyes were intense and appraising, like she was calculating his usefulness in a dark scheme.

"Yeah, it happens," Ned said. Without a word, he went inside but Cherry lingered.

"Nice to meet you," Isaiah said. Cherry was a stone effigy, a steel castle, a bulletproof vest.

"Yeah, me too."

Cherry watched Isaiah drive away. The Mustang disappeared down the road, and she listened to its engine fade in the distance. She went inside. Ned was where he usually was, molded to the beat-up yellow couch with his head back and his feet stretched out. The beer bottle looked like part of his hand. Overall, he was a useless bum, but he was King Kong in the sack and he could read her moods. She started to say something but stopped and stared into the unlit fireplace.

"What?" Ned asked. She didn't answer. "Cherry? What's up?" he said, his tone rising. "You're making me nervous."

"Isaiah," she said. "I've seen him somewhere before."

CHAPTER SEVEN: WHERE'S MY SAMITCH, BITCH?

Isaiah got home from Ned and Cherry's, tired and disappointed. He wished Duke had been his dog. He was putting the key in the door when he heard a crash. He hurried inside and heard another crash. He rushed into the kitchen. The window and the fridge door were open. A young man was on the floor, trying to get up, slipping on the yam casserole he'd dropped.

"Stay there," Isaiah said.

The kid was in his late teens, early twenties. Except for the yams on his clothes, he was neat and clean, a smiley face T-shirt, a complicated black watch and near new sneakers. Not a drug addict and not a punk vandalizing for fun.

The kid looked spent, desperate and afraid. His shirt was torn, there were twigs in his hair. "I'm really, really sorry," he said.

"Who are you running from?"

"Me? I'm not running from anybody."

"You have no money or you'd have bought some food and you have no phone because you didn't call your family. What's your name?"

"Billy," the kid said, like it was the worst name in the world.

"Tell me what you're running from, Billy, or I'll call the police." The kid was one of those people whose every emotion could be seen on his face, every intention in his eyes. "You're about to tell me a lie," Isaiah said. "Don't. I wasn't bluffing. I *will* call the police."

Billy lowered his head and mumbled, "I was in the neuropsychiatric wing at the county hospital."

"What for?"

"A ninety-day psych evaluation," Billy said, adding quickly, "It's bogus, completely bogus."

Isaiah's reaction was visceral, an immediate antagonism to anyone who needed help; anyone needing a ninety-day psych evaluation. Isaiah had encountered a lot of troubled people on his cases. He asked what he always asked when confronted by someone unstable.

"Did you take your meds?"

Billy was surprised, hesitating before he shook his head. "No, but I'm okay, I really am. I'm not crazy. Can I get up now?"

"Yes, but sit in that chair." Billy obeyed. Isaiah tossed him a dish towel to wipe off the mess. There was only one option, Isaiah thought. Call the authorities and let them deal with it. "You have to go back," he said. "You won't last very long, running around stealing casseroles. I imagine your family's worried about you too."

"Please don't call the cops," Billy said, like he was pleading for his life. "I have things to do. *Important* things. My friend might be in danger and I have to help her." Isaiah's antagonism was growing into repugnance. Maybe that was true, maybe not, but it sounded like a case; one more pathetic soul in deep trouble of their own making.

He restrained himself from asking, What friend? What danger? Danger from who? Instead, he said, "That's too bad, but you have to go back. I can make the call or you can."

"Wait, let me explain."

"I don't want an explanation."

"I'm not crazy," Billy said adamantly. Anyone who has to tell you he's not crazy probably is, Isaiah thought. "I didn't belong in a hospital," Billy went on. "It was a conspiracy."

Conspiracy? Get this kid out of here,

84

Isaiah thought.

Billy continued. "Cannon — that's the sheriff — convinced my mom that I was" — he made air quotes — "*a danger to myself and others.* What a load of crap! And you wanna know why?"

Could this get any worse? Isaiah thought. Cannon was involved. That this was turning shitty wasn't a surprise, it was the speed of it. "No, I don't want to know why," he said. He raised his hand to shut Billy up. "Make the call or I will."

"Let me just explain."

"I just said —"

Billy blurted out, "A serial killer is coming to Coronado Springs!" You could tell he didn't want to say it; that it made him sound unhinged. Isaiah reminded himself not to ask the kid why he believes this or where he got the information or anything else. It would only make the situation more intriguing.

"You have to go back," Isaiah said.

Billy started to cry. "I can't. My friend is following him — the serial killer, I mean. Don't you see? She could get killed! I have to help her! Please don't make me go back."

The kid's fear and sense of urgency were real, Isaiah thought. But lots of things seem real when your mind is full of voices and

85

the only solid ground is your imagination.

"His name is William Crowe," Billy said. "He's AMSAK. I can prove it. I have his records and everything!"

AMSAK? Isaiah thought. Billy is either delusional, paranoid or both.

Billy read his expression. "It's complicated," he said. Crazy people are always complicated, Isaiah thought unkindly.

Billy went on. "Crowe killed my friend Ava's sister. Ava is following him in her car and that's why she's in danger. He might catch her and then what? See what I mean?" *Don't fall for it, Isaiah. Get him out of here.*

"You have to go back," he said again.

"No, no, I can't!" Billy shouted. "I've got to help Ava!"

This was getting worse, Isaiah thought. Like Alicia and her goddamn lemonade. Drink it and you'll die of diabetes. Don't drink it and you make a six-year-old girl cry her eyes out. Then it occurred to him. This wasn't his decision.

"Look, I don't care if you go back to the hospital. It's up to your family. Is there somebody responsible you can call?"

Billy brightened.

"My sister, Irene! She's the only one who listens to me." Isaiah gave him his phone and Billy made the call. He turned away and talked in a steady stream, like he didn't want his sister to think about what he was saying.

"Tell her to bring your meds," Isaiah said. Billy ended the call and started to speak, probably a thank-you. "Don't say anything," Isaiah added sharply. "Just sit there and shut up."

Twenty minutes later, the doorbell rang. Isaiah opened the door. He couldn't hide his disappointment. Irene couldn't have been more than fifteen or sixteen. She was very thin, not soft, sinewy, like a high jumper or a marathoner. Great, Isaiah thought, the only one who listens to Billy is a girl barely out of middle school.

"You're Irene?" Isaiah said, hoping she'd say no, she was Sally, the little sister. Her big sister Irene was right behind her.

"Yes, I'm Irene," she said forthrightly. "Is Billy here?" Isaiah let her in. "I'm very sorry about this," she said. "It's a big imposition. I'll get him out of here as soon as I can."

Billy came to meet her. They hugged for a long time.

"Talk somewhere else," Isaiah said.

They went out on the back stoop. They argued, Billy shrill and beseeching, Irene stern and exasperated. She sounded like the older one. Billy shouted, "You have to believe me, sis! You have to!"

Billy believes in things that aren't there, Isaiah thought. He remembered his clients, Lester Collins who stabbed a hallucination that turned out to be his neighbor and Missy Laws who drowned her baby girl in the toilet because she thought it was poisoning her milk and Jake Lamont who jumped in front of an Amtrak train because he thought he was Iron Man.

Irene returned. "I'd like to talk to you, Mr. Quintabe. Is that all right?" Irene was unassuming, obviously intelligent, in that space between plain and pretty, the kind of standout you had to look for. Nevertheless, Isaiah really, truly didn't want to hear what she had to say. He said nothing. She sat down.

"Billy told me about the serial killer. He thinks AMSAK is someone named William Crowe." She sounded weary and frustrated. She wrung her hands, the long fingers wrestling with each other. "Frankly, I don't believe him, but I want you to know, Billy is not mentally ill. He's lost and confused but he's not sick."

"Your brother was in neuropsych. Doesn't that tell you something?"

"It was a mistake. Well, not really a mistake."

"What do you mean?" Isaiah said. Inwardly, he slapped himself in the face. Questions only encouraged her.

"Billy always wanted to be a hero," she said. "You know, like the kid who stepped in front of the terrorist or went back into the fire to save the dog. Maybe it was because Mom was disappointed with him, and he got bullied a lot. He told tall tales. He saw a spaceship land on Sugar Mountain. He was going to catch the murderer, the politicians were trying to stop him from exposing corruption. Things like that. No one believed him." She had a water bottle and paused for a drink.

"Then I think he got angry," she continued. "He started messing with people's heads, doing things for shock value and taking stupid risks. He rode his skateboard down Watershed Hill. It's incredibly steep, hairpin turns. No one was crazy enough to do it except Billy. He nearly killed himself, but he got it on video. That was the important thing." Irene stopped, sighed, readying herself for what came next.

"He put on a puppet show for schoolkids. Hansel and Gretel, the fairy tale? Both of them were naked and anatomically correct. He snuck into the church before choir practice," she continued. "There was a microphone on the pulpit. Billy replaced it with a plastic turd, one of those novelty things? Reverend Anders was outraged and drop-kicked the thing across the chapel. Every couple of Sundays, Billy would do the same thing, and the reverend would react the same way. I think it was the fifth time or sixth time Billy did it," Irene cringed. "He used a real turd. I guess you can imagine the rest.

"The kids started seeing Billy in a different way," she went on. "He wasn't an idiot, he was outrageous, he was a freak, but in a good way. The kids made him a folk hero. And he loved it. There was no reason to stop. Dead cat in the bakery window, red dye in the water main so anybody who took a shower thought they were bleeding to death. At the school talent show, he performed a rap song called 'Where's My Samitch, Bitch?' and got a standing ovation. The principal suspended him. Kids started singing the samitch song on the playground and at parties and around the house. Parents were pissed off."

Gretta was humiliated, Irene said. Cannon was furious. The offenses were minor but they were happening on his watch. Cannon got written up in the *Eureka Examiner,* the article titled TOWN SHERIFF INVESTI-

GATES PLASTIC POO POO. It was published in other newspapers too. The city council was outraged. Billy's antics were making their town look ridiculous. Everywhere Gretta went she got looks. *She's the attorney with the crazy son.*

"Billy dropped out of school," Irene said. "He had nothing to do. He got into fights. He was arrested for shoplifting, public intoxication, urinating in a mailbox, sleeping in someone else's car and other petty offenses. His pranks continued, but without an audience of high school kids, they went largely unnoticed. He worked sporadically at menial jobs. Basically, he was a bum, living at home. Gretta gave up on him. Everyone gave up on him.

"Except me," Irene said. "But Billy went too far. He re-created a scene from *American Graffiti.* You know, the one where Richard Dreyfuss attaches a steel cable to a police car?" Isaiah knew the scene. Once the cable was attached, Dreyfuss drove past the cops at high speed. The cops took off in pursuit, and the whole axle was ripped off. "Unfortunately, it was Cannon's patrol car," Irene said. "Of course, Billy videotaped it and posted it on YouTube. It went viral, like worldwide viral. Lots of people love that movie." Billy was arrested and charged with vandalism, assault on a police officer and destruction of public property. The press was all over it. That Billy's mother was an assistant DA made it all the more intriguing.

"When Billy was out on bail, he was arrested again," Irene said. "He was drunk out of his mind, wandering around on the interstate. He nearly got run over a dozen times. With permission from Judge Marsten, Gretta's longtime friend, she had Billy committed for a ninety-day psych evaluation. It made everybody happy. There would be no trial, Billy was removed from public view, and in the meantime, they'd work out a plea deal. That's Billy's story in a nutshell."

Isaiah was expressionless. "What about it?"

"What about it?" She was surprised by the question. "I guess what I'm trying to tell you is that Billy's got problems, but he's not insane. He doesn't drink anymore. He's done playing pranks. He's lost and needs therapy, but he shouldn't be stuck in a hospital."

"What's this have to do with me?" Isaiah said. He knew, of course. The girl was setting him up, trying to tell him Billy wouldn't be a lot of trouble. She was going to ask him if Billy could stay. Let her ask, he thought. The days of saying yes to this kind of bullshit were over.

"Could you let Billy stay with you?" Irene said. "Just for a couple of days? He's been cooped up in the hospital for weeks. It's probably why he's like this. Frustration sets him off. If he has some breathing space he'll calm down, and I'll take him to the hospital myself. I promise." Isaiah started to reply, but Irene cut him off. "I brought his meds, phone, laptop. He'll be quiet and he can sleep in the basement or the garage. I'll come every day and check on him. I have money for food." She smiled, as if to say, I've taken care of everything! No worries, sir! "He won't be any trouble," she added.

Yes, he will, Isaiah thought. He'll be all kinds of trouble.

"I don't know," Isaiah said. Shit. He shouldn't have said that. I don't know means you're thinking about it, that the idea is on the table.

Irene was tearful and clutching his arm. "He has no one else, and it's just a couple of days," she pleaded. "I promise he'll behave himself. Really, Mr. Quintabe, you have my word." Isaiah looked at her, this girl who loved her brother and didn't want him to suffer or be humiliated. Isaiah knew this would end in unqualified disaster. He absolutely knew it. It was guaranteed, fated, as certain as catching a cold.

"Okay, but just for a couple of days." Irene thanked him profusely and left. Alone again, he thought about the shit that was bound to come. The old adage was true. No good deed goes unpunished. The only questions were what form the punishment would take, how long it would last and whether violence would be involved. Billy came in.

"Thank you. I really, really mean that. You're saving my —"

"Stop. I don't want to know what I'm saving," Isaiah said harshly. "I don't want to know anything. Whatever's happening with you, keep it to yourself. I want no involvement of any kind."

Isaiah was uninvolved for exactly forty-six minutes, because that's when Sheriff Cannon showed up at the door. "Mr. Quintabe," he said gruffly. He held up Billy's mugshot. Great, Isaiah thought. His houseguest had a criminal record.

"His name is Billy Sorensen," Cannon said. "Have you seen him? He escaped from neuropsych. Somebody saw him around the area." *Tell him, Isaiah! Tell him Billy's in the kitchen!* "He's not dangerous," Cannon said, "just an asshole that stirs up trouble. He's also a pathological liar." Isaiah hesitated. "Well?" the sheriff said, impatiently. "Have you seen him or not?" *Tell him! Tell him, goddammit!*

"I, uh — no, I haven't," he said. Cannon stared a moment, turned, and walked away. Isaiah closed the door.

"What the fuck have I done?" he said aloud. Billy came out of the kitchen, grinning, about to say something. Isaiah cut him off with a glare. "Don't say one fucking word. Just get out of my goddamn sight." Billy slunk away.

Isaiah was disgusted with himself. He hated his gooey, stupid heart, his compassion and kindness, his compulsive need to be the Good Samaritan. Grace loved him for it, but it made her angry too, deliberately inviting danger, thinking he was immune, threatening himself and their relationship. Now the relationship was gone and so was his career. He knew he was feeling sorry for himself, but knowing that didn't make the feeling go away. Insights like "You're feeling sorry for yourself" just added to your misery. Not only are you a friendless outcast, you're a weakling and a crybaby. You're a man without a dog.

He found a support group in Clarkson, on the Nevada side. It met in the evening at the senior center. The room had one small window, a circle of metal chairs and a coffeemaker on a folding table. It made the meeting seem clandestine. Six men and one woman. They were grim, disheveled, downcast eyes, arms folded tightly across their chests. He wanted to be an observer instead of a participant. In a gesture he knew was pathetic, he pulled his chair back from the circle a foot or so.

The therapist was a man named Hank. Heavyset, friendly, a leather vest over a blue shirt and a silver earring. He welcomed everybody, nodding at Isaiah, the new guy. He went around the circle and everyone said their names. Isaiah said his was John. Hank asked if anyone would like to speak first. A fortyish guy with a gray ponytail said he was afraid of sleeping because of his nightmares. He tried to stay awake with coffee and amphetamines, but they made him jumpy and gave him the sweats. He called people for no reason. He had fits of temper and broke things.

He said he was in Afghanistan in 2004, drove a convoy to Fallujah. He saw the four contractors who were killed by the insurgents, charred black and hung from a bridge. Of all the horrors he saw, that's what traumatized him, that's what razed his mind and leveled his soul for all these years. He sought escape in suicide twice. Every morning he'd wake up thinking, *Shit, I'm still alive.* His wife, that bitch, said he just wanted the attention he never got in life; that it was an act of anger, like fuck you, you'll miss me when I'm gone. She never understood that suicide was about stopping the pain. Suicide was not being able to take it anymore.

Hank asked Isaiah if he wanted to say something but he declined. He left before Hank led the group in prayer. He drove fast like he had when he'd fled LA. The night was moonless, the sky, black as a raven. The drone of the engine made his head thrum, the headlights reducing the world to a white line on black asphalt. He began to panic, as if his very self was dissolving, his life evanescing into the cold mountain air. His hands shook, he nearly missed a turn and ran off the road. He pulled over and stopped. He closed his eyes, telling himself repeatedly that he wasn't actually dissolving. He was safe no matter how he felt. He turned off the ignition. He turned off the lights. He sat in the quiet for a long time, the occasional car swishing past. He thought about his choices. He was healthy, unattached, money in the bank, there were a hundred things he could do. But he could only think of one. Going back home. Going back to Grace. The gangs and bounty hunters would be waiting. He wondered what difference it would make. Dying here or dying there. It didn't really matter, he decided. He started the car and drove on.

CHAPTER EIGHT: ROCK CLIMBING

Gloria was sitting on a lawn chair, sipping a cold Corona. It was very refreshing. TK kept them on ice in a Styrofoam cooler. You couldn't get them that cold in the fridge. TK was holding a beer with one hand and tending the barbecue in his easy, patient way. Their brief courtship had been combustible, but everything had turned out fine. She'd been reluctant at first. Afraid was more like it. Her husband of twenty-seven years had left her for a barmaid. From then on, love was a cuss word and men were worthless scoundrels, objects of punishment and little else. Until TK came along. He convinced her otherwise with his sweet nature and loving heart; with a little red bird and dancing elephants.

"Why is the chicken taking so long?" she said. "You should put some more coals on there."

"You're talking about grilling. This is

barbecue," he said.

"Well it's still taking too long," she grumbled. She was in a bad mood despite the pleasantness of the day. It was all Juanell's fault. Thinking about him made her anxious.

"What do you say we go somewhere? Take a little vacation," TK said. That instantly brightened her mood.

"That's a lovely idea. Let's go someplace sunny and warm. What about Hawaii?"

TK shook his head. "Not for me."

"Why? What's wrong with Hawaii?"

"I don't need a tan. Do you?"

She spit up her beer and laughed. "See what you made me do? Now my dress is wet."

"Leave it like that. I believe I see some cleavage."

"Stop it," she said. But she didn't dry it off. They sat there awhile, looking out at the wrecking yard like it was a sandy beach on Waikiki. Love can do that to you, she thought.

"How's it going with Dodson?" TK asked. Gloria huffed and shook her head.

"We start his education tomorrow, and I'll tell you this. That young man needs a lot of work."

"Dodson's been Dodson a long time.

You're trying to turn a bicycle into a pickup truck."

"I'm not saying it will be easy. Juanell is so stubborn. You'd think change was some kind of torture. He's so hardheaded." TK didn't say anything. Gloria looked at him. "I'm not like that. I'm not like that at all."

"I didn't say you were," TK said, tucking away his grin. "Uh-oh. I think my chicken's burning." He handed her his beer and got up again. TK did that, confronting her without confronting her. She was learning from him, and that hadn't happened in a long time. She finished her beer and finished TK's too. Tomorrow was going to be a war.

Cherise was at work. Dodson and Gloria were facing each other across the breakfast table, Gloria's posture as straight as the high-backed chair she was sitting in. She was looking at him like he was a fecal sample. "Let me understand," she said. "You want me to teach you how to behave properly and be presentable in public, is that right? How to be civilized, dignified and normalized so you can join decent society like a regular human being? Are we on the same page?"

He inhaled so deeply he thought the Cocoa Puffs would come flying out of the box. "Yes, we're on the same page."

"You realize that I'd rather put my head in the microwave than spend time with you. If there was a choice between cutting off my foot or talking to you for five minutes, I'd go out right now and buy myself some crutches." The feeling's mutual, Dodson thought. *Please, God, get this over with.* Gloria went on. "I have never met anyone in my life with lower moral standards or a higher likelihood of going to prison, and the only things I can think of with less intelligence are my dead Uncle Dewey and a pound cake."

"I thought you might feel that way," Dodson said. "I don't know why. Maybe I'm psychic. Are you going to help me or not?"

"I'll do this for one reason and one reason only," Gloria said. "Cherise and the baby."

"That's two."

She glared and snapped back, "Although I might change my mind if you get smart with me. And I have conditions. Are you listening to me?"

"I'm sitting right in front of you. How could I not?"

"Condition one. You will not talk back to me. None of your lip, none of your smart remarks. Do you understand?" Dodson nodded so slightly it might have been a tic.

Gloria scowled. "I said, do you understand?"

"Yes, I understand."

"Second condition. You will do exactly as I say. No attitude, no objections, and no negotiations. I say it, you do it. Is that clear?"

"Yes, it's clear." He wondered if there was a way to kill Gloria and get away with it. Stick a black widow spider into her ear or put Super Glue in her toothpaste. She might not die but she'd shut the fuck up.

"Do I have your word on that?" Gloria said. Dodson said something inaudible. "What was that, Juanell? I didn't hear you."

He mumbled, "Yes, you have my word."

"Louder, please. I need to know you mean it."

"Yes, you have my word." He could hardly keep from screaming.

Gloria got up and smoothed down her dress. "We're going out."

"Out? Out where?"

"Wherever I say. Go put your shoes on and not those ridiculous glow-in-the-dark sneakers."

They went to the Suit Store on Atlantic Boulevard. "How can I help you today?" the salesman said.

"We're looking for a business suit," Gloria

replied. She hesitated, like saying the words might hurt or cause a landslide. "For my son-in-law. Something conservative. No stripes, checks, logos, gold buttons or anything else."

"Can I choose the color?" Dodson said.

"Yes, you can. You can choose between charcoal gray and charcoal gray."

"How about a three button?"

"No. Two."

"How about a vest? I've seen professional people wear them."

"You mean like a waiter or a riverboat gambler? No."

"How about a yellow tie?" Dodson said, getting desperate. "Yellow and gray go good together."

"Maybe if you're a taxicab or cockatoo," Gloria said. She turned to the salesman. "Something medium blue with a small pattern."

They bought shoes, black oxfords. Dodson wanted the ones with perforations in the toe cap but Gloria said no. "A man's got to have some kinda style," he complained.

"Yes, some men need style but that's not you. You have too much style. You have extra style. You have style you need to get rid of."

Dodson stood in front of the three-way

mirror. He was horrified. "I'll have to move out of Long Beach and live someplace where they ain't no black people."

"Your posture is terrible," Gloria said. "Don't lean on one foot, make your shoulders level, and stand up straight. Now shake my hand and say, good afternoon, Gloria, it's very nice to meet you — don't look off somewhere, look directly at me. What are you doing, watching for a drive-by?" She smoothed her dress again. "Okay, go ahead."

"Good afternoon, Gloria, it's nice to meet you."

"Now shake hands." Dodson bent his elbow, his hand curled.

"Stop right there," she said. "People in the business world don't shake hands like that unless they're a rapper or basketball player. Now shake the normal way." He took her hand like it had mud on it and shook. "That wasn't so bad, was it?" No, it was worse, he thought. Like touching a corpse or an alligator. She looked at him in the mirror again and frowned.

"What's wrong now?" Dodson said.

"You look like you stole that suit. Something isn't right."

"Of course it's not right. It's like a Japanese tourist wearing a cowboy hat. Some things are just wrong." Gloria wasn't listening. She was still looking at him, lips pursed and nodding. A horrifying thought occurred to him. He backed away, his palms out protectively. "No, please, Gloria, I'm begging you."

Twenty minutes later, they were approaching Pete's Place. "Don't do this," Dodson said. "Let me keep my dignity, that's not too much to ask, is it? I'm begging you."

"Oh, you hush now. You're being melodramatic." They stopped at the doorway.

"No, that's it. I refuse," Dodson said.

"Well, that's fine with me," Gloria said. "Do you know a good motel? Because that's where you'll be living if I tell Cherise."

The barbershop was a familiar place. Pete was slow, withered, had Don King hair and smiled every other Tuesday. Old Man Dupree was sitting in one of the shoeshine chairs, reading the *Racing Form*, a pipe between his teeth. Dodson had never seen him shine shoes or do anything else for that matter. Two other barbers worked for Pete. They looked too young to be entrusted with a grown man's hair. No, they should stick to carving gang signs into the side of your head.

Gloria took Pete aside and spoke to him in hushed tones. At one point he laughed, but she silenced him with a look that made him take two steps back.

"Let's go, Dodson," Pete said, dolefully. Dodson's hair was relaxed and straight. He wore it combed back like Pat Riley. He knew it was old school, but he liked that. It made him stand out in a world of deep waves, sponge twists, frohawks and box fades. It made him look too cool to care. He lowered himself into the chair like he had a severe case of hemorrhoids.

"I don't want to look," he said. Pete turned the chair around.

"Okay," he said with a sigh. "The big chop." Dodson closed his eyes, clenched his fists. He heard the scissors working, felt swatches of hair fall on his shoulders. "Could you stop moving around?" Pete said. "I might make a mistake."

"The whole goddamn thing is a mistake."

"Don't listen to him, Pete," Gloria said. "You're going in the right direction." Lord have mercy, Dodson thought. What direction is that? *Oh, please, God, don't let it be Will Smith.* The big chop was done. Pete moved Dodson to a sink and washed his hair with a special shampoo. He left it there for five minutes and rinsed it out. Back to the barber's chair. Pete cut his hair again, carefully this time, then he washed it a second time and dried it. He whipped off the barber's apron and said, "You want to take a look?"

"Should I?" Dodson said.

"Not for me to say."

Dodson nodded, and Pete turned the chair around. Dodson's first impulse was to say, who the fuck is that? It was a plain old haircut. No waves, twists or surgical lines. Just his natural hair cut very short. With the exception of Gloria, everybody in the place was either stifling a laugh or pointedly looking away.

Dodson said, "I look like Will Smith." And the whole barbershop burst out laughing. Old Man Dupree laughed so hard the pipe fell out of his mouth and he burned a hole in his pants.

"How could you do this to me, Gloria?" Dodson said as they walked out the door. "What have I ever done to you?"

"You married my daughter."

Dodson was waiting for inspection when Cherise got home from work. He was wearing the suit, the shiny black oxfords and the new haircut.

"An improvement, wouldn't you say?" Gloria said. Cherise's lips curled in, her forehead wrinkling so she wouldn't start laughing.

"What's so funny?" Dodson said.

"You look like Will Smith!" She laughed so hard she went into the bedroom waving one hand in the air.

"Thank you for your support," Dodson called after her.

Gloria went home. Dodson stood on the balcony. He ran his hands through the hair he didn't have anymore. The makeover had left him feeling naked and vulnerable. He didn't realize how much he'd invested in his appearance. It reflected a particular image of himself, one that proved convincing to others and himself. He had become that image. He was what he imagined himself to be. Gloria had blown that to shit in one afternoon. She didn't realize what she was doing, or maybe she did. She'd put wooden wheels on a lowrider and turned it into a metal-flaked donkey cart. He shook his head ruefully. This wasn't the worst of it, either. This was the start of it.

Dodson used to enjoy sitting in the kitchen. A comfortable place where you could come up with ideas, think about your agenda, your plans, your goals for the future or nothing at all if that was your pleasure. He especially liked eating Cocoa Puffs at the breakfast table. You could listen to the sounds of your teeth crunching on the cereal and taste the chocolate melting on your tongue and the cold milk carrying it down your throat. Now the kitchen was like a robbery in progress. Somebody dangerous and unpredictable ordering you to take all the self-respect out of your pockets.

Gloria cleared her throat and began. "How you speak tells people who you are, where you're from and your level of education. As soon as you open your mouth, folks know you are a hoodlum from the ghetto who dropped out of high school because you were dull-witted and couldn't compete."

"Soon as I open my mouth, huh?" Dodson said.

"Your pronunciation and vocabulary are decent, but your grammar needs work and you use run-on sentences far too often. The graphic images will have to go as well as your use of street jargon and profanity."

"All that?" Dodson said. "That crimps my game, woman. Won't be nothing left to say 'less I'm fakin' jacks. Maybe I'll be an intern at the goddamn zoo and conversate with the animals, bark like a seal or screech like a muthafuckin' howler monkey — what? What'd I say?"

When Cherise came home from work, Dodson and Gloria were practicing proper speech. Dodson looked like his spirit had left him for someone else.

"How's everything?" Cherise said. Gloria nodded at Dodson, urging him with a wide-eyed glare.

"Everything is — fine," Dodson said, haltingly. "We was — were — doing — I mean having, lessons on communicating right — I mean correctly."

"Oh, really? And how did that go?" Cherise said. Another glare from Gloria and Dodson reluctantly went on.

"The lessons was — were very pleasant. I didn't have no — any problems at all. I be — am, making progress, you feel me — I mean, don't you think so?"

"Well, the grammar's better," Cherise said, "but he sounds like he lost twenty-five IQ points."

"I know. He's a slow learner," Gloria said.

"There must be some other way."

"I've been thinking about that, but he's so hardheaded."

"Do y'all know I'm here?" Dodson said. Cherise thought a moment. "You know what? My friend Kumiko learned to speak English by watching TV." Dodson perked up.

"I like TV."

Dodson's assignment was to binge-watch *Friends.* He was to say everything the characters said exactly the way they said it. Dodson watched the opening of the show; six white people jumping around in a fountain. "One thing for sure, none of those people can dance," he said. "Who is that fool in the water doing the twist?"

The episode began and Dodson echoed every line.

"It's a shepherd's pie! It's got layers of meat, cheese, sponge cake, hot dog mustard, preserved pork fat, and blueberry jam!"

"Is the shepherd dead or is he still okay?"

"My list of boyfriends includes a dog walker who growled when he answered the phone, a little person who punched me in the kneecaps because I thought his shoes were for a baby, and the mascot for the Mets. You know, the guy that runs around dressed as an apricot?"

"Was the apricot a good kisser?"

"Everybody knows what turns a woman on. You've got zones A, B, C, D, and W."

"Why W?"

"Because it's way the hell down there."

When Dodson was done watching, he wanted to drown Ross in the fountain, choke Chandler to death with that sweater-vest, smash Phoebe's guitar on Joey's empty brain cavity and swing the smelly cat at Monica and kill her. Dodson wondered why there were no people of color on the show. The Friends lived in Manhattan after all. There weren't any blacks, Puerto Ricans, Sikhs, Filipinos or any other ethnicity that made the Big Apple big except an extra or two in the coffee shop. The fuck was that about?

The lessons with Gloria went on. And on. Every day, taking orders from a woman who didn't like him, trust him or regard him in the slightest way. Today's session began in the living room. Gloria was sitting on the sofa, Dodson standing in the doorway, wearing his suit and tie.

"All right," she said. "Walk over there and sit down in that chair — and remember, keep your head still, stop nodding and take that hitch out of your stride. You look like a pimp prowling around the bus station."

Dodson thought a moment, taking in all the instructions. He proceeded so cautiously he stumbled and nearly fell. He felt better when he sat down in the chair. It's hard to fuck that up. Gloria was shaking her head.

"Don't stick your legs out, and sit up straight," she said. "No, don't cross your arms over your chest. You look like you're waiting for your parole officer."

"Where am I supposed to put them?"

"See those armrests?" Gloria replied. "They're for your arms."

They were in a booth at Denny's, looking over the menus. Gloria said, "When you're with people from the office, don't order anything that's awkward to put in your mouth, makes your hands greasy or drips down your chin. Hamburgers, fried chicken, gravy, onion rings, burritos, tacos, French fries, maple syrup, wings, spaghetti or anything with sauce — and, oh yes, don't order anything with the words hot, garlic, spicy, super, Southwest, ultimate, jalapeños or skillet in it, and never, ever order dessert."

The server arrived. Dodson said, "Could I please have a bowl of dry oatmeal, an empty glass of water, a side of Handi-Wipes and a hazmat suit? And could I get that oatmeal medium rare? Thank you so much." Gloria said grilled chicken was a good choice. It came with a zucchini and rice pilaf. Dodson had a few bites and wondered where the flavor went. Maybe they left it in the kitchen. Gloria didn't let up.

"Don't run your tongue over your teeth, and take smaller bites — oh for goodness' sake, chew discreetly, you look like you're eating taffy. No, no, don't cut your meat all at once. You're not making lunch for your ninety-year-old grandfather. Cut a piece, eat it and then cut another. Could you please slow down? Eating is not the same as running from the police."

"I'm trying to get this over with."

"Don't bend your head down to the plate," she continued. "That might be appropriate if you were in Beijing eating noodles but not here in America eating grilled chicken at Denny's — and *dab* with the napkin. You look like you're erasing your lips."

Dodson put his fork down. "You know what? I'm not gonna eat anymore. It's too stressful. The only way to make you happy is to die from starvation."

"If you weren't Cherise's husband, I'd say that was a good idea."

On the drive home, Gloria brought up another topic. "Music. That's important," she said.

"I like music," he said. He remembered saying that about watching TV. He shouldn't have said anything at all.

"You know all those rappers you like?" Gloria said. "Forget them. From now on Ice-T is ice tea and ice cubes are in your freezer. I want you to find some singers you can be familiar with so if somebody asks you what you like you won't say Mister Assault Rifle or Overdose Willy or whoever those people are."

Dodson said, "Overdose Willy?"

He listened to some music on Spotify. Ed Sheeran? First of all, the boy looked like a leprechaun or a toadstool or a leprechaun sitting on a toadstool. All the money he makes and he can't buy some decent clothes? Who cut his hair? His mom? A samurai? His gardener and a Weed Eater?

Dodson had heard the name Taylor Swift but that was all. One thing for sure, this girl should start her day with a few bowls of Cocoa Puffs and follow it up with a double-meat Fatburger and some chili fries. Dodson had a closet rod with more curves. She sang okay, but two high notes from Jennifer Hudson would blow her skinny ass right out of her Tesla. And by the way, who is Adam Levine and why does he have his shirt off? Dodson liked Gwen Stefani. She had style and attitude when she wasn't singing with her countrified boyfriend. Dodson couldn't listen anymore. If somebody asked him what music he liked he'd say jazz and leave it at that. Nobody knew shit about jazz.

They were in the kitchen again. "Conversation is very important," Gloria said. "What you talk about is as revealing as how you talk. Subjects to be avoided. Drugs, gangs, guns, your past, your nonexistent job history, your friends, your criminal record, your business failures, your experiences as a convict, and of course, politics goes without saying. Stick to safe things like sports. Do you golf? Never mind. Do you work out? Lift weights? Run on a treadmill?"

"No, I don't work out or lift weights. I don't need to," Dodson said, "and if I'm gonna run somewhere, I want a destination. I want to be somewhere. You could run on a treadmill all damn day, and where are you when you get off? The goddamn treadmill. That's a waste of my time."

"Then say you ride one of those fancy bicycles," Gloria said, impatiently, "or you like to go rock climbing."

"Rock climbing?" Dodson said, his voice rising. "Did you say *rock climbing?*"

"Yes," she snapped. "That's what I said. Do you have a problem with that?"

Dodson was fed up. His blood pressure was so high he thought his eyeballs would explode. It was time to speak his mind, fuck the torpedoes and get the hell out of my goddamn way.

"When's the last time you seen a nigga rock climbing?" he said. "I got all kinds of danger in my life without hangin' my ass off a goddamn mountain. Where the fuck are them people climbing to anyway? Ain't shit up there but snow. You can find snow at sea level if you know where to look. You wanna know why you don't see more than two or three mountain goats at a time? Cuz most of 'em slip up, fall and break they mutha-fuckin necks, that's why. *Rock climbing.* Really now. What kind of pointless shit is that? What else will white people think of next? Rock climbing backward? Rock climbing buck naked while you drinkin' a cappuccino? It's just like all the other bullshit they make up. Like ice fishing. *Ice fishing.* Have you seen that nonsense? First you

118

gotta drill a hole in a frozen lake — that's some crazy shit all by itself. Then you gotta dress like you dog sleddin' across Siberia and fish with a fishing pole that ain't no bigger than an ice-cream stick. And for what? To catch a fish? I got news for you. You can go to the store and buy a goddamn fish and you don't even have to wear a sweater. Come to think of it, you can buy a fish that's already cooked. Muthafuckas never heard of Mrs. Paul? You don't have to find, catch or clean a box of fish sticks. All you gotta do is turn on the toaster oven and open the bottle of tartar sauce. And what was that other thing? What's it called? *Curling.* Yeah, that's it. I ain't never seen a nigga curling and I hope I never do, slidin' down the ice with a muthafuckin broom sweepin' shit nobody can see. You might as well dust the furniture while you moonwalkin' or wash your car while you doing reps with a cast-iron frying pan. You know what I seen on ESPN? Some white people kayaking in the goddamn white-water rapids. You believe dat? First of all, if you take a kayak in the rapids you deserve whatever happens to you. You know you shouldn't be in there with all them rocks and currents and shit. You could die. Use your damn head. Drive a couple of miles to the lake where all the black folks is swimmin' around and having picnics. I'll tell you something else too. Any time you need a helmet to go in the water you know you 'bout to do something stupid. What if somebody told you to wear a bulletproof vest before you got in the Jacuzzi or strap on a Glock nine when you're 'bout to take a shower? Wouldn't that give you pause? Wouldn't you think maybe I'll stay dry today? You wanna know what I seen on TV? A white boy had a goddamn lion for a pet, named him Chauncy and treated him like a great big kitty cat. Wrestlin' around, playing with each other, this stupid muthafucka talking 'bout how they were true friends and bonded on a spiritual level. Yeah, he said that shit right up to the day that lion ate him like a Chinese chicken salad and spit out the bones. His wife said she couldn't believe Chauncy would do something like that. Ain't that some shit? You know a black woman wouldn't say nothin' like that. If you can't believe a goddamn lion wouldn't eat a big juicy steak that come into his house and plays with him every day, you are too stupid to be alive in the first goddamn place. Somebody like that shouldn't have a bedbug for a pet. And one more thing —" Dodson stopped. Gloria was gone. "Well, all right, then," he said.

He went out on the balcony and brooded awhile. He'd learned something about himself. He was afraid of the unknown. Strange, for somebody who grew up on the streets where unpredictable shit happened all the time, but in that context, you expected it. Every day was a safari. You didn't know where the quicksand was, but you knew there was quicksand and you knew to look out for it. A cape buffalo could charge out of the jungle at any moment, but you knew there was a cape buffalo and you knew he'd charge. This shit was altogether different. Tomorrow was his first day at Apex. There'd be no map, no road signs and no idea what form the quicksand and the buffalo might take. He called Isaiah.

"You okay?" Isaiah said.

"Fuck no," Dodson replied. He told him about Cherise, the internship and his makeover. He got no sympathy. Isaiah laughed as hard as Cherise.

"I feel so much better now, I'm so glad I called," Dodson said.

"Sorry, sorry, but I haven't laughed like that since I left Long Beach," Isaiah said.

"You want to see something even funnier?"

"Is there such a thing?"

Dodson texted him a photo of his new look. Cherise had insisted on taking it. The sounds Isaiah made weren't laughter. They were more like a police siren with the hiccups or a goose with hay fever. "Oh, God, my stomach hurts."

"I'm glad I can bring so much entertainment into your life," Dodson said. "How are you?"

"I'm in trouble."

"Is that supposed to surprise me?" Dodson said. "I didn't expect you to say anything else. What is it this time? Army ants? Dracula? Hurricane Cleo?"

"A serial killer."

"I'm not surprised by that either. It was only a question of time before you got mixed up with one of them crazy muthafuckas. How many of them are there?"

"Just the one."

"Well, that's a relief. I thought you might say a family of 'em or a serial killer basketball team, something like that. And while I'm thinkin' on it, did it ever occur to you to leave wherever it is you're at? Unless you're tied to a radiator with a ball gag in your mouth, get your ass outta — shit, what

122

am I thinking? You *are* tied to a radiator with a ball gag in your mouth."

"In a way, yeah."

"Anything I can do?"

"No, I don't think so."

"Have you talked to Grace?" Dodson asked.

"You know I can't."

"I don't know that at all. You gave up too soon and you know it. The both of you did. You broke up because you wanted to."

"That's not true," Isaiah protested. "Why would I want to do that?" Dodson had lost patience with his two friends. They needed each other like he needed Cherise.

"You and Grace been alone your whole lives. It's what you know. It's what you're comfortable with. You like it that way — no, let me finish. Are you telling me, the great IQ with his freakishly large brain couldn't think of any other way to deal with his problems than leaving town? Don't even try to explain. You know you can't bullshit me." Getting on Isaiah's case was making Dodson feel better, but he didn't know why.

"Good luck tomorrow," Isaiah said.

"Change the subject if you want to, but the girl's waiting for you to call. I know she is."

"I have to go."

"Ease on down the road, Q."

"I'll try."

CHAPTER NINE:
WELCOME TO THE GHET-TOE, HONEY

Deronda was shorthanded. She was working with Grace cleaning the food trucks; scouring the cutting boards, wiping down every surface, mopping, loading pots, pans and utensils into her car to be taken home and washed. Deronda didn't mind doing this kind of work. The sweating and the back pain reminded her to keep her head straight and keep her ego in check. If you're from the hood, there's only one thing you know for certain. No matter how good your shit is, life can snatch it away from you in less than a blink. It reminded her of a nature program she'd watched with Janeel. The episode was about a green lizard that hunted with its tongue. There you were, a happy little cricket sipping nectar out of a rosebud, minding your own business, and *flick,* just like that the lizard's stomach acid was reducing you to a wing and an eyeball.

Deronda's boyfriend, Robert, was an

analyst at a tech company. You couldn't hide anything from him. Give Robert the name of a pygmy in the rainforest and two days later he'd have a dossier on the little guy. What hut he was born in, which cologne he preferred, how many goats he traded for his ol' lady and whether he liked his eggs over easy or sunny-side up. She'd asked him to dig up something on Bobby James, but he'd come up dry. The worst thing Robert could find was that Bobby had been arrested at a political rally for failing to disperse. There had to be some dirt on him somewhere, Deronda thought, and if it wasn't on the internet, you had to go to the source.

For the third night in a row, Deronda and Grace sat in Grace's car, waiting for Bobby James to come out of his house. Who knows? Maybe he liked to flash truck drivers or poison cats. It was a desperate, futile thing to do. They'd been there for a couple of hours already, restless, ready to pack it in.

"We should go," Deronda said. "You should be painting."

"I don't have the light and this is more important," Grace said. Her eyes widened. "There he is!" Bobby emerged from the house, got in his dusty blue Prius and drove away. They followed him south on Long

Beach Boulevard, turning east on Coast Avenue. A two-lane street and dark. The streetlights were far apart. Bobby approached the intersection of Coast and West Lantana, a notorious drug corner. Three young guys were out there, servicing their customers.

"He's not gonna stop, is he?" Deronda said eagerly. Bobby stopped. One of the guys looked in the passenger-side window, there was a brief exchange, and something changed hands. "Oh, my muthafuckin' God," Deronda said, delighted. "Bobby James just bought some heroin!" Grace laughed and they bumped fists.

Bobby drove on, leading them to an address on Morrel. "The heart of darkness," Deronda said. "The police send robots in there." Three dying palm trees marked the entrance to a crumbling two-story apartment building, THE DOLPHIN in wrought-iron script hung over the vestibule. All the apartments faced the cement courtyard, empty except for a mangled bicycle and a washing machine with no door. They looked like casualties. At the center was a fountain filled with cement and assorted trash. Bobby had already disappeared into one of the apartments. Deronda and Grace stayed in the lightless vestibule. "So Bobby buys heroin and then he comes here for what?" Grace said. "Is he trading drugs for sex?"

"Let's hope so," Deronda said.

"How do we find out which apartment Bobby visits?" Grace said. "Wait until he comes out?" Deronda shook her head.

"It's dangerous, not for me, but for you."

"Should I wait in the car?"

"You know what?" Deronda said. "I know that dude." A man was sauntering up the street. He was wearing an orange velour tracksuit, a gold rope chain too thick to be real gold, and a leather Kangol cap.

"Who is he?"

"Spenser Witherspoon. They call him Spoon." Deronda gave him a big smile. "Whassup, Spoon? How you been livin', son?"

"I been livin' how I been livin'," Spoon replied warily. Apparently, he wasn't used to people being glad to see him. "Is that you, Deronda?"

"Yeah, it's me. You still a pimp?"

"Why does everybody call me that?" Spoon said indignantly. "For your information, I'm a personal manager."

"I'm sorry, Spoon," Deronda said quickly. "My mistake."

"Do you happen to be in need of my services? I have an opening in my organization that would be perfect for your royal bootiness."

"Not today, Spoon," Deronda said. "You ever seen this dude?" She got out her phone. She showed him a photo from a Wells Fargo brochure. "His name is Bobby James. He's trying to take my baby away."

"Yeah, I seen him around," Spoon said. "Muthafucka lucky nobody's robbed him yet."

"Who does he come here to see?" Deronda asked. Spoon hesitated, frowned, seemingly thoughtful. He wants something in return, she thought. "You heard about my food trucks?" she said.

"Hell, yes!" Spoon said enthusiastically. "I been to the one in the Vons parking lot. Sheeit. I'd throw my mama out the window for a three piece and some collard greens."

"Tell you what," Deronda said. "Tell me who Bobby visits and I'll serve you up our Happy as a Muthafucka Meal. Whole chicken, collard greens, yams, a drink, mac and cheese and a double peach cobbler."

"Now you speaking words I understand," Spoon said, rubbing his palms together. "Good thing you don't want me to kill that muthafucka or he'd be dead right now."

"Tell me."

"It's a ho named Sandra somethin'. She's

129

strung out. I don't know how she's making it. She ain't on the stroll. She used to be a porn star. Called herself Wanda Wonder Lips. She was one of my favorites, but you can't even recognize her now. She looks like a tree fell on her and she had to crawl her ass out. She's in 207."

"Thank you, Spoon."

Grace said, "Okay, so Bobby's girlfriend is a junkie and a prostitute, but we can't tell that to a judge. We need evidence."

"Like what?" Deronda said. Grace had no answer.

"May I offer a suggestion?" Spoon said. "What you need is some pictures, like the two of 'em buck nekkid and Sandra got a needle in her arm."

"You know what? That's not a bad idea," Grace said.

Deronda had to get home. The babysitter was threatening to leave. Grace said she'd stay and take pictures.

"Forget it. I told you it's dangerous," Deronda said.

"It sho' the fuck is," Spoon agreed. He smiled. "May I offer another suggestion? Y'all could take pictures from my apartment. You could see Sandra's place real good from my living room. However —"

Spoon wanted another Happy as a Muthafucka Meal as compensation.

"Take care of my homegirl, Spoon," Deronda said. "Anything happens to her I'm coming back here with Michael Stokeley."

Spoon reacted with alarm. "Don't bring that crazy muthafucka nowhere near me. You might as well bring some wild dogs in here and let 'em eat my ass to death."

Deronda left. Grace readied herself. She was going into a pimp's apartment. Spoon opened the door. The place was dark, lit only by the TV. One of those survival shows was on, the kind where they give you spaghetti if you hit a coconut with a spear. She waited for her eyes to adjust. The room was close, warm, and smelled heavily of weed, alcohol and fabric softener. She wanted to open a window.

"Let's have a cocktail," Spoon said. "You ever heard of Parks Punch?"

"No, I haven't," Grace said.

"Well, you're in for a treat. Please, make yourself comfortable." Spoon went into the galley kitchen and started getting things out of the fridge. The room came into clearer view. It was a studio, cramped and messy, a bed in the center of the room. Two women wearing housecoats were sitting on the sofa, watching the TV. One of them was large, like three beanbag chairs stacked on top of each other. The other looked anorexic. Thankfully, she wasn't suffering from the condition, eating big handfuls of Doritos from a family-size bag and drinking a Big Gulp as big as a wine barrel.

"Hello," Grace said. "I'm Grace."

"Mary," said the big one, her eyes never leaving the TV.

"Vivian," said the skinny one, her eyes never leaving the TV. Grace looked for somewhere to sit, but there was only the bed and the sofa. No chance she was sitting on the bed, with its twisted sheets, squished pillows and stained comforter.

"You want to sit down?" Mary said.

"If you don't mind," Grace said.

"Sorry. Ain't no room."

Spoon came back with a red plastic cup and a dubiously washed water glass. "You gonna love this." He handed her the glass. Only the best for company. Grace noticed Spoon had a large garish ring on every finger and several bracelets on his wrists. She wondered how he washed his face. She took a sip of the drink and paused as flavors so grotesque filled her mouth she wanted to borrow Spoon's toothbrush.

"What's in this?"

"Vodka, Crystal Light lemonade powder,

margarita mix and Coca-Cola," Spoon said. "It's good, ain't it?"

"Excellent." She looked around for a planter to dump it in, but there were no plants except a bag of weed on the coffee table. She opened the drapes as if that might clear the taste out of her mouth. Sandra's apartment was directly across the courtyard. Spoon said he had business and left. As soon as the door closed, Grace poured the Parks Punch down the sink. She stayed by the window, her phone at the ready. She thought about Isaiah. What he was doing, whether he was safe, if he'd found another girlfriend, if he'd found another life. She was on the verge of tears, something that happened a lot these days.

The residents of the Dolphin came and went. Black and Latino rap fought for dominance. There were cooking smells. A little boy in a jumper pedaled around the courtyard on a tricycle. Why isn't he in bed? Grace wondered. It was nearly ten o'clock. Three teenage girls in tight jeans and tank tops went past Spoon's window.

"No shit?" one girl said. "Treyvon shot the muthafucka? For what?"

"Fool was Crip Violator," the second girl said. "Shouldn't have been where he was at."

"Where's Treyvon now?"

"At the police station, where you think?"

A couple walked through the courtyard, a woman in a thin dress and flip-flops, the man, limping, oil splotches on his coveralls and no shirt. They were sullen, like they were mad at each other. A loud argument broke out in 212. A drunken man came wobbling out backward with his hands up.

"Hey, come on, Carmen, don't be like that." A beer bottle went whistling past his head, shattering in the courtyard. "Okay, okay, I'm going, okay? I'm fucking going."

A cluster of gangstas emerged from a downstairs apartment, talking loud and laughing. White T-shirts, bling, expensive sneakers, sinewy arms, veins like subterranean tunnels, their brown skin nearly black with tats. There was a feral, unbound quality to their swagger. They were scary, Grace thought, but that was the point. The little boy in the jumper came running around a corner and nearly ran into them. He stopped, looked up, awed and terrified.

"The fuck you lookin' at?" a gangsta said.

"Don't just stand there, nigga," a second gangsta said. "Get the fuck out the way." The boy turned and ran. The gangstas laughed and disappeared into the vestibule.

A minute later, a middle-aged man in a

hoodie hurried up the steps, knocked on the door of a neighboring apartment. "Nicky, you in there?" he said. His voice was husky and furtive. "Nicky? You holding? Come on, man. I'm dying out here. Nicky? Don't fuck around." He cursed, hurried down the stairs, crossing the courtyard, passing an old man shuffling along. Layers of filthy clothing. No shoes, rags tied around his feet. He was having a heated conversation with himself.

"No, sir, no, sir, that is not what happened!" he said, adamantly shaking his head. "You wrong, you wrong, you wrong. That's not even close to the — why should I go?" He stopped, incensed, hands on his hips. "I'm staying right on this spot, you hear me? And I — am — not — moo — ving!" The little boy in the jumper returned. He had his arms out like wings and was flying around the courtyard. "Don't do that," the old man snapped. "That's crazy behavior!"

A couple of young men sat down on the edge of the fountain. They were in their twenties, athletic-looking, ubiquitous white T-shirts and baggy shorts. They passed a forty-ounce Miller back and forth and argued about Kyrie Irving, whoever that was. Two women came through the vestibule, probably hookers given how they were dressed, one of them holding her high heels like a briefcase. They were sharing a joint. They looked bone weary.

"Park it over here, baby," one of the young men said. "I got somethin' good to show you."

"I already parked it there, Jerome," one of the hookers replied. "And there wasn't shit to see." The man's friend and the other hooker laughed.

"You can't play it off like that," Jerome protested. "You don't remember you was hollerin' and digging your nails in my back?"

"That's what I do when I'm tryin' escape somewhere," the hooker said. More laughter.

"Gimme a hit off that tree," Jerome said, serious now, not liking her comebacks.

"You better get your own tree, you broke-ass bitch."

Jerome raised his voice. "What'd you say?" The courtyard went still. The words and tone were a signal. Some shit was about to happen.

"I *said,*" the hooker replied, "you better get your own tree, you broke-ass bitch."

"Damn, man," Jerome's friend said, falsetto. "You gonna let that ho talk to you like that? That's disrespectful."

Jerome stood up, jaw clenched, forehead furrowed. People were coming out of their apartments to watch.

Mary said, "Come on, I want to see this." They went outside on the walkway. Jerome was in the hooker's face, head cocked to one side, his fists curled.

"Say that again, bitch," he snarled.

"I already said it twice. You deaf as well as stupid? Now get the fuck outta my way." Smiles and chuckles around the iron railing. They were playing to the crowd. Nothing to do now but watch the fight.

The hooker tried brushing past Jerome, but quick as a hand clap, he slapped her hard, the sound harsh and ugly. Grace turned away, her hand over her mouth. Violence is gut-wrenching no matter what the degree. There were *oooh shits* and laughter from the crowd.

"Yeah," Jerome said, nodding, "You ain't so roughshod now, are you, bitch?"

The other hooker said, "Damn, Jerome, why you wanna do that?"

At first, Grace thought the first hooker was crying, but it was a cover. She slipped her hand inside her beltline and whirled around with a box cutter. She slashed Jerome across the chest. "OH, SHIT!" he screamed. He staggered back, looking down at himself, hands clamped over his wound, a bloodstain expanding around it. The crowd was startled, shocked; some were even laughing but no one was surprised.

The hooker paced back and forth. "Uh-huh! Uh-huh!" She shouted. "Whatchoo got to say now, nigga? Come on and hit me again!"

The crowd was lit. *Ooh shit, go on, Lucida! Cut that muthafucka to death! That's what you get, Jerome, you punk-ass bitch!! I hope that nigga bleeds out, I swear to God I do. Hey, Jerome, you got health insurance? Hey, Jerome, can I have your TV?*

Grace looked at their faces. People were watching like it was nothing more than a close playoff game. No horror. No disgust. A few of the women were nodding with satisfaction as if Jerome, and anybody like Jerome, deserved to have his chest split open with a box cutter.

The hooker and her friend had disappeared. There was terror in Jerome's eyes, his mouth open, hands still over his wound, his clothes a mess of blood. He fell to his knees. "I need help. Somebody help me." He sat back on his haunches and keeled over onto his side. A couple of people said they called 911. Jerome's friend took off his T-shirt and held it against his wound saying, "Hold on, J, hang in there, man."

The crowd was drifting away, Jerome's life or death not entertaining enough to keep their attention.

"Where are the paramedics?" Grace said.

"They take their time comin' here," Vivian said.

Grace saw the little boy in the jumper. He was hanging on to his mother's hand, watching Jerome writhe and bleed and cry. The boy was all of six years old. His face was blank, studious, like this was something he should pay attention to. A pang of sadness went through Grace. They went back inside. Mary and Vivian returned to the sofa. Grace stood there. She couldn't get over what happened.

"Whas' the matter with you?" Mary said.

"I can't believe everyone was so matter-of-fact," Grace said.

"Welcome to the ghet-toe, honey," Vivian said. "We see that shit every fucking day."

People from the suburbs would be disgusted by the residents of the Dolphin, Grace thought. Look at them, they'd say, so callous and bloodthirsty. Animals, they'd say. They can't help it, they'd say. They're just like that, they'd say. Yes, they're like that because they see this shit every fucking day. That little boy in the jumper will see this shit every fucking day; stabbings, shootings, beatings, whores and pimps, drunks and crackheads, killers and crazies and abject cruelty. Grow up like that little boy, people of the suburbs. And see what happens to you.

Mary got a text, looked at it sourly. "Spoon's pissed. Wonders why we ain't out on the block."

"Cuz my feet hurt," Vivian said. "And if I see another dick today I'm gonna shoot myself in the pussy."

Dutifully, Mary and Vivian got their things together and dressed. Mary in a miniskirt and fishnets, Vivian in short shorts and patent leather thigh-highs. It dawned on Grace that these women weren't being stoic. It wasn't like they recognized the fucked-up nature of their lives and decided to accept it. There were no decisions, there was no recognition. This is what you did. This is what you do.

"What are you looking at, bitch?" Mary said. "Where the fuck are my shoes?"

Grace couldn't imagine it. Standing on a street corner in those ridiculous clothes, yelling "Need a date, baby?" at the passing cars and getting in with some stranger who might beat you or rape you and driving into an alley and giving him a blowjob, furiously bobbing your head up and down with the shifter hitting you in the chest, this mother-fucker taking forever to get off, the car heating up, sweat running down your neck, the smell rank, afraid you might choke to death. Yeah, try that, people of the suburbs, Grace thought. Try it twenty-five times a day and see what you become.

Grace went out on the walkway and watched Mary and Vivian cross the court-yard toward the vestibule. They were talking easily with the occasional laugh, Mary putting her hand on Vivian's arm. They could have been schoolteachers or bus drivers or traffic cops or anything but among the most brave, exploited, heartbreaking people Grace had ever met. If their lives ended in suicide she wouldn't be surprised. She'd be surprised if they didn't.

The man in Sandra's apartment left. Grace was caught off guard. She took a video but it was murky, blurred, and didn't show his face. Was it Bobby? She ran after him but by the time she reached the street he was gone. "Fuck you, Grace," she said. "Fuck you to death."

She was walking back to her car when she saw Spoon, coming the other way, doing that pimp walk thing and bobbing his head to his headphones. The sight of him made

141

her angry, this unfeeling bloodsucking leech bastard strolling along like he was a human being. She stopped, reached down and found a gravelly fragment of cement just big enough to close her fist around. Spoon came closer, saw her and grinned.

" 'Sup, baby? Did you enjoy your cocktail?" Grace smiled. If Spoon knew her better, he might have recognized the smile as her evil one. She hit him in his stupid face, knocking his head sideways, the headphones flying off. He fell into a chain-link fence and slid down to the ground. He looked up at her, confused and in pain.

"The fuck did I do?" he said, and she walked away.

Chapter Ten:
The Stark

Skip drove past Isaiah's place. A FOR SALE sign on the front lawn, a blue sticker on it that said SOLD. There were flyers stuck in the door screen, litter on the lawn. No one home. Skip parked and thought about it. How would he find that asshole? Maybe he was in another city or had moved out of state. Skip didn't know any of his friends or where he hung out. He fumed for a while and then looked at the sign again. On the bottom it read: TUDOR REALTY. Skip looked up the address and went over there. He told the woman at the desk he was interested in Isaiah's house.

Otis J. Tudor thought he was a big shot, sitting behind a glass desk the size of a dining table in a chair that was more like a throne. He wore a shiny green suit, gold chains, tinted glasses and alligator shoes.

"It's a pleasure to meet you, Mr. Hanson," Tudor said, in a voice that suggested the pleasure should be yours.

"Yeah, me too," Skip said.

"Miriam tells me you're interested in the house at 221 Draper Street."

"Yeah, that's the one," Skip replied. Tudor was smiling, but he seemed suspicious. Maybe he's reacting to your clothes, Skip thought. Worn-out jeans and a faded T-shirt that said ALPO and in smaller letters GRAVY CRAVERS, or maybe it was his shaved head or the dog-bite scars on his arms or the prison tats that showed above his collar. "Yeah," Skip went on. "My friend used to live there, Isaiah —" He hesitated. He didn't know how to pronounce Q Fuck's last name. Stupidly, he said again, "Isaiah."

"Yes, he's quite a young man," Tudor replied knowingly.

"Do you know where he is? I'd like to say hello." *You said it too fast, Skip, he's onto you.*

"How do you know Isaiah?" Tudor asked. The smile had gone.

"Uh, well, you know, around the neighborhood."

"Really?" Tudor replied, amused. "You lived in East Long Beach? Where?"

"Uh, you know — over on that, uh, whaddayoucallit, big street." Tudor wasn't buying it. Skip kept trying. "Yeah, yeah, it was, uh

144

— shit, I can't remember. It was a long time ago."

Tudor pursed his lips and sighed. "All right, Mr. Hanson, if that's your real name. What is it you really want?"

"Forget it," Skip said. He went back to the car, drove to the Dairy Queen and had a cup of soft ice cream. He was frustrated. How was he going to find that bastard? Who could he ask? It had to be somebody who wouldn't be so suspicious, and he needed a better cover story. He finished the ice cream and smiled. He had an idea. He stopped at a drugstore and bought a box of business envelopes. He put in some ones and fives and sealed it shut.

A Mexican woman was sweeping her walkway. Her house was right across the street from Isaiah's. Skip had waited over an hour for something like this to happen. He got out of the car and walked toward her, smiling, giving her a friendly wave. The woman's expression darkened. She stopped sweeping, wary of a stranger who looked like an ex-convict.

"Sorry to bother you," Skip said apologetically. He nodded at Isaiah's place. "Isaiah, he helped me out, you know? That guy would help anybody. Even a bum like me that was broke and couldn't pay him."

The woman relaxed a little and smiled. "Yes, Isaiah is a good man."

Skip tried to look sheepish. "Uh, here's the thing, see. I was in trouble, you know? But I'm okay now because of Isaiah. I've got a job and everything. I'd like to pay him what I owe, but I don't know where he is." He took the envelope out and showed it to her. "Do you happen to know where I could find him? I really want to pay him back."

"Nobody knows," the Mexican woman said. "Bad people are after him, and he left. Maybe he is hiding."

"Bad people?" Skip said.

"Yes, there are many," she said sadly. "That's what happens when you are good. They try to stamp you out."

"Do you know where he went?"

The woman shrugged. "No, I'm sorry."

"Okay, thanks." He turned and walked away, wondering what he would do next.

"You know what?" the woman said brightly. "Maybe Grace knows."

Skip stopped, turned around. "Grace?"

"She's his girlfriend. She works in a food truck, the one in the Vons parking lot."

Skip stood in line and watched Grace. She took orders, handed out Styrofoam boxes, took money and made change. She didn't

146

look too happy about it. Probably a smart-ass if she was with Isaiah. She was white, and that surprised him a little. She looked okay, nothing special except for the green eyes. They were striking, the kind you noticed, the kind you didn't want looking at you. Other than that there wasn't much to her. Skip was all adrenaline. Calm down, he told himself. But he couldn't. The need to find the man who took his dogs away, took his life away, was overpowering. He was third in line. Then second.

Grace was at work at the service window, tired and pissed off. Her heart was bleeding for Deronda. Her friend had worked so hard to make herself a success, to give Janeel a good life and future, and all of it was threatened by Bobby Fucking James. It wasn't right. It wasn't fair. She wanted to be at Bobby James's house choking him to death with an electrical cord.

"Uh, let me have a three piece with macaroni salad and yams," the man said.

"Anything to drink?" Grace asked.

"Lemonade."

"That'll be sixteen twenty-five." The man gave her twenty dollars. She made change, her artist's eyes giving him a once-over. Scruffy, dirty-blond hair, a ghost of a soul patch, neck tats, stupid T-shirt, Crocs. A peculiar look on his face, eager and excited, too much for someone ordering fried chicken. *Be alert, Grace. Something's wrong here.* "What's your name?" she asked.

"Name?" he said, like it was none of her business.

"So I can call you when your order's ready." *Duh,* she thought.

"Oh. Yeah. Sure. Um. Eddie. My name's Eddie." Isaiah had taught her about things like this, somebody stumbling over their own name. This asshole was up to something. A lurker maybe or some delusional asshole who thought a girl who sold fried chicken at a food truck had to be lonely. "It'll be just a few minutes, Eddie."

"Say," he said, like he just remembered something happy. "You're Isaiah's girl, aren't you?" *Ding, ding, ding, ding! Danger! Danger!*

"Isaiah? Who's that?"

"Come on," he said with a coaxing smile. "No need to be embarrassed about it. Isaiah is a great guy."

"Sorry. My boyfriend's name is Fritz." She looked over his head. "Next in line?"

"No, no, I've seen you together," the guy insisted. "I'm a friend of his. Eddie! You know, *Eddie*! From the old days."

"Could you step aside, *Eddie*? I want to take the next order."

The guy acted like he hadn't heard her. "Say, how's he doing anyway? I was wanting to buy him a drink or something, catch up, talk about old times."

"I don't know anybody named Isaiah, okay?" Grace said. "Now could you step aside, please? Your order will be ready in a few minutes." She looked at the customer behind the man. "Oh, hi. Sorry, I'll be right with you."

This moron was fucking oblivious. He kept pushing. "No, no, really, Isaiah will want to talk to me. Just tell me where he is and I'll do the rest." She was pissed now.

"I don't know any Isaiahs and your name's not Eddie, asshole, and whatever you want it's bullshit."

The guy's smile was gone; his voice had teeth in it. "I just want to talk to him, okay? Tell me where he is, and I'll go on my way."

It suddenly dawned on her. She knew who he was. "You're a Stark, aren't you?"

"A what?"

"Don't play dumb with me. You're a white nationalist. A racist shit-eating Nazi pig asshole. Well, I've got news for you, dickhead. We're not in your fucked-up clubhouse in El Segundo, we're in East Long Beach where troglodytes like you are trespassing." She grabbed some bills out of the register and threw them at him. "Here. Take this and buy yourself a new swastika, mother-fucker. We don't want you here."

Suddenly, the guy jumped up on his tiptoes and heaved his face through the window. He looked crazed. He looked insane. "Listen, you cunt," he spat. "I know who you are, I know where you live, I know what you —" It happened so fast. One second, the guy was halfway through the window and the next, he was looking up at Michael Stokeley with a sawed-off shotgun jammed under his chin.

"They all out of chicken, muthafucka," Stokeley said. "And if I see you round here again, I'll stick this in your eye and blast the back of your head off." Stokeley shoved the guy away, and he hurried off. Odeal Wood-son leaned out of the window.

"Michael, is that you? What did I tell you about playing with guns? Go on home now. Shoo!"

CHAPTER ELEVEN:
FLYING FREE

Dodson got up early, dressed and left while Cherise was still sleeping. He didn't want hugs, and he sure as hell didn't want to hear her say, good luck, honey, and I know you'll do great, honey. The last thing you need when you're nervous and anxious is a goddamn pep talk. It was distracting, the other person trying to ease their own nervousness.

The Apex Advertising building was all glass and aluminum. Nothing special, but he'd been less intimidated getting processed into Vacaville. He drove into the garage. The first thing he noticed were the executive parking spaces. RESERVED FOR E. NEWBERG. RESERVED FOR Z. SANDLER. RESERVED FOR M. LUPICA. That was cool. Like having your own table at Roscoe's Chicken N Waffles. He was way early so he waited in his car and listened to Tupac. Mister Assault Rifle and Overdose Willy weren't on his playlist.

He went through the heavy revolving door and down a short staircase into the lobby. It was immense. You could play soccer in here if you didn't slip on the marble floor and crack your skull open. He stood there a moment, watching well-dressed people going back and forth, filling the space with echoing footsteps and low chatter. He was glad he was wearing the suit. The majority of the people were white but there were lots of black and brown faces too. Maybe it wouldn't be so bad.

Two security guards were sitting behind a reception desk as big as a fallen redwood, nothing on it but a clipboard. A white woman and a black man. Dodson chose the brother and stepped up to the desk. The man was doing something on a laptop and didn't look up. Dodson waited. Did this guy know he was an imposter? An unqualified former crack dealer trying to hustle his way into a real job? The guard looked up, but he didn't seem to register someone was there.

"Identification," he said. Dodson handed it over. The guard scanned it and checked a screen. There was a tiny camera on the desk. It blinked and the guard printed out a pass, your murky image and a bar code. The pass got you through the turnstile. The elevator took you up to your floor and your floor only. They didn't mess around about security these days. Goddamn terrorists were everywhere and most of them were home-grown. Dodson's appointment with Human Resources was at nine. He filled out forms, received a packet of information about the company and an employee handbook. It took a long time. He was told he should report to his new boss directly. His name was Arnold J. Stimson and his office was downstairs, B223.

B223 was in the basement. Dodson rode down in the elevator, wondering if his tie was straight and swallowing dry. All the shit he'd been through and he was nervous about meeting some guy named Arnold J. Stimson? That fear of the unknown. He couldn't shake it. He got off the elevator. There was a large bullpen, rows of desks, people on their cell phones, talking into headsets, shuffling papers and typing on their computers. Almost everyone was dressed casually, and there were all kinds of hairstyles. Buzz cuts, pompadours, tapers, dreadlocks, cornrows and seven different kinds of fades. Gloria was wrong. The makeover had been for nothing. He got directions to Stimson's office: around the bullpen, left, then a right and down the hall.

The hall was a long stretch of green carpet and harsh fluorescents, office doors and interior windows on one side. It looked institutional.

Stimson's office was at the very end. The reception area in B223 was small, like laundry room small. No one was at the desk, and there was nothing on it, not even a landline. Dodson knocked on the inner office door. "Excuse me? I'm supposed to meet Arnold Stimson." There were noises. Squeaks and creaks like someone had suddenly sat up in an office chair. There was a pause. A man cleared his throat and said, "Uh, yeah, come on in."

Dodson opened the door. Arnold Stimson was standing at his desk, trying to blink the sleep out of his eyes. He was in his sixties, verging toward fat, not enough hair for a comb-over. He wore a baggy gray suit and scuffed loafers. He'd apparently tied his tie while he was driving on the freeway. He had a look on his face like Dodson was a Jehovah's Witness with an earnest smile and a handful of pamphlets.

"Hello, I'm Juanell Dodson. Your new intern."

"Yeah, that's, um, sure," Stimson said. "I'm Arnold Stimson. I didn't expect you so early." It was a quarter after ten. Stimson put a hand on the small of his back and stretched.

"Oh, man," he groaned. "My back is killing me."

On the desk were a large monitor, a coffee mug that said YOU ARE MY SUNSHINE, some spreadsheets, pencils in a water glass and an open newspaper. It was dim in the office. Only the lamp was on. The furniture was spare. File cabinets, a drawing table, an easel, a small sofa and a coffee table. A dead rubber tree stood in the corner. The two men shook hands and sat down across from each other. Stimson's chair squeaked and creaked. Dodson didn't know what to say and apparently neither did Stimson. He glanced at the newspaper. "Senator Michaels has a son who snuck into Syria and tried to join the Taliban. They wouldn't accept him because you have to be a Muslim and have a history of resistance."

"What was the son before he went to Syria?" Dodson asked.

"A surfer," Stimson said. He went on. "I must say it's unusual to have an intern with no résumé or references. I take it you know someone." He wasn't resentful, just curious.

"Laurie Singer. Friend of my wife's."

Stimson sighed. "I'm going to miss Laurie, I really am. The last thing she did was bring you on as an intern."

"Laurie's not here anymore?"

"Friday was her last day, God bless her," Stimson replied. "I mentored her when she was starting out. I always knew she'd be going places." Not good, Dodson thought. If Stimson was unprotected, so was he.

Dodson thought the architects who planned the building must have been high. Ground level cut right across the middle of the one big window. The top half looked onto the bottoms of tree trunks, ferns, bushes and a layer of dead leaves and twigs. The bottom half of the window was solid dirt with roots burrowing and squiggling through it.

"Yeah, it's unsettling but you get used to it," Stimson said. "Once a mole made its nest right in the corner there. Fascinating little thing, had babies too."

"What happened to it?"

"A snake ate the whole family." Stimson took a sip from his coffee cup and made a face. "Let me tell you what I do here. I'm a creative executive. My job is to develop advertising campaigns." There were posters of various products on the walls, none of which Dodson had heard of. Kiss Me More Lip Gloss, Persian Lite Seven Grain Pita Bread, Uncle Buck's Feral Hog and Sweet

Potato Dog Food and a few more.

Stimson continued. "The creative director gives me an assignment and it's my responsibility to develop a campaign that targets the appropriate consumers and get them to buy the product." Dodson nodded. "A lot of people think it's easy," Stimson said dolefully. "But take my word for it, it's not." Stimson had been here too long, Dodson thought. Put out to pasture while he was still in his office.

"I'm hungry. Do you mind?" Stimson said.

"Not at all," Dodson said.

Stimson found a camera bag in a desk drawer. "Let's go," he said. "I'm supposed to take the stairs." They'd gone up one level to the lobby and he was already winded. "Maybe this isn't a good idea." They went into the lobby itself and waited at the elevator. "There's a rooftop garden. It's got a great view," Stimson said.

A man appeared beside them. He was late thirties, fashionably thin, sharp suit, grooming by *GQ* and a cutting expression. He looked like Jared Kushner if Jared Kushner was black and hostile.

"Stimson," the man said. "Hard at work as usual." He glanced at the camera bag. "Doesn't your wife fix you breakfast?"

"Brad Hampton," Stimson said. "I'd like you to meet my new intern, Juanell Dodson. Juanell, Brad is my creative director."

"Good to meet you," Dodson said. Brad gave him a quick glance. He didn't say anything or offer his hand. It was a short but uncomfortable wait. Brad's animosity and impatience were almost audible. The doors finally opened. Brad got on, turned and put a palm out. "Private call, take the next one." As the doors closed, he added, "I'm expecting big things from you on the Skechers campaign. I'm looking forward to your presentation." The doors closed. Stimson sighed, relieved. They waited for the next car.

"I'll be straight with you," Stimson confessed. "I am the last person in the whole building you want to be working for."

"Oh, yeah? Why's that?" Dodson said.

"I've been here for twenty-nine years," Stimson continued. "I started as an assistant, then assistant copywriter, a junior creative, then half of a two-man creative team. That's where you want to be. You're actually creating campaigns. Dennis Rogers was my better half. He was the art director. We were really good." Stimson smiled nostalgically. "We were servicing major clients. Dove soap. GM trucks. Tide detergent. Hershey bars. Coca-Cola." The elevator came and they got on. "But times changed as they usually do, and the products changed too," Stimson went on. "All the new stuff, electronics, phones, cloud services, video games. Dennis and I couldn't keep up. Our mindset was stuck in 1995. I'll let you in on a secret. I have a collection of Michael Bolton albums." Dodson had never heard of the guy.

They reached the top floor and went out on a roof garden. Green plants. Tables with umbrellas. Great view. The ocean in one direction, the city stretching to the horizon in the other. They sat down and Stimson opened his camera case. He took out a sandwich neatly wrapped in wax paper. Old school, Dodson thought.

"Want a half a sandwich?" Stimson said.

"No, thank you."

Stimson continued. "When Coke started putting rappers into their commercials, I knew Dennis and I were done. He took a buyout. I couldn't afford to. I fell out of favor and wasn't given another partner. My assignments got less and less prestigious. I got a pay cut. Two of them." Stimson ate the sandwich like it was the best thing in the world. "Marge can really make a sandwich. Sure you don't want some?" Dodson shook his head.

"I would have been fired but I had friends in high places," Stimson continued. "But they're retired now or they've gone on to other jobs. Laurie used to be my creative director. Brad took her place and now I'm a pariah. That's why my office is in North Mongolia and they replaced my assistant with an intern." He opened a little thermos. "Apple juice?"

"No, thank you," Dodson said. "Brad said you were making a presentation?"

"I'm supposed to, but I've got nothing," Stimson said. "Skechers wants a print ad for their walking shoes. Their brief says they want cool, edgy and relevant. For walking shoes? I don't even know what that means. It's also a test. If we give them an ad they like, they'll give us more business. If we don't, a multimillion-dollar client goes down the drain."

"When's the presentation?"

"Tomorrow, doomsday," Stimson said. "I'll have zip, and Brad will convince Matsumoto to let me go. Ed Matsumoto, Brad's boss. I've known Ed for years. I don't know if that helps or not." Stimson finished the sandwich. Then he refolded the wax paper and put it back in the camera bag with the thermos. Really old school, Dodson thought.

They went back to the office. Stimson worked on his campaign and Dodson spent the rest of the day taking files and drawings from one office to the next, adding up Stimson's expense receipts, copying documents, reading company memos and filling out activity reports that Stimson said didn't matter.

Dodson met people. Some were friendly, others were busy and distracted. *Hey, you're the new guy, aren't you? Good to meet you, Juanell. If you have any questions just ask. It's boring around here but you'll get used to it. You're Stimson's intern? Oh, that's, um, that's great. What's he working on now? Thumbtacks? Doorknobs? Just kidding.* Nobody seemed to care about his age or how he spoke. Nobody asked him about Taylor Swift or rock climbing. The talk was general, everyday chitchat. Last night's game. Traffic. Where to eat. Posts on Facebook, one executive or another. To Dodson's surprise, people tried to clue him in. *Zack Sandler is the executive art director. CPM means cost per thousand clicks. Bounce rate means how many times a consumer looked at a web page and didn't engage. Brad and Walsh are freaking out about Skechers.* There was racism everywhere you went but Dodson didn't see it here, at least on the surface.

When he returned to the office, Stimson was slouched in his chair, facing away. Drawings and partial drawings were scattered around. The wastebasket was full of crumpled-up paper. There was a large sketch pad on the easel. The drawing had been x-ed out several times.

"Mr. Stimson?" Dodson said. Slowly, Stimson revolved in his chair. He looked as gray as the dirt window, the bags under his eyes like hammocks with people sleeping in them.

"We have plans, me and Marge. Did I tell you she was sick?" he said. "Immune deficiency disease. She's just starting to get symptoms. We both pretend they're not there. The doctor says she's got two years, maybe three, before they get really bad."

"I'm sorry to hear that."

"If I get my pension, we'll buy a Winnebago and travel until . . . until we can't anymore. Marge is really looking forward to it." Stimson smiled dreamily. "Wouldn't that be great? No clocks, no phones, no campaigns, no Brad. At age sixty-five I'll be happy for the first time since I was a teenager."

"Why wouldn't you get your pension?" Dodson said.

"Brad hates me."

Stimson sent Dodson home, saying he was pulling an all-nighter. Dodson wished him luck and told him to call if there was anything he could do. He felt sorry for the man. Desperate, fearful, his idea of happiness a Winnebago and no phones. Stimson was whipped. He had to go on but the juice had been squeezed out of him a long time ago.

He told Cherise about his day. "Uncle Buck's Feral Hog and Sweet Potato Dog Food?" she said.

" 'Fraid so."

"Well, I hope you haven't hitched your wagon to a dying mule."

"Me too."

"Was it anything like you thought it would be?" she asked. "The people I mean."

"No, not really. As long as you don't mess with them or loaf around, they don't care who you are. They got their own lives to handle."

"I know," Cherise said.

"Gloria was wrong about damn near everything."

"I know that too."

"Then why'd you let me take them damn lessons?"

163

"I wouldn't have," Cherise said, "but you were so insistent that white people would be condescending, I wasn't going to convince you otherwise. And then you went on and on about needing to learn things and I figured fine, if that's what will make you feel better. I wasn't planning on my mother getting involved. That just happened."

Dodson loved that his wife was so smart. He was impressed with her, proud of her. But there were times when he wished she'd bump her head, be less smart and give him a fucking break. They went to bed, but he couldn't sleep. He wished he had some weed, but he'd stopped buying it. He felt guilty about spending the money. He paced, watched TV, had a bowl of Cocoa Puffs, played Madden and Call of Duty. He put on a robe, went out on the balcony. The sun was rising. It was six in the morning.

The neighborhood was quiet. Rare and pleasant unto itself. On the rooftop across the street, Bolo Wakefield was tending his pigeons. He'd been doing it for decades. Bolo was stooped and gray haired, wearing a straw hat, coveralls and no shirt. He held his head at an odd angle. Bolo had had a couple of strokes. The right side of his face sagged and he couldn't see out of that eye. He had a tough time keeping his balance. A week ago, Dodson carried a thirty-pound bag of bird feed up to the roof for him, learning more about homing pigeons than he wanted to know.

Bolo had built what he called a loft, a wire cage really, with a corrugated metal roof. It was big enough for him to move around in. "You start with young pigeons that have never been outdoors," he said. "And you feed them at the same time of day. Do it by hand so they get to know you. Then you don't feed them again until the next day."

"Seems like a long time between meals," Dodson said.

"It is," Bolo said. "When you come in the next day, the birds are damn near starving. You do this for two months." Dodson almost said it sounds like animal abuse but held his tongue. "At the end of the two months, you open the door and move away so they can't see you. Then you let 'em come out by themselves. Mess with 'em and they'll likely be traumatized and not come back."

"I've got to go now, Bolo."

"This is the good part," Bolo said. "Watch this." He had to turn slightly so he could see with his good eye. He unlatched the loft and opened the door. The pigeons were excited, walking back and forth, cooing and bobbing their heads. In a flurry of flapping and feathers, they flew out, a couple dozen of them. They climbed, swooped, careened across the clouds, winged over the rooftops and disappeared into the sky. Must feel good, Dodson thought. Flying free.

Dodson's day with Stimson had affected him. Made him think about himself, his future, where he wanted to be in five years, ten years and on down the road. It didn't used to matter until he'd married Cherise and now there was Micah to worry about. He'd learned a lot from watching Isaiah. His mindset, his attitude, how he conducted his life. Isaiah was happy in his way. Happy wasn't doing nothing. Happy was doing the thing you loved to do. It might not be fun or exciting to someone else, but that didn't matter. If you found that thing you were lucky. Like most people, you put a toe in the water, got pulled in by the river of life and ended up in the Baltic Sea or the Gulf of Mexico or some other place you never thought you'd be. Dodson shook his head at the phrase "finding your passion." It made it sound like you'd be riding the bus one day and see your calling on a billboard.

Isaiah didn't discover his passion. He followed his gift. He became an investigator by investigating, and the more he did it, the better he got, and the better he got, the more he wanted to do it because he was good at it. It was satisfying. Isaiah grew his passion like a rosebush, trained it like a racehorse. The result was expertise. Kids were always looking for something "cool" to do. Actor, singer, model, writer, entrepreneur, even though they had no talent for it or the drive to learn the profession. That's your problem, Dodson thought. Looking for a cool career that got public attention. But Isaiah had taught him coolness was being an expert. Be the one they turn to when no else can solve the problem. Didn't matter if your world was shoemaking, shooting pool or flying a helicopter. If you were an expert, you were cool.

Why not follow Isaiah's lead? Dodson thought. Start with the talents you already have and see where they take you. What exactly are your talents? Dodson wondered. What do you do that comes naturally, that's instinctive? That was easy. Selling. It was the basis of all hustling. Dodson had always been exceptionally good at convincing people to buy, sell, give something up, take a chance or get something for nothing. Hustling and advertising were the same things except the goods were legal and actually existed. Kale is a superfood. Oh, really? You mean like collard greens? If that was the case, black people would be leaping tall buildings in a single bound. Women like the smell of your deodorant? No shit? Then why not cut to the chase and spray it directly on your dick? Call it what you want but that was Hustling 101. Why would walking shoes be any different?

Stimson said Skechers wanted something cool, edgy and relevant. Cool and edgy, Dodson understood. But what did relevant mean? He looked it up in the dictionary. *Appropriate to the current time, period or circumstances; of contemporary interest.* Dodson read the newspaper and he watched the news. He knew what was current, he knew the issues of the day and what people were talking about. But how do you incorporate all that in a commercial about shoes?

He had to use his imagination. He had to be creative. Grace said creativity was everything you experienced in your entire life brought to bear on a single problem. When she was deciding about a shape or a color she wasn't choosing from a list. Her life was the sun shining through a magnifying glass, the beam narrowed and focused on one spot until there were flames, until she decided on a shape or a color.

Dodson looked back over his life and thought about his relevant experiences. Then he gathered his own sun and narrowed the beam. His heart was going faster. He looked across the neighborhood and smiled.

He called Grace. "It's Dodson," he said.

"Isn't it the crack of fucking dawn?" she replied, sleepily.

"I need a solid."

"Happy to help. Can it wait until after breakfast?"

"No. I'm coming over."

She hugged him as he came through the door. "I'm so glad to see you!"

"Yeah, me too," he said. Grace was straight up and a badass in her own right. He liked her a lot. She glanced at his hair but didn't say anything. An act of kindness, he thought. He told her about the internship and Cherise's ultimatum. She didn't judge. She didn't say, it's about time, or you only have yourself to blame. She felt for him and he was grateful.

"How's it going?" she asked.

"I really don't know yet. It's something new," Dodson said. He looked at her and frowned. She looked worn-down and worried and she'd lost weight. He'd return the favor, he thought. Nobody wants to be told they look like shit, but she brought it up herself.

"Yeah, I'm not doing so hot," she said. She told him about the show. "I'm behind on my work. I could do a show with fewer paintings, but I don't want to disappoint the gallery owner." She looked like she had something else to say but didn't.

They went into the kitchen and she made coffee. "Isaiah says my coffee is awful but I don't think it's bad for instant." She offered him a cup.

"No, thanks, I've had it before," Dodson said. "If a taster had a choice, it wouldn't be your coffee." She smiled and took an extra-big sip.

"So, what's this thing I have to do before breakfast?" she asked.

Dodson told her about Stimson and the Skechers ad. He explained his idea. "Do you like it?"

"Like it?" she replied with a grin. "I fucking love it." She got to work and drew a preliminary sketch. Dodson was thoroughly impressed.

"You know your shit, don't you?" he said. She smiled, pleased that he was pleased. He knew what she wanted to ask.

"I talked to Isaiah," he said.

"How is he?" she said, unformed tears in her eyes.

"He's aight. He's traveling, getting some head space, Northern California somewhere." This was no time to tell the truth, he thought.

"Did he say anything . . ." she began.

"About you? Yeah. He asked how you were. I said, Do you want me to reach out? He said no, but he wanted to say yes, just like you. You gonna call him?"

"I can't, and you know why."

"I don't know why you fightin' it," Dodson went on. "Y'all gonna be together sooner or later. Why not sooner? It's like Cherise and me. You'd have to kill both of us to keep us apart." Grace closed her eyes, took a breath and opened them again.

"Give me some room, Dodson. I'm going to paint now."

Chapter Twelve:
Dumb and Dumber 5

It was a little after ten at night. Deronda walked into the Dolphin courtyard, dragging her feet, pretending to be tired like everybody else in the place. Tired of your shitty job, tired of fighting with your old man, tired of your kids, tired of being broke, tired of struggling for every fucking thing you needed to live a decent life.

She'd dressed down for the occasion. Old hoodie, old skinny jeans and old Converse All-Stars. She went up to the second floor and picked a spot on the railing, near Sandra's apartment. She lit a joint. Something called Train Wreck she'd bought from Raphael. The smell was strong, like a skunk got shot in the ass with Michael Stokeley's Mossberg. She puffed but didn't inhale. She didn't want to be high.

People passing through the courtyard glanced at her, expressionless. She could have been chewing gum. She saw the bloodstains on the cement where Jerome had been cut. Grace had told her what happened. And there was the boy in the jumper, doing little hops and talking to himself. The jumper was stained and too small for him. There was something sticky on his face, lint in his hair. That could be Janeel, Deronda thought. One more accidental, overlooked child who might as well call up Vacaville and make his reservation now. It took less than five minutes for Sandra to open her door, the smell of weed an aphrodisiac.

"Who are you?" Sandra said, warily.

"Who are *you*?" Deronda said, without turning around.

"Ain't no need for attitude," Sandra said, apologetically. "I was just askin'." She came out on the walkway, leaned against the railing. She sneezed, found a tissue in the sleeve of her too-big sweater and wiped her nose.

"You live here?"

"Visiting my cousin, Jerome," Deronda said. "A fool if there ever was one."

"You know he got cut up, right?"

"Yeah, and everybody in the family is wondering why it took so long." Without looking, Deronda held out the joint. Sandra took it, her hand shaking.

"Thanks, that's real nice of you." She sucked in a monumental hit, held it and

173

blew it out again.

"What's your name?" Deronda said.

"Sandra. You?"

"Tiana," Deronda said. She didn't want her name getting back to Bobby. They took turns with the joint. Deronda took a side-long glance. A junkie, no doubt. Heavy-lidded eyes, gaunt cheeks, it was seventy-five degrees and the girl's wearing a sweater and hugging herself. Antsy too, shifting her weight around like her clothes had hair in them. She sneezed a second time. Her nose was running, and there was a light sheen of sweat on her face. That's how it goes, Deronda thought, hot-cold, hot-cold.

"Where you from?" Sandra said.

"Lawndale."

"Is it nice there?"

"Not the part I'm from. Ain't no better than here."

"You got a job or something?" Sandra asked.

"Stripper," Deronda answered.

Sandra smiled. "Yeah? Where?"

"The Kandy Kane. Man, it's fucked up over there. Offstage fees is high, extras in the VIP rooms, dressing room ain't never clean and too many gawkers, cheap-ass muthafuckas. I hate them table dances, didn't you? Trying to balance yourself in them heels, a nigga lookin' up at your business and eatin' pizza at the same time."

"I worked at the Wild Child, over in Carson?" Sandra said. She smiled, looking back in time. "Yeah, I was fine too. I wasn't nothing like this. I had me some titties, girl, and I could *daaaance.* Did all kinds of pole tricks too. Muthafuckas at the tip rail be hollerin' jack, throwin' that money at me, niggas wouldn't even sit down!" She laughed. Deronda laughed too, remembering the feeling. They were silent a few moments, the memories fading into the fucked-up present.

"Damn, I'm bored," Deronda said. "I don't know nobody and got nowhere to go. You got somethin' goin' on?"

"I wish I could help you, but I got something to do."

"Yeah, it's cool. Maybe I'll see you around." She gave Sandra the joint. "Keep it." She went down the stairs and crossed the courtyard. She glanced back. Sandra was holding the joint, puzzled, as if she'd never gotten something free before.

"Nice meeting you, Tiana," she said.

"Yeah. You too."

Deronda went to the car, a junker she'd borrowed from TK. No chance she was parking her Lexus around here. She'd hoped to get more personal with Sandra and talk about Bobby James, but there was no way in. She was banking on Sandra's habit; the chills, the restlessness, the sneezing, the sweat, were all signs it was "nighttime," what the addicts call withdrawal.

It was right after high school. Deronda had been living with Dodson in Isaiah's apartment. Isaiah was weird now, but even more back then, obsessed with finding his brother's killer and ignoring everything else. Isaiah and Dodson had their run as the Battering Ram Bandits, then a whole bunch of other shit happened, and Dodson kicked her to the curb.

As a parting gift, he gave her five thousand dollars and sent her on her way. That hurt. It would've almost been better if he'd given her nothing. Almost. She loved Dodson, at least she thought so at the time. To this day, she felt a little twinge when she saw him with Cherise. The breakup taught her a lesson though. Love wasn't heaven. Love was Training Day. Love toughened your ass up for the shit to come.

Her reaction to the breakup was to party and go through boyfriends like regular meals. They were a blur, but Melvin Mitchell was a standout and not in a good way.

176

He looked and acted normal, but he was a dedicated junkie. Heroin was always around. Deronda dibbed and dabbed. She snorted lines, chased the dragon around the block, and at Melvin's insistence, she shot up three times. That was her limit. Then it was four. Then five. Maybe more. She lost track. Then Melvin was arrested and there was no more dope. He was the one who scored. She had no idea from who or where. No big deal, she thought. She didn't need dope to live. What was all this addiction bullshit about anyway? And then she got the chills and the sweats and the runny nose and everything ached and she couldn't stand being in her own skin. You were nothing but want, nothing but need. There was no discussion. You weren't thinking about quitting or other drugs or if it was worth the risk hitting the street and looking for a dealer. You were fucking starving. That was what it was like; famine in Africa and you were one of those ashy, drawn-out faces with horses' teeth and bones showing through your skin. It was survival, son. You see a rat, you eat the rat. All you had to do was find the rat in the first fucking place and you were cool.

Deronda went out and scored, not as hard as she thought. Long Beach was the biggest port on the West Coast and heroin was smuggled in by the megaton. Cooking was a problem. Melvin had done all that rigmarole, tying off your arm, doing the filter and the spoon, heating the shit up, et cetera fucking et cetera. He even did the injecting. It wasn't something you could practice, and it was hard to do when your hands were shaking. She fucked up a vein or two before she actually fixed. The shot knocked her out. Like out. Maybe she took too much, she didn't know.

Nona woke her up, they were roommates then. She was groggy, half-conscious. Two other girls were there too. Her cousin, Sheila, and Nona's sister, Katrice. They weren't sympathetic or even worried. They were pissed off. They screamed at her, telling her she was a stupid bitch and what the fuck was wrong with her and did she want to die and they would kill Melvin as soon as he got out of County. Nona picked up the tiny envelope and shook it. There was a little bit left. "I'm flushing this down the toilet."

"The fuck you are," Deronda said. She got up off the couch and Nona hit her. Hit. Her. With a closed fist. And then all three girls beat on her until she was crying and curled up on the floor. Then they took her clothes off, stuck her in a cold shower, dried her off, dressed her in a housecoat and put her to bed. It was a cold but brief turkey. One of the girls stayed with her 24/7. Mostly Nona. Brought her soup and saltines, the only things she could keep down, rolled her joints, took her to the bathroom to throw up. Love Nona. Love that girl to death.

Deronda sat in the car, wishing she hadn't given the joint to Sandra. It was a chilly night for LA. She wanted to turn on the heat, but a parked car with no lights and the engine running was asking for some shit to happen.

Sandra came out of the Dolphin in the same baggy sweater, looking frantic and talking on her phone. She hurried south and turned onto Argento. Deronda got out of the car and followed her. There were bad parts of East Long Beach and there were really bad parts, and this was one of them. There was only one streetlight every two or three blocks, the street itself a fucked-up stretch of burglar bars, security gates, gang graffiti and overflowing dumpsters, more trash and broken glass than asphalt. Sandra arrived at a loading dock, lit by a yellow floodlight. A couple of junkies were camped out there, two zombies with sores on their faces, clothes so dirty they could walk around by themselves. They mumbled and shrugged and shook their heads. Sandra cursed and hurried away. She met another junkie in front of a liquor store who had no answers either. She stamped her foot, turned in a circle and covered her face with her hands. She cried for a minute and got on the phone again.

"Come on, Luis, pick up. It's Sandra," she said. "Please pick up. PLEASE!" Luis didn't pick up. Deronda followed her to a building that was almost identical to the Dolphin, except there was no fountain. Sandra disappeared through the vestibule, and by the time Deronda caught up, Sandra wasn't there. No way to tell which apartment she'd gone in. Deronda waited. Like music in a movie, an argument faded up. A man and a woman. First-floor apartment, on the other side of the courtyard. Deronda got closer. The woman was Sandra. The man was screaming. She was hysterical. Pleading, explaining, crying.

"I'm sorry," Sandra sobbed. "I'm really sorry, but I couldn't think of nobody else."

"So you come to me?" the man said. "You already owe me money, you stupid fucking puta!"

"I'm sorry, I'm sorry. Please, please, Luis. Gimme a dime bag — shit gimme a deuce, that's all. I'll bring you the money tomorrow. I swear I will!"

"No, you won't, you fucking liar!"

"Come on, Luis, I'll suck your dick. I'll do it real good!"

"Get out!"

"Please, Luis! It's only a deuce!" There was a sound Deronda knew well. Knuckles hitting flesh and bone. Sandra screamed. Furniture was being thrown aside. He was chasing her. Deronda pounded on the door.

"Sandra? Sandra, are you all right? Come on outta there!" A moment later, the door swung open. Luis was a short, fierce motherfucker in boxer shorts; bald, meth eyes, muscled up and pouring sweat.

He leaned into Deronda and shouted in her face, "Who the fuck are you?" He was rocking his head from side to side, fists bunched up.

"I'm her friend," Deronda said.

"Oh, you're her friend? Her friend?" he screamed, spit flying out of his mouth. "Her fucking FRIIEEENDD?" Deronda didn't move, kept her face calm, her shoulders relaxed, her hands stuck in her front pockets. If you don't want to get hit, don't look hostile and don't look like you're expecting it. One more lesson she'd learned the hard way.

"How much does Sandra owe you?" she said.

"Sixty!" Sandra blurted out.

"Seventy-five or she stays here with me," Luis said.

Deronda brought some folded cash out of her back pocket. "This is a hundred and thirty, something like that. Here. Take it. Give her a twenty-dollar bag, and we'll get the fuck outta here."

Deronda refused to let Sandra fix in the car, and they drove back to the Dolphin. Sandra had her knees pulled up to her chest, her arms inside her sweater. She was shivering like she'd just been rescued from an ice floe.

"You always carry that much cash?" she said.

"I do if I had a good night at the strip club," Deronda said.

"I 'preciate what you did, but was you following me?"

"No," Deronda said. "I was gonna get something to eat and I saw you go in there, thought I'd holla at you." That was enough curiosity for Sandra. She closed her eyes, bowed her head and breathed in slow deep breaths.

Sandra hustled into her apartment. Twenty dollars bought you a sandy-colored pebble of Mexican brown. Heroin was getting more popular these days. Kids were afraid of meth and crack, and opioids were too expensive. As soon as Sandra got out her works, she went from a sweaty malaria victim to somebody working an assembly line. Quickly, efficiently, she prepared the fix. Deronda turned away, she didn't watch Sandra search for a vein, desperately inspecting her arms, hands, feet. Melvin had a friend who shot up in his groin, hit the femoral artery and died a minute later. Melvin had another friend who shot up in the neck and lost his ability to speak. As the heroin was heated, there was that nasty vinegar smell mixed with the musty air. Deronda wanted to leave.

Sandra was mumbling, *"Please, please, please, please."* Please what? Deronda wondered. Please work faster? Please be good dope? Please not be mixed with fentanyl and kill me? Deronda turned around. Sandra was leaning back on the sofa, her eyes closed, her body relaxed. She wasn't high, really. For a junkie like her, it was about not being sick.

Deronda looked around and was sorry she did. Imagine being someplace where there was no order of any kind. Shit piled around you without regard to what it was or where it should be or whether it was washed, unwashed or needed to be refrigerated. And there in the middle of it was a soul so lost, so ravaged, so hopelessly messed up you wanted to cry. Deronda couldn't stand it anymore. "Sandra? I'm gonna leave you my number, okay? You want to get together, call me." Deronda got a pen out of her bag, wrote her number and the name Tiana on a napkin. She turned for the door. She saw a shadow move past the front window. Then a knock and a voice.

"Sandra? Open up. It's me. Bobby."

"Oh, shit," Deronda whispered.

"Sandra," Bobby said. "Don't make me stand out here."

It was a studio apartment, like Spoon's. There was a galley kitchen separated from the living room by a short counter. Hide behind it? No, Bobby might want a drink. The bathroom? No, Bobby might take a piss. The closet had no door and there was no room under the bed.

"Sandra," Bobby said, knocking louder. "Hurry up, will you?" Sandra opened her eyes extra wide and blinked a few times, her head reeling like a drunk waking up in a chair. Deronda was scared. She'd just bought heroin for Bobby's drug-addicted, prostitute girlfriend. That wouldn't sound too good in court. She had to do something.

"Goddammit," Bobby yelled. "Open the fucking door!" Sandra got up and let him in. "Christ. What took you so long?"

"I went as fast as I could," she said. "And don't be startin' up on me. I don't want to hear that shit no more."

Deronda couldn't see anything. She was standing behind the curtains. They weren't floor length, her calves down to her shoes exposed. It was like *Dumb and Dumber 5* starring a black girl from the hood. In her favor, it was dark, the only light coming from the TV. Her best camouflage was probably the mess. Why would a pair of Converse All-Stars be any more noticeable than all the other shit piled everywhere?

It sounded like Bobby had a shopping bag. He set it down somewhere. "Have you been seeing johns?"

"No. And even if I did it wouldn't be none of your damn business."

"Well, don't, that's what the money is for. Do you want something to eat?" He started emptying the bag.

"No, I ain't hungry. Did you bring the dope?"

Bobby groaned. "Can't you clean this place up? I'll pay someone to do it."

"No, I told you fifty times already, I don't

want nobody messing with my stuff. I don't even know why you come here. You say the same things every time."

"I've gotta stop this," Bobby said, mostly to himself. "It's ridiculous. I don't know why I do it."

"You do it cuz you *lovvvve* me," Sandra said, mockingly.

"No, I don't love this you," Bobby said. "I love the other one. The one that was beautiful and smart and —"

"Don't be talkin' 'bout all that. The only one you got is the one sittin' here. You don't like it you can take your love and get the hell out my apartment."

"And if I do, you'll die," Bobby replied.

"Most likely." Sandra was disdainful, skeptical, like when you're challenging somebody to put up or shut up. "What y'all gonna do then? Come to the funeral? Throw some dirt on my grave?"

"I can't deal when you're like this," Bobby said, a tremble in his voice.

"You don't have to deal with nothin'," Sandra said. "You can take your ass back to your office and go fuck yourself."

If there was room for Deronda to shake her head, she would have. Here's a miserable-ass junkie, deep in need and messed up beyond measure, telling her baby daddy to go fuck himself. Goes to show you. Your pride might be gone forever, but you'd fake it when you had to.

"Christ!" Bobby shouted. "Can't we get some air in here?" He charged over to the window. Deronda was behind the left curtain. *Shit, I'm so busted!* Bobby grabbed the right one and yanked it open. He was two feet away. If he looked sideways, she was done. *Your mommy messed up, Janeel. She's very, very sorry.*

"Close that!" Sandra snapped. "That window don't open no way." Bobby cursed, closed the curtain and moved away. Deronda took a deep silent breath and tried to generate some moisture in her mouth.

"Wait a minute," Sandra said. "What happened to Tiana? She was here a minute ago."

"Who's Tiana?" Bobby asked.

"This girl I met. She was here right 'fore you knocked on the door."

"Well, she's not here now."

"She got to be," Sandra said. Deronda heard her get up from the sofa. *Please, Sandra, sit your dumb ass down.*

"Well, I'm going," Bobby said.

"Whatever," Sandra said. Bobby left. It was silent except for the TV. Moments went by like minutes. Sweat was running down Deronda's face, but she couldn't reach up to wipe it off. Her nose itched. Was Sandra looking for her? Was she standing there scanning the room inch by inch, her eyes about to land on the All-Stars? The quiet was nerve-racking. For some reason, the TV made it quieter.

"See, I knew she was here," Sandra said. She must have found the napkin. "I wish she woulda stayed. I thought I had me a friend." She went into the bathroom and closed the door. Deronda had been standing there so long, the blood had pooled in her legs and she was light-headed. She shoved the curtains aside and got out of there, breathing deeply as she flew down the stairs.

"It was so fucked up," Deronda said. "I heard everything but I couldn't record it." She was home with Grace.

"But you got useful information," Grace said. "Bobby is supporting his girlfriend, a drug-addicted prostitute. He buys her drugs and gives her money. That doesn't sound like father material to me. What I don't understand is, what's Bobby doing with her? He works in a bank."

"I think they met at the strip club," Deronda said. "He was a regular, came in and only saw her, spent everything in his wallet before he went home. The stripper's dream."

"That happens?"

"Oh, yeah. I had a few customers like that. Dudes get obsessed. They think they love you, want to meet you outside the club, buy you presents, make all kinds of promises. It's a hard line to walk. You want nothing to do with 'em, but you gotta keep 'em thinking you do."

"Yeah, go on."

"So Bobby gets obsessed with her, right? But Sandra's playing him. She's already got a man, some dude named Peaches or Mr. Hat. He gets her hooked on dope and gets her to do porn, and when her looks go, he turns her out. When she's too skanky even for him, he dumps her. What she gonna do now? She's got no man and no money."

"She calls her favorite customer," Grace said.

"Hey, Bobby," Deronda said in a cooing voice. "It's Sandra. Did you miss me? I missed you."

"Even though she's messed up?"

"*Because* she's messed up," Deronda said. "That rescue thing. Lots of men are into it. At the club, we called them white knights."

"And there's Bobby's fantasy girl as

messed up as she can be."

"Uh-huh," Deronda said. "He'll save her, get her back on her feet, and she'll be so grateful she'll keep house and blow him night and day."

"But we can't tell that to the judge. We need some kind of proof."

"Like what?" Deronda said. Grace thought for a long moment.

"I don't know," she said.

Bobby grew up in East Long Beach just like Deronda. Same struggles, same teetering on the poverty line, same limited prospects. Growing up hard does something to you. You worry about survival all the time. Whether you know it or not, your gut tells you to forget your wants, your needs come first. Put your desires in the passenger seat, son, you've got work to do. Did you want to get a degree in business finance? No, you didn't. Why did you? Because you had your cousin's notes, and he graduated with honors. How do you think the grade point average went from 2.0 to 3.0?

After you got your degree you had a choice. Be the business manager of a start-up or work at a bank. Working at a bank was at the bottom of your shitty job list. But survival demanded a monthly paycheck, a pension plan and medical insurance. It was a solid, safe choice. Aspirations were nowhere to be seen. But what had all your solid, safe decisions come to? An ordinary boring life. In a damn cubicle all day, opening IRAs and checking accounts, which amounted to no more than filling out a mountain of forms. People didn't know this, but you were under pressure all the time. Management pushed you into opening accounts and issuing credit cards to customers without them knowing about it. They made money by charging unwarranted fees. To hit your sales target, you had to create phony PIN numbers and email addresses to enroll people in online bank services. Was that rewarding? Satisfying? Did it utilize any of your intelligence and creativity? Was it something you could be proud of? No, it wasn't. Bobby was on the lookout for an opportunity.

Bobby first got onto Deronda because he subscribed to the *LA Times*. He read the article about her and the food truck business. He remembered the name and her world-famous backside. He saw the picture of Janeel and thought, what if you were the father? What if you wanted custody? How much would Deronda pay to make you go away? Didn't matter if Bobby wasn't the father. With what he had in mind, she'd have to capitulate. She was trapped.

Seeing Sandra was depressing. Bobby was at home, making himself a grilled-cheese sandwich. He was worried about time. The hearing was in four days. Deronda was desperate. She might do more than worm her way into Sandra's apartment. For all Bobby knew, she would drive her car through his front door or get her friends to beat him into the sidewalk. He had to shut her down once and for all. But how? What was Deronda thinking? He wondered. Obviously, she wanted something to hold over your head and make it a standoff. There was nothing in your past to use as leverage.

That's why she was in Sandra's apartment. She was looking for dirt. Okay, Bobby thought, if you're Deronda, what do you know or think you know? What did you hear while you were hiding behind that curtain? Bobby visiting a drugged-out hooker. Bobby bringing her dope and money so she wouldn't have to trick. Bobby pleading with her, using his love to coerce her into another life.

Bobby absently took a bite of the grilled cheese and burned his tongue. He drank some water and let the sandwich cool off. The realization came to him and he smiled.

Okay, if you're Deronda, what do you do now? Bobby thought. You try and get evidence, of course, but how would you do that? He smiled again. You'd want to take pictures.

CHAPTER THIRTEEN: STEALTH DOG

Skip was back in his moldy motel room, eating a cold Quarter Pounder with Cheese. John Travolta in *Pulp Fiction* said in France they call it a Royale with Cheese. Some name for a burger. The shit that happened at the food truck had rattled him, that scary fucker sticking the barrel of a shotgun under his chin. He was just like the black dudes on the yard at Vacaville, the ones who lifted weights until they looked like armored vehicles.

Skip hated Grace almost as much as he hated that goddamn Isaiah. She would definitely have to pay. *Oh, my God,* he wished Goliath was here. He'd grind that bitch into hamburger, stick her in a Royale and let the dog eat her with Secret Sauce. The Mexican lady told him Isaiah left. If that was the case, he only had one option. Scare Grace, intimidate her, break her

194

down. Make her go to Isaiah or Isaiah come to her.

Next day he went to Fry's, bought a GPS unit and put the app on his phone. Keeping track of Grace would be easy. The blue dot told you where she was and where she was going. You could also set up zones, boundaries covering her usual routes. If she left that zone to meet Isaiah, you'd get an alert. If Isaiah came here, it was a different situation. The Mexican lady said bad people were after Isaiah. If that was true, he wouldn't stay at Grace's house. He'd hole up someplace else and Grace's driving pattern would change. Instead of home to work and back again, she'd go visit him.

Skip drove over to the Vons parking lot. Grace was working at the service window, passing out food and making change. He had to wait a couple of hours before she got off. He followed her to a house on Mayfield. She was living with some black chick who drove a really nice car. Skip had some time to waste. He went to the movies. Another fucking Godzilla. Really? All those supposedly smart people in Hollywood and that's the best thing they could come up with?

He went back to the motel, drank some, watched TV and slept longer than he'd wanted to. He woke up at four a.m. He put on some dark clothes and drove over to Grace's house. He didn't take the gun; there was no need. He got to the house around four-thirty. The street was dark and quiet. No traffic, no people. The moon was almost full but it was cloudy, the light faint.

He parked three houses down, got out of the car, walked normally until he reached Grace's driveway. Then he got low, scurried to her car. The Jeep had a lot of ground clearance. He crawled underneath and turned over on his back so he could see the underside of the car. He attached the unit to the frame. Then he turned over and started crawling out again — and froze. A black dog was sitting on the front steps. Just sitting there, panting. It must have been sleeping and getting under the car woke it up. It was looking at him.

The dog was mostly in the dark, but Skip could see its shape and the gleam of its teeth. It looked familiar. Very familiar. The big square head, the curled-over ears, the squat body. Skip mouthed the words *Ohh fuck.*

It was a goddamn pit bull.

Skip squiggled back under the car and stayed still. He didn't know what to do. If he made a run for it, the dog would be on him before he reached the sidewalk. You could kick and punch a pit bull all you wanted but once the dog clamped on to your arm, shoulder, wrist, hand or ankle, you were done. A pit will never let go. You'd have to jam a spike down its throat, stab it thirty times, or shoot it in the head.

Skip's mouth was dry; he was starting to sweat. His heart was thudding. He noticed something strange. The dog hadn't barked, growled or even come over to investigate. Skip had never seen a pit bull or any other kind of dog act like that. A goddamn Labradoodle would at least be barking. Calm down, Skip thought. Wait it out. See what happens.

It was hard to tell how much time went by. Two minutes, ten minutes, and the dog was still sitting there licking its balls. Was there something wrong with it? Was it sick? The dog stood up. *Oh, shit, here we go.* It was standing at a different angle and Skip could see it better. He knew a lot about conformation, the way a purebred is supposed to look. This wasn't a purebred. It was mixed with something. There was some dewlap, wrinkling on its forehead, the legs were a little long and the tail had a curve in it. Skip gasped and felt a burst of high-voltage fear in his chest. *It was one of Go-*

liath's kids! And Goliath wasn't just big. He'd been bred from a long line of fighting dogs and then crossbred with Presa Canario. The Presa was a hulking beast, like a bull mastiff, bred for ring fighting and killing predators. It had an unpredictable temperament and was human aggressive. In the dog world it was described as a "pit bull on steroids."

Oh, shit, it's coming over here! Nothing for Skip to do but scramble out of the other side and run like hell. He wished he hadn't parked so far away. He was about to turn around, but the dog had already arrived. Skip went still, sweat running down his temples. The dog stood there panting. *Heh-heh-heh-heh.* A sound he once enjoyed sounded like a car chugging carbon monoxide into his skull. The dog was a little bigger than average, seventy-five pounds or so. That Goliath chromosome. Even so, it could easily get under the car, but if it did, it would have a hard time manuevering, Skip thought. If he could swivel around, he could kick at the dog and keep it off him — until the dog got hold of his foot, ate the toes and tore off the rest.

The dog stuck its nose under the car. *Heh-heh-heh-heh.* No growls, no barks. All it did was sniff a couple of times. Then the dog raised its leg and pissed on a fucking tire! It finished, trotted back to the front steps and sat down again.

The hell was this? Skip thought. He was freaking out. The dog was definitely freaky, but so far seemed harmless. He started crawling out and stopped again. He thought of something. Isaiah. He was as smart as he was sneaky. Skip huffed and nodded to himself. Yeah, the fucker. You know what he did? That son of a bitch had trained a *stealth dog*! It sat around like it didn't care, but as soon as you were out in the open, it attacked and ripped you to shit. *So now what, Skip?* Knowing that didn't really help. He was thirsty, cramped, hungry, and he needed to piss. It got lighter. It was dawn.

Now the dog was lying down with its chin on his paws. It was looking at him with its eyes open. Take a chance? Run for the car? He remembered Goliath killing an entire herd of goats and chasing a mail truck for four miles, all the way to the landfill, the driver screaming the whole way. All Skip could do was wait until somebody came by and distracted it. *Oh, shit.* What if Grace found him, cowering under the muffler? She'd let the dog eat his organs. Jesus, he *really* had to pee. He was on his stomach and couldn't open his zipper. He held it a while longer, but his bladder was about rupture. Fuck it. He peed and felt its warmth spread over his groin. *Christ, Skip, you pissed on yourself!* He couldn't deal with this. He didn't know what to do. Run, stay, run, stay. The piss was turning cold. He felt like crying.

And then — hope! Skip saw the mailman, halfway down the block and coming this way. He must know the dog and it didn't seem to bother him. Maybe it wasn't a stealth dog. Maybe he was making that up. Yeah, sure, you dope, it'd be really hard to train a dog like that. He started to move but stopped again. What if he was wrong? Suppose it *was* a stealth dog. He wouldn't attack the mailman because they knew each other. Skip could smell the piss, his whole crotch was freezing. It was so depressing it made him want to do nothing.

The mailman approached. "How you doin', Ruff !" The dog was suddenly energetic, wagging its tail, hurrying over to him. The mailman gave him a treat. "Here ya go, buddy. Special just for you." Christ, that's no stealth dog. You're a fucking idiot, Skip. He crawled out from under the car. He smiled cheerily and dusted off his hands. The dog didn't care but the mailman was staring at him.

"Grace asked me to look at the muffler," Skip said. "Too bad, I think she's going to have to replace it."

"Have an accident?" the mailman said, nodding at the piss stain that went from Skip's waist down to his knees.

"Oh, that," Skip said, with a weak chuckle. "It's just, uh, water." He hurried back to his car.

He got to the motel, left his pants outside the door and took a shower. That was one of the worst things that had ever happened to him. He lay down on the bed. He couldn't sleep. He stared at the ceiling fan, patting his groin to see if the piss stain was still there. He thought of Grace. He thought of Isaiah. His anger came from a distance, thundering war drums and crackling cymbals, billowing storm clouds rolling off the desert hills, an advancing army dressed in black, blotting out the sky and shitting rain, drenching you, drowning you, washing you into a river, dark as gunpowder and pulling you under.

Skip said, "Time for the pain."

Chapter Fourteen:
Bona Fides

Isaiah slept miserably. When he awoke, two voices were nagging at him. One of them said, *Be strong, don't give in,* and the other said, *Get it over with and you'll be done.* Strength and control were far and away the better option. Good, you've decided, he thought. There were other things to do. He could look for another dog, read, play with Alicia and Juana or take a hike somewhere. For the moment, why not make yourself some coffee and breakfast? It might improve your mood. He had his coffee and breakfast but his mood was worse. *Get it over with* had made a comeback. Grace once told him he was like Coltrane's music. Seemingly unstructured and directionless, but underneath, a hidden current of discipline and rigor, of forward movement in calculated beats. She said the current always flowed whether he knew it or not. Abruptly, he stood up. He put his hands in his front pockets and stood there. He could feel the Demon, itchy and restless, yanking on its chain.

He entered the garage, angry and impatient. "You said you had Crowe's records," he said, accusingly.

Billy was lying on the narrow cot, listening to his headphones. Startled, he sat up. "Um, what?"

"You said you had William Crowe's records. I want to see them."

"I didn't even think you heard me," Billy said.

"Are they on your laptop?"

"Yes, but why —"

"Give it to me," Isaiah said sharply. "Now."

He brought Billy's laptop into the kitchen and plunked down at the breakfast table. He hated himself for doing this, for failing to deny the Demon Curiosity. The PTSD hadn't stopped his driving need to know, find out and reveal, however sickened he was by the prospect. The question to be resolved: did William Crowe kill Ava's sister, Hannah, or was it made-up bullshit?

Isaiah looked at Crowe's mugshot. He had an oblong face, jowly and unshaven, double chin, thick lips, his eyes dull and too close together. There were surveillance photos of him standing at an intersection waiting for the light to change. According to his file, he was six foot, 232 pounds. He towered over the people around him. His body was like an upright gorilla. Huge torso, short legs and long arms. There was a brutish, mechanical quality about him. Like he'd do whatever he wanted without thought or feeling, and there was no one who could stop him.

The police files were daunting. Hundreds and hundreds of pages, photos, notes and exhibits. When Isaiah had a vast quantity of data to read, he used speed-reading techniques. He formed an objective. What was he seeking? In this case, he wanted information that would confirm or vindicate Crowe as Hannah's killer. Knowing that, he narrowed his focus. For the entire afternoon and into the early evening, he skimmed the paragraphs to see if they were relevant so he could either skip them or read for more detail. He widened his visual field to take in whole sentences and used his finger to guide his eyes over the text. His finger moved faster than his eyes would naturally. He looked for conclusions, theories, the bottom line. He could read over seven hundred words per minute instead of the usual two-hundred-plus. He skimmed Crowe's background, the forensic reports, case notes, photos, witness interviews and the key evidence, all of it circumstantial. Crowe was a reasonable, even likely, suspect, Isaiah decided.

Ava's twin sister, Hannah, was twenty-one years old, blond, slim, five-four, 113 pounds. When she left work at six-fifteen, it was dark. She walked home as she usually did and was kidnapped before she got there. Police found an empty lot on her route. The evidence indicated she'd been knocked unconscious and dragged across the ground to a vehicle parked in the alley behind the property.

Isaiah looked at photos of the drag marks. He noted they were interrupted by frequent stops, as if the victim had been too heavy to drag continuously. Understandable, Isaiah thought. Deadweight is much harder to lift and maneuver. A fifty-pound box of auto parts is manageable. The same parts in a laundry bag is another matter. The man had been walking backward, the body obliterating his shoe prints.

Isaiah thought of something. Crowe was six foot, 232 pounds. One of the detectives described Crowe as "physically intimidating." A man of his size could have easily dragged a 113-pound woman across an empty lot, or a football field for that matter. Hell. He could have thrown the girl over his shoulder and carried her. Something you couldn't do if you were a smaller, weaker man who had to rest a few times before going on. Crowe was not small and weak. Crowe didn't kill Ava's sister; someone else did it. Billy was chasing a fantasy and so was Ava. Satisfied and very relieved, Isaiah closed the laptop.

He went for a run. He took a trail behind the house, jogging through the woods, the air crisp, sunlight piercing the trees, his shadow like a friend. It was invigorating, but it didn't stop the Demon. The bastard was stepping on his heels and yelling in his ear. "Leave me alone," Isaiah said. He went to the gym. He lifted weights, practiced his Krav Maga moves and rowed the rowing machine nearly to Long Beach. He discovered you couldn't sweat the Demon away or even make it breathe hard.

He went back to the fucking kitchen, sat down at the fucking breakfast table and opened the fucking laptop. There were other ways to explain the drag marks. Maybe Crowe had an injury. Maybe he was all bulk and no brawn. Isaiah knew guys like that. Or maybe there were two killers, like the Hillside Strangler case, Kenneth Bianchi and Angelo Buono, the cousins who killed ten victims together. In that scenario, Crowe's partner drags the body to the alley, Crowe waiting in the getaway car. But the question remained. Did Crowe kill Ava's sister or not? Isaiah was pondering how to approach the data when Billy came in.

"Excuse me, but are you still using the laptop?" he asked. Isaiah looked at him a moment, considering, Billy intimidated.

"Something wrong?" he asked.

"Sit down," Isaiah said. Billy withheld his next question and quickly sat down.

Isaiah let him sweat a second or two. He said, "How do you know Crowe killed Ava's sister?"

In high school, Ava Bouchard was one of the cool kids. She was pretty, popular, always in the mix and seemed always to be having fun. Her crew hung out under the pergola where it was shady, they ate lunch in the cafeteria at their own table, and they were always going to parties. Billy was an anonymous fringe kid who huddled with other anonymous fringe kids in the corner of the library. They ate lunch on a bench behind the gymnasium, listened to bands that nobody ever heard of and watched their teenage years zip past like scenery from a moving car. Billy had two classes and study hall with Ava. He made it a point to sit near her. She hardly seemed to study, too busy being popular and happy. They knew each other to nod hello, but that was it.

Algebra was Billy's favorite class because he sat directly behind her. He could smell her soap, see the shine on her hair and the soft fuzz on her earlobes. One day, he overheard her saying she wasn't prepared for the test. She had to pass or take the class over in summer school.

A few minutes later, Mr. Fujimoto passed out the tests. Billy tapped Ava on the shoulder and said, "I'll help you with the answers."

"What? How?"

The test began. Billy used his finger, and with a light touch, drew a 1 on Ava's back. She flinched but didn't turn around. Then he drew a C. For question 1, the answer was C. She shook her head slightly; she didn't understand. He did it again. She hesitated, and nodded. Her elbow moved; she was filling in the little box. They went on to question 2. They did the whole test that way, like some strange version of Anne Bancroft and Patty Duke in *The Miracle Worker,* a buzz of electricity coursing through Billy every time his finger tripped over her bra strap. Afterward, she turned to him, offered him a brilliant smile and said, "Thanks, Billy. That was very nice of you." He realized he was holding his breath.

"Uh, sure," he said.

The next day, they got the test results. She got an 82, he got a 78. He'd intentionally answered a few wrong so they wouldn't have the same score. When the bell rang, she turned to him again, smiled that smile again and said, "That was the coolest thing ever."

"Uh, sure."

They continued the routine for the rest of the semester, Ava's average test score rising to a solid B. After one test, Mr. Fujimoto said, "Quite an improvement, Ava," and she burst out laughing. They became friends of a sort, waving and grinning whenever they saw each other. They might have been closer, but their cliques were like herds on the Serengeti. Gazelles over here, wildebeest over there. She invited him to her birthday party, but he didn't go. Her friends were other cool kids, jocks and hipsters. He'd be intimidated, wouldn't say anything and feel like a dummy.

At the graduation ceremony, she sought him out, hugged him and said, "You're so sweet, Billy. I wouldn't have made it without you." Billy's friends stared like he'd been blessed by the pope. After that, they lost touch, but he thought about her all the time. Ava. The dream girl who got away because he was a nerd and a nobody.

It was three weeks before Billy was committed to the hospital. He'd been following a story about a serial killer the media called AMSAK because he dumped his victims' bodies near the confluence of the American and Sacramento Rivers. The article was captioned AMSAK TAKES 17TH VICTIM.

A young woman named Hannah Bouchard was found drifting in the current, her body snagged in a tangle of low branches. Like the other victims, she'd been raped, tortured and mutilated before a horrifying death. Parts of her body were missing. Bouchard, Billy thought. That was Ava's last name. Was it possible they were related? He did a search. They were twin sisters. Billy had never met Hannah. According to the newspaper bio, she had attended Sacred Heart Catholic School. Why wasn't explained. At the time of her death, she worked as a nursing assistant, attending classes at night to become a licensed nutritionist. Of course, the sisters looked very much alike. Billy thought he could tell them apart if they wore the same clothes and their backs were turned.

He saw a live news clip of Ava. She was walking from her house to her car, a reporter sticking a microphone her face.

"Is there anything you'd like to say to the public, Miss Bouchard?" he said.

"Yeah," she replied, her eyes blistering the camera lens. "If anyone out there has information about that miserable cocksucker —"

"Miss Bouchard, we're live on the air."

"I don't give a shit. That motherfucker killed my sister."

"Miss Bouchard, please —"

"Are you listening out there, you fucking cockroach?" she said to the camera. "One day, they'll catch you and when they do? I hope they burn you at the stake and flush your fucking ashes down the toilet. I wish I could do it myself." To the reporter she said, "Get away from me, you fucking vulture. You live off dead meat."

Billy's outrage converged with his feelings for Ava. He wanted to get back in her life. He wanted to rescue her from her sorrow. Be a hero. He used a web app and got her email address, but what would he say? Hi. I'm the guy who wrote on your back in algebra class and I want to help? He needed to bring something to the table. Something to get her attention. He read all the articles he could find about AMSAK. At least seventeen murders were committed over a nine-year period. Two more may have been copycats. The killer still hadn't been identified. Ava must be incredibly frustrated, Billy thought. If you were her what would you be thinking? The same thing you'd be thinking if someone killed Irene. You'd want to catch the son of a bitch. The police never said anything about ongoing investigations. Billy wanted to know what they knew.

Billy's mother, Gretta, was a public defender for Pumas County, which included Coronado Springs. She had use of state law enforcement databases as well as CLETS, the California Law Enforcement Telecommunications System. CLETS provided access to national databases maintained by the FBI. Hardly anybody outside law enforcement knew about CLETS, but it was accessed three million times a day. Who would notice Billy logging in, especially when it was coming from his mother's IP address? To get the password, Billy planted a hidden camera in a row of law books behind Gretta's desk. It was focused on the monitor and keyboard. She spent long hours there working on cases. It took patience, but Billy got the passwords.

He downloaded all the AMSAK police and FBI files into the cloud. They were voluminous. Ten phone books' worth of incident reports, autopsy reports, chrono reports, DNA tests, evidence analysis, marks analysis, witness statements, victim backgrounds, crime scene photos and on and on. There was too much data. What would be of the most interest to Ava? he wondered. It was terrible to think this way, using her sister's death to make contact. And the plan could backfire. The massive files of information might only serve to confuse and overwhelm her, make her grief all the more painful.

Billy had a moment of conscience, but it didn't stop him. He knew his ploys pissed people off, even Irene, but he couldn't help it. Dr. Schaeffer said he had Narcissistic Personality Disorder; grandiosity, a lack of empathy, and an obsessive need for admiration that outstripped his moral imperatives and anything beyond his own self-interests. If that were true, Billy mused, lots of rich people had the same condition. Yeah, yeah, he knew Schaeffer was right, but it hardly mattered. It was like being an alcoholic and somebody tells you not to drink. Yawn. I've heard it all before.

His immediate problem was establishing

his bona fides with Ava. He'd send her something from Hannah's file, something official. The autopsy report was horrifying, even in the spare, bureaucratic language. *Strangulation, sexual assault, severe hemor-rhaging, sharp force injuries, fifty-eight punc-ture wounds, bones severed, six teeth re-moved, the murder weapon was a large knife, possibly a Bowie knife.* The crime scene photos were obscene, repulsive, as if all the evil in the world had gathered in Sacra-mento to tear Hannah apart. Whatever hap-pened, Billy thought, Ava would not see her sister's file.

Okay, something else then. A suspect file. Less horrifying and more intriguing. There was a list of three that hadn't been cleared. Billy selected one at random. Charles Lantana. A grim-looking man with Elvis Presley sideburns and an ear that was half torn off. Billy wrote Ava an email. The subject line: URGENT. THIS IS NOT A HOAX.

Dear Ava,
My name is Billy Sorensen. We were classmates at Windemere High. I was the kid who helped you with algebra. I read about your terrible loss. It must be extremely frustrating, not knowing what's going on or whether the police

are making progress. Don't ask me how, but I have access to the AMSAK case files. This is not a prank or a hoax. I wouldn't do that to you or anybody else. I have attached one of the files. Look it over. If you think it's legit, give me a call. I want to help.

Sincerely.

Billy

Forty-five minutes after sending the email, Ava called. "Billy, is that you?" He was flustered a moment.

"Yeah, it's me," he rasped.

"Oh, my God, I can't believe it."

"Me neither."

"The file, you got it from your mother, didn't you?"

"How do you know?"

"She's an attorney for the county and I know she didn't give it to you."

Nonsensically, Billy said, "I'd rather not say." Ava's voice sounded the same but different. Deeper, throatier, slightly hoarse, simmering emotions beneath.

"Billy, I appreciate this very much, but you're taking a big risk. You could go to jail for this."

"I know and I don't care," he replied. He liked saying that. He wondered if she could hear the longing in his voice.

"Do you have all the suspect files?"

"Yes, and I'll send them to you." There was a lengthy pause. "Ava? Are you still there?"

"Why are you doing this, Billy?" she said, an edge to her voice. "What do you want?"

"Nothing for myself. I want what you want."

"Well, I want to catch the fucker."

"Then so do I." Billy smiled, greatly relieved. For once, he hadn't humiliated himself.

"Billy, do you have Hannah's case file?" Ava asked.

"Yes, but I won't send it to you."

"Why?" she said in a flash of anger. "She's my sister."

"Because you don't want to see it. I swear, Ava, you really, really don't. If things were turned around, you wouldn't send it to me." She thought a few moments.

"Okay," she said quietly. There was a pause. He thought she might be crying. "Where do we start?" she said.

Billy had thought about this. "I think we should start with the short list of suspects."

"What if AMSAK isn't one of them?"

"The police have had nine years to catch him. Nine years of intense investigating by

216

dozens, even hundreds of detectives and FBI agents. They've collected thousands of pages of evidence, and they've gone back over that evidence again and again. They must have some idea of who he is by now. There might not be enough evidence to make an arrest, but one of those guys could be AMSAK."

"You sound really sure," Ava said.

"I could be wrong, I probably am, but we've got to start somewhere." Ava agreed. Billy would send her the files of the suspects. They would read them and talk. That was the plan until they changed it.

"Thanks for this, Billy," Ava said. "I really mean that." The call ended. He sent her the files. The suspects who hadn't been cleared were Charles Lantana, a fifty-four-year-old plumber who had replaced the garbage disposal in Hannah's apartment. Frank Saltair, a thirty-nine-year-old welder, part of a crew that put up an apartment building right across the street. And William Crowe, forty-five years old. He worked at the garage where Hannah had her car repaired. All had lengthy criminal records. Only Saltair had an alibi that could be verified. Billy had just started reading the files in depth when Ava called, excited, breathless.

"I've seen one of the suspects before!" she

said. Billy was bowled over.

"Who?"

"William Crowe."

"You saw him where?"

"I can't remember," Ava said, exasperated. "It was a while ago, before Hannah was . . . it was for like two seconds, but I know I saw him."

"When was this?"

"I don't know, it was a while ago."

"What makes you think it was Crowe?"

"Did you look at his photos?" she said. There was an assortment of mugshots, surveillance photos and video freeze frames in the file. "If you see a face like that you remember it," Ava said. Billy was overjoyed. Maybe they could actually nail this bastard, and he could be a hero.

William Jeffrey Crowe's criminal record started when he was a teenager. He was one of those kids Sacramento police officers knew by name. Vandalism, breaking and entering, drugs, cruelty to animals and arson. He set fire to some brush in an empty lot and a house burned down. He was still a minor so he got off with a stint in a juvenile detention center. His mother and father were mentally unstable and abusive. Crowe grew up in an atmosphere of violence, drug abuse and neglect. As an adult, Crowe's crimes got more serious. Voyeurism, selling stolen property, indecent exposure, assault, assault and battery and spousal abuse. His last arrest was for a bar fight.

Hannah had disappeared somewhere between work and home. On the same night, Crowe was picked up by a store camera two blocks from Hannah's apartment. Crowe's house was searched. They found a box of latex gloves and a roll of duct tape, suggestive but that was all. They also found a cheap pair of handcuffs still in their bubble packing. When asked about them Crowe said, "I like to play cops and robbers." No handcuff marks had been found on any of the victims. There was nothing in Crowe's car.

The police interviewed him several times but got nothing. He didn't ask for a lawyer. He taunted them. *You think I'm going to answer that? You guys are a joke. You have no idea what you're doing, do you? You've got no evidence or I'd be in lockup. You're full of shit, you know that?* Interest in him was keen, but while he was in prison on the bar fight charges, there were two more killings. The MOs were close. Whether it was AM-SAK or a copycat was never resolved. Police interest in Crowe waned, the surveillance ended. There were still a lot of questions so he hadn't been cleared.

"He's gotta be the guy," Ava said. "The arson, cruelty to animals, the history of mental illness, all early warning signs of a serial killer. Plus, the other things. Contact with Hannah at the garage, the duct tape, gloves, store video, the fucking handcuffs. It's him, I know it's him."

Billy was argumentative by nature. Even if someone's views coincided with his own, there were still objections to be made. "Are you sure that you saw him?"

"Yes, I'm sure, of course I'm sure."

"This was in Sacramento?"

"Yes, Billy. He's from Sacramento and so am I."

"Where did this happen?"

"I don't remember, but it doesn't matter. If I saw him, I saw him."

Had she really seen him? Billy wondered. She didn't know where or when. Maybe she saw someone who looked like Crowe or saw no one at all. This had happened to Billy many times before, wanting to believe something and creating his own affirmation.

"Don't be offended," Billy said. "But Crowe looks how a serial killer should look. Maybe you glommed on to that."

"No, Billy. I wasn't conjuring up something, I recognized him. There's a difference."

"The evidence is pretty circumstantial," he went on. He felt silly saying it. His entire belief system was based on circumstantial evidence.

"Circumstantial is another way of saying coincidental," Ava said, getting heated. "I don't believe in coincidences. Do you?"

"But what about the other two murders when Crowe was locked up? He couldn't have committed them."

"They were copycats," Ava said with a little less conviction.

"Maybe, but the police have lost interest."

"Not completely." She was angry now. "And I don't care one way or the other, Billy. I saw him, and that means he was stalking Hannah or maybe me. I'm not arguing anymore. Are you with me or not? Make up your mind."

Billy was in a panic. He'd gone too far. "I was playing devil's advocate," he said with a fake laugh. "Of course I'm with you."

Isaiah and Billy were still at the breakfast table. The pause had started a minute ago, Isaiah saying nothing, the tension of silence making Billy sweat.

"Can I have some water, please?" Billy asked.

"No, you can't," Isaiah replied. He returned to his reverie, piecing together what he'd read with what Billy told him. "You said Ava is following Crowe?" he asked.

"Yes. They're coming south on Highway 185 from Sacramento. Another 150 miles and they'll pass through Coronado Springs."

Going where? Isaiah wondered. He brought up a map on the laptop. Pass through town and there was only one logical destination. Lake Tahoe. There were only truck stops between here and there. It seemed unlikely Crowe was headed for a truck stop, and if he wanted to go to Tahoe, Highway 80 was a much more direct route. It would save him a couple hundred miles.

"Crowe's destination is here, Coronado Springs," Isaiah said.

"Here? Why?" Billy asked. "Are you sure?"

Isaiah worried. If you're following someone over a long distance it is very hard not to be spotted. Crowe might be watching for a tail as a matter of course. He'd been on a decade-long murder spree and hadn't been caught. He was cunning and vigilant, if nothing else. "Call Ava," Isaiah said, urgency in his voice. "Tell her to back off and we'll pick Crowe up when he arrives here."

"Ava will not back off," Billy said firmly. "She doesn't want Crowe to be arrested, she wants to kill him."

"Damn," Isaiah breathed. He rose. "I've gotta go."

"Go where?" Billy said. Isaiah didn't answer. He went into the living room and gathered his things off the coffee table.

"You're going to meet them, aren't you?" Isaiah didn't answer. He pushed through the screen door and headed for the Mustang, Billy trailing.

"Please let me go with you," Billy pleaded. *"Please."* Isaiah got in the car and sped off.

CHAPTER FIFTEEN:
COME AND GET ME

Ava had Crowe's routines down. At eight a.m., he left the house, arrived at the garage at eight-thirty. He changed tires and oil, installed air cleaners, swept up the parking area and did other menial tasks. He took longer breaks than he was supposed to, looked pissed off all the time and generally did as little as possible. At six, he left work, stopped at Bigelow's for a shot and a beer, talked to no one and then went home to his wife, Shareen. She was a big woman with a big mole on her upper lip, her bramble of salt-and-pepper hair un-brushed and crooked as an untrimmed hedge. She looked like the prototype of disappointed and stubborn.

Shareen's house had wooden fences on either side of it. No one could see you creeping along the side, peeking in windows and eavesdropping, especially at night. The couple seemed to fight more than anything else. Second on their list of activities was eating, third was sitting on the sofa three feet apart and watching TV. They had sex with surprising frequency, especially for two people who clearly didn't like each other. Neither seemed to be enjoying it. A quick, standing hump while Shareen was ironing. A quick, clumsy grapple in the morning, or a quick up-and-down on the sofa while Crowe peeked under Shareen's armpits at the TV.

One morning, Crowe came out of the house with a battered suitcase and no ankle monitor. Ava was surprised and confused. Crowe was on parole; what was he doing? He put the suitcase in the trunk, then Shareen came out toting a big handbag. She yelled at him, but Crowe ignored her. Frustrated, she got in the backseat. He ranted at her for five minutes, but she didn't budge. He gave up and they left. They drove north on 185, out of Sacramento for a hundred miles or so. They stopped at a gas station. Ava was filling up, Crowe on the other side of the pumps. He was on the phone, talking heatedly, fiercely, trying to keep his voice down. She could only hear a phrase or two. Shareen was in the backseat of the car, morose and glaring at nothing, her arms folded tightly across her chest.

Ava's phone buzzed. It was Billy. She sent it to voice mail. He was getting to be a distraction.

She had to get nearer to Crowe, but she needed a reason. She thought a moment. The air hose! It was closer to Crowe, and the pumps wouldn't be in the way. He might have seen her on TV so she pulled her Dodgers cap down low. She messed with the hose like she didn't know how to use it.

Crowe was walking in circles. "You can't do it; you can't fucking do it!" he shouted. "Why? Because you're going to fuck it up, that's why!" He listened, getting angrier and angrier. He shook the phone and roared into it, "Yes, I'm giving you an order! Don't you fucking hang up on me! DON'T YOU FUCKING HANG UP ON ME!" Ava wanted to run. The man was terrifying.

Even in his rage, his dull eyes were fixed, the thick lips wet, a snarl like a claw across his face. He was a creature, she thought. Something damaged in the womb, born defective, vicious and implacable. This was the animal that had killed Hannah. Fury banished Ava's fear. She had to force herself not to douse him with gasoline and set him on fire. Crowe was still talking. "Just wait for me, okay? You can do that, can't you? I'll be there in — what was that? No, you can't do that! Just stay there until I — hello? Hello?" He swore, a molten stream of invective, the veins in his neck bulging. He glanced at Ava. She quickly pulled out the air hose, turned and kneeled beside her car. She heard him arguing with Shareen.

"You can't go with me. You have to go back," he said.

"Not until I know what you're up to," she said.

"I told you, it's a business thing."

"What business thing? You change tires for a living."

"I'm gonna drop you at a bus station."

"There ain't no bus station out here."

"Get out of the car, Shareen, I'm warning you."

"Warning me?" she said. "I got news for you. This is *my* car, paid for with *my* money, and if anybody's getting out it's you."

"I swear to God I'm gonna drag you out of there," he snarled.

"Oh, really? Who's on parole, me or you? You touch me and I'll call the cops and you won't have to worry about your *business thing* no more. You'll be in handcuffs on your way back to Quentin." Crowe clenched his teeth and growled at the sky. Then he got back in the car and they drove away.

Ava hurriedly returned to her car, a white

Chevrolet Spark. It was tiny, but it got great mileage. The gas nozzle hadn't been returned to the pump.

"Shit!" She jumped out, returned the nozzle to the pump, got in and raced out of the gas station. She thought about what Crowe said on the phone. Was that why Crowe had left Sacramento? To stop someone from doing — what? What could be so extreme that a serial killer was trying to hold you back?

She'd been driving for ten minutes. The road ahead was straight and empty. Had she lost him? "GODDAMMIT!" she shouted, and tromped on the gas.

Shareen was pissed off. Everything was better when Crowe was in prison. Everything was better when he was an idea, or like an actor on TV. She remembered the good parts; telling her funny stories, being nice to her, telling her she was beautiful and writing all those romantic letters. And he was the one that was needy. She liked that. No man had ever needed her before. Her friends told her she was out of her mind, but Crowe didn't scare her. All the things he'd done before didn't bother her at all. For one thing, he was a changed man, and for two, he was behind bars. He didn't tell her he was getting out on parole so when he showed up at her door it was a big-ass surprise. What else could she do but let him in? They were husband and wife.

At first, she was happy. Crowe was glad to be out and appreciative of everything she did. And the sex. My, oh my, he was like a moose during mating season, the big bull trying to fuck the whole herd, but in this case, the whole herd was her. He was quick about it but frequent. Like all the damn time. He was wearing her junk into scrap metal. But then things started to change. He hardly talked, kept to himself. No more *I love you baby, you're beautiful baby, I need you baby.* All that nicey-nicey stuff was just an act. He'd turned into one more man, one more slob, one more do this, do that. The only thing Crowe had on her ex-husband Maurice was that he had to have a job. Then something weird happened. One afternoon, a white man showed up at the door. He didn't say his name or anything. He was nervous and had a creepy smile. She couldn't believe it when he took Crowe's ankle monitor off.

"The hell are you doing?" she said. The man didn't say anything and left. It scared her. Without the monitor, Crowe could go wherever he wanted. He could leave her.

She asked him about it.

"I'm off parole," he said, but she knew that wasn't true. The next day, he said he was going on a trip.

"What trip? To where? For what?" she said. He said it was a business thing. "What business thing? You don't have any business."

Maybe it was a good idea, she thought. With Crowe gone, the house wouldn't look like an earthmover had rolled through it, she wouldn't have to cook, and she could go a half day without getting boned. But she knew from years of living in an empty house that loneliness was a bitch and a half. Love the one you're with, she thought, because there's nobody else to love.

Crowe wouldn't say anymore. While he was putting stuff in the trunk, she came out of the house with her biggest handbag and climbed into the backseat of her metallic red Jetta. She'd saved for over a year just for the down payment, and she wasn't leaving until hell froze over and everybody went ice-skating.

"Get out," Crowe said.

"Tell me where you're going."

"I told you already."

"You mean your business thing?" she scoffed. "You think I'm a fool? Whatever you're up to it's criminal. What else could it be? You've never been anything but a criminal your whole damn life."

"Shut up, Shareen, and get out of the fucking car."

"*You* shut up, and if you want me outta here you better have a baseball bat. I don't play that shit, mister man. Mess with me and see what happens." Crowe pleaded, threatened and cajoled. Finally, he got in the car and they drove off.

"Where're we going?" she asked. When he didn't answer she added, "Well, fuck you then."

They left the gas station and drove a half hour, the elevation climbing, deep forest on either side. Shareen's ears popped. Crowe still hadn't said anything, but he didn't have to, sighing every seven seconds, shifting around in his seat, glaring bullets at her in the rearview mirror. He wants to get rid of you after all you've done. It was humiliating. You give somebody all you got and find out all you got ain't good enough. The only reason Crowe waited while she was in the bathroom was because she threatened to call the police and report the car stolen. If you have to threaten your husband to keep him from ditching you at a gas station, you are a sad, sad case. As the miles went by, her anger swelled. Another man jerking her around, making her feel bad and kicking the shit out of her dignity. Crowe might be leaving her, but it wouldn't be on his terms.

"Turn the car around. We're going home," she said.

"No, we're not," Crowe said.

"Well, this ain't your car now, is it? And by the way, you just bought gas with my credit card because the money you make wouldn't get us around the block."

"Shut up, Shareen."

"Fuck you, Crowe." She looked at her phone. "Too bad you can't get cell service up here or I'd be calling the police right now." Crowe went quiet. That always shut him up, the bastard. She almost laughed. They didn't talk for a while, and then he did a weird thing.

He said, "Okay." But not to her. He said it like he was answering somebody else's question.

"Okay what?" she said. Crowe said nothing. He drove, looking right and left, slowing nearly to a stop before turning off the highway onto a dirt road.

"Hey," she said. "Where're we going?"

Ava drove fast. There were some wide

bends, but the highway was mostly straight. She saw nothing. *Damn you, Ava, you lost them!* No, wait. They couldn't have gotten that far ahead. They must have turned off somewhere. She did a U-turn, raced back but saw nothing but the blur of trees. She pounded on the steering wheel. "SHIT! SHIT! SHIT!" She jammed on the brakes and skidded to a stop. A dirt road cut into the forest. There was still dust in the air.

"Oh, no," Ava said. Crowe had no reason to go in there unless he was going to kill Shareen. What now? she asked herself. Go after them? Go after a serial killer? No, that was crazy. Call the cops? No cell service. They wouldn't be in time anyway. Ava sat there, her conscience and common sense pulling in opposite directions. She couldn't let Shareen be butchered. She took a deep breath and made the turn. She drove down the road at walking speed, trying to see around the curves. She was afraid Crowe would hear her coming so she pulled over into a clearing. She went around to the trunk and lifted the spare tire. The Sig Sauer was wrapped in a towel.

As soon as Crowe turned off the highway, a sneaking suspicion crawled up Shareen's spine and crawled back down again. She thought about the crimes he had committed and the warnings from her friends. She should have listened to them. *You're in trouble, Shareen, you're in deep-ass trouble.* The road got bumpier and more narrow. She could see him in the mirror. His face blank and staring straight ahead. If he felt something, it wasn't an emotion. It was dim and gloomy in the forest, trees blocked the sunlight, thick brush all around.

"What's in here?" Shareen asked hoarsely. "We going camping?" He didn't think that was funny and neither did she. "Uh, you know, I was just kidding about calling the cops. I was just messing with you! You know me, I'm always joking around!" She tried to laugh, but it sounded like she was panting. Branches scraped against the side of the car. She could already see the scratch marks on the beautiful red paint. The ruts made her sway back and forth. She was getting carsick. "I swear, Crowe, I would never call no police on you! I'm your wife, remember?" She smiled at him in the mirror. She couldn't see herself, but she knew it looked fake.

The sweat had soaked through her clothes and her heart was beating fast. She could feel her pulse in her throat. She had to get out of the car, but how? If she jumped out, she'd break an arm or a leg or some other body part. If she waited until they stopped, she'd have to run for it. She wished she hadn't worn flip-flops and stuck with Weight Watchers. She felt her anger returning, her gumption. *Fuck you, Crowe. One of us is walkin' outta here and it ain't gonna be you.* As casually as she could, she reached into her big purse and found her makeup bag. Crowe glared at her in the mirror. She found a small package of tissues and dabbed her face. "Hot in here," she said. There were stumps to drive around, and Crowe's eyes went back to the road. Shareen put the tissues back in the makeup bag but kept her hand in there, her fingers fumbling around until they found the cuticle scissors. They were small but sharp. But were they sharp enough?

Shareen could see an open space ahead. The road dead-ended. *Oh shit. It's now or never, girl.* She pushed the seat belt down below her breasts, making a little sound to indicate it was too tight. She leaned forward and swung the scissors as hard as she could. She was aiming for Crowe's neck, but the seat belt held her back and she stuck him in the shoulder.

"FUUUCKK!" he screamed. He stepped on the gas, the car lurching forward and slamming into a tree. Crowe's airbag went off. Shareen untangled herself from the seat belt, got out of the car and ran.

Ava reached a bend in the road and peeked around it. Crowe's car had crashed into a tree, and the doors were open. She crept up on it, holding the gun tight. She could hear movement somewhere off in the trees. She heard Crowe shouting. She followed the sounds. There was no trail. She pushed her way through the branches and bushes, ducking and shoving them aside. Some were impenetrable, and she had to go around. She heard Crowe shouting again. She was going in the wrong direction. The trees dispersed the sound. She swore, changed course and kept going.

Crowe bulled his way through the brush, getting scratched to shit and wheezing for breath. It was frustrating, but in another way it was good. The hunt, the rage, the lust, the unrelenting need to kill was overwhelming. Shareen wasn't Shareen anymore. She was a thing, an object, a locked box that held unspeakable pleasure. He couldn't wait. He went faster. "Aww, fuck!" he said. He forgot to bring his knives. He didn't want to drag Shareen back to the car.

He'd have to just kill her. He saw a flash of movement. He was gaining on her. A flood of adrenaline coursed through him. He cupped his hands around his mouth and shouted, "YOU CAN'T GET AWAY FROM ME! I'M COMING FOR YOU, BITCH!"

Ava was exhausted, desperately thirsty, sweat stinging her eyes. She put her hands on her knees and gulped air. She was covered with tree sap, dust and sweat. She heard Crowe yelling. She made her best guess and fought her way forward. *Keep going, Ava, don't stop.* She saw light through the trees. A clearing. Was that where the voice was coming from? She clenched the Sig tighter and forced herself to go faster, slowing to a creep as the light got brighter. She reached the edge of the trees. She steeled herself, took a breath and stepped into the clearing. "Stop," she shouted, swinging the gun left and right. "Leave her alone, Crowe!" She lowered the gun. No one was there.

Shareen couldn't go on. Her lungs were in cinders, her legs wobbling, she was bleeding from the scratches all over her body. She fell to her knees and flopped onto her side.

She curled up and waited. There were pebbles and dirt stuck in her skin, a roaring sound in her ears. She couldn't get enough air. She thought her heart would pound itself apart. She wondered how she'd gotten here, helpless and waiting for death. All she'd ever wanted was love. That's not a lot to ask, is it? Or maybe it was. Maybe it was everything. She saw Crowe coming, heard his heavy breathing, dust rising from his clomping footsteps. He stood over her, the sweat from his face dripping into her eyes and making them sting.

"Yeah, bitch," he growled. "Got anything else to say?" He nudged her with his shoe. "What's that? I can't hear you." She closed her eyes. There was nothing she could do. Crowe picked her up by the armpits and dragged her. She didn't know where they were going until she saw the edge of the cliff and there was nothing underneath her and she heard herself scream and saw the ground, hurtling up toward her.

Ava was still in the clearing, wondering which way she should go, when she heard Shareen scream. It was coming from far away. Crowe was killing her. "Oh no," Ava said, and she started to cry.

■ ■ ■ ■

The wound in Crowe's shoulder was superficial, but it hurt like hell. Shareen had a first-aid kit in the car. He cleaned the wound with a bottle of water, slathered on Neosporin and covered it with gauze and a bandage. It was sloppy but the best he could do. He took her credit cards and money and threw the bag away. That was over and he felt good about it. It would be a long time before Shareen's body was found if it was ever found at all. She'd bumped and rolled down the cliff, disappearing into the trees. Coyote food, he thought. Eat up.

Crowe sat on the bumper and took a breather. All this mess, all this bullshit, and why? *Warren.* Fucking Warren. For some reason, the moron got it into his head that he had to kill "EX." He said it stood for "execution." Going after EX was a stupid, risky thing to do, not to mention pointless. Warren was certifiably insane, like, can't-function-in-the-real-world insane. Take one look at him and you knew he was a lunatic. Some random urge would flash in his head and he'd follow it like a goddamn lemming. He was too far gone to be careful. No thinking, no planning. He would see EX and attack. Then he'd get caught and make a deal with the prosecutor. Give me life in prison instead of the death penalty and I'll give up AMSAK. Warren had to be stopped, Crowe thought. Warren had to die.

Crowe drove back on the dirt road. The car was running okay, but there were noises coming from under the hood. He passed an open space and saw a little white car. He stopped. It wasn't there before; it must have come in after him. Did somebody see him kill Shareen? No, couldn't have. The driver would have had to run down the road, fight through the brush, somehow locate Crowe and follow him without being seen or heard. Crowe sat there, the car idling rough like his brain. Should he ambush this guy before moving on? Naah. If the guy didn't see anything and couldn't find her body, then he wasn't a threat. Anyway, Crowe's shoulder hurt and he was starving.

He returned to the highway. A hundred and ten miles to Coronado Springs. He drove on. Still, it bothered him. That car. He'd seen it before, but where? The gas station, yeah, he remembered it now. A coincidence? What were the odds of seeing a little white car pumping gas next to you at an Exxon station and then parked in the woods while you're throwing your wife over a cliff? There was a girl at the gas station too, she was wearing a blue cap and fucking around with the air hose. Had he seen her before? Hard to say. Maybe if he got a good look at her. He glanced at the rearview mirror. The road was empty, but he knew she was after him. He smiled and said, "Come and get me."

Isaiah drove north on 185. Crowe was coming south. They'd meet — no, not meet, pass each other at seventy miles an hour. Isaiah could pull over and wait for him but he nixed that. He wanted the killer as far away from town as possible. So what are you going to do, Isaiah? Stop the guy? Stop a serial killer? How? Maybe let him go past you, follow him and force him off the road. Then what? You get out of your car, he gets out of his car and stabs you fifty times with his Bowie knife?

Isaiah was afraid. His heart was skipping beats. Why was it his job to stop Crowe? He'd sworn off this shit forever. *Turn around, you idiot! What the fuck are you doing?* Hysteria was taking over. *Oh, shit. What's that? It's a goddamn car! Fuck, it's coming fast! Think, Isaiah, think, goddammit!* He had nothing, his head was empty, the oncoming car nearly on top of him. He screamed as the car sped past. Some kids in a pickup truck.

His hands were greased with sweat, his shirt stuck to his chest. A monster who had killed seventeen women was on his way and Isaiah didn't know what to do. A long straightaway lay ahead of him, a red car just coming over the rise, a half mile away, the sun reflecting off its windshield. *Can't see the driver, squint, shade your eyes, still can't see, can't see, goddammit! Is it Crowe? Is it the serial killer?* The red car was closing in. *Is it him? Is it? YES, IT'S FUCKING HIM!* Isaiah swerved in front of Crowe's car and immediately swerved back, saved by a millisecond of rational thought. The red car shot past, the horn honking, fading until it was gone.

Isaiah pulled over to the shoulder and stopped. He could barely breathe, forehead on the steering wheel, sweat like he'd been blasted with a fire hose. He'd almost killed himself. Was he like the man in the support group? Did he want to end his life to stop the pain? No. What he wanted was to give up. To stay here in the car with his eyes closed and let the rest of the world speed past while he slept, alone and at peace. Crowe would be nearing Coronado Springs by now, or maybe he was already there, scouting around for his eighteenth victim, smelling blood, grinning as he sharpened his Bowie knife. Isaiah sat up, drew in a long breath and put the car in gear. Then he checked his rearview mirror, made a wide U-turn and drove back toward town.

Chapter Sixteen:
Lebron

Dodson's second day on the job and he forgot to set the alarm. He got to work at nine-fifteen. The Skechers meeting was at nine-thirty. He walked into Stimson's office and found him in his chair, slouched and facing the wall of dirt. He was on the phone.

"Oh, it's going great, Marge," Stimson said. "I think I've really got something here. It's a winner, all right."

There were dozens of drawings scattered on the floor, the table, the sofa. A few were pinned to the corkboard, more spilling off the easel. To Dodson's eye, they were ordinary and boring. A young couple walking on a boardwalk wearing Skechers. A happy group of millennials hanging out in a pub, everybody wearing Skechers. An attractive young woman strolling through a college campus wearing Skechers. No black or brown characters. It was like *Friends* all over again. There were captions: SKECHERS

WALKING SHOES, THE MOST COMFORT-
ABLE SHOE IN THE WORLD. SKECHERS:
TAKE THEM FOR A WALK. The rest were just
as humdrum.

"Yeah, Brad's really going to be surprised," Stimson said to Marge. "I can't
wait to see the look on his face. What? Oh,
sure, meat loaf is fine. Okay, I'll see you
tonight. Love you." He ended the call. Stimson turned his chair around. He looked like
he'd spent the night in a clothes dryer,
tumbling around with the socks and under-
wear. Some men seem more masculine
when they're unshaven. Stimson looked like
a hobo. He read Dodson's expression and
sighed.

"Yeah, I know. They're all crap. I don't
know what I'm going to tell Marge. She's
so sensitive. I hate to see her cry." Stimson
was silent a moment. In almost a whisper
he added, "I really do hate it."

"Got something to show you," Dodson
said. He put Grace's poster board down on
the desk. Stimson stood up and leaned over
it. He stared at it. And stared at it. He hates
it, Dodson thought. Thinks it's bullshit.
He's hesitating because he doesn't want to
embarrass me.

Stimson laughed, delighted. "This is
amazing! I'm completely blown away! How

245

did you come up with this?" Dodson was pleased but managed to keep his composure. Cool is cool. He shrugged.

"I just did."

Stimson came around the desk and gave him a sloppy hug. "Thank you! Thank you so much!" Suddenly, he pulled away. "Wait a minute. I can't use this. It's yours."

"It's yours now."

"No, I couldn't," Stimson said firmly. "It's not right."

"It's right if I say it's right. Besides, you don't want to disappoint Marge, do you?" Tears ran down Stimson's cheeks.

"I can never repay you!" he gushed. He was going to hug Dodson again, but Dodson put his palms up.

"Skip all that, will you? You're gonna be late for the meeting."

"Boy, oh, boy," Stimson said as he left. "Boy, oh, boy."

Dodson made the calculation. If Stimson got fired, he'd get fired and he'd be back cleaning food trucks for Deronda. If Stimson succeeded, Dodson succeeded, and if that happened, maybe he'd get bumped up to an assistant and from there, who knows? He was starting to think like Cherise. He was nervous. Stimson liked the idea, but given his track record, he wasn't much of a judge. Would Brad and Walsh go for it? The heavy hitters? Would the idea stand up to that kind of scrutiny? Dodson had never been in a situation like this. Doing something he was proud of and having it judged by people who knew what they were doing. Who had expertise. He hoped the meeting didn't take very long.

Brad grew up in Beverly Hills and lived a Beverly Hills life. His father was a Beverly Hills attorney, his mother, a Beverly Hills real estate agent. They were severe and big on discipline. Brad was the youngest of three brothers. They were only a year apart and intensely competitive. Intensely. Their parents encouraged it. They saw it as preparation for a cutthroat, competitive world. There were rewards for winning, consequences for losing. Attention and affection were similarly dispensed. They were chickens in a behavior modification experiment. Peck the right dot and get a kernel of corn. Peck the wrong one and you went hungry.

That's how Brad felt most of his waking hours. Hungry, as if more accomplishments could fill the void left by the past. The brothers competed fiercely in every aspect of growing up. Grades, test scores, chess, ping-pong, body mass index, number of pull-ups, number of offices held, time in the 400-meter dash, who dressed the best, who had the prettiest girlfriend, whose car was cooler, who went to a better university. They even compared scores on their driving tests. Now that they were adults, it was who was more successful. Theo was a neurosurgeon at Johns Hopkins. Randle was, literally, a rocket scientist at NASA. Brad was middle management at an advertising agency that wasn't even in Beverly Hills.

It had always been that way, Brad routinely coming in last. Figuratively speaking, he was on the practice squad, the third string, the bronze medalist. His parents were greatly disappointed in him. The consequences weren't draconian, but they were pointed. A 95 on the algebra test? No ride to school. Take the filthy bus with a bunch of deadbeat commuters. Learn how it is to be ordinary. You entered the annual chess tournament in a field of forty-eight. You had three losses. Theo had two. Randle won the whole fucking thing. A 4.0 grade point average? Impressive, except it was an unweighted score and didn't account for the difficulty of the classes. Compared with his brothers, 4.0 was tantamount to a mental disability.

What really hurt was baseball. Brad had been a dedicated fan since he was old enough to watch TV. His brothers didn't play the sport and he couldn't wait to join a Little League team. Unfortunately, he was a terrible fielder and his batting average was a subpar .178. Embarrassed, his parents made him quit. His favorite mitt was thrown in the trash, the posters of his favorite players torn down. He was forbidden to watch the sport on TV, his memorabilia given away. He hid something from his parents. An autographed baseball, Nolan Ryan's loopy signature scrawled on it in blue ink. These days, he kept it on his desk in an acrylic cube.

Brad had learned that it didn't matter how hard you worked. Nobody gave a shit about effort. Nobody cared that you were exhausted, discouraged, and alone. His brothers were simply smarter and more talented and that was it. They were merciless in their taunts, sneers and insults. Brad felt like a snail, a zit, a gum wrapper in a mud puddle. If he wanted a smile from his parents, he had to bully, sabotage, oversell, tell ridiculous whoppers and blame others if something went wrong. He had to take credit for things he had no part in and distance himself from anything that smelled of failure and defeat. Brad hated to see his brothers win, and as he grew older, he hated anyone who was smarter, more talented, or who got more attention than he did.

Brad loathed Stimson. The man was a slug and a waste of a salary. There was also the pension issue. If Stimson got his contract renewed and retired with full benefits, hell, he could live another twenty years. That amounted to a considerable sum. And for what? To support a guy who should have been fired a decade earlier? He should be paying them back for the time and money they'd already wasted on him. Stimson was a living example of what could happen to you if you weren't a hard motherfucker, if you weren't ruthless, opportunistic and devious, if you didn't put a boot on the ambitious ones and undermine the ones in front of you. Stimson was a portent, an omen, your worst nightmare in a rumpled suit and a cheap tie, and really, Brad thought, who needs to see that every fucking day?

Ted Walsh was executive VP in charge of campaign development and everybody's boss. He sat at the head of the long white conference table in his dark gray suit and his mightier-than-thou attitude, his bulk and bloodhound face heightening the illusion of power. A large monitor was on the far wall. Presentations were digitized. No more easels, drawing pads, and overhead projectors. Brad resented Walsh. There was no question the younger man should be in charge. Walsh was getting too old for the sticky, unpleasant aspects of management. Cutting staff, cutting costs, cracking the whip. Better to let his ruthless, demanding attack dog do it. That was fine, Brad thought. It made Walsh look soft and Brad like a leader. The partners were starting to notice. Brad was their man of the future. He was blunt, abrasive, and nobody liked him, but he got shit done. He knew his business too.

Also at the meeting were Marty Lupica, executive art director, Zack Sandler, the project manager, Erica Newberg, the account director, plus a strategist, someone from Advanced Planning and a couple of assistants. And there was Stimson in all his broken-down glory. God, he looked like he'd slept curled up on a bus bench with a newspaper over his head. Brad had convinced Walsh that this campaign was Stimson's do-or-die. The doofus either came up big, or he could pick up his pink slip.

Brad stood up. "Let's begin, shall we? I don't have to tell you how important Skechers is to the company. If we succeed, they will bring us other business, maybe all of their business. Millions and millions of dollars are resting on this one ad. Dunheath, Navarro, you're up first." Brad wasn't naïve enough to rely on Stimson. Kameron Dunheath and Isaac Navarro were two hipsters who thought a lot of themselves. Dunheath had a James Harden beard, nerdy sunglasses and peg-leg pants that ended at his sockless ankles. Navarro wore suspenders, a wrinkled check shirt, jeans so tight they could have been a body tattoo and chukka boots worn down to a shine. They were pretentious assholes but they did good work.

Navarro typed on his laptop. A digitized image appeared on the wall monitor. A beautiful young couple walking the red carpet. A crowd of paparazzi taking their pictures. She was wearing a hot, sequined dress. He was wearing a tuxedo and both had on Skechers walking shoes. The scene cut to the same couple sitting courtside at a basketball game, cheering the home team on, the same couple at a hip nightclub dancing with drinks in their hands. The same couple in hiking clothes, holding hands and taking in a spectacular view. In every scene they wore Skechers. The caption:

SKECHERS WALKING SHOES
They'll take you places.

"I'm underwhelmed." Brad sighed. "It has some of the elements but it's soft. No edge, no zeitgeist."

"We needed more time," Dunheath said.

"You didn't have more time," Brad snapped. Disaster, he thought. Now it was up to Stimson, who was guaranteed to have shit. The room was tense and disquieted. There was a sudden interest in fingernails, loose threads and water spots on the table. No one wanted to see the old guy humiliated again.

"All right, Stimson, the floor is yours," Brad said.

Stimson stood up, exhaling with his cheeks puffed out and his brow furrowed. My God, is he sweating? Brad thought. Couldn't he *pretend* to have his shit together?

"Yeah, I've, um, got something here," Stimson said. He reached down and brought up a poster board. Poster board? What the fuck was this all about? Brad couldn't see it at his angle. He glanced at Walsh and raised his eyebrows.

"This should be interesting," he said.

"I didn't have time to have it digitized," Stimson said. "So you'll just have to, uh, you know, look at it." He handed the poster to Sandler seated next to him. Sandler held it up with two hands like he was looking at himself in a mirror.

"Oh, my God. This is too much," he said. Brad couldn't tell if that was a compliment or condemnation. The people beside Sandler leaned in to look. They seemed puzzled a moment, then they smiled and burst out laughing; the others started leaving their seats to cluster around the poster.

"That's too cool," Lupica said.

"They wanted edge, this is edge," Navarro said with an admiring nod. Brad wondered what the hell was going on.

"Well, let's see it," he said irritably. The poster board was passed to him. He held it up so that Walsh could see it too. The scene was a big city. Tall buildings in the background. A young black man was standing at the curb. He was well groomed, nicely dressed and wearing Skechers walking shoes. His hand was raised, signaling for a cab, the beginnings of disappointment on his face. A cab was going past him, the service light was on. The driver, of indiscriminate race, was pointedly ignoring him. The caption:

SKECHERS
When you really need to walk

Brad couldn't believe it. Stimson did this? It was exactly what Skechers wanted. "All hail Stimson!" someone shouted. And the room responded, "All hail Stimson!" They were happy for him, rooting for him; why was unfathomable. Even Walsh was smiling. Look at that doofus, Brad thought, all red-faced and sheepish. He looks like a god-damn hero.

Walsh turned to Brad. "This is exactly what Skechers wanted. Don't you agree?"

"Uh, yes, yes, I do," Brad said. "It's very good work." Brad lowered his voice and with feigned modesty said, "It was my idea, but Stimson really took the ball and ran with it."

"That's what I like to see. Teamwork."

"I don't mean to be a spoilsport," Brad continued. "Stimson did great work, but frankly, it's a one-off for him, Ted. He's never done anything like that in his life."

"No, he hasn't," Walsh said, frowning.

"I still say we don't renew his contract. There's no reason to think he can do this again." Walsh thought a moment.

"Give him another assignment and then we'll see."

255

The room was clearing. Stimson saw Brad and hesitated, like he didn't know whether to go or stay. Brad kept his face blank and the doofus left.

Everyone was gone. Brad was infuriated. How was it possible for Stimson to come up with something like that? The ad reflected a black experience. What did Stimson know about it? It was confounding. It was like an over-the-hill benchwarmer with bad knees coming off the bench and scoring forty-five points in a playoff game. Even if that were possible, it was zero on the likelihood scale. Brad shook his head. This is bullshit. Stimson was running a very clever scam. A week before contract time and he suddenly comes up with a brilliant ad? This would not stand, Brad decided. Stimson was going down.

Brad stood in the doorway of Stimson's office. The idiot was in his chair, facing that ridiculous wall of dirt and talking to someone on the phone.

"Brad went for it, honey," Stimson said excitedly. "Yeah, just like I said he would. Everybody loved it. I mean they really loved it! Winnebago, here we come!" He swiveled his chair around and saw Brad. "I've gotta get off now, sweetheart. Okay. See you at home. Love you." He ended the call.

"Making plans, are we?" Brad said.

"Just, um, sort of." Stimson waggled a pencil nervously between two fingers.

"Well, congratulations. It was quite a surprise."

Brad meandered around the office, looking at the drawings, taking his time, humming tunelessly, picking up one, studying it briefly and picking up another, holding it up to the light and then moving to the next. Occasionally, he'd glance at Stimson appraisingly, skeptically, and go back to the drawings. Stimson looked stricken, as if at any moment Brad would find the bloody glove.

"Are these the preliminary drawings?" Brad said. "They don't look anything like the ad."

"Oh, those," Stimson said, like he just remembered them. "Yeah, I, uh, I left them at home." The pencil was waggling faster.

"I'd like to see them. And I'm curious. Where did you get the idea? It seems a little out of your wheelhouse."

"The idea?" Stimson repeated. Brad looked at him sharply.

"Yes, Stimson, the idea."

Stimson looked caught. Busted. "I, um, I

have a friend. He's black — African American. He told me the cab thing happened to him."

"What's your friend's name?"

"His name? Um. Lebron."

"Lebron," Brad said flatly. He snorted and made his favorite expression. A sardonic, suspicious, deeply disappointed glower. The pencil was a blur, like an airplane propeller at takeoff. "Stop that," Brad said. The pencil flew out of Stimson's hand, hit the wall of dirt and clattered to the floor. The sound seemed to echo. "If you're through doing circus tricks I have another assignment for you," Brad said.

"So soon?"

"You didn't think we'd renew your contract on the basis of a single idea, did you?" Brad replied. It was a trap. No way "Lebron" could create two hits in a row. Stimson would have to complete the assignment himself. He'd be exposed as the useless slacker he was.

"What's the assignment?" he asked.

"Bayer aspirin." Brad was contemptuous. "Have you seen their ads? Two carefree senior citizens, gazing into each other's eyes and dancing in their living room, as if to say, see? Take Bayer aspirin and you can have fun like us! Frankly, the association makes me wince. It's distasteful, like Ovaltine. You drink it because you're old."

"I take aspirin," Stimson said.

"Is that what you think is needed here? Associating aspirin with you?"

"No, I guess not."

"Bayer wants a sixty-second commercial," Brad continued. "Something to do with reducing strokes but not so literal like their usual crap. And another thing. They want to link the product with environmental concerns."

"Environmental concerns? With aspirin?" Stimson said.

"Don't you keep up with trends?" Brad said. "Why am I even asking? A lot of major companies are using the environment as context. According to the data, it's effective with millennials. Like that Exxon commercial, all those aerial shots of green meadows, forests and majestic mountains. It looks like Julie Andrews will show up singing 'The Sound of Music.' Somehow, they forgot to mention the Exxon Valdez."

"When do you need this?" Stimson asked.

"The Bayer people want to see something on Monday." That wasn't really true. Bayer didn't expect anything for weeks.

"Monday? That's not possible."

Brad ignored him. "Bayer has a slot ahead

of the Masters golf tournament. It was a sudden thing, something to do with the network screwing up. The data is in the brief. Remember, Stimson, golfers are an older demographic, high net worth, second homes, top management. In other words, they work a lot and may or may not be in good health. They don't want to watch a commercial that says, hi, you're gonna be dead soon. Why don't you dance with your aging wife in the living room?" Stimson looked like he'd been diagnosed with liver cancer.

"No excuses," Brad said. He left Stimson's office and went down the long hallway. It was creepy down here, the fluorescents lighting a carpeted green road to anonymity. He stopped at the men's room. It was as depressing as the hallway. Small and cramped. Two sinks, one stall, two urinals, and checkered backsplash tile in beige and brown. He stepped up to a urinal and unzipped. Someone else entered the room and took the urinal beside him. Christ, he hated this. You were in such close proximity. Your shoulders were nearly touching. Cardinal rule for urinals. Never look anywhere but down. At the edge of Brad's vision, he could see the man was black. That made him more uncomfortable, but he didn't know why. Brad and his neighbor finished their business at the same time. Simultaneously, they moved to the sinks. Was this some sort of herd behavior? If there were ten black men in here would they all move in synchronicity? He had a sober moment. Why the antipathy? You don't even know the guy.

Now they were standing side by side with a goddamn mirror in front of them. What were you supposed to do, ignore each other? They looked at their reflections, made eye contact, and for some inexplicable reason Brad smiled, however wanly. Disturbingly, the man smiled back, like really smiled, as if they were fishing buddies or fraternity brothers.

"Whassup, man. How you doin'?" the man said.

"Fine, thank you," Brad replied. Automatically, he added, "And yourself?"

"I'm doin' aight," the man replied, as if it were a surprise to them both.

The vernacular, Brad thought. He's from the so-called street. His ensemble was off-the-rack, but he was presentable. At least he wasn't sporting one of those ridiculous haircuts. The whassup and aight were a little much. What was he trying to do? Send a message? Assert his blackness? Did they know each other? Had they met?

They started to wash their hands and, of course, there was only one soap dispenser. They had to take turns. Brad quickly went first to avoid the awkwardness. He pumped several times, but there was no soap. God, he couldn't just leave. Like twins in a sitcom, the two men rinsed their hands at the twin sinks, their movements nearly identical. It seemed to take a long time. What were they doing, Brad wondered, proving to each other they were sanitary?

"I like the people here," the man went on. "I'm learnin' my way around, but I've got a long way to go. You know how it is." You know how it is? What does that mean? Brad thought. Were they supposed to have some commonality of experience? Like what? They both got scholarships to Cal Arts and vacationed in Montreal? Brad gritted his teeth and almost cursed. There were no goddamn paper towels, only a goddamn industrial hand dryer, the kind that makes your tie flap around and sounds like an F-15 at takeoff. He gestured magnanimously.

"After you."

The man nodded his thanks and went first. That was something at least. The noise precluded introductions. What did the man say again? You know how it is? Ah yes. You're both black and therefore you were supposed to acknowledge a bond existed, a birds of a feather sort of thing. Yes, we're both black, Brad thought, but that doesn't mean we're the same.

He took the elevator to his office. He'd met the man before but couldn't recall the circumstances. It seemed very recent. He prided himself on his memory. It gave him a kind of power, knowing names, remembering details about where and how he'd met someone. It made him seem omniscient. *Ah yes, Roger, we met at the social media conference in Philadelphia. How is your son? Going to Columbia, isn't he? Say hello to Linda for me, will you?* It was annoying that he couldn't remember. It's nothing, Brad thought. Forget about it, you're being ridiculous.

Dodson left the men's room wondering what Brad was so uptight about. It wasn't pissing side by side, his vibe was about more than that. The man actually flinched when you said aight. It wasn't deliberate or maybe it was. A way to say, you're at the top, and I'm at the bottom, but we share the same struggle, don't we?

Stimson gave him the Bayer aspirin brief,

explaining the assignment and the environ-mental angle. "I'm sorry to do this to you, Juanell, but will you take a crack at it? I'll work on it at home too." He shrugged help-lessly. "I'll try anyway."

The brief contained the commercial's objectives, target audience, strategies, time frame and costs. Not really helpful. Aspirin was about headaches and heart attacks and that's it. An environmental angle? It was like linking the environment to toothpaste or deodorant.

Dodson went home, talked as briefly as he could with Cherise and played with Micah for ten distracted minutes. He went out on the balcony and leaned against the railing. He looked out over the neighbor-hood. Bayer aspirin prevents strokes, he thought. Who did he know that had a stroke? Mr. Yamashita, the roofer, and Penny Ventner, a waitress at the Coffee Cup. Both were confined to their houses. Must be terrible locked up like that. He thought about Bolo Wakefield tending his pigeons with his blind eye, turning his head sideways so he could see what he was doing. Strokes limit you. Strokes are a cage. An idea was coming together. Dodson could see it unfolding in his head. He smiled and nod-ded his approval. This might work. He told

Cherise about it, and then he called Grace.

"Kinko's," she answered. "How can I help you?"

Chapter Seventeen:
Peter Oh Who?

Janeel was at Nona's house. Deronda was home. She'd stopped speaking altogether. She thought she might have forgotten how. Bobby James had created so much fear and anxiety she couldn't do anything but sit on the sofa with her arms around her knees. Grace was in her room, listening to some of that fucked-up white people's music. Somebody named Radiohead. That boy needed to get his head out of the radio and listen to some hip-hop.

Her phone buzzed. Unknown Caller. She answered.

"Hello?"

"Tiana? It's Sandra," Sandra said. "You remember me?" Deronda nearly gasped. She had to stay calm, control her voice.

"Hey, Sandra," she said, all warm and casual. "How you doing?"

"I'm doin' how I do. I just wanna thank you for what you did for me. Wasn't for you steppin' up I might be dead right now."

"Wasn't no thang. I was happy to do it," Deronda said. She hurried to Grace's room and knocked on the door. Grace stuck her head out. Deronda put her finger over her lips and put the call on speaker.

"I gotta a little present for you," Sandra said.

"Aw, y'all didn't have to do that."

"Can we meet someplace tomorrow?"

"How about the Coffee Cup?" Deronda said.

"Okay, thas' cool," Sandra said. "How 'bout around one-thirty — no wait, that's out. I gotta meet Bobby."

"Who's Bobby?" Deronda said, glancing at Grace.

"My baby daddy. He's why I don't need to trick no more. I'm meeting him in the park at two. How 'bout we meet at three?"

"Sho' nuff," Deronda said. "See you then." The call ended. She grabbed Grace by the elbows, elated. "We'll get some pictures! Show them to the judge! Bobby James and his baby mama, a junkie-hooker-ex-porn-star!"

"Exactly what we needed!" Grace said, laughing. She thought a moment and frowned. "But how do we get pictures without Bobby seeing us? The faces will have to be clear. We'll have to see their expressions. Otherwise, the judge won't know how they feel about each other."

"How come you always see the problems?" Deronda said.

"It's a gift."

Deronda called her boyfriend, Robert, and told him what she needed. Robert was out of town on a project, but he said he'd have something sent over. Two hours later, a messenger delivered a drone. It was small; you could hold it in one hand and it weighed three pounds.

"Speed, twenty meters per second," Robert said. "A twelve-million-pixel camera. You can shoot in bursts or take HD color video. You can zoom in close enough to see if Bobby shaved."

"I don't know how to use no drone," Deronda said, but Robert had already ended the call.

It was seven in the morning. Sandra and Bobby were showing up at the park at two. Deronda and Grace had seven hours to get the drone up and running. How hard could it be? Grace thought. We're smart and we can read directions. She'd seen little kids fly drones. Turned out, being smart and reading instructions weren't enough. If the online user's manual was on paper, it'd be thick as a T-bone steak. The controls were indecipherable. Elevator trim. Power trim. Throttle control rod. Flaperon/screw switch. They spent an hour just trying to identify them and memorize what they did.

"Jesus," Grace said. If you wanted to take pictures or video, you had to download an app on your phone. The app had more selections than the menu at the Mandarin Palace.

Maiden flight. The drone didn't so much take off as it did rise straight up and rocket away horizontally like the Road Runner. Deronda was barely touching the controls and the damn thing swooped, rolled, banked and zigzagged all over the goddamn park. The squirrels took cover. The winos threw rocks at it. Grace wasn't helping, yelling, "More pitch! More yaw!" Though she barely knew what the words meant.

Deronda paid a kid five dollars to retrieve the drone from the trees. After six or eight perilous climbs, the kid's face was scratched, his pants torn, his hair tangled with leaves and twigs. He demanded and got ten dollars a trip. Once he had to get the drone down from the roof of the restroom. He fell and skinned his knees. That cost Deronda another twenty. The kid was making enough coin to buy a fleet of drones.

Deronda took pictures. She got some great shots of grass, the insides of trash cans, azalea bushes from two inches away, pigeons looking up, and a fantastic shot of Mo sleeping on a bench with his zipper wide open.

"We need some help," Grace said.

"Lord, do we ever," Deronda replied. They were glum and defeated. They would never figure out this complicated piece of shit. They were packing the drone away when Grace grinned and said, "Wait a minute. I know somebody!"

Grace hadn't seen Gilberto Cervantes for two years. She'd met him when he was in middle school. Gilberto and his friend Phaedra Harris were representatives of the Carver Middle School Science Club and Isaiah's ex-clients. He helped them with a problem, and in return, they acted as eyes and ears on one of his cases. They were the smartest kids Grace had ever met and the strangest. Their combination of maturity, pretentiousness and naïveté was as ridiculous as it was hilarious.

At the time, Gilberto was president of the chess and computer science clubs, captain of the debate team and vice captain of the academic decathlon team, only because Phaedra got two more votes. Gilberto had also been the student rep on the community outreach program. He eschewed the latter, expressing a clear dislike for young children and the elderly. "Doesn't matter," he said. "They all drool." He only volunteered because it would plump up his college applications.

Grace and Deronda were on a slope, hidden in a copse of trees. They saw Gilberto entering the park, carrying a briefcase and looking around distastefully. Stylistically, he had discarded his tax attorney look for Ralph Lauren casual. A three-button herringbone sport coat, an off-white shirt under an orange cable-knit sweater, chinos, deck shoes and zany-colored socks.

"Oh, my muthafuckin' God," Deronda said, "He might as well wear a sign that says, will somebody please kick my ass and take my money?"

"Thank you so much for coming," Grace said as Gilberto approached. "It's very nice of you to take the time." She'd had to beg, plead and use Isaiah's name before he agreed.

"I've never been to this park and now I see why," he said. He looked like he smelled a dead fish in his pocket.

"Gilberto Cervantes, this is Deronda Simmons."

They shook hands, their fingers barely touching. They were two completely different species, Grace thought. Like a penguin meeting a kangaroo.

"I'm sorry this is happening to you, Deronda," Gilberto said. "This Bobby James character is an absolute scoundrel! I haven't been so outraged since the Pizza King was nominated for the Federal Reserve Board."

Deronda looked at Grace. "It's a long story," Grace said.

Gilberto eyed the drone skeptically. "I see. A Phantom 4 Professional Quadcopter. A decent unit, I suppose." He fussed with it awhile and put the app on the iPad he carried in his briefcase.

"I appreciate you doing this, Gilbert," Deronda said.

Gilberto stiffened. "It's Gilberto. Never Gilbert."

Gilberto turned out to be Charles Lindbergh, Chuck Yeager and that guy who landed a jet on the Hudson River all rolled into one. *What's that, you say? You want a tracking shot of that dog chasing a tennis ball? No problem. Excuse me? You want a close-up of that empty wine bottle so you can read the label? No sweat. Say again? You want to hover over that bald guy and count the freck-*

les on his head? You got it. Gilberto handled the drone like his own personal falcon. It did everything but kill a pigeon, land on a treetop and eat the thing for lunch.

"They're here!" Deronda said. Bobby and Sandra entered the park and walked leisurely along the path. He had on a polo shirt and jeans. She was wearing frayed shorts, a faded tank top and flip-flops. They were holding hands, talking, animated, smiling and laughing. They looked like they were in love.

"I'm seeing it but I ain't believin' it," Deronda said.

"Is that the miscreant?" Gilberto said. "He looks like my father's golf caddy."

Gilberto had the drone hovering high overhead. Grace and Deronda were watching Gilberto's iPad, the shots clearer than Deronda's HDTV. You could see the chipped red polish on Sandra's toenails and the hole in her shorts.

"You know, I never thought they'd be all lovey-dovey like that," Deronda said. It struck Grace too. Somehow, it seemed wrong. The assistant manager at Wells Fargo and a drug-addicted prostitute holding hands?

The couple sat down on a bench. Bobby whispered in Sandra's ear. She smiled. He kissed her on the cheek. Deronda was astonished. "Did you get a shot of that?"

"Try not to insult me," Gilberto said. "Technologically, this is no more difficult than feeding a goldfish."

Grace didn't like it. Sandra's smile looked fake. She was anxious, a bead of sweat trickling down her temple, hands scratching her thighs. Grace didn't know much about it, but Sandra seemed like she needed a fix. "She looks like she's in withdrawal," she said.

"Who gives a shit?" Deronda replied.

"I've never seen two such unsavory individuals in my life," Gilberto complained. "I only hope I don't catch something."

"How? From the camera?"

"Germs travel on air currents just like pollen," Gilberto replied, "or that annoying leaf in *Forrest Gump.*"

Bobby had a fold of cash in his hand. He slipped it to Sandra and she stuffed it in her pocket. The shot was so vivid you could see the dial on Bobby's watch. He kissed her hand.

"I can't stand it," Deronda said. "This is too good."

"Yeah, it is," Grace said.

"What's that supposed to mean?"

"Why would Bobby do that?" Grace said.

"If he was going to give her money, he could have done it at her apartment or in his car or anywhere. Instead he does it in a public park? It makes no sense."

"Don't matter," Deronda said. "It makes sense to Bobby."

"And he kisses her hand? Peter O'Toole in a movie, maybe, but Bobby James?"

"Peter oh who?"

"I think Bobby knows we're here," Grace said.

"Will you stop raining on my damn parade? I got Bobby by the balls, and you know what I do with balls." Deronda was referencing a tussle she had with a drug dealer named Junior. He tried to push her head into his lap, and she gave his nuts a crank like she was opening the hatch on a submarine.

Deronda's wary, streetwise self had abandoned her. You couldn't blame her, Grace thought. Janeel was everything. Her friend was ecstatic, walking in circles and woo-hooing. Bobby and Sandra left the park, but Gilberto kept the drone on them. As soon as they were on the street, everything changed. Bobby dropped Sandra's hand, scowled and sucked in a big breath, like whew, I'm glad that's over. Sandra was wheedling him, desperate, tugging on his sleeve.

This is wrong, Grace thought. Very wrong. Gilberto stopped shooting and put the drone back in its case. Deronda was trying to thank him, but he was saying things like, "Yes, yes, that's all well and good," and "It was nothing, and I'm not kidding."

"I'll be leaving now," Gilberto said.

"Can I give you a lift?" Deronda said.

"What kind of car do you drive?"

"A Lexus."

"Then I agree."

They walked toward the exit. Grace looked back at the bench where Bobby gave Sandra the cash. She felt a growing dread. She wished Isaiah was here.

CHAPTER EIGHTEEN:
I AM NOT HIM

Grace was tired. If she wasn't working at the food truck, she spent every minute prepping for her art show. The gallery owner wanted seventeen of the twenty paintings Grace had showed her. The gallery owner wanted five more. Usually, Grace painted at a leisurely pace. She didn't want to force it, letting her art unfold in its own time. But she was on a time clock now. A whole different thing. Art as a business. She had to hurry without hurrying, and how the hell do you do that? Deronda told her to skip work, but she wouldn't. It wasn't right. She'd freeloaded off her friend Cherokee for weeks at a time and felt really horrible about it. She wouldn't, couldn't, do that again.

She left work and headed home, taking the route she always did. There was a four-way stop at Waverly. She braked, waited for her turn to cross. She saw the Stark sitting

277

on a bus bench not ten feet from the car. He was staring at her, unblinking, smiling, amused and threatening. He wasn't wearing a shirt, a spiked dog collar around his neck. This asshole was nuts.

She stared back, a stone-faced fuck you. A horn honked behind her. The Stark waved bye-bye and she drove on. It was freaky, seeing him like that, and what was the dog collar all about? Obviously, he was pissed because Stokeley had made a fool of him. Let him be pissed, Grace thought. Fuck him.

Later on, she was shopping at Vons, pushing her cart, getting things on a list. She was in the produce section picking out some apples when she saw him again, leaning against a display, piles of potatoes and onions behind him. He was smiling that smile and still wearing the dog collar. "Hello, Grace. What's for dinner?"

She said, "This, motherfucker." She picked up an apple and threw it at him, hard. It hit him in the chest, but he didn't wince, didn't stop smiling, like he didn't even feel it. He leaned down, picked up the apple and took a big bite, looking at her while he chomped.

"Mmm, good," he said. She tried to look bored and moved on.

She stayed in the market, shopping as usual, not giving him anything. This was some kind of stalking campaign, she thought. This guy didn't want to get physical so he was taking his revenge by intimidating her. Good luck with that. It was unnerving, but she'd never let it show. She kept the collapsible baton on the coffee table just like Isaiah did. She took it to work too. She thought about telling Deronda, but she had her hands full with Bobby James.

The encounters with the Stark continued. At the food truck, he'd stand off a ways, eating a taco, that same look in his eyes. He'd smile and give her a little wave. At night, she'd see him parked across the street. She wished Ruffin was an actual guard dog. She bought some things at Rite Aid, and when she got back to her car there was a dead sparrow on the seat. This is movie stuff, she thought, but it was getting to her. She was starting to feel afraid.

When she saw the Stark, it was harder and harder to maintain her composure. He had to be following her, she thought. She took different routes to and from work. She made sharp turns and kept her eye on the rearview mirror, but she never saw him. She came home one evening and Ruffin had a ribbon tied around his neck and a Christmas tag dangling on a string. It said, TOO BAD IF HE GOT RUN OVER. She went inside, infuriated. Threaten the dog? Threaten *the dog*? It was time to hit back. But what could she do? Call the cops? Get a restraining order? She didn't even know the Stark's name. She didn't know what to do.

The Stark was really screwing things up. She couldn't sleep her usual five hours a night. She was anxious and too distracted to focus on her painting. This was her first show. Her chance. She had to get rid of this guy, do something devious and intimidating. She was capable but didn't have the energy, especially alone. She smiled. Why not leave it to an expert?

"Dodson," she said.

She invited him over to the house. Deronda and Janeel were out. She told him about the Stark, popping up everywhere wearing a dog collar. "This guy is shredding my nerves. I can hardly function." Dodson thought a moment.

"Did you say he wears a dog collar?"

"Yes, the spiky kind they put on an attack dog."

After she described him, Dodson said, "That dude ain't no Stark. That's Skip Hanson." He told her about Skip and his pit bulls and why he hated Isaiah.

"He's really a hitman?" she said.

"He's good at it too. You say he's not following you?"

"Not that I can see."

"Then how does he know where you're gonna be?"

She thought a moment and said, "Grace, you're a stupid cow." They went outside. She crawled under the Jeep with a flashlight. "There it is. A GPS unit." Skip had been tracking her. He knew her every move. "I'm going to remove it," she said.

"No, leave it there," Dodson said. She slid out from under the car.

"Why? If it's there he'll know where I am."

"Yeah," Dodson said with a smile. "But we'll know where he is too."

Dusk. The day's last light glimmered faintly through the trees. Grace sat on a bench pretending to read something on her phone. When it was dark, she got up and left the park. She could feel Skip following her, gleeful, eager to scare her to death. She wore earbuds, but there was no music. She walked a ways and turned down a side street. Would Skip make his move? No, not yet. There were a few pedestrians and an occasional car. She walked two more blocks, approaching a patchy lot where swap meets were held and kids played soccer. She was wearing jeans and a dark blue hoodie. She tried to walk normally, her right hand down by her side. She crossed the field, reaching the darkest part. *Okay, Grace. Wait for it.* It was quiet, and then she heard him coming. He was behind her, running full out, his footsteps getting louder.

Skip followed her from the park. She didn't take her car. What was that about? She walked at a normal pace, no hurry, nothing was going to happen to her, right? She was Isaiah's girl, she was invincible. No, you're not, Skip thought. But why was she making herself a target? Was she stupid? Then it came to him. She thought he'd given up!

Ha! What a joke. He'd never give up. He was excited, adrenaline pumping, body tensed and ready for violence. He felt good, like he did in the old days when he killed people for a living. He would come up behind her, get her in a chokehold, drag her someplace, slap her around and threaten to rape her. Maybe feel her up a bit and put the gun to her head, tell her he was going to shoot her on the count of three unless she gave up Q Fuck. Then make her take her clothes off and leave her there crying like the cunt she was. The police? The bitch didn't even know his name. She thought he was somebody named Stark. He grinned. She was crossing the lot. Nobody around, the only light from the surrounding buildings. He was twenty yards behind her. The bitch wouldn't hear him, she had on earbuds.

He took a deep breath, leaned forward and started to sprint. Faster and faster, sneakers flying over the ground, her silhouette getting bigger and bigger. He was six feet away when she turned to face him. She did something with her hand. He heard a *snick* and she raised something over her head. THWACK! Something whipped him across the shoulder.

"MOTHERFUCKER!" he screamed. He spun around, holding himself. THWACK! She whipped him across the thigh. THWACK!

"OH, FUCK!" he yodeled. Across the elbow. "FUCKING SHIT!"

It was a goddamn police baton. The gun was in the back of his pants. He reached for it, but she kept hitting him, backing him up, his forearms raised to protect his head. THWACK! THWACK! He was getting her timing down. *Fuck it. Fuck the pain.* She raised the baton to strike him again. He caught her wrist and twisted the baton away.

She yelped in pain.

"I'm gonna beat you to death," Skip snarled. He reared back with the baton, but somebody punched him hard on the cheekbone, then another to the stomach. Wheezing, hurt and in agony, Skip staggered back into a wall. Someone appeared beside Grace. Whoever it was reached around and took the gun. How the hell did he know it was there? Skip's eyes had adjusted to the dark. It was a black guy.

"I hope your punk-ass learned a lesson," the black guy said.

"Who are you?" Skip said.

"Isaiah's homeboy. You don't remember me, Magnus?" He held his phone up to his face. Skip opened his mouth and gawked.

"You're him! You came to my place with Isaiah!"

"Uh-huh," the black guy said. "I was there, and I saw all them dogs you bossed around like slaves and your fucked-up house way the hell out in the middle of nothin' and I seen that hibachi where you cooked burgers for your nonexistent gun club."

Grace huffed and shook her head. *She's laughing at you, Skip. This fucking bitch is laughing at you!* The black guy went on.

"Be sensible, Skip. Grace can't give up Isaiah because she doesn't know where he is. Think about it. The less she knows, the safer he'll be. You get that, don't you?" Skip was in too much pain to speak. "My work here is done," the black guy said. "You?"

Grace leaned in close and said, "The word is out, Magnus. Everybody in the hood is on the lookout for you. Remember the guy who stuck the shotgun under your chin? Him too. Stay the fuck away from me." And the two of them walked away.

Grace and Dodson crossed the street. Dodson ejected the magazine from Skip's gun, popped the shell out of the chamber, then tossed everything into the gutter. He and Grace got in the car. They grinned at each other and bumped fists. "You are amazing, Dodson," she said.

"Yes, I am," he replied with a hustler's smile. "But don't tell nobody."

Skip stayed leaning against the wall, letting his breathing level out and the pain go down some. He limped to the park to get his car. He stopped at the liquor store to buy a bag of ice and a fifth of Jose Cuervo. The man behind the counter said, "I hope you won the fight."

Skip got back to the motel. He took a couple of Vicodin and iced himself down.

The black guy was right. If bad people were after Isaiah, he wouldn't tell Grace where he was. It wouldn't make sense. Everything Skip had done was for nothing. He filled a Styrofoam cup with tequila and drank it in three gulps. Bile came surging up his throat like an oil gusher. He choked, stumbled into the bathroom and vomited green slime into the sink. Groaning, he went back and sat on the bed. He was beat to shit, defeated, sapped of energy, red welts throbbing all over his body. Was it worth it? he thought. Was all this time, energy and bullshit really worth it? If he'd been picked up packing a gun, it was a return trip to Vacaville. What was he doing anyway? Fuck Isaiah. That shit was in the past. He should be rebuilding Blue Hill and getting in touch with his connections. He should start working again and getting his shit together — but those thoughts lasted less than a lit match. Fuck no. FUCK NO!

Humiliation and loneliness had been a way of life for Skip. As a kid, he'd always been on the edges, a pathetic outcast peeking over the fence at the fun. Magnus Vestergard, the loser with the stupid name. It was an image of himself he hated and tried not to remember. Memories were nothing but pain. Sometimes it would come to him, the realization that everything he did, then and now, was a way of saying, *I am not him. I am not Magnus Vestergard.* But Isaiah smashed that image over his head and let the mess drip down his face. He'd never give up. Fuck the risk, fuck Blue Hill, fuck everything. He would either put Isaiah and that bitch in the ground or stick a gun in his mouth and leave his brains splattered all over this shitty little room.

CHAPTER NINETEEN:
EX

Ava was upset about Shareen, but what could she do? Tell the police Crowe had killed his wife even though she hadn't seen it? Even if the police believed her, she couldn't take them on a path through the woods because there was no path. She'd heard a scream but didn't know where it came from. Then she'd have to explain how she found out about Crowe in the first place, and why she knew so much and where she got the information and Shareen would still be dead. She'd tell the police later, she decided. She talked with Billy on the phone.

"Crowe's destination is Coronado Springs," Billy said. "He's coming here to kill someone." She wanted to ask him for more details, but she'd get them later. She had to get some rest, shower, change her clothes. Billy said he was staying at his friend Isaiah's house.

"Who's Isaiah?" she asked. She didn't like this, more people knowing what they were up to.

"He's a good guy, you'll see," Billy said. He gave her the address. He started to say more, but she said they'd talk when she got there. She ended the call. She wanted to get on with the mission. She drove faster.

Crowe entered town on Coronado Boulevard. He drove two blocks, took a right, made a U-turn and parked. He was facing Coronado. He'd wait here for the girl. She'd go right by him. In less than ten minutes, she drove past in the Spark. He followed her to the Treeline Motel, a dump but it was probably cheap.

"Lucky me," Crowe said. Warren's car was in the same parking lot, in front of 103. The girl's was in front of 105. She was getting things out of her trunk. Yup. It was her, blue cap just like the girl at the gas station. Mmm, juicy, Crowe thought. Wait a second. He recognized her! It was their last victim, Hannah something. How could she still be alive? No, wait. She had a twin sister. Crowe had seen her on TV saying shitty things about him. He couldn't remember her name. He watched how she moved and felt the need like heat from a blast furnace.

Warren came out of his room, looking like he always did. Gaunt, stupid and half in the bag. He was scrawny, his chest concave, his shoulders hunched the way people do when they don't want to be seen. Yeah, that works. Warren reminded Crowe of that guy who played George McFly in *Back to the Future*. Crispy something, except Crispy's face wasn't sweaty, his eyes weren't bugged out, and he didn't look insane.

Warren glanced and then stared at the girl. "Don't do it," Crowe said aloud. Will the crazy fucker drag her into his room? There were people around, the cops would come. It would be a disaster. Warren walked away. Crowe blew out a stream of air like he was cooling his coffee. He wondered how the girl had gotten onto him in the first place. Pretty ballsy, following him all the way from Sac Town.

If the girl wanted him arrested, she'd have called the cops by now. What was she after? he wondered. To hurt him? Catch him in the act? Kill him? If she'd made it this far, it was possible. He and Warren had murdered her sister after all. Crowe wouldn't give a shit if somebody killed Warren, but it takes all kinds. He smiled. This was working out better than he thought. He had to kill the girl for practical reasons, and he could satisfy his fantasies at the same time.

Crowe always heard his fantasies before they took over. It began with a single note, someone humming and holding it, growing in intensity and volume until it oscillated the air like a tuning fork, shifting into a monk's drone, nasal and monotonous, the pitch rising higher and higher, stretching into a keening so sharp it pierced your skull, splintering into a squall, hissing and raspy, getting louder, ever louder, until you saw them, your fantasies, charging out of the blackness, a horde of screaming chimpanzees with bloody eyes and bloody teeth riding eyeless horses with dead women in their mouths. The monk was droning.

Warren was watching TV and eating the shittiest pizza he'd ever had. He wanted to take it back and make the kid behind the counter choke on it. How did people live out here with all the fucking trees and shitty pizza? He was out of beer and would have to get some more. The drapes were closed. They held in the smell. Mold, bleach and BO. He only had dirty clothes, and they were scattered all over the floor.

This morning, he'd followed EX from the house to the office. It took everything he had not to ram that fucking Subaru broadside. He'd seen the daughter too. Juicy, as Crowe would say. He'd do the daughter first and make EX watch.

Crowe and Warren had different fathers, men who probably parked their eighteen-wheelers at the Road Stops Here truck stop, conveniently located where Interstate 5 meets 80, the main arteries into and out of Sacramento. They probably took advantage of their mother's fire-sale prices and quick service. She killed herself when the two boys were in middle school. They were bounced around to different foster homes and institutions, eventually losing track of each other.

When Warren turned eighteen, he was no longer the state's responsibility. He did a little of everything to get by. He dealt meth and Oxy, robbed people, broke into houses, stole cars and burglarized stores. He lived in his sister's basement. She wouldn't allow him into the house. There was nothing there except a water heater, piles of junk and a cot, not even a microwave or a TV. Almost everything he ate came out of a bag or a box. He watched TV at Tango's, a bar near the house, but after a while he quit going. His neck hurt from looking up and half the time it was a soccer game. He was in and out of prison. This was his life, and he never expected more.

Warren turned thirty-four when he made the biggest mistake of his life. He'd gone to Tahoe to gamble, and predictably, he lost everything. He was heading back to Sacramento and stopped in Coronado Springs for a burger. He saw a girl in the parking lot. He grabbed her, dragged her into his car and assaulted her. He was caught, arrested and tried in the county courthouse. According to Warren, EX "destroyed" him. Ask him how this happened and his answers made no sense. The screaming didn't help and neither did the drugs.

They shipped him off to San Quentin where he reunited with Crowe. Crowe was big, violent, and he didn't back down, qualities that earned you a lot of respect among the inmates. He kept Warren safe, but it almost wasn't worth it. Since they'd last seen each other, Crowe had become more of an asshole than he was when they were kids. Bragging, telling whoppers, putting you down, threatening.

"Give me shit, okay, Warren?" he would say. "And I'll turn you over to the niggers."

Crowe was released first. He rented a house — no, not a house, a shack with holes in the floor, newspaper taped on the windows and no hot water. Crowe worked at a garage changing tires and he sold meth on the side. When Warren got out, they lived together. It was a parole violation, but their parole officers had too many clients to stop by. Warren's PO said she had over a hundred.

Warren knew Crowe was into something bad, but he didn't know how bad until they were roomies. Some whore had rejected him, laughed at him, called him a creep and a psycho. Crowe went fucking ballistic. Like insane ballistic. Stomping all over the house, breaking shit and yelling about ripping the bitch's head off and eating her tongue. Crowe asked Warren for help, hinting that if he refused, he'd get thrown out. Why not? Warren thought. He didn't mind seeing women getting beat up. He'd beaten up a few himself. The whore's name was Dixie. She was skinny with sunken cheeks, a brass-colored wig and a mean face. Crowe always said he had "high standards" for whores. What a laugh.

Warren pretended to be a john and got Dixie into the car. As they were driving, Crowe popped up in the backseat and grinned at her in the rearview mirror. The bitch screamed, but Crowe put the Bowie to her throat and told her to shut up.

The car was a junker. Crowe said it was cheap and it ran okay. He said he used it for this and nothing else. Warren wondered what "this" was. Crowe said it was one of his safety precautions. All the evidence would be in this car and not the one he drove every day. Evidence? Warren thought. Evidence of what? He realized Crowe wasn't going to beat the girl up. *He was going to kill her.* Warren's pulse sped up, his mouth was dry.

Crowe told him to drive to the highway.

"Where are we going?" Warren said.

"To the place," Crowe said, like it was holy or something. The place? Warren thought. What place?

They drove way out into the desert somewhere, and now they were off road. The girl knew she was in deep shit. She was crying softly, saying something to herself.

The "place" was nothing but a rusty, beat-up trailer parked in a deep arroyo. It was behind a hill so you couldn't see it from the highway even if the lights were on. It had a generator and running water from a tank you had to fill every once in a while. Crowe said you needed water to clean yourself up. The woman was lying in the dirt, not moving, murmuring something to herself. Oh, shit, Warren thought. This was going to be fucked up.

Crowe brought out his tackle box. His knives were in there. The first time Warren saw them he whistled like they were a girl with a big ass. There were two of them. They were gigantic, something you'd throw at a whale or hack into a fort with. Crowe told Warren about them. It was just after Warren had moved in. He remembered because it was the one and only time Crowe had said something interesting.

They were in the shack, sitting on the cushionless couch watching a hockey game. Neither of them knew shit about hockey, but they had nothing else to do. Crowe was sharpening one of his "beauties" on a gray whetstone. He spit on the stone first, saying it worked better than water. Warren wondered what "better" meant. The spit was slimy and yellowish because they'd eaten mac and cheese out of a box. Crowe drew the blade back and forth across the stone, applying a little pressure with his off hand. He said the angle was important, twenty degrees was best. Warren wondered if he was making that up.

"This is a Bowie knife," Crowe said it like he was a tour guide. "It was named after a man named Jim Bowie, a famous knife fighter that died at the Alamo. He didn't invent the knife, it was around long before him."

"Then why did they name it after him?" Warren said. Crowe gave him a look. Questions were not appreciated. He continued. "This is back in Louisiana, the 1800s. There was this famous fight, called the Sandbar Fight. Two families were warring over some land, so they met on a sandbar in the middle of the Mississippi River." Warren was going to ask why, but Crowe interrupted him.

"The sandbar was outside the jurisdiction of the law," he said. "It was going be a duel and they had laws against dueling." He said it like Warren was supposed to know about dueling laws a million fucking years ago.

"Didn't you just say it was a knife fight?" Warren asked. Crowe gave him that look again. He turned the Bowie around in his hand. He went on. "So the families and their supporters met out there, fifteen, eighteen people, something like that. Bowie was there to back up one of the families. The two leaders had their duel, but they were too far away and missed each other. Twice."

Warren chuckled. "What a bunch of idiots. What happened after that?"

"They shook hands, okay?" Crowe said,

297

copping an attitude. "Is that what you wanted to know? They shook hands. Are you satisfied now?"

"Okay, okay."

Crowe continued. "Well, the two sides were still pissed at each other, and they got into a brawl. Bowie charged into the middle of it, and a man from the other side shot him in the hip and knocked him down. But guess what?"

"What?" Warren said. He wasn't supposed to ask that either.

"Fucking Bowie gets up and charges the guy!" Crowe said like it was the most amazing thing in the world.

"Fucker had balls," Warren conceded. Crowe shifted his shoulders around, sighed and went on.

"Like I was saying. Bowie charges the guy who shot him, but the guy hits him with the gun and knocks him down again. And then a second guy shows up, shoots at Bowie but misses!"

"And Bowie's on the ground? Were all these guys cockeyed?" Warren said. Crowe hefted the knife like he was thinking of using it.

"I'm getting to the good part," he said through his teeth.

"Fine, so what happened?" Warren said

impatiently.

"So then this guy, the second guy, draws a sword and stabs Bowie right in the fucking chest! But it didn't go through because it hit his sternum. Right here." Crowe put his finger on Warren's sternum.

"Fuck man, how lucky is that?" Warren said, batting the finger away.

"Be quiet, okay?" Crowe was mad now. The asshole was so touchy. Crowe smiled and shook his head like Bowie was his kid or something. "But Bowie's not done. He grabs this guy by the shirt, pulls him down on the knife and fucking kills him!"

"Atta boy!" Warren hooted. "Go get 'em, Bowie!"

"And then a *third* guy comes up behind Bowie and shoots him again!" Crowe said, laughing. "And you know what Bowie does?" He was grinning, like Warren would never guess.

Warren blurted out, "He cuts the guy's arm off?" Crowe went still. He looked like a soccer ball with no air in it. He looked like he'd dropped his birthday cake. He held the knife in the stabbing position. His jawbone was moving around. "Yes," he said stiffly. "Bowie cut the guy's arm off."

"I knew it! I knew it!" Warren said, bouncing up and down. He couldn't remember the last time he knew an answer ahead of time. "Did the guy die? The guy who got his arm cut off?" Crowe slipped the knives back in their sheaths and put them in the tackle box. "Wait, don't go yet," Warren said. Crowe didn't answer, shutting the lid with a little extra snap. "Where're you going?" Warren said. Crowe got up and walked out of the room, Warren calling after him, "What about the Alamo?"

A spotlight was bracketed to the roof of the trailer. The light was white and hard, bugs flying around. Everything around them was dark. The whore hadn't moved, staring at something far away. She'd given up. It was time to die and she knew it. Crowe was standing over her, holding the Bowie. He taunted her, called her names and waved the knife. Warren wondered why Crowe had brought him here. He said he wanted a lookout but a lookout for what? Rocks? Bats? Cactus? Then it came to him. Crowe wanted someone *to watch.* He was going to put on a show, and he needed an audience. And what a fucking show it was! Warren had never seen anything like it. He couldn't take his eyes away, even though he was scared and the screaming was loud and blood splattered on his shoes.

In the middle of it, Crowe said, "Want some?" And Warren thought, why not? He wanted to see what it was like. Crowe gave him the other Bowie knife and it was a fucking trip! You could do whatever you wanted. *You could do whatever you wanted.* No rules, no watchers, no cameras, no zip.

Later, they cleaned themselves up. They wore latex gloves and wrapped the woman in a plastic tarp. They drove to an isolated section of the Sacramento River and set the body adrift. Warren asked why they didn't just leave her in the desert. Crowe said he wanted the police to find the body. He wanted to mess with them, shock them. He liked the idea of those assholes looking for clues when there weren't any. Why the river? Warren asked. Crowe said the Green River Killer was famous and he wanted to be more famous than him. He wanted headlines. He wanted to be at the top of the news. He said he wished he could tell the cops his real name.

Warren's first two kills with Crowe had been the best. It was way better than fucking and way better than drugs. The third was a disappointment. Not the same high, not the same rush. The time between killings was worse than withdrawal. Warren had never felt this low in his life, and there were a lot of low points to choose from.

Warren's need to kill grew stronger. It felt like something was alive inside him, some kind of animal with fangs. It was blurry at first, but Warren decided it was a wolf. A big fucker, all black with glowing blue eyes like a malamute, growling and snapping its jaws and gnawing on Warren's bones. At night, it howled for blood, wanting more, wanting it now. Warren could feel the wolf taking over.

Crowe drove him crazy. He took forever to find a victim. He was so picky. They'd be out trolling the streets and pass up a perfectly good black chick. If you complained, Crowe would say, "Don't you get it? She has to be perfect." What was perfect? Warren asked. First of all, she couldn't be a slut, Crowe explained. What a fucking joke. Crowe fucked slutty whores whenever he had the money. The perfect girl was also white, in her mid-teens, slim, pale skin, medium to long brown hair, and she had to be "classy." "You know, a regular girl," Crowe explained. "Nice and clean, from a good home, not all gooped up with makeup and tight clothes." Warren thought that was the stupidest shit he'd ever heard. A good home? What the hell did that mean? You had to meet her parents? You only saw girls like that around high schools or the mall, and they were usually in packs.

Crowe was such a hypocrite. After driving around for an hour or two, he'd decide a black chick was okay and so was short hair and a few extra pounds and caked-on makeup, a ring in her nose and gang tats everywhere. Finally, he'd say, okay, okay, let's do it and Warren would say it's about time, and Crowe would get pissed. Crowe had a bunch of other stupid requirements. Where and when to kidnap the girl, what they would wear, how to get her in the car blah blah fucking blah.

If you complained, Crowe would say, "It's my thing," and he was "allowing" you to participate. You were a "guest" and he could "disqualify" you any time he wanted. He'd been killing damn near a decade and hadn't been caught. "You want to know why?" Crowe would remind him every other god-damn day. "Me. Not you. Me."

They had one last kill together. It was just before Crowe went to the joint for a stupid bar fight. It was evening, dark because it was late in the year. Crowe was driving around the edges of downtown Sacramento. He was super excited, making lefts and rights that made no sense. Warren was hyped and jumpy. He'd snorted a few long lines of coke.

"What are you doing?" he said.

"We're early," Crowe said.

"Early for what?"

Crowe had that scary gleam in his eye. "I found a new one. Number seventeen. You won't believe it, Warren. She's a nurse! I love those fucking uniforms. I wish hers was white, but it's a shitty green color."

"What's so special about her?"

Crowe laughed. "She's got a twin! Yeah, no shit! Her sister looks exactly like her. I saw them at the Capitol Mall. They were holding hands." He smiled at the memory. "I pretended to bump into them just to get a look. It was amazing! Except for their hair they were —"

"Identical?" Warren said.

"Yeah," Crowe said, not getting the joke.

"So? What's the big deal?"

"Don't you see? You kill one of them but you're actually killing two!"

"No, you're not, you're killing one," Warren said.

Crowe sulked. "Forget it, okay? You have no fucking imagination." He glanced at his watch. "It's time." They reached an isolated stretch of Hanover Avenue. It was a short block. No houses, only commercial buildings, the kind that sold plumbing supplies and wholesale furniture.

"It's a shortcut for her," Crowe said. "She goes this way, makes a right and she's home. Otherwise, she'd have to go around." Crowe was an asshole, but he did his homework, Warren thought.

They drove past an empty lot, nothing there but construction debris. The only light was from the windows across the street, fluorescents left on for the night. Crowe drove around the block, turned into an alley and parked at the rear of the lot.

"This time you do the work," he said. "I've set everything up, everything's ready. You grab her, I'll be waiting in the car."

"What kind of bullshit is that?"

"It's not bullshit. You have to pull your weight, okay? You can't just do the fun part, you have to — she'll be here any second, Warren! Go! Hurry!"

There was a dumpster near the front edge of the lot. Warren got out of the car, ran and took cover behind it. A woman was coming up the street. You'd never know she had a twin; she looked like everybody else. She was wearing a puffy vest over green scrubs and carrying a big bag. There was no one around. They hadn't seen anyone since they got here. Crowe had picked a good spot. The woman was talking on the phone, chatting and laughing. You should look where you're going, Warren thought. He was less nervous about grabbing her than he was about Crowe, his fat ass waiting for him to fuck up.

Warren lost focus for a moment — the woman was right in front of him! He made his move a moment too soon. She was parallel, not past him. She turned her head and saw him coming. She didn't scream, she ducked. Warren hugged air and she darted out from under him. He reached out, grabbed the collar of the vest and yanked her back. Her feet went out from under her, but Warren held on. The vest was pulled up to her throat. She had both hands on it so she wouldn't choke. She started screaming and kicking her legs. He couldn't hold on and get to his Bowie at the same time.

"Shut up!" Warren hissed. He saw a truck was two blocks away. Its silhouette was big and square, its engine loud and guttural. The bitch kept fighting and screaming. "SHUT UP!" Warren hissed louder.

Crowe was in the alley, watching from the car. He nearly laughed. The bitch ducked and Warren almost missed her. What a fucking moron. Now he was trying to drag her onto the lot. Not easy. She was on the ground and he had her by the collar. Deadweight. He should have hoisted her over his shoulder. Crowe heard a truck. It was close, maybe on Hanover. *Oh, shit.*

"Hurry, Warren, hurry the fuck up!" Crowe shouted into the windshield. Warren couldn't hear him. He was still struggling with the woman, taking quick glances at the truck, getting closer, the engine noise louder. There was a line where the light ended and the darkness began. Warren had to get the woman across it before the truck's headlights hit him.

"HURRY UP, WARREN!" Crowe screamed. Warren had half her body over the line. She was twisting, trying to turn her body over. "Here I come!" Crowe said. He leaped out of the car, the truck noise instantly louder. Warren was jerking and yanking the woman's collar. You could feel the truck's vibration through the ground. Crowe was running. "Hurry, Warren! Hurry!"

Warren pulled the woman over the line. A few seconds later, the truck went by. The woman had stopped screaming. Warren probably hit her. Crowe stood in the middle of the lot, teed off, breathing hard and shak-

307

ing his head.

"Can't you do anything right?"

Warren began dragging the woman again, stopping every few yards. He was wrung out and slimy with sweat. "How about giving me a hand?" Crowe looked at him disgustedly.

"Do it yourself, asshole." He went back to the car.

A few days later, Crowe got into his stupid bar fight and went to jail. Warren was relieved. He had the shack to himself, he could do what he wanted and didn't have to listen to Crowe's endless bullshit. Then he realized he wouldn't be able to kill again until Crowe got out. The need was strong and Warren couldn't wait. Besides, who needed that prick anyway? You know what you're doing. He went out by himself, trolled Village 5. It was on a list of Sacramento's worst neighborhoods. He picked up a hooker, knocked her out, took her to the place and did his thing. It was good, he thought afterward, but it wasn't great.

He went out again, nabbed a housewifey-looking woman. She fainted so it was easy. He had her halfway into the trunk when she opened her eyes. She'd been playing possum. She kicked Warren in the face and nearly escaped, but he gave her a judo chop and knocked her to the ground. He had to fight hard to get her back into the trunk. It was exhausting. He took her to the place and did his thing.

Warren went back to the shack and smoked a cigar-sized spliff. That could have turned out bad, he thought. Maybe he needed Crowe, and he missed the shared adrenaline, the insane laughter, the looks they exchanged when they were covered with blood.

While Crowe was in prison, he married a woman named Shareen. She was heavy and sweated a lot. She didn't know how to do anything except fry baloney and nag. Warren couldn't believe Crowe would marry a lump like that. Crowe said living in an actual house, eating fried baloney sandwiches and watching Netflix with Shareen was better than living in a shack with his half brother, eating frijoles out of a can, and watching the same six channels because they couldn't afford cable.

When Crowe was released, he found out about Warren's killing and the near miss. He called a bunch of times, yelling and complaining, his voice like a hacksaw cutting through a lead pipe. Warren wanted to go out again, but Crowe told him no. The time "wasn't right." More bullshit. The asshole was worried he wasn't the boss anymore and didn't want you doing stuff yourself. To hell with it, Warren thought. You don't need him anymore. You already proved it.

He went out by himself again. He prowled the streets of South Haggenwood and Ben Ali, other names on the worst neighborhoods list. It was closer to the shack than Crowe would have liked but so what? Warren wanted a woman. Didn't matter if she was old or young, hunchbacked or blind and in a wheelchair. The goddamn wolf was chewing through his rib cage.

He drove around for hours but couldn't find a woman who was isolated enough to grab. He kept driving, craning his neck like that would help him see better. He was about to go home — and there she was, walking down Curson. There were streetlights, but they were far apart. Everything in between was dark or had a bunch of shadows.

The wind was gusting hard. The girl was wearing a hoodie cinched tight around her face, hands in her pockets, leaning into the wind. Anything that wasn't tied down was rustling and flapping, trees bending, shit tumbling down the sidewalk. There was an old man on the other side of the street trudging along, head bowed, eyes down. A kid was up the block a ways, riding a bicycle in circles as if to say fuck the wind. I'm here, goddammit.

Warren knew he should wait until the street was completely deserted, but who knew when that would be? The wolf was climbing out his chest with its fangs dripping, and then Warren *was* the wolf, and he was going to eat this bitch down to her socks. He pulled the car up behind her and got out fast. He clamped one hand over her mouth, put the Bowie knife to her throat and told her to be quiet. But the stupid bitch started fighting anyway, thrashing around, trying to pry his hand off her mouth, going "MMMMFFFMMMM-FFF." He could barely hang on to her.

"Cut it out or I'll cut your goddamn throat," he growled. She bit his hand. He yelled, but he didn't let go. The old man was pointing at them and looking around for someone to tell. The kid was riding in circles around them and yelling for help. And then a black guy in a do-rag came running right at them.

"The fuck are you doing?" he shouted.

Warren let the girl go and flashed the Bowie. The guy stopped but he wasn't scared. He said, "You done fucked up altogether."

Warren backed away. Then two more black guys joined the first one, and they kept coming, challenging, gesturing with their hands, talking shit like black guys do. Warren reached the car. He got in quickly and put the knife on the seat beside him. He'd left the engine running, but he still had to put it in gear and release the hand brake. Before he could do it, one of the black guys smashed the windshield with a brick or a rock, the glass shattering. The second guy was getting in the passenger door. Warren grabbed the knife and slashed at him, cutting him across the shoulder. The guy screamed and fell back. The third one opened the driver's-side door. Warren tried to bring the knife around, but he banged the blade on the steering wheel and dropped it. The guy tried to drag him out. Warren yanked himself away, released the brake, put the car in gear and stomped on the gas, running over the one who broke the windshield, all of it happening in seconds.

The third guy wouldn't let go. He had his feet on the door sill, one hand on the door, the other clamped on to the steering wheel. Warren fought him for control, the car swerving, heading for a building. He hit the brakes hard. The guy was thrown forward into the door, releasing the steering wheel as he was thrown back and onto the pavement. A crowd was running toward the car, screaming and throwing bottles and rocks. Warren put the car in reverse, cranked the wheel to straighten out, the crowd right outside banging on the windows. He stomped on the gas and sped out of there.

Warren got home, scared and shaken. He took a couple of nembies, smoked a joint and had a few beers. He knew he'd messed up. Next day, the news was everywhere. For the first time in his life, Warren bought copies of the *Sacramento Bee* and the *LA Times*. AMSAK SUSPECT STRIKES AGAIN. SEARCH FOR AMSAK SUSPECT INTENSIFIES. The story was on the local stations and CNN as well.

There was good news, if you could call it that. Warren hadn't killed anybody and the police didn't have a license plate number. The description of him was vague. Warren drove the car out to the desert, wiped it down and left it in a dry creek bed far from the highway. He had a bicycle strapped to the bumper. It took him half a day to reach a bus stop and it nearly did him in.

Crowe came over to the shack. He was

really pissed. "What the hell is wrong with you?" he shouted, waving the newspaper. "Have you lost your goddamn mind? How could you be so stupid?" Something about that word had always bugged Warren. Of all the words there were, that one reduced you the most.

"Don't call me stupid," he said. Crowe was in his face, aiming his fat finger at him.

"You *are* fucking stupid. Do you want to go back to jail for a hundred years? Christ, how could you be any more of a screwup?"

"I said don't call me stupid." Warren slapped the fat finger away. Crowe was red-faced and sweating.

"You do as I say!" he screamed. "It's my operation. I was the one who brought you into it! Remember that, *stupid*?"

Warren's hand shot out and grabbed Crowe around the throat, squeezing hard before pushing him away. Warren wasn't as strong as Crowe, but he was strong enough. Crowe stumbled back, coughing, tripping over the coffee table and falling on his ass. Warren laughed. Crowe got to his feet, his mouth open, his eyes shining like there was a fire inside his head. His knife was on the floor. He picked it up. He looked at Warren and made a sound, too deep to be human, like something coming from a cave or a crack in the earth. Warren drew his own knife. He carried it with him all the time just like Jim Bowie.

"That's my knife. I gave it to you," Crowe said.

"Well, I'm not giving it back, asshole." They looked at each other. If he takes a step forward, it's kill or be killed, Warren thought.

Crowe said, "You wait, Warren. You just fucking wait," and he left the room.

The next day, Crowe kept bitching. They couldn't use the car anymore, they'd have to wait a long time before they could kill again. The cops were everywhere. Crowe blamed him in a hundred different ways — but he didn't call him stupid.

Warren stayed home, three days, four, five days, then a whole week. The wolf was pacing, snarling and tearing at his stomach lining. The goddamn thing was hollowing him out. He couldn't eat or sleep, tempted to slip into the night and find a girl. But reality was too big and loud to ignore. He could get caught, go to prison again. He'd spent eleven years of his life locked up in a cage. He never got used to it, never adapted, scared out of his mind every second, waiting for somebody to stab him or a bunch of gangsters to drag him into the utility room.

Going back terrified him. He'd kill himself before that happened. But the wolf didn't give a shit. Fear and common sense had no effect on the beast. It was so big now, Warren could hardly breathe. He walked around the shack, the lights off, raving, stabbing the air with the Bowie, his urges like violent orgasms.

Warren didn't know how it happened, how the wolf turned its anger on EX. He thought about what happened back then, playing the scenes in his mind, each frame a slash with the Bowie. EX had to be gutted, strung up and hacked to death. He made the mistake of calling Crowe.

"We could do it while we're waiting for shit to cool down," Warren said. "EX lives in Coronado Springs, it's like a four-, five-hour drive. Nobody's gonna connect that with us." Crowe said no, absolutely not. He was on parole, and he was wearing an ankle monitor. He couldn't go anywhere except to work and back. Anyway, they couldn't make plans for a strange town. They'd have to do it on the fly, a sure way to get caught.

"There's no reason to do this, Warren," Crowe said.

"I have to."

"Why? You keep saying that, but it doesn't make any sense."

"I don't care."

"No, I forbid it!" Crowe shouted. "What if you get caught, huh? What if they offer you a deal? We'll knock ten years off your sentence if you tell us who your partner is. You'd give me up in a second!" Warren didn't say anything. Crowe was right. He'd have no problem flipping over like a blueberry flapjack if it came to that. Warren hung up, but Crowe called him back.

"You'll mess everything up like you always do!" he roared.

"Not always," Warren said. He wasn't good at arguing.

"Yes, always! You're not good for shit! All you do is get in my fucking way! And now you're going to do something stupid like this? Yeah, you heard me. You're stupid and you've always been stupid and you'll fuck this up because you're a stupid goddamn idiot."

"I don't give a shit what you say, I'm going," Warren said. Crowe was screaming as the call ended. When this was over, Warren thought, he would scalp that asshole and cut out his Adam's apple so he couldn't talk anymore. He was going to Coronado Springs to kill EX and nothing was going to stop him.

■ ■ ■ ■

Warren hated his room at the Treeline. The bed was buckled in the middle. It was hot and suffocating and the smell was bad. The heating-cooling thing under the window didn't do anything but rattle and blow dust around. He needed more beer. Maybe get a Styrofoam cooler and some ice so he wouldn't have to drink it warm. He put on his pants and a sleeveless sweatshirt. He'd go to the liquor store, move around a little, get some blood flowing. Then he'd go looking for EX. The thought of it excited him.

He left the room and saw a girl, two doors down, jiggling the key in the lock and cursing. She was wearing a blue baseball cap, jeans and an old flannel shirt. He wondered what her tits were like. Warren felt the wolf lunge, jaws snapping shut an inch away from the girl's neck. She'd never know how close she came to getting dragged into his room. Maybe later, he thought. When it was dark.

CHAPTER TWENTY: SIDE HEADING

Isaiah was still shaken. That he'd nearly killed himself was devastating. He'd always been in control of himself. Maybe not his emotions but his actions, his decisions. Now he was subject to impulse and delusion. He couldn't trust himself. A knock on the door startled him. He crossed the room and opened it. A young woman was there, haggard and pale. She had the beaten, beseeching look of someone in terrible trouble. Go somewhere else, he thought. We're all out of kindness, patience, sympathy, empathy, a sense of justice, social responsibility or anything remotely to do with helping someone besides myself. The cupboard is bare, folks. The cupboard is burnt to shit.

"Mr. Quintabe? I'm Ava Bouchard," she said. "My friend, Billy Sorensen, said he was staying here. I was wondering if I could see him." He looked at her with barely disguised animosity. This, of course, was the friend who was in so much danger that Billy escaped from the hospital to help her. If Isaiah's experience was any guide, the danger would be right behind her. She stood there, waiting to be invited in. Let her sweat, he thought. Finally, she asked, "May I come in?" He made her wait another moment before stepping aside. A new course of anger swept through him. Billy and this girl had brought a serial killer to his doorstep. The very essence of everything he was trying to get away from. The bottom of the septic tank, corruption in its most virulent form. His fury rose. He closed the door behind her.

"I'm sorry for the intrusion," she began.

"Call the sheriff and tell him about Crowe," he said, bitterly. "Get out your phone and do it right now."

"I can't, Mr. Quintabe. I have to —"

"I don't care. Call him."

"You don't know what you're asking. You don't understand."

"I don't want to understand," Isaiah replied. He could barely keep from screaming at her. "Call him right now or I'll call him myself, and if I do it I'll turn Billy in and give you up too." He glared at her and she glared back. She got out her phone.

"I'm calling him, *okay*?" She was incensed. He didn't care.

"And after you're done? You and Billy get out of my house. I don't care what you do or where you go. Just get out."

Sheriff Cannon was at his desk, ready to go home. It had been a long, irritating day. Mrs. Landy had called and said she'd had a break-in. She didn't. An errant baseball had broken her window. George Alpin called and said kids from the high school were smoking weed in the park. Cannon didn't care, but he was up for reelection. He went out there and told the kids to take it indoors. Max Grabie had dementia and wandered away from home. Cannon found him in the drugstore, standing in the cold and flu aisle looking around like he'd landed on Pluto. Cannon's daughter fell down and bruised her shoulder. Cannon knew she was okay, but Marcie insisted they take her to the emergency room. And Billy. That stupid kid. Gretta kept calling and asking what was happening and if the department was doing anything to find her son. Cannon didn't care if her son had been eaten by a cougar. He'd had enough of Billy's bullshit.

Loretta stuck her head in the office. "Call for you. She says it's urgent."

He picked up the phone. "This is Sheriff Cannon."

"Hello, Sheriff. I have something to report." A young woman's voice.

"Your name?"

"I'd rather not say, but it's important."

"Okay. Go ahead," Cannon said.

The young woman, who sounded rational, told him a long story about her sister being murdered by AMSAK. She said AMSAK was a man named William Crowe, and he was in Coronado Springs. Cannon was skeptical. She sounded reasonable, but lots of crackpots sound reasonable.

"So you think this Crowe is the killer or the police do?" he said.

"He's on their short list of suspects."

Cannon's pulse took a bump. "How would you know that? That information is confidential."

"I have the police files."

"The police files? Where did you get them?"

"I can't tell you."

"If that's true, you're in a lot of trouble, young lady," Cannon said.

"I accept that, Sheriff," the woman replied. "But there's a serial killer in your town, and it's your responsibility to arrest him."

"If you don't mind, I'll decide what I'm responsible for," he said. This was beyond far-fetched. He didn't believe this girl had the police files; there was no way to access them. She was making this up and for some reason she was fixated on somebody named William Crowe. He was probably an ex-boyfriend or it was a mistaken identity or her sister was murdered by somebody else or her sister was alive or maybe she had no sister. Something occurred to him.

"Are you by any chance a friend of Billy Sorensen?"

"Yes, I am. But that doesn't mean —"

"Well, you have a nice day, miss," Cannon said. She was still talking when he ended the call. He started to get up from his desk but sat back down again. What if she wasn't a crackpot? What if she was right? Due diligence, asshole. This kind of crap always comes back to bite you. He looked up Crowe's sheet. He was actually a suspected serial killer. Could the girl's story be true? He called the local motels. No one named William Crowe or anyone of his description had checked in. He called Crowe's parole officer.

"Harrison Pearce," Pearce said.

"Hi. I'm Ron Cannon, the sheriff over in Coronado Springs. I'm wondering if you could do me a favor."

"Sure," Pearce said, a little too eagerly. Maybe talking to a real police officer was exciting. "How can I help you?"

"Could you check out one of your clients for me? His name is William Crowe. I heard he was in my town."

"What a coincidence." Pearce chuckled. "I saw him just this morning. He was at work, right where he was supposed to be. I searched him too. The most dangerous thing on him was some loose change." He chuckled again. "Tell you the truth, I was almost sure Crowe would screw up, but I was wrong. He's been straight as an arrow."

That was what Cannon wanted to hear. Pearce's chuckle sounded forced, but he had confirmed Cannon's suspicion. The girl was a crackpot.

"Okay, Mr. Pearce, I appreciate your help."

"My pleasure, Sheriff, call me anytime."

Crowe watched Ava come out of her room at the Treeline. She'd ditched the blue cap, and her hair was wet. She'd taken a shower. Christ, he wished he'd been there. He followed her to an outlying neighborhood. She stopped in front of a house. She seemed to be confused about the address. Crowe hastily parked and got out of the car. If she was on foot, he would be too. Years of following women around had taught him a few things. She was puzzled a moment, then walked around the side of the house. Crowe moved quickly, crouched, staying behind her. She crossed the backyard toward a tiny guest house, deep woods behind it. She knocked on the door. A black guy answered. They talked for a moment, the black guy not happy to see her. He let her in.

Crowe was worried. Pearce texted him. Sheriff Cannon had called. He wanted to know Crowe's whereabouts. This girl had already involved the cops. He had to shut her up. Killing her was easy enough, but now there was the black guy. He couldn't do this alone.

"Yeah, what do you want?" Warren said. That's how he answered the phone. If he knew God was calling he'd say the same thing.

"We're being followed," Crowe said.

"We?"

"I'm here in Coronado Springs," Crowe added. Warren didn't say a thing. "I'm not here to hurt you or take you back," Crowe said. "I'm here to protect us. Hannah Bouchard's sister followed me here from Sacramento. She needs to be gone."

"What's this gotta do with me?" Warren said.

"If she's onto me, she's onto you. My parole officer got a call from the sheriff. The cops are involved. Do you want to go back to Quentin, Warren? We have to take her out."

"I'll think about it." That was Warren's way of saying fuck you. When he's like this you can't push. You have to lead.

"Remember the girl two doors down from you at the motel?" Crowe said. "She was getting things out of her trunk. That's Hannah Bouchard's sister. Juicy, huh? Perky tits, right?"

"You think I'm gonna fall for that? I've had enough of your bullshit."

"It's not bullshit, I saw her five minutes ago." Crowe's voice got low and husky. "She's in a guest house, Warren. I'm looking at it right now. She's in there alone, and there's nobody around. Did you hear me? There's *nobody* around. You can do anything you want. Think about it, Warren. You can do anything you want." He let that hang in the air.

Warren said, "Come pick me up."

Isaiah was homesick. He wanted desperately to see Grace, Dodson, TK and Deronda.

326

He wanted to see Mrs. Marquez, Mo the wino and Beaumont, now dead and gone. He missed Verna and her croissants made from warm snowflakes and a tub of butter. He missed the hood, depressing as it was. That was his home, where he'd lived for twenty-nine years. He was alone, lonely and depressed, the PTSD pulling him further and further into the abyss.

He had to leave, get out of Coronado Springs. He'd go find Grace and to hell with the rest. It was suddenly urgent. He rushed into the bedroom, found his duffel and began stuffing his clothes. He felt afraid, like he was coming apart, like his chest was splitting. A panic attack. "I've got to get out, I've got to get out!" he shouted. Fuck clothes. He shoved the duffel aside and patted his pockets, no car keys. He looked around. Not on top of the dresser, not on the floor, not on the bedside table. He ran into the living room. He swept everything off the coffee table and flung the cushions off the couch. "Where are my fucking keys? Goddammit, where are they?"

He stormed into the kitchen. No keys. Mindlessly, he opened drawers and cupboards and slammed them shut. He was sweating and trembling. The keys were his escape from this town, from PTSD. "Where are they? WHERE ARE MY FUCKING KEYS?" His phone buzzed. It was stuck in his pocket sideways, and he couldn't get it out. "Come on, come onnn! Fucking shit! Fucking shit!" He couldn't stand it any-more. He put a hand over his face and sobbed. "I have to go, I have to go . . ." The phone kept buzzing. And buzzing. He screamed, tore it out of his pocket, rearing back to throw it against the wall. He stopped. The caller ID said GRACE.

"Grace?"

She was crying. "Why didn't you call me, you son of a bitch! What do you think I've been doing all this time? I've been waiting to hear from you! Why didn't you call me? What's wrong with you?"

"I'm an idiot," he breathed.

"Yes, you are. Goddamn you, Isaiah!"

"Yes, goddamn me."

They were silent a moment. In a small voice she said, "How are you?"

"I'm okay, I'm fine." Saying I miss you seemed so obvious it was moronic. She told him about living with Deronda and working at the food truck and how it was great and how much she loved Janeel. She sounded like she was holding something back. She choked up.

"I have my own show, Isaiah. Just me and

nobody else." He felt her pride, her relief, her happiness.

His voice cracked. "That's amazing . . . I'm so . . . I'm so happy for . . ." His words were so inadequate he was ashamed of them. He could feel Grace beaming through the phone, and he hoped she could feel him too. She was in Ojai for the opening. She'd be there a day and take off the next morning.

"I can't wait!" she said.

"Me either."

He decided not to tell her about the PTSD or Billy and Ava or William Crowe and Sheriff Cannon. He talked about the drive here. The forest, the mountains, Lake Tahoe, Rush Creek, the decision to stop at Coronado Springs, the Ortegas and their daughters.

"I'm not going to be IQ anymore. I'm done," he said.

"I'm so glad! Oh, my God, I've been waiting so long to hear that." A pause, then, "You're not okay, are you?"

"No, I'm good. I'm fine."

"No, you're not. I can hear it in your voice. Something's wrong, I know it is. You're in danger, aren't you? You're either chasing someone or they're chasing you. If you don't want to be IQ anymore, you're off to a terrible start." He had no answer. She added, "If you get killed before I see you I'll kill you again."

"I'll help you," he said.

There was silence instead of I love yous. They said their goodbyes and the call ended. He sat down. The kitchen felt empty, like people had been there and now they were gone. He should have told her not to come. He had some time. She was leaving for Coronado Springs the day after tomorrow. If Crowe and Warren hadn't left or been arrested by then, he'd meet Grace somewhere else, Tahoe maybe. He grinned. He was going to see her! Be with her! He was thirsty. His throat was dry from screaming.

Isaiah's garage was dim and cool, milky windows, low ceiling, smelling of dust, concrete and cardboard. Billy was lying on the cot, talking to Gretta on the phone. She'd called ten times so he finally answered.

"Are you all right?" she said.

"Yeah, I'm fine."

"Tell me where you are, and I'll pick you up." Billy could hear it plain as day. It was the last thing she wanted to do.

"No, I'm busy," he said. Gretta breathed a

familiar sigh, equal parts disappointment, resentment and exasperation. They had an unwritten rule. Billy didn't talk about what he was doing, thinking or believing, and his mother didn't ask.

"You have to go back to the hospital," Gretta said. This isn't good for you. Your stress level is probably sky-high and you know what happens —"

"Yes, I know what happens," Billy said, his voice hardening.

"The sheriff is looking for you. He called me."

"I don't care, Mom. What I'm doing is important and I'm sorry if I make you look bad in front of the whole town."

"I said that once Billy, and I was upset," Gretta said, Billy noting she didn't add *I didn't mean it* or *I'm sorry.* Silence and another sigh. "I don't know what to say," she said.

"Yeah, me neither," Billy said, and he ended the call. It was pointless trying to mend fences. The bond between them was too far gone. All they did was fight because it was all about winning the argument, not coming together. There was nothing left but contempt. He was supposed to go camping with Gretta and Irene, do the happy family thing. That wasn't going to happen.

Gretta was right about the stress, though. It was spilling over the dam and roaring down the riverbed. He closed his eyes and tried to even out his breathing. *Easy, Billy, come on, stay in control, stay in control, you're all right, everything is fine.*

"Billy?" a voice said. It was Ava. He scrambled off the cot.

"Holy shit."

"Yeah," she said with a smile. "Holy shit."

Ava was no longer radiant. Everything about her was weary and tense and underneath it all, a scalding hatred that clouded her eyes and banished happiness forever. *You're going to come through for her no matter what, Billy.* She walked over and hugged him and cried into his shoulder. All the years you dreamed about her, and here she was with her arms around you. When, if ever, did your dreams really come true?

Their first conversation was more awkward pauses and perfunctory questions than anything else. What have you been doing? Are you working now? Do you remember so and so? Billy said he was a student at Golden State University. He was home on semester break. He said that he worked as a lab assistant in a genetics research program. Ava seemed uncomfortable, restless, nodding frequently. It was hard talking in a garage so they went outside and sat on two white plastic chairs.

"Thank you for everything, Billy." She put her hand on his. Aside from his burning face and thumping heart, all he could feel was her skin on his. "Before we get into this, I know about your problems."

"Oh, that," he said, pawing the air. "It's not as bad as they make it out to be." He'd never been as humiliated as he was right now. Not only did she know his pitiful history, he'd lied about it.

"I don't care, Billy. I really don't," Ava said. "I know what kind of a person you are and that's all that matters."

He got up and turned away from her, his fists clenched at his sides. "God, I'm such a loser!"

She was suddenly annoyed. "Billy, one of the things I really don't like is when somebody feels sorry for themselves."

"I'm not." He sulked.

She took a deep, preparatory breath. "This thing we're doing? I'm going to go on by myself." He couldn't believe it. He was as hurt as he was outraged.

"Go on by yourself? You can't!"

"You're a liability, Billy. The police are looking for you."

"Who told you?" Billy said, angrily. "Isaiah?"

"It was on the radio."

"Shit."

Ava went on. "Isaiah made me call Cannon. I told him about Crowe, but he didn't believe me. I think he's preoccupied looking for you. If we're together, I'll be caught too. I can't let that happen. Do you understand?"

"Sure I do." He backed away from her. "The nutcase from Schizo Central might go bananas and mess things up. Well, go on then! Do what you want!"

He stormed away, heading for the trees. There was a picket fence between the garage and the next house over. He caught a glimpse of two men standing still, like a freeze frame, like they were caught off guard. Ordinarily, he would have stopped and questioned them, but he was too pissed off. He kept going and felt the temperature change as the dark canopy of trees fell over him.

"Who am I anyway?" he muttered. "I only brought her into it in the first place. She'd be nowhere without me. She'd be back in Sacramento doing nothing, that's what." He heard her call out.

"Billy, wait!" She was coming after him. Serves her right. He slowed his pace.

Isaiah was at his kitchen window, drinking a glass of water. The lost keys seemed silly now. He was going to see Grace. The first thing he had to do was get Billy and Ava the fuck out of here. Then he had to clean up the place, get some new bedding, fill the fridge with her favorite foods, and detail the Mustang. He saw Billy in the yard, pissed off, charging into the woods, Ava going after him. What a mess. Their mess. He was done.

Then two men appeared from the neighboring yard. They kicked and stomped their way over the picket fence, walking fast and stiff legged, like running would be too obvious. The bigger one had a big knife in a sheath and a gun. Isaiah recognized him from his mugshot. It was Crowe. The second man had an identical knife. They were excited, eager, laughing as they disappeared into the woods.

Isaiah raced into the living room and grabbed the collapsible baton off the coffee table. Then he ran out of the house and into the woods. He stopped. There was a path that forked right and left. Everybody who lived on the street used the path as a shortcut; to picnic spots, drinking spots, places to make out, or just for a walk in the woods. There were a lot of footprints. He cupped his hands over his mouth and shouted as loud as he could. "Billy! Ava! Crowe's here! Run!" He shouted it several times, but there was no way to know if they'd heard him. *Shut up and go to work, Isaiah.*

Crowe and Warren started off running, but neither of them were in shape and the altitude here was like outer space. After the first forty yards they were heaving with their hands on their knees. They heard the black guy shouting.

"Who's that?" Warren said. He thought a moment and glared. "You didn't tell me about him, did you, you asshole?"

"One of us has to go back for him," Crowe said between gasps.

"You," Warren said, and before Crowe could react, Warren went after the couple, calling over his shoulder, "You're bigger and you've got a gun."

There was a time during the Walczak case when reading footprints would have been very useful. Since then, Isaiah had studied up on the subject, like he always did when there was something relevant to learn.

Crowe and his friend would be moving the fastest. They were the most likely to leave traces that would indicate direction. Unfortunately, most of the ground was covered with dry pine needles that wouldn't take a print. There were only patches of dirt. He'd stick to those.

Arbitrarily, Isaiah went left and began "side heading," turning his head sideways and low to the ground. The bottom eye scans the ground. The top eye sees a few feet ahead. Ridges and shadows are more visible this way. When you're running, your feet scuff the ground, and dirt is thrown out of your tracks. Sometimes you can see the scuffs, if they're reasonably fresh. But the dirt patches were dry, and there were dozens of prints going in both directions. Isaiah moved with agonizing slowness, on his hands and knees, his head three inches above the ground and angled sideways. *Patience, Isaiah.* Inch by inch, he continued. It was hot, his neck hurt. His face was so close to the ground he was inhaling dirt. He kept stopping to wipe the sweat out of his eyes. He had to stay focused and concentrate or the kids would most certainly die. But how far should he go before he tried the other path? His neck was cramping. *Focus, Isaiah, focus.*

He saw what might be a fresh track. He stood up and looked down on it. Yes, it was fresh. Part of the sole pattern was still there. It was a sneaker. Both men were wearing sneakers. Did it belong to Crowe, his friend or someone else? If the print was complete, it would be about eleven inches in length, and that translated into a size ten and a half shoe. The corresponding heights ranged from five-ten to six-two. Crowe was six-two. His friend was shorter, but the print fell within the parameters. The ball of the foot was the deepest. An indication that the person was running. Isaiah took off.

Warren was ready to drop. He wasn't walking so much as he was staggering. He was light-headed, and his lungs sounded like worn-out brakes. He stopped. He saw them. The boy and the girl. They were forty, fifty yards ahead, talking, no idea he was there. The girl was the one he'd seen at the motel. Juicy, just like Crowe had said. He wondered how to do this. He couldn't run up on them, he could barely walk, and they'd hear him long before he got there. It was hard to think when you could hardly fucking breathe. Something came to him. They were too far away to shout at. He had to keep going.

■ ■ ■ ■

Isaiah trotted along the path, his breathing steady. He'd adapted to the altitude. He was scared, expecting at any moment to see Billy and Ava lying in the dirt, cut to pieces, Crowe and his buddy standing over their bodies, waving their bloody knives. He hoped he'd read the prints right. He smelled pine needles, tree resin and dust. Lots of dust motes were hanging in the air. He was going in the right direction.

This section of the trail was slightly downhill. He sped up, grateful for the help. He caught another smell as he approached the next bend. It was human. It was sweat. Someone was on the other side of the bend. He tried to stop, but he was going too fast. He slipped in the dirt, his feet going out from under him just as the blade of a big knife sliced through the space he'd just vacated.

"Godammit!" Crowe shouted.

Isaiah fell on his butt, scrambled to his feet and reached for the baton. He'd dropped it. Crowe came toward him. He was much bigger in person, his hair plastered to his wide forehead, breathing in huffs, his thick lips dry and chapped, his pupils filling the whole eye. He looked like a mutant hyena.

"Forget something?" Crowe said. He kicked the baton away. The Bowie was in its sheath. He raised a gun. "Before I kill you, who are you? What do you want?"

"I'm nobody," Isaiah said. "I just want to keep those kids out of harm's way. That's all. Nothing else."

"Do you know who I am?"

"I know you've got a gun and a knife. Other than that, nothing."

Crowe gestured. "Down there." Off the trail, maybe thirty yards away, was a gulley. He grinned. "A good place to hide your body."

CHAPTER TWENTY-ONE:
BE COOL, ISAIAH

Billy and Ava turned around and headed back to Isaiah's house, Billy slowing the pace, drawing it out.

"I'm not going back to the hospital, Ava," he said. "I can't. I won't."

"Then what? Be a fugitive? I mean, I can't stop you. It's your choice, but eventually they'll catch you."

"I want to help you get Crowe."

"You already have, Billy. You're making this harder."

The words slipped out before he could stop them. "I want to be with you." There was an awful silence. "Never mind," he mumbled.

She put her hand on his shoulder. "It's okay, Billy. Let's talk about it later, okay?"

A man was lurching toward them. "Help, I need help." His hair was greasy, his whole body was weeping sweat. His chest going in and out like he was sucking air through a

341

straw. His shirt was open. His ribs and clavicle stuck out.

"Are you okay?" Ava said. She started to move toward him, but Billy grabbed her arm. His innate suspicion was on high alert. What was this guy doing out here? If he needed help why was he going farther into the woods?

"What's the matter?" Billy said.

"I'm sick, I'm really sick," the man wheezed.

"Sick how?"

"I don't know, I'm just sick."

"You don't know how you're sick?" Billy said. He noticed the tattoos on the man's arms; crude, thick lines, little detail. Prison tats.

"I'm just sick, okay? I'm fucking sick!" the man said. "I need help, okay?" Embarrassed, Ava tugged on Billy's sleeve.

"Billy, I think he's really sick."

"See?" the man said. "Listen to your girlfriend."

This guy is bullshitting, Billy thought. "If you need help you should go back in the other direction. You know, where the people are?"

"Are you gonna help me or not?" the man said, his expression darkening.

"Help you how?" Billy said. "We're not

doctors, and we don't have any water. Like I said, go back the way you came." The man took a few steps forward. Billy backed up, taking Ava's elbow and pulling her with him. "Come on, Ava, something weird is happening."

The man's face was crinkling and buckling. He looked like an invisible hand was crushing his head like a soda can. His teeth looked loose, his gums were black. He slipped his hand behind him.

"He's got a weapon, Ava! Run!" Billy shouted. She raced off. The man started after her, but Billy didn't move. The man had a knife. It was big and shiny. Billy recognized the shape. A Bowie.

"I'm gonna cut your goddamn head off," the man said.

AMSAK's victims were killed with a Bowie. That couldn't be a coincidence. This guy and Crowe were buds. "Oh, I get it now," Billy said. "You were the copycat, weren't you? You're Crowe's partner." The man started forward, waving the blade back and forth. Billy retreated, keeping the same distance between them. He wanted Ava to get well away. The man hawked up a loogie and spit. It landed on his shoe.

"Fuck," he said. Billy heard Ava coming up behind him.

"Are you okay?" she said.

"Go back, Ava. This asshole has got a knife!" Billy shouted. "Hurry, get out of here!" She was beside Billy now. She saw the Bowie knife. Her eyes narrowed. She didn't budge.

"Who is he?" she said.

"Crowe's partner."

"Then he killed Hannah too."

The man was reeling. "I'm going to get you. I'm going to slit you down the middle."

Ava was expressionless, save for her eyes, so focused and concentrated Billy wondered why the man didn't detonate. The rest of her was like the bow of a battleship, cutting through a heavy sea, impenetrable, unforgiving and coming right at your shitty little rowboat. She started toward the man.

"Ava?" Billy said. He took her arm, but she shrugged him off.

"Stay out of this." She went closer until she was a body's length away from the man. He lunged with the knife. Billy cried out, but Ava dodged away, stirring up a haze of dust.

"Ava, please don't do this!" Billy said.

She circled around the man, nodding, still expressionless, still the battleship. The man turned with her.

"Ava, come on, I'm begging you!" Billy

pleaded.

"I said stay out of it, Billy!"

Ava kept circling. The man couldn't keep her in front of him.

"Stay still, goddammit!" Clumsily, he charged.

"Watch it, Ava!" Billy shouted. Deftly, Ava stepped aside.

"Shut up, Billy."

The man charged twice more but didn't come close. The air was cloudy with dust, the sun bright and hard. Ava was tight but under control. Her breathing was harsh but even. The man was drooling and making animal sounds.

"You bitch. I'm gonna get you!" he blubbered. He gathered what was left of himself and gave it one more try, plodding toward her, screaming and holding the knife like he was giving her change. She backed up, backed up, letting him build up speed. He was almost on top of her, when she quickly stepped aside, the man going past her, tripping over a tree root and smashing headfirst into a stump. There was an ugly *thud,* the knife flying away. Billy winced. The man curled up like a mealworm, groaning, both hands on his head.

Ava stood over him. "You killed my sister, didn't you? You killed Hannah."

"No! No! It was Crowe! He did everything!"

"And where were you?" Ava said. "Watching? Is that what you did? You watched my sister die?" She fell to her knees beside him. "Did you hear me? I said, *did you watch my sister die?*"

"You're too close to him, Ava. Get back!" Billy said. She ignored him and pried one of the man's hands loose. "You killed her too, didn't you?"

The man's groans were mixed with sobs, his face caked with sweat and mud and blood. He shook his head. "No, no, no . . ." Ava grabbed a bunch of his hair, steadied him, then scooped up a handful of dirt and shoved it in his mouth. It was more shocking than a gunshot. The man thrashed, choked, sitting up to spit and claw the muck out of his mouth. He was hysterical, making strangling sounds and coughing violently. Ava stood up and searched around with her eyes.

"What are you looking for?" Billy asked. She picked up the Bowie knife. "No, Ava!" She gave him a look so heated he stepped back two paces. She stood over the man and glowered down at him. Her teeth were bared, her face a mess of sweat, dirt and rage, her eyes blazing like road flares. She nudged him with her foot.

"Look at me," she said. "I said look at me!" The man had curled up again, his filthy hands over his face. He peered up at her between his fingers. "Do I look familiar?" she said.

"What? I don't know."

"You don't know? That's funny. Because Hannah and I are twins. I loved her. Hannah was the best thing in the world and you and Crowe murdered her!"

"No, no, I swear I didn't. Crowe did everything!"

"Liar!"

The man turned over on his stomach and started to crawl away. She fell on him, her knee in his back, pinning him to the ground. He grunted, the wind knocked out of him. She hit him viciously with the heavy butt of the knife. "Tell me what you did!" she snarled. He cried out but didn't speak. She hit him again.

"Stop! Please stop!" he sobbed.

"I'm going to ask you one more time, and if you tell me the truth, I'll be satisfied and let you go."

"You will?" he croaked.

"Yes, I will." The man didn't reply, making a raspy *uhhhh* with every breath. "I meant what I said," Ava said, reassuringly.

She put the point of the knife in his ear. "But if you lie to me . . ."

"Okay, I did it," the man said. "I did it with Crowe." Ava's eyes turned black. Her nostrils flared, the slack snapped out of her body, all quivering sinew and unleashed fury. She screamed and raised the knife over her head with two hands.

"Ava, don't!" Billy shouted. Ava hesitated, shaking, savage. "Ava, please!" She hesitated, then stood and threw the knife away. The man had passed out. A quiet fell, the kind you only hear in the forest, where every shifting breeze, creaking branch and humming insect played a symphony of peace. Ava stood there, motionless. Billy tried to hug her, but she wrested herself away and walked off down the path.

Isaiah slogged through the trees toward the gulley, Crowe behind him with the gun. "How's it feel, huh?" the killer said. "Knowing you're gonna die? Most people cry and scream and beg. What are you, a tough guy? We'll see about that." Isaiah wanted to provoke him, make him mad. Make him use the knife.

"All those women you killed," he said. "Takes a big man to do something like that. Takes a lot of courage."

"If I were you, I'd shut up," Crowe said.

Serial killers define themselves by their fantasies. *No one can stop you, you're too smart, too powerful. The whole world is afraid of you. You are the king, master of all you see. Bow down, motherfuckers.* So they don't really like it when you challenge that fantasy. It yanks them back to reality and calls them out as losers and cowards who slaughter the helpless. They have to prove you wrong. They have to preserve the fantasy. If they don't, they are what you say they are.

"Proud of being a murderer? A filthy shit people think is garbage?" Isaiah said.

"I'm gonna fuck you up so bad you'll be crying for Mama," Crowe growled.

"You're about to shoot me in the back, aren't you?" Isaiah stopped and turned around to face him. "You don't have the guts to go man to man. You're a pussy, Crowe. You couldn't hurt me with that knife if I was blindfolded." Crowe's grip tightened on the gun, a fluttering tic under his eye. *He's gonna shoot you, Isaiah. He's going to fucking shoot you!*

"I'm telling you, asshole," Crowe snarled. "Shut your mouth."

Isaiah gestured like he was helping Crowe park. "Come on, you coward. Do something." Crowe raised the gun and aimed it at Isaiah's face. *He's going to shoot you, he's going to blow your fucking head off!* "What's the problem? Afraid to use that big bad knife? Good thing for you. I'd take it away and jam it down your throat."

"Oh, you think so?" Crowe said. Veins were popping out on his forehead, his sweat like three coats of shellac. Isaiah had seen a lot of terrifying expressions before, but Crowe's was an abomination, the semblance of a human face after the blowflies had gone, grotesque and decaying, sockets for eyes, hate pouring from the hollows.

"If you're afraid to use it, you might as well throw it away," Isaiah said.

"I'm not afraid of anything," Crowe said.

"Except me."

Crowe jammed the gun in his belt and slowly drew the Bowie. You knew it was deadly sharp. You knew its heft would cut deep and go all the way to your spine. Crowe tested the point with his fingertip.

"Let's go," he said. He came forward, smiling, knees bent, the knife in front of him. Isaiah backed away, considering his next move. He knew about knife fighting. Ari, his Krav Maga teacher, had taught him. You have to be close in to stab somebody, the length of your arm, and ironically, Isaiah needed Crowe that close to defend himself.

Wait for an attack and you were done for. You had to act preemptively, a split second before your opponent makes his move. Isaiah knew the gulley was close behind him. He couldn't see it, he had to sense it. He took smaller and smaller steps. He felt the ground sloping and stopped. It wasn't more than a foot behind him. The distance between himself and Crowe was closing, the killer's grin more gruesome than the blade.

"Well, shithead," Isaiah said, "what are you waiting for?"

Crowe screamed and came forward, his feet wide apart, shifting his shoulders, drawing his elbow back to thrust the knife forward. In the same instant, Isaiah stepped in to him, his left hand shooting out, grabbing Crowe at the crook of his elbow, trapping the knife against his side. Almost simultaneously, he threw a right that hit Crowe in the throat. Crowe choked and gagged. He staggered sideways and fell into the brush. He thrashed and floundered, trying to get up and draw the gun out at the same time. Isaiah raced away, Crowe shooting at him, BLAM! BLAM! BLAM! bullets cutting branches as he wove through the trees.

He met Ava and Billy on the path. They

351

exchanged quick stories and hurried back to the house. Nobody said anything until they were in Isaiah's kitchen, drinking water and breathing hard. He didn't think the killers would come back. They were too beat up.

"You have to call Cannon," he said.

"We're not exactly credible," Billy said. Isaiah shook his head disgustedly. He patted his pockets for his phone. He'd left it on the breakfast table.

"So the gang's all here," Cannon said as he came in the front door. Billy and Ava were sitting on the sofa looking at their knees. "What's up, Billy boy? I should have known you'd be here, and you must be the young lady who called me and told me Crowe was here in Coronado Springs."

"I told you the truth. He's here," she said.

"No, he's not," the sheriff said. "I called Crowe's parole officer and he told me Crowe was in Sacramento right where he was supposed to be. Saw him in person."

"Crowe and his buddy tried to kill us," Billy said.

"Be quiet, Billy, I've had enough of you," Cannon snapped. He looked at Isaiah. "I did a search on you, Mr. Quintabe. You're supposedly a smart guy and quite the detective. For somebody they call IQ, I'm surprised you got involved with these two knuckleheads."

"You'll just have to see," Isaiah said. The three of them led Cannon into the woods and along the path, Isaiah explaining what happened. They reached the gulley, but there were no footprints, no scuffs in the dirt, the pine needles were undisturbed, the surrounding foliage looked like surrounding foliage.

"I don't see anything to indicate a knife fight happened here," Cannon said. "I don't see anything at all."

"They cleaned up," Isaiah said.

"Is this after the fight or before?" Cannon sneered. Isaiah didn't say anything. Without evidence, what would be the use? They tried to find the spot where the other man had attacked Billy and Ava, but everything looked like everything else. The path was the path, the trees were the trees. They couldn't find the man's knife or any blood on the ground.

"Okay, that's enough," Cannon said.

When they got back to the house, Cannon said, "You're all under arrest for lying to a police officer and filing a false report."

"But —" Ava began.

"Shut your mouth, young lady, and don't open it again until I tell you to. I'm disappointed in you, Mr. Quintabe. I don't know what you're up to, but this is pretty stupid for a guy they call IQ." Cannon used snap ties to cuff their hands behind their backs. He ushered them to his SUV. He took their belongings, put them in paper bags and tossed them on the passenger seat.

Cannon drove, the prisoners squeezed together in the backseat. The doors were locked and the meshed partition was up, but not all the way. The air-conditioning, Isaiah thought. The sheriff is letting the cool air through. He doesn't want you to die before he locks you up.

They had gone less than a mile when Cannon said, "Oh, hell." A traffic accident. A pickup had T-boned another car. A third car had swerved to miss them, run over the curb and smashed into a chain-link fence. People were hurt. Cannon radioed the dispatcher and said he was on the scene. He stopped the car but kept the engine running. "Don't leave, kiddies." He got out and and walked toward the accident, talking on his radio.

"I'm sorry about this, Isaiah. I really am," Billy said.

"Me too. We really screwed things up," Ava said.

"The best thing you can do is shut up so I don't kill you right now," Isaiah said. The engine idled, the air-conditioning droned steadily. Billy coughed. Ava cleared her throat.

Isaiah couldn't believe it. He'd come all this way to get locked up, charged with felonies and sent to prison with a bunch of guys he'd sent there. A wave of paralyzing hopelessness washed over him. The PTSD had won. He would never be himself again. He would be nothing. He would be — *Snap out of it, asshole. Grace is coming.* He had to escape, call her and warn her off. He took a careful look around the car. He looked at Ava. She was long-limbed and Olive Oyl skinny. What did she weigh, a buck-oh-five? The partition had been lowered, but the gap was a little more than a foot.

"Ava, do you think you can get through there?" Isaiah said.

She stared at the partition a moment. "Let's find out." She got her head and shoulder through the opening, tearing a button off her shirt. That was the hard part. The rest was wriggling like a salamander and squeezing herself through.

"Way to go," Billy said.

It took a lot of grunting and maneuvering, but she got her back turned to the passenger-side door and opened it. She nearly fell out but righted herself. She went around to the driver's-side door. Again, with her back turned, she found the switch that unlocked the back doors. Isaiah and Billy scootched out. They took the paper bags that held their belongings and ran for the guest house.

They had to get the snap ties off. Isaiah kept his toolbox in the garage. It was on the floor. He had to sit with his back to it, open it and, with directions from Ava, find the wire cutter. Then he stood back to back with Billy. Ava directed Isaiah's hands until the wire cutter found Billy's snap tie. Isaiah snipped them off. Billy freed Isaiah and Ava.

"We've got to get moving," Isaiah said. "Cannon might be on his way right now." They hurried out to their cars. They heard a siren, getting closer and louder. Ava and Billy drove off in Ava's car. Isaiah got in the Mustang and sped away.

He drove out of town a ways and then onto a logging trail he'd scouted before, driving slow, wincing every time the oil pan scraped against the ground. He came to a clearing and parked. He rested and drank some water. He got his phone out to call Grace and stopped. It was the biker couple he saw about the dog.

"Be cool, Isaiah," Ned said. He had a gun and so did Cherry.

"Move it. And don't make me shoot you," she said.

CHAPTER TWENTY-TWO:
THE BLACKULA OF EAST LONG BEACH

Brad had few if any scruples. He routinely took credit for work done by others, for which he was universally despised. What he couldn't stand was being shown up, whether in public or in private. If the quality of someone else's work exceeded his own, he was outraged. If they did something noteworthy before he did, he went apeshit, as if it were a personal insult, a measurement of his own competence and abilities. His lack of character or any semblance of ethics was an industry joke, an anecdote to tell over lunch, passed from one person to another until it was common knowledge. *Do you know he . . . I heard he . . . I'm not kidding, he actually . . . No shit? That really happened? How does he get away with it? Why does management stick with him? Are they blind?*

Management stuck with Brad because he was good with clients. He smoothed, appeased, promised and bent reality to suit whatever the client wanted to hear. He also lied with impunity. Brad was consistent with management's image of a tough, take-no-prisoners executive who got shit done. People said Brad didn't speak softly. He carried a big stick and a spare. But he got results. His creative teams produced great work whether they were credited or not.

Brad was well aware of his reputation. He alternately wore it as a badge or hid it away, depending upon the circumstances. Sometimes he passed over his ruthlessness as a necessary attitude for success. But in his rare reflective moments, he knew his personality was a reflection of his shitty past. Day to day, it didn't seem to matter. Like everybody, his past was intertwined with his present so seamlessly it was all one flow. You were you and that was all.

The same people were at the meeting. Brad was confident. Whatever Stimson's scam was, he couldn't possibly pull it off twice. Sixty-second commercials took weeks to come together. The room was buzzing, everyone eager to see what the doofus came up with. Even Walsh seemed excited. Brad heard people were calling Stimson "Don," after the Don Draper character in *Mad Men*. Ridiculous. And the amazing thing was, nobody was suspicious. They were blinded because they wanted that asshole to succeed. After the Skechers ad, they said Stimson was reborn, that this was his comeback, that he was returning to his old self again. Bullshit, Brad thought. Even when Stimson was his "old self" he'd never done anything remotely as good as the Skechers ad.

The doofus came in, carrying a stack of storyboards. Storyboards? This was prehistoric, Brad thought. Didn't the putz have a computer? Everyone smiled and greeted him. He was embarrassed, red-faced, hunching his shoulders.

"Okay, let's get right to it," Brad said. "What have you got, Stimson?"

"Uh, I'm going to put these down in order. There are a lot of them." People got up from the table, and Stimson laid down the storyboards going from left to right, everyone lining up to see them in the correct order. Brad watched. The staff reacted to the first ones with puzzlement, and as they moved along, there were curious smiles, and when they reached the end they looked — what would you call it? Surprised, yes, but something else. They were moved.

What was going on? Brad thought. He was at the end of the line with Walsh. As they went from one storyboard to the next, Brad pitched the commercial to himself.

Point of view. The screen is dark. We hear footsteps walking over rough ground, a light breeze is blowing, leaves are rustling. The footsteps stop, and suddenly, something lifts and there's light! Blue sky, puffy white clouds and shimmering aspens. It's a gorgeous day! Another angle. A hawk is perched on a falconry glove, shaking its head, a man's weathered hand just removing its hood. The same hand unties the tether around the hawk's leg. The man, nearly choked with emotion, says, "Okay, old friend. I'll miss you." The man lifts the glove and the hawk takes off, the man shouting in a trembling voice, "Go boy! Go! Go! Go!" The hawk soars. We can feel its exuberance and power as it glides effortlessly over pristine forests, sparkling lakes and majestic mountains. And as it disappears into a breathtaking sunset, the graphic:

FLY FREE
Bayer Aspirin
Reduces the risk of stroke by 22%

The room was nearly silent. Newberg said, "It's beautiful, Stimson." And everyone burst out talking, their praise effusive, shaking their heads as if to say, whoda thunk it? That sly dog. He's been waiting in the

361

weeds to fool us all. Walsh was staring at the last board. He touched it with his finger. He too was moved.

"Well done, Stimson. Well done indeed," he said.

"Thank you, Ted. I really appreciate you saying that."

Walsh said quietly to Brad. "Another one of your ideas?" Brad shrugged modestly.

"I guess so. I don't like to take credit in front of the staff. Listen, about Stimson's pension. I still think —"

"Renew his contract," Walsh said, and he left. Brad could barely suppress the torrent of outrage churning in his guts or the need to slap the shit out of Stimson. The room was clearing.

"Stay, Stimson," Brad said. They were the only ones left. Stimson didn't seem happy or smug, like he should be for pulling this bullshit off twice and making a fool out of him. "We're renewing your contract," Brad said. "Congratulations. I guess you'll be getting that Winnebago after all."

"That's great," Stimson said, almost inaudibly. Still, no happiness. What an oddball. "Thank you," he said. Brad gave him a look and stalked out of the room.

Brad had just entered his office when Walsh

called. Strange. They were sitting next to each other five minutes ago. Walsh said a situation had arisen, an emergency. He explained and added, "This is a top priority, Brad. You and Stimson get on this immediately. Don't let me down. I'll be very disappointed if you do." The call ended.

Brad was stunned. Walsh saw them as a team! The old geezer had gotten it in his head that they'd come up with the Skechers and Bayer ads together. Okay, maybe it was because he took credit for the ideas, but that was irrelevant at this point. Walsh's tone was as alarming as it was clear. *If we lose this account, I'm not taking the blame. Do you understand, Brad?* His job is at risk. Can you believe it? After what he'd done for the company? He took the autographed baseball out of its box and turned it around in his hand. Of all the great pitchers in the history of the major leagues, only one had thrown two no-hitters back to back. Johnny Vander Meer in 1938. Not Nolan Ryan, Pedro Martínez, Randy Johnson, Sandy Koufax or anybody else. Three in a row? Everybody in baseball, past and present, agreed that three in a row would never happen. But it had to, Brad thought. Or you're done.

Stimson rode up in the elevator. Brad had

called him up to his office. The anxiety was killing him. He never imagined this arrangement with Dodson would morph into a bizarre version of Cyrano de Bergerac. Dodson was elevating Stimson's career, a career he didn't want and wanted out of. Now he was the Golden Boy when all he wanted was to drive down the highway with Marge in a Winnebago, Brad in the rearview mirror giving him the finger. What could that mean little prick want now? The receptionist told him to go in.

"There's an emergency, Stimson," Brad said. "BeHeard is a major company and our biggest client. As you know, or maybe you don't, they create software programs for marketing, financial management, automation, resource deployment, retention tools and a number of consumer products. The bad news is, BeHeard may be leaving us and taking their business to Ogilvy. The loss would be devastating."

"That's too bad," Stimson mumbled pointlessly. Brad breathed a deep sigh and went on.

"You have to come up with a killer campaign," he said, almost adding *you and Lebron.*

"But I just did the Bayer commercial,"

Stimson said.

"Doesn't matter. The company needs you so you'll do it."

"What's the product?"

"Voice-to-text software."

"Voice-to-text software? But it's —"

"Not sexy, I know," Brad said. "People use it primarily for dictation — and other things too, emails, texts, keeping notes. Technologically, BeHeard is marginally better than its competitors, but numbers won't help us here. All the programs do virtually the same things. And they're boring."

"Voice to text," Stimson said distantly. It was the assignment nobody wanted. Voice to text was a simple product everyone knew about. There was nothing to add, no image to project, no advanced features to laud. It was like advertising flowerpots or manila envelopes.

"We need a hook," Brad continued. "We need warmth, emotion, something human. The relevancy factor goes without saying."

"Warmth, emotion and relevance," Stimson said blankly.

"I need it on Friday," Brad said, and this time it was true.

"Friday? That makes no sense. How could they possibly expect a presentation on Friday?"

"They don't," Brad replied. "One of my spies tells me Ogilvy is making a presentation to BeHeard on Monday. If we make ours on Friday, we'll beat them to the punch."

"Is anybody else working on it?" Stimson asked.

"Dunheath and Navarro are on vacation, and the other creatives are in critical stages of their own campaigns. A warning, Stimson. If we lose the BeHeard account, I'll have to cut staff. People you know. People that are your friends." Brad couldn't believe he was saying the words. "Is there anything I can do for you?" Stimson seemed more struck by the offer than the assignment.

"Um. No. Thank you."

"That will be all," Brad said. And the putz walked zombie-like out of the room. "This is ridiculous," Brad said aloud. He was actually dependent on the doofus! Can you imagine? Everything you've worked for is riding on that moron. And the worst part? If you get fired, you'll have to listen to your brothers.

Dodson was sitting at Stimson's desk, reading through the BeHeard brief. Stimson was staring at the wall of dirt as if there might be a tunnel he could use to escape. "Voice-

366

to-text software," Dodson said. "What do they expect you to do with that?"

"Something miraculous," Stimson said. "I ran out of miracles when I was born. I know I have no right to ask you this, but could you take a shot at it? I've already had my contract renewed, but if we lose BeHeard, Brad will cut staff. People I know and care about. People I've known for years. Their jobs depend on this commercial." Dodson didn't answer. "I realize I'm really taking advantage of you," Stimson added.

"Don't nobody take advantage of me. I do what I do for my own reasons," Dodson said. "But I'll give it a try."

Cherise was thrilled for her husband. She was overjoyed he was enthusiastic and going to work every day. She'd never seen him like this, except when he was partnered with Isaiah. She wanted to congratulate him, say she was proud him, that she knew he had it in him. But telling him those things would seem condescending, as if she was surprised her husband could handle himself in the mainstream. In truth, she was surprised. In fact, she was blown away. The Skechers ad he'd come up with was smart, clever and funny as hell. Where in the world had he found these new capabilities? His idea for the Bayer commercial was inspired. Of course, she had to seem like she'd known it all along, that this was what she expected. So she kissed him when he went out the door, made sure supper was waiting, even if it was takeout, and listened attentively when he talked.

The family Cherise had always wanted was falling into place. A beautiful child and a husband who was a good provider and a responsible adult. What worried her was the future. She worked at a large law firm and saw it every day. People putting in sixty- to seventy-hour weeks, everything else a distant second or third. Marriage, kids, fun, love. They became obligations, more like chores. *Ah, hell, I forgot her birthday. Ah, hell, the kid's soccer game is in twenty minutes. Ah, hell, it's fucking date night.* Work was more satisfying. The objectives were clear, the methods were tried-and-true. You did it and were done. Home was a morass of grueling relationships and conflicting agendas. Judging by Cherise's superiors, a great career was a four-lane highway to living parallel lives. Is that how the Dodsons would end up? One more married couple going through the motions?

Juanell was brash, impulsive and free-wheeling. He was independent and resentful of authority. Some people thought outside the box. Dodson had no box. Most of the time, he believed he was the smartest person in the room, and most of the time he was wrong, unless you were on the street somewhere. In that context, he was Warren Buffett or Stephen Hawking. There should be a statue of him in the Hustlers Hall of Fame.

Dodson was also loving and fiercely loyal to those he cared about. Other people were a different story. He wasn't helping Stimson because they were friends. He was helping him because it would prove to himself and to his family that he could hang at Apex or anyplace else. She'd been wrong to doubt him. But what worried her most was the day of reckoning. It would be hard, soul-wrenching and a lose-lose for everybody concerned. Whatever happens, Cherise thought, don't break his heart.

Dodson thought all night about the voice-to-text commercial. It was again early morning when the idea came to him. It wouldn't be easy. It would require all his hustling skills plus a few more. He was intimidated, but he made the call.

"I have something to ask you," he said. "It's about work."

"Ask me what?" Gloria said. "Should you blow your nose during a conference call? Scratch your privates when you're talking to your boss? Yell 'fire!' and pass gas when you're in a crowded elevator?"

"Can I come over?" Dodson said meekly.

"To my house? Certainly not."

"You've been to my place."

"I've been to Cherise's place. You just live there."

Swallowing his pride, tail and all, Dodson said, "Gloria, please."

"Did you just say please?" she said in disbelief. "I was wondering which would come first. Death or you being polite."

"It's not for me. It's for Cherise and Micah."

"Well, in that case," Gloria said. "But if you're not here in the next ten minutes I'm not answering the bell. I have better things to do than listen to you talk about —"

"Mister Assault Rifle and Overdose Willy. You told me."

Gloria lived in an apartment two blocks away from the Coffee Cup. She and Verna had been friends for decades. People said Verna got her croissant recipe from Gloria, but Dodson didn't believe it. Nothing that good could have come from the Blackula of East Long Beach.

"Come in," she said sharply. "And don't touch anything." She looked him over and scowled. He was in his street clothes. He should have worn the suit. "The shoot-out is thataway," she said. Her living room had as many hard edges and sharp angles as she did. It was like a storehouse for T-squares, isosceles triangles, armrest covers, and the color brown. Whoever heard of a brown corduroy sectional lined up like a row of cardboard boxes or a brown pillow shaped like an arrowhead?

Gloria also collected things. In the main display case, there were snow globes depicting winter in Vermont and Denmark, a small army of owl, elephant and dog figurines. Delicate teacups from faraway Macy's, a carved wooden bust of MLK, a set of frosted mugs from the A&W Root Beer factory, a President Obama commemorative plate, an etched glass award for Teacher of the Year, three blue ribbons for the best minced pie and a marble statue of Jesus. If it wasn't for the brown motif, it could have been a gift shop on a dying pier.

"May I sit down?" Dodson said.

Gloria thought a moment; apparently this was a difficult decision. She nodded at a plain wooden chair. It was for a child, maybe a foot off the ground. She waited, daring him to stay standing or sit someplace else. He sat down. His knees were nearly in his face. Gloria smoothed her dress and sat at the far end of the sectional. She was wearing a brown dress and seemed to blend in with the upholstery. If you closed one eye you almost couldn't see her. "Now, what is it you want, Juanell? And please be brief. Your voice is very annoying."

Dodson explained his problem and what he wanted from her. Flames of outrage leaped from his mother-in-law's eyes. She jumped to her feet.

"Get out!" she yelled. "Don't say anything, just go! I have never heard such a vile suggestion in my life!"

"Vile?" he said, shocked. "Who said anything about vile?"

"Have you no sense of propriety? Of common decency? If Cherise doesn't divorce you, I'll hang Micah out of a window until she does!"

"I have no idea what you're talking about!" Dodson said. He tried to heave himself to his feet, but his legs were cramped. He plunked back down, his center of gravity shifted, and the little chair tipped backward. He fell into the display case and a lifetime's worth of knickknacks came raining down upon him. There was a moment of quiet. Almost everything was broken. Stunned, he lay there amid a thousand pieces of shattered memories. He had a bump on his head where the marble statue of Jesus hit him.

Gloria was horrified, her hands out in supplication. Perhaps she was beseeching Jesus, who was presently on the floor and unable to help. She kept swallowing and blinking, her head was trembling sideways. She couldn't seem to focus her eyes, her vision split between a cracked root-beer mug and Dodson's throat.

Gloria was moving her mouth, trying to say get out. He decided not to wait for a complete sentence and sprinted the hell out of there. He was nearly at the elevator when he heard a terrifying screech, and Our Lord and Savior's left arm and shoulder flew past him so close it put a skid mark on his haircut and broke a mirror at the end of the hall.

Dodson was home. He was sitting on the sofa, still in shock. He wanted to sit at the breakfast table, but it had become the dunking chair at a carnival or a coach seat on a thirty-two-hour non-direct flight to Ukraine. Cherise was pacing, talking to Gloria on the phone.

"Vile?" Cherise said. "What in the world are you talking about?" She stopped and glared at Dodson. "Did you say you wanted to videotape my mother naked?"

Dodson's eyes widened to the width of his forehead. "I never said anything like that in my entire life! I've never even thought about it." And then he did, a flash image so horrifying he wanted to blind himself. "She's crazy!" he shouted. "She's out of her damn mind!"

"Shush, Juanell," Cherise said. "Mama, Mama, please stop, he didn't mean anything of the — no, no, this has nothing to do with your — I realize they're not where they used to be but — yes, I remember, you were Miss Earl's Auto Shop of 1955 but — yes, I know you still have the sash and I know Josiah spilled Thunderbird on it but that doesn't — Mama, will you *please listen*!" A pause.

"The video is for a commercial," Cherise said. "Part of Dodson's work. You must have misheard him, no nudity is involved — yes, you can wear a fur coat and a ski mask if it will make you feel better. You want him there in ten minutes? What's that? I'm sorry, Mama, but who is Overdose Willy?"

The knickknack genocide had been partially cleaned up. Jesus's head sat accusingly on the mantel. Dodson would have sworn the Son of God was watching him. Gloria managed to restrain herself from killing him, probably because the Son of God was watching her too. Dodson explained what he wanted and why. She was surprisingly cooperative. Afterward, she seemed glad to have done it. It was upsetting, she said, but upset was a way to never forget.

He called Grace.

"Technical support. How may I help you?"

"I need you to edit a video."

CHAPTER TWENTY-THREE: I WILL KILL THE JUDGE WITH MY SHOE

There was a swing set in Deronda's back-yard. Grace was pushing Janeel higher and higher, the boy happy like only kids can be. She couldn't wait to get into court tomorrow. See Bobby's expression when the judge saw Sandra's mugshot and criminal record. She thought about what her lawyer would say: *Your Honor, Mr. James's girlfriend is a junkie and he supplies her with heroin. Said girlfriend is also a self-employed ho and used to be Spoon's favorite porn star, Wanda Wonder Lips. I submit this box cover to the court as Exhibit 1A, and please note, Your Honor, the video is titled* Wanda Wonder Lips Does the Philadelphia Eagles.

Deronda was thinking up lines to say like, if you want half of something, Bobby, I'll buy you a donut. Or — why don't you blackmail a car dealer and get half a Toyota? Her phone buzzed. Sandra again. She probably wanted to apologize for her no-show at the Coffee Cup. She was crying.

"Hey, girl," Deronda said. "You okay?"

"No, I'm not okay. I'm fucked up," Sandra sobbed.

"You mean you need a fix?"

"No. I mean I'm fucked up," Sandra said. "It was fake, Deronda. Me and Bobby in the park? All that cuddling and shit? He made me do it. He knew you was gonna take pictures and he wanted you to think we was in love."

This can't be true, Deronda thought. "But why would Bobby have to make you do it? Y'all are together, ain't you?"

"No, we not," Sandra said. "I'm not Bobby's girlfriend, I'm his sister." Deronda almost dropped the phone. Grace saw the change in her. She lifted Janeel out of the swing and came over.

"What's happening?" she said.

"Really, Deronda, I'm so, so sorry. I really am," Sandra said. "I hope it didn't cause nothin' bad —" Deronda ended the call.

"Are you all right?" Grace said.

"Bobby James," Deronda said. "He scammed us. Sandra's not his girlfriend, she's his goddamn sister." Grace recoiled.

"What?"

Ten minutes later, Deronda got a text from Bobby. *Last chance to settle. Meet me*

*in the hallway outside Courtroom 7. 9:45
sharp. Make sure your attorney is there.*

It was later that evening. Deronda was on
the sofa, humming softly and cradling Janeel
in her arms. She was smiling, the boy's head
underneath her chin, his pudgy cheeks in
full bloom, long eyelashes over unsullied
eyes, unaware there was such a thing as evil
in the world. It was one of the saddest
things Grace had ever witnessed. There was
nothing she could do or say that would
console her friend. She couldn't watch
anymore and went back to her room. She
couldn't stand it. Deronda would have to
give up half her business. She knew life
wasn't fair, but couldn't it give honest, loving, hardworking folks a fucking break? She
wished the situation was reversed. She'd
give up the art show or anything else if
Deronda could keep her business.

The unlikely pair had grown close over
the last couple of years. Cherokee was a
friend, but their relationship was more col-
legial, they were pals. There was more to it
with Deronda. No, they weren't like sisters.
It was something else, some kind of nexus
between hardship, struggle and love won
and lost; an invisible bond of compassion
and respect. And like most things human,

words only made it seem trite.

Grace couldn't calm her anger, she didn't want to, but the inaction was burning her up. She wondered what normal people would do in a situation like this, people who were sociable and likable and who weren't lifelong misanthropes. *They'd ask for help, you mope.* From who? she wondered. The situation demanded someone smart, devious and duplicitous, someone who thought a line in the sand was a line in the sand and that rules were made for people who obeyed rules. She smiled. It was so obvious. "Dodson," she said aloud.

Dodson came over. He looked tired and his eyes were bloodshot, his body limp with fatigue. Deronda was so upset she didn't notice his haircut. She told him about Bobby James, his threat and their court date tomorrow.

"Well, what do you think?" she said.

"Have you got any coffee that Grace didn't make?" Dodson asked.

"You want coffee now?"

"Yes, I do. I've had a very long day."

Deronda grumbled and went off to the kitchen. Grace stayed. She didn't know what to do with herself except sit there and shred a half a box of Kleenex. Dodson didn't seem worried at all. He was weary, but he still looked confident, in control. He looked like Dodson.

"How did it go with the Bayer commercial?" she asked.

"It went great, and I appreciate your help. I'll give you the full story some other time." He nodded at the tissue shreds all over the floor. "Does that help?"

"No," Grace said. "It doesn't do anything."

Deronda brought in the coffee. She handed him the mug. "Okay. Will you please tell me what you're thinking? This is my life, Dodson. I'm begging you. Please don't mess with me."

"Ain't nobody messin' with you," Dodson said, annoyed. "Sit down. You're interfering with my process." He thought a long moment. "You got two problems. The first one is dealing with Bobby's case."

"What's the other?" Deronda said.

"Later. We gotta stick to the matter at hand." Dodson sipped his coffee and seemed to drift off.

"Dodson, please. Don't make me beg," Deronda said.

"Don't nobody want you to beg." He yawned, adding, "If anybody's gonna beg it'll be Bobby James." He got up.

"Where're you going?" Deronda said, alarmed.

"I have an idea, but it's not fully formed just yet. I need my hustler's hat and I left it at home. I'll have it worked out in the morning. Right now, I need some sleep." He moved for the door. Grace couldn't believe he was going.

"*Please,* Dodson," Deronda said, tearfully. She nearly fell to her knees. "You've gotta help me!"

"I *am* gonna help you," Dodson said. "But if I don't shut my eyes now, I'll shut 'em in the courtroom. Do you trust me or not?"

"No, I don't trust you at all, but I need your help anyway."

"See you tomorrow." He left. Deronda started to cry.

"I know we been enemies, but I didn't think he'd be like this. He was my last hope."

Grace put her arm around her friend. "Dodson will come through. I know he will." But she didn't know that at all.

Deronda and Grace held hands as they walked down the wide hallway to Courtroom 7. People were milling around, sitting on benches, waiting, anxious and sullen. Most were women and children, hoping

381

they'd see Daddy even if he was in hand-cuffs.

"Bobby James is gonna ruin me," Deronda said, getting tearful again. "I worked so hard . . ."

"It's gonna be all right," Grace said, though she had a feeling it wouldn't be. "Dodson's smart. He'll come through."

It was 9:45. Bobby James and his brother-in-law, the attorney, were waiting. No Dodson. The hearing was at ten.

"Shit," Deronda hissed. "Dodson ain't here."

"Where's your attorney?" Bobby said as they arrived.

"He's not coming."

"Well that's stupid of you. You'll have to go it alone, I guess." He glanced at his watch. "The courtroom opens in a few minutes. Do I get half the business or do I go in there and ask for a paternity test? Make up your mind, Deronda. What are you going to do?"

"Okay," she said almost inaudibly. She was trembling, fierce and helpless. Grace could not fucking believe it. Her teeth were clenched, her body like a coiled snake. *Oh, my God,* she wanted to floor this shameless, greedy son of a bitch bastard. Bobby noticed her glaring at him. He was flustered a moment and turned away.

"I have papers here for you to sign, Miss Simmons," the attorney said. "I'm a notary public as well."

Dodson arrived. "I'm sorry," he said. "Deronda won't be signing any papers today."

"Dodson? What are you doing here?" Bobby said. "This is none of your business."

"Are you an attorney?" the attorney said. "If you're not, you have no legal standing."

"I'm a friend of the family," Dodson replied with a friendly smile. "And as I said, she won't be signing anything."

"You realize of course what that means," the attorney said. "If we continue with the proceedings Bobby will officially become Janeel's father and Deronda's tawdry past will be on the public record forever."

"Yes," Dodson said pleasantly. "That's exactly why we want to proceed. You see, on top of caring for Janeel, Deronda is running a very successful business. It's become impossible for her to care for him the way a mother should. And that's why we're gonna give you what you want, Bobby James. Custody. Split right down the middle, fifty-fifty." Bobby and the attorney looked confused. Deronda and Grace glanced at each other and smiled.

"I don't understand," Bobby said. "What are you talking about?"

Dodson went on. "Deronda will have Janeel for two weeks, and then he'll be with you for two weeks. Naturally, this means you'll be sharing Janeel's expenses. Food, clothing, medical care, transportation and whatever else comes up." Bobby and the attorney had gone still. It was as if they'd been freeze-dried like Grace's coffee, right there in the hallway. "Will you be able to take Janeel to and from preschool every morning and afternoon?" Dodson said. "It's tedious, what with the traffic and all — oh, I almost forgot. Do you have a spare bedroom? If not, you'll have to share yours with your four-year-old son."

"He only wets the bed once in a while," Deronda said. "There's sharing the bathroom too. Just this morning, I cleaned up a whole bottle of shampoo off the floor."

"What else was there? I'm forgetting something," Dodson said.

"Vacations!" Grace said gleefully.

"Thank you for reminding me, Grace. Deronda will take Janeel with her on her vacation, and you will take him on yours."

"My vacation?" Bobby said. "Take a little kid on *vacation*?"

"Janeel wants to go to Disney World,"

Deronda said. "The one in Orlando? He must have asked me a hundred times."

"Nothing like a four-year-old on a five-hour plane ride," Grace added.

"The poor child doesn't have a father figure," Deronda said. "He'll love going with his daddy. He'll be stuck on you like a sucker-fish on a shark, twenty-four hours a day, morning 'til night. Don't worry. He's a good kid. He loves to laugh and run around, screaming and knocking things down and digging shit up. Y'all gonna have a wonderful time!"

The attorney was frowning, his chin tucked into his chest. Bobby looked dazed, like he was in the witness box and the judge was a box of Wheaties.

"I think that's everything," Dodson said. "We'll explain to his honor that we've agreed to terms and you'll officially be Janeel's daddy, legally responsible for his care and happiness for the rest of your fucked-up life."

"No, not forever," Deronda said. "Only 'til he's eighteen. Don't worry, Bobby, the time will go by so fast you'll wish you could keep him around forever." Something sticky seemed to be holding Bobby's mouth closed. He finally got it open.

"What if I say fine, let's do it?" he said.

Bobby and the attorney were nodding at each other, smiling with their eyes wide, a feeble attempt to encourage each other.

"Go on and do it," Deronda said. "And you know what's gonna happen? You'll take care of Janeel for what, I don't know —"

"Two hours, tops," Grace said.

"By that time, you will have sewn your lips together so you can't scream anymore," Deronda said. "Then you'll thank your lucky stars you brought him back before you put a rag in his mouth and stuffed him in the garbage disposal. Whichever way you go, life as you know it is long fuckin' gone." The courtroom doors opened. She grinned and said, "Well, Bobby James. Do you have the nuts or don't you?"

Bobby agreed to withdraw all rights and obligations to Janeel and to have no contact with him. The judge was notified and the agreement was accepted. "The court is adjourned," she said. Grace had her hand over her mouth, face wet with tears, joyful.

Dodson and Deronda exchanged a long hug. "You a bad muthafucka, Dodson," she said.

"You don't have to tell me," Dodson said. "I know what I am."

Grace hugged him too. "You're the greatest, Dodson. You truly are." She thought he was choking up, but he turned his head away.

"I don't know how I'm gonna pay you back," Deronda said.

"Well that hug ain't gonna do it," Dodson said. "I think a fee would be appropriate." The attorney was packing up his briefcase. "How much do you charge?" Dodson asked.

"Seven fifty an hour," the attorney said.

"How long did it take me to wrap this up?" Dodson said.

"Well, there was last night, and I'm assuming you thought about it at home," Grace said. "And there was this morning too."

"Put it all together and you've got what? Three hours?"

"Call it four," Deronda said. "Come by and I'll write you a check." She paused a moment, looked at him quizzically. "Can I ask you something, Dodson?"

"What's that?"

"The fuck happened to your hair?"

Bobby was still seated at the plaintiff's table. He'd developed an intense interest in something scratched into the wooden surface. It said, I WILL KILL THE JUDGE WITH MY SHOE. Bobby had been staring at it since the hearing ended. "I'm not done yet, Deronda," he said. He looked at her, venom spewing out of his eyes. "Not even close." He got up and left the courtroom.

"I think he means it," Grace said. "What if he spreads that stuff around anyway?" Deronda exchanged a knowing glance with Dodson.

"What?" Grace said.

It was nearly eight by the time Bobby got home from work. He had to stay late because of the hearing. He crossed the lawn with his head down, his eyes burning up the dandelions. "That bitch. That fucking bitch!" He was going to punish her, starting now. He'd make a thousand copies of the material he'd collected. Everybody in Long Beach and beyond would see her for the ho she was. Janeel only had his mother to blame.

Bobby fumbled with his keys, cursed and opened the door. The lights were on. He always turned them off when he left. Puzzled, he blinked and looked around. Was he in the right house? Two men were lounging around the living room watching Bobby's TV and drinking Bobby's beer. They had on wifebeaters, gold chains and big shorts. One of them was missing his left hand, a large set of pliers in its place. The second man had a patch over one eye. His other eye was apparently wild and appeared to be looking out of the window.

"Uh, excuse me, but this is my house," Bobby said. No reaction. "Hello? I said this is my house. You don't belong here." Still no reaction. "Did you hear me? I said —"

A third man came in from the kitchen, eating an immense sandwich with ingredients from Bobby's fridge. He had mayonnaise on his mouth. He was bigger than the others and a terrifying sight, right out of a documentary about Pelican Bay; giant muscles, a welted scar on his angry face, fists like small cars. The mayonnaise looked like ghost blood.

"You know who I am?" the man said. He sounded like he had nails in his throat. Bobby stared. He was starting to look familiar, from somewhere in the past. Yes, it was coming into focus. Bobby saw the man as a teenager, beating the shit out of somebody with a tire iron. He saw the teenager punch the biology teacher in the chest so hard, dust puffed out of the man's suit. The teacher crashed into the terrarium and three tarantulas skittered across the linoleum, everyone running for the door. Bobby saw the teenager grab a screaming meter maid by her weave and sling her into a hedge. He saw the teenager pick up a mini fridge and hurl it into the window of a moving car. It was *Michael Stokeley.*

"Oh shit," Bobby said. Suddenly, he felt weak, his lips were quivering.

"You know who I am?" Stokeley repeated.

"Y-y-yes, I do. You're Michael Stokeley."

"Then you know I don't play."

"Yes, I know that," Bobby whimpered. "But could I ask what you're doing here?"

"No, you can't," Stokeley said.

"Of course, sure, sorry I asked." Stokeley looked at the others. They groaned wearily, finished their beers and reluctantly got to their feet. They were like a herd of something, bison or delivery trucks. They bum-rushed Bobby out of the door, threw him in the trunk of a car and drove off. Bobby knew how to open a trunk from the inside, but it seemed safer where he was.

Twenty suffocating minutes later, the car stopped and Stokeley yanked him out of the trunk. They were in what looked like a wrecking yard; stacks of crushed cars, broken glass on the ground, the smell of oil and rust, a crane looming against the night sky. Stokeley held Bobby up by the collar and frog-marched him around a mountain of tires, the crew following behind. It was very dark. Bobby was so scared his throat had closed. They stopped.

390

"That's it," Stokeley said, nodding at something decisively.

What's it? Bobby wondered. The thing they'll use to kill you with?

The crew stuck him in the driver's seat of an old station wagon and duct-taped his hands to the steering wheel. "I already have a car," Bobby said. Nobody laughed. The crew pushed the station wagon deeper into the yard, through a chain-link gate and into a metal container of some kind. It was closed on three sides and big enough to house the station wagon. Bobby's window looked out onto a small clearing, lit by a single floodlight. Stokeley and the crew were standing there, passing a joint around. With them was an old man, the white girl from court, and Deronda. Fucking Deronda. This was her doing.

"Deronda? What is this?" Bobby said, outraged. "You know this is kidnapping, don't you?"

She didn't answer. The old man had some kind of control box, a heavy extension cord coming out of it. He turned it on, whatever it was. Bobby heard a loud buzzing and the rumble of a diesel engine. He felt the box move around him, clanking, grinding, metal banging into metal. Something seized the entire car. The roof began buckling, the windows cracking. A hot blade of panic cut through Bobby's heart. *He was in a car crusher.* He screamed but couldn't hear himself over the noise.

The group watched as the roof closed down on him, the B pillars snapped, the tires exploded and the doors crumpled. "Help me! Help me!" Bobby screamed. Everybody was smiling and chuckling, as if getting pulverized in a car crusher was a skit on *Saturday Night Live.* The roof touched the top of Bobby's head. He had to angle it sideways so it wouldn't break his neck. *Oh God, oh God, I'm gonna die in a goddamn car crusher!* The windows were squashed, he couldn't see out of them anymore. He smelled the godawful release of a giant fart. That goddamn Deronda. *She's actually murdering you!* Was she that evil? That insane? "HELP ME! SOMEBODY PLEASE HELP MEEE!" Bobby couldn't move his neck anymore. He felt the ligaments straining. *Oh God, oh God, I'm going to fucking die I'm going to fucking die!* The crusher stopped, the engine sputtering as it wound down.

It was quiet; the only sounds were creaking metal and tinkling glass. Sweat and grime greased Bobby's face. His legs were cramping, his neck ached. He heard someone approach the passenger side.

"Hello? Hello?" Bobby shouted. "Please, please get me out of here!"

"Here's my last word," Stokeley said. "If what you have on Deronda shows up any-where? I mean *anywhere,* your shit is over. Even if you didn't do it, you'll be right back where you are, 'cept there won't be no car. You feel me?"

"Yes! Yes! I feel you! I feel you all over!" Bobby shouted. "I feel you everywhere! Oh, God, please let me out of here!"

"I'm sorry about Sandra," Deronda said, "but you fuck with a mama and her baby? Mess with that connection in the least kinda way? Shit will fall on you heavy as the Long Beach Freeway. TK will give you some water and let you out in the morning."

"The morning?" Bobby cried. "*The morning?* Are you out of your mind? I'll be dead by then!"

"Maybe, but I doubt it," Deronda said. "You take care now." Bobby heard them walk away. He screamed and screamed until his voice abandoned him and his lungs had collapsed. He fell into a dark, futile silence. He'd never felt despair before, such over-powering fear. Well, he thought, at least you survived, Bobby James.

Chapter Twenty-Four: The Ballsack of the Universe

Sureños gangs did business with the Hells Angels. Drugs and guns. Each had conduits to buyers the other didn't have. Isaiah's wanted poster had been circulated. Ned and Cherry saw it on a blog. Cherry called the number and talked to Manzo, leader of the Locos. Isaiah had betrayed him, Manzo said. It was personal. The gang leader wanted him back "by any means necessary." Manzo told Cherry that a Locos affiliate gang was coming over from Clarkson on the Nevada side. CTA 13, the Clarktown Asesinos 13, would dispatch members to bring the money and take Isaiah back to LA.

Isaiah learned all this on the drive to Ned and Cherry's house. They took him into the backyard at gunpoint and shoved him into a dilapidated one-car garage. The garage had double doors that were locked on the outside with a chain and a padlock. The place was full of motorcycle parts. Everything was cobwebby and rusted. An engine block, wheels, tires, a battered car seat, tools, an acetylene torch, a car jack, miscellaneous junk. Ned and Cherry debated whether to duct-tape Isaiah's hands behind or in front of him.

"The back is more secure. It's obvious," Cherry said.

"Are you going to hand-feed him? Hold his dick when he pisses?" Ned said. They duct-taped his hands in the front. They left him alone. Isaiah sat on the car seat. The garage was hot and close, the gasoline and oil smells were nauseating. There was a small gap between the doors. He put his face next to it and breathed in the fresh air. The garage was made from solid wood planks and two-by-four crossbeams. No chance you could kick your way out. There was one window on a side wall, but it was caged in with burglar bars.

Grace dominated Isaiah's thoughts. He had to stop her before she left for Coronado Springs. Cherry had taken his phone away and stomped on it. Even if he escaped, he'd be on foot, wandering around in the mountains with no way to communicate and twenty miles away from town. Ned and Cherry had left the Mustang in the woods.

Ned wanted to take it, but Cherry said it was too flashy and Cannon might know the car. They'd come back for it later.

Someone was opening the padlock, the chain clanking. "Get away from the door," Cherry said. "Sit down and don't move." Isaiah did as he was told. Cherry came in with a gun, a bottle of water and a Snickers bar. She tossed the last two in his lap. She looked smug and confident.

"The Asesinos are on their way."

"The deal will never happen," Isaiah scoffed. "They aren't coming here with twenty-five grand."

"Oh yeah? Why's that? Manzo said he wants you bad." Cherry leaned back against the wall, crossed her ankles, gun by her side.

"How would that work? Manzo sends the Asesinos twenty-five thousand dollars by Western Union? Even if he could he wouldn't. He wouldn't trust a Nevada gang to pay him back. The alternative is the Asesinos putting up the money themselves and trusting Manzo will give them a refund. Come on, Cherry, you know neither of those things are gonna happen." Isaiah's plan depended on what Cherry did after she left the garage.

Cherry stirred, uncrossed her ankles. "Those gangs are tight. They're not going to start a war."

"They start wars with each other all the time," Isaiah replied. "When I was leaving LA, the Westside Locos were warring with Azusa 13, Temple Street with Puente, 18th Street with 38th Street." It wasn't true but it sounded true. "Who did you talk to in the Asesinos?"

"Shot caller. Del Rio," Cherry said.

"When are they supposed to get here?"

"He said they'd leave right away."

Isaiah laughed. "So Del Rio gets off the phone, goes into his sock drawer, finds twenty-five K in cash and then jumps in his car so he can hand-deliver it to you?" Cherry pursed her lips and looked at the floor. Isaiah continued. "If the Asesinos are from Clarkson, they're probably a small set. Fifteen, twenty guys, most of them teen-agers. They wouldn't have that much cash if they sold everything they owned."

"Okay, so what are you saying?" Cherry said, on defense now.

"I'm saying they're coming here to kidnap me, shoot you in the process and collect the reward themselves." Cherry thought about it, grim-faced, her aging eyes seeing how it would play out.

"You think you're smart, don't you?"

"I am smart, and so are you," Isaiah said.

Cherry stood away from the wall, looked at him a moment. She went outside, put the chain and padlock back on the doors and left.

The bastard was right, Cherry thought. She kicked herself for being so naïve. What now? They could leave, which meant the Asesinos would trash the house and take Ned's bike. It wasn't running, and they didn't have a trailer. If they stayed, they'd have a fire-fight on their hands. She found Ned where he always was, doing what he always did. He put down the beer.

"What's wrong?" he said.

"We need reinforcements."

Isaiah heard the rumbling of motorcycles. Three bikers pulled into the yard, Hells Angels emblems on their helmets and clothes. Two of them looked like brothers. They were driving traditional choppers. The big guy was driving a vintage, full-dress Electra Glide. Gleaming red and white paint, full windshield, whitewalls, lots of chrome and color-coordinated saddlebags. A bike meant for cruising. They parked next to Ned and Cherry's bikes. The couple came out of the house and passed around beers. The group talked awhile. They had guns. They sat around drinking more beer, loading magazines and taking aim at imaginary gangsters.

It was an eight-hour drive from Clarkson to Coronado Springs. About seven hours had gone by since Cherry had talked to Del Rio. The Asesinos would be here in an hour, give or take. Cherry had a brief argument with Ned that ended with her saying, "You are one useless asshole." She and the new arrivals went in the house. Ned, not embarrassed at all, stayed on the back stoop and popped open another beer.

Isaiah looked through the tools and found a hacksaw. He clamped it into the table vise, blade side up. He put a hand on either side of the blade and sawed through the tape. He paused for a drink and the candy bar. He peeked through the doors again; Ned was still there. There was nothing more to be done until he left. Isaiah sat down on the car seat and waited.

Cherry and Jesse were on the front porch, waiting for the Asesinos to arrive. On their side of the railing, a protective wall had been jerry-rigged. An old file cabinet on its side, the drawers filled with dirt. There were stacks of cinder blocks and firewood, the hood of an old car, an oak tabletop and a half dozen sandbags. Blankets were draped over to hide the barricade. Jesse was even and quiet like he always was. If he trimmed the mountain man beard and took off the red bandanna and the rings, he'd look like your jolly uncle. But nothing about Jesse was jolly. When somebody needed a beat-down, Jesse volunteered. If there was a shooting, he was the prime suspect. If there was a bar fight, he started it. Cherry knew he was in love with her and would do anything to protect her. "Thanks for doing this, Jess."

His eyes were on the road. "No problem." Jesse's favorite weapons were his matching Heckler and Koch .45s. He was proud of them, all oiled up and shiny. Cherry didn't care about brands, calibers or anything else. Who cared about whether a gun was a .44, a .55 or made by Mongolians? If the guy you were shooting at was dead it was a great gun.

The Waylon brothers, Solo and Reems, were inside, watching through the windows, the space underneath them reinforced like the porch. They were reliable, tough as prison barbells and veterans of gang wars and shoot-outs.

"Where the fuck is Ned?" Reems said.

"Rear guard, unless he fell asleep," Solo answered.

Predictably, they heard a million-watt amp pumping out rap music. Cherry hated that shit no matter who it was coming from. If she met Kid Rock, she'd beat him to death with his golf clubs. "It's them," she said.

Isaiah watched Ned. He was still on the stoop, almost inert, like doing nothing was his career.

"Go inside," Isaiah hissed, but Ned yawned and opened another beer. He didn't look like he'd get off his butt any time soon. Actually, it didn't matter. Isaiah hadn't figured out how to escape. The chain and lock on the door were inaccessible. The hand tools were useless. There was the acetylene torch but the fuel tank was empty. There was no way to make another opening. He had to use the one that was there. The window and those damn burglar bars. *Come on, Isaiah, focus. Grace is coming.*

Cherry watched the cars come out of the woods and drive slowly down the barely paved road. The lead vehicle was a canary-yellow Malibu with shiny rims, blacked-out windows, lowered nearly to the ground. Behind it was a black Impala with blacked-out windows, shiny rims, a voluptuous woman painted on the side. Mexicans loved those old Chevys the way bikers loved old Harleys. The cars stopped in front of the house. The windows were open, cholos in there giving them hard looks. A skinny, shirtless vato with a six-pack and six thousand tats got out of the Malibu. He was cocky, smiling, running his hand over his fuzzy head.

"I'm Del Rio," he said. He announced it like, I'm Denzel Washington. The music was so loud he had to shout over it. "You're Cherry, huh? I bet you're sweet like one too. That's cool, man. A chica in charge? You must be a badass, mamacita." The guys inside the cars laughed. "That ink on your head don't exactly look feminine," he went on. "What's your old man think? Can he still get it up for you?" *He's trying to provoke you, Cherry. Make you show your hand.*

"How about turning the music down?" she said. Del Rio ignored the request. "I want to see the money," she said.

He grinned. "You got it, chica."

Cherry's antennae were up. Why hadn't Del Rio asked to see Isaiah? Wouldn't that be the first thing you'd do? Three homies emerged from the Impala, all of them high school age. A tubby kid went off to the side, turned his back and started taking a piss. The second kid took a shoe box bound with a rubber band out of the trunk. He brought it to Del Rio. The third kid stayed by the trunk. It was hot, but all of them were wearing gangsta flannel. To hide their guns, Cherry thought. The whole thing looked choreographed. *Something's wrong, Cherry.* The music was too loud even for gangstas and why was Del Rio still talking?

"How do you fucking live out here?" he said. "There ain't shit to do. All you got is trees and shit. No taco stands, no clubs. What do you do if you want something from the store? Do you get cable out here?"

"The money," Cherry repeated.

Del Rio held the box out with one hand. "Twenty-five grand, chica. All for you."

"Open it."

"Anything you say, mamacita." The realization came fast and all at once. The music and Del Rio's monologue were distractions. The one guy stayed by the trunk because there was a gun in there. The guy who'd brought the shoe box was standing almost behind Del Rio. When he drew his gun, you wouldn't be able to see him. Cherry looked between the tubby guy's legs. He wasn't pissing, he was flanking them. In every drug-money transaction Cherry had ever seen, the cash was in some kind of bag or stuffed into a manila envelope. Not in a fucking shoe box. *There's a gun in there!*

"It's a setup!" Cherry shouted, and she dropped behind the railing. Del Rio took a pistol out of the shoe box. The homie behind him was drawing a gun. The one near the trunk whipped out a pump-action shotgun. The tubby turned around with a gun in his hand.

"Fuck 'em up!" Del Rio shouted. The Mexicans barely got off a few shots before they were hit by a nonstop barrage. The guys inside the cars got out on the other side. They dived, dodged and ran for the trees. Del Rio and the guy behind him were hit multiple times. The homeboy with the shotgun was driven back behind the car. The one who wasn't pissing was crouched and hurrying away.

"Run for your lives, you assholes!" Cherry shouted.

"Hallelujah," Isaiah said. The shooting woke up Ned. He rushed inside the house still holding the beer. Isaiah picked up a wrench, broke the window and cleared the glass fragments out of the frame. There were four heavily oxidized burglar bars. They were do-it-yourself, made from heavy angle iron. The welds were sloppy but looked strong.

The car jack was on the floor. It was an ordinary scissors type, the kind you'd find in the trunk of your average Toyota. Isaiah inserted the crank into the jack and turned the handle, raising the height of the jack to around eight inches or so, roughly the same width as the space between the bars. He flipped the jack to vertical and wedged it between two of the bars. It was hard getting it into position. Isaiah reinserted the crank and started turning it. Even a simple jack like this one could lift a car weighing three or four tons. It was slow going. The jack was extending sideways. You don't have the same leverage as you would if the jack was on the ground. The bars screeched and yawned but they didn't move. Isaiah kept at it, grunting with every turn, his T-shirt like a wet paper towel, his arms and shoulders burning. Then what he hoped would happen, happened. A bar broke loose from its weld with a dull bang. Isaiah gathered up a few tools, pushed the bar out for more space and wriggled out sideways.

The blank, gray sky was filled with shouting and gunfire, an acrid cloud of gun smoke obscuring the view. The Mexicans had dispersed into the woods. It was hard to tell if anybody was hit or where the return fire was coming from. The front of the house was ripped to shit with bullet holes. Reems and Solo shot up the Asesinos' cars just for fun. They screamed *Death to your pinche madres* and worse.

Cherry stopped shooting. She sat with her back against the file cabinet and shook her head. What a fucking disaster. She was broke, two dead guys were lying in the yard, and the house was shredded. What had she expected? That everything would turn out fine? It was amazing how dumb you can be when you think there's an easy score. There was no such thing as an easy score. Something always went wrong, because that's what happens when everybody you know, love and do business with is a ruthless fucking criminal.

"Ned," she shouted, "get some more ammo!"

Isaiah ran over to the row of motorcycles parked on the cement apron. He had tools he'd taken from the garage. The first bike in line was a red Sportster with high-rise handlebars and a seat so small it looked like it belonged on a bicycle. It was fifty years old, the electrics much simpler than they were now. Isaiah looked under the headlight and found the ignition wire. He pulled it out a few inches and cut it. Inside it were three more wires. One for ignition, one for power and a third for the headlight. Isaiah separated them and touched the ends together. The power bypassed the starter and the bike's ignition clicked on.

The bike had a kick starter, never easy on an old Harley. Isaiah mounted up and stood on the pegs, one foot on the starting lever. He plunged his foot down like he was trying to smash it through the cement. The engine sputtered, coughed and died. He tried it again. Same thing. He tried it again. Same thing. The shooting was sporadic, everyone was probably running out of ammo. Sooner or later, somebody would come back here to get more. At last, the Sportster started. Ned came out the back door with a beer in his hand.

"You know why you're not getting out of here?" he said with a lazy smile. "Because I want your car."

The bike's engine died again and Isaiah quickly dismounted. Ned crossed the cement apron surprisingly fast for somebody who was half drunk. The speediest thing Isaiah had seen him do was sit down. Ned threw a big right hand. Isaiah ducked under it, grabbed Ned by the thighs and hoisted him over his shoulder. Ned went crashing into the red bike, which crashed into the bike next to it and then they all went down like dominoes. Only the one at the end was left standing.

Ned was sprawled on top of the red bike, out cold, gash on his head, his arms and legs tangled up with the handlebars. Isaiah couldn't move him and the bike was leaking gas. He jogged over to the last bike, the Electra Glide. It was as old as the Sportster but looked new. It was a bulky thing, much bigger than the Sportster. The wiring was virtually the same, but you had to take the dashboard off, a chrome cover that held the speedometer. Unscrewing it took forever. Isaiah got the cover off. He did the same with the ignition wires as he had on the other bike. The ignition clicked on. He mounted up and stomped on the starter lever. There was a deafening backfire, as loud as a .45, but the bike rumbled to a start. He pulled in the clutch and put it in gear. He had to keep revving it or the engine would die.

A big guy with a beard and a red bandanna came lumbering out of the house. "Ned, are you fucking with my ride?" he said angrily. He saw Isaiah and stopped. His voice was low and gutteral and menacing. "Get off the bike," he said. Isaiah was corralled on three sides by a barbed wire fence, an empty chicken coop and the downed bikes. The only way out was through the guy. "You hurt my bike, and I'll bury you, mother-fucker."

If Isaiah went right at the guy, he would sidestep, grab him as he went by and knock the bike over. Try to go around him, and it would be even easier for him. Isaiah thought a moment. He'd done this before on a Kawasaki, but it was built low with low handlebars for street racing. The Electra Glide was wider, nearly three times as heavy, and it had regular handlebars. Was it even possible? It was all about timing. *Here we go.* Isaiah let out the clutch and rolled slowly toward the big man, revving the engine, higher and higher. The big man was gesturing with his hands, inviting him to bring it. Simultaneously, Isaiah cranked the gas, let go of the clutch and jerked hard on the handlebars. The bike burned rubber, rose back and *wheelied!* The big man's eyes went wide. The front wheel was coming right at his face.

"Oh, fuck!" he shouted. He had to side-step and duck at the same time, no chance to grab Isaiah as he roared past, touching the brake to bring the front wheel down.

He drove over the grass and around the house to the road, hearing gunshots as he sped away.

Cherry packed her things in boxes and stacked them in the living room. They had to move before the landlord or the law came by. She heard an engine popping and blatting. Ned had fixed his bike. They were going to Reno. Fucking Reno. The ballsack of the universe. Ned had buddies there. And then what? More squalid living, long scorching rides, stripping in some shitty club and eating Hormel Chili and white bread on a paper plate? There had to be something else, Cherry thought. There had to be.

Hmm, what are your choices, Cherry? You could stay here and live with Jesse, but why would that be any different than living with Ned? It would be like jumping from the frying pan into another frying pan. Or she could go live with her mom in Fresno, listen to her constant bitching and get her job back at the DMV. Ned, on the other hand, was as wretched as she was. He didn't hassle her or judge her. She wondered what would happen if she didn't choose from the obvious and struck out on her own. Ned was shouting, impatient to get going, yelling over the engine noise.

"Cherry! For fuck sake, what are you doing?"

"Okay, okay, I'm coming."

She went to the front door and opened it halfway. Ned was sitting on his bike, revving the engine in short bursts. "Come on, Cherry! Why are you just standing there?" Her bike was next to his, the handlebars and the narrow seat beckoning. He'd started the engine for her. Easiest thing in the world was to mount up, take off and let the wind clear the shit out of your head. She didn't move, fixed to the spot.

"Cherry, what the fuck, huh?" Ned said. He kept twisting the throttle, the bike's exhaust snarling at her, telling her to get on her fucking bike. "Cherry, are you coming or not?" He was angry now. "The fuck is wrong with you! I'll leave you behind, I swear to God I will!" She stood there. Ned screamed at her. "CHERRY, ARE YOU COMING OR NOT!" She stood there.

Chapter Twenty-Five: Puff Adder

Brad was in a state. He'd been grinding his teeth since he woke up this morning, and he was eating Tums like Raisinets. The meeting was at eleven and Stimson hadn't arrived. Seven minutes to go. The BeHeard people had come in force. Brad hadn't expected so many. An art director, copywriter, project manager, account manager, two creatives, three assistants and Vice President of Campaign Development Seth Adder, "Puff Adder" to his friends. He was Walsh's counterpart.

By all reports, Adder was a rude, impatient, abrasive, unreasonably demanding asshole. People said he made Brad look like Andy Griffith. Adder had been a star from the beginning. Creative executive at nineteen, creative director at twenty-five, a VP at twenty-nine, and an executive VP at thirty-five. His looks belied his personality. He had soft eyes, set in a round, benign face, square tortoiseshell glasses, his hairline retreating fast. He dressed like a teenager. Chick-fil-A T-shirt, gold chains, tight jeans and patent leather sneakers. He looked like Sidney Lumet in Justin Bieber's wardrobe. When Brad met Adder in the lobby, the first thing Adder said was, "This better be fucking good. I hate wasting my fucking time."

Everyone had seated themselves at the long white conference table. Adder said, "Can we get on with this? What am I waiting for?" Brad was overcome with anxiety. It was two minutes past eleven. Where the hell was Stimson? Earlier, they had talked on the phone. Brad wanted to see the presentation first, but the doofus said it wasn't ready yet.

Adder was already agitated. "Well?" he said.

Walsh looked sharply at Brad. "The creative should be here shortly," Brad said. *Where the hell are you, Stimson?* An endless thirty seconds went by, everyone restless, listening for footsteps, waiting for Adder to explode.

Adder stood up. "Okay, we're going."

"Come on, Seth," Walsh said. "You've been here five minutes. Have a little patience, will you?" Adder heaved a sigh that was almost a groan and sat down again.

413

Walsh leaned over and whispered to Brad. "Where's Stimson?"

"He should be here any second."

"This is your idea too. Why don't you pitch it?" Walsh said.

"Stimson's got the visuals."

"You're a professional, aren't you? Pitch it," Walsh demanded.

Slowly, Brad stood up. "Okay. Well. The creative is a little late so I'll get started." He paused, poured himself a glass of water and took a very long drink.

"Do you want something to eat?" Adder said.

"Brad," Walsh said, impatiently. "Let's begin, shall we?"

"Right," Brad said. He was rarely lacking for ideas, but his mind was so empty his breathing echoed. "So, um, what we've developed here is a sixty-second commercial for BeHeard's new voice-to-text software, version two point one."

"Thank you, Brad," Adder said. "We didn't know that. Why don't you tell us the ladies' room is for ladies or how many twos there are in one two three?"

"Right," Brad said again. "Um, what we're going for here is a fresh take, a unique perspective on voice-to-text software. What is beyond, what it can be." Everyone sat rigid with fear. Adder was breathing deeply, glaring at his hands, folded on the table. They seemed to be choking each other. He was like that comedian who slips a balloon over his head and blows it up, the balloon expanding and expanding and you're cringing because you know it's going to pop but you don't know when. Brad went on. "We here at Apex want to elevate voice-to-text software to something approaching the first computer or the introduction of the cell phone or —"

"A can of pork and beans!" Adder shouted. The balloon popped. "GET THE FUCK ON WITH IT OR I'M OUT OF HERE!" Brad felt himself shriveling into his shoes. Walsh was furious, Adder was getting up. Stimson stumbled in, red-faced and sweating.

"Seth," Brad said, so relieved he might have fainted. "This is the creative executive on the project, Arnold Stim —"

"I don't care what his fucking name is!" Adder said. "Just fucking start!"

Stimson was fumbling with his laptop, in a panic, typing furiously. "Just a second! Just a second! I'm getting it."

"That's it," Adder said. He stood up and his entire entourage stood up too, feet shuffling, deep breaths, muttering and chairs scraping against the floor. It sounded like a flock of flamingos taking off. "I told you not to waste my time, Brad," Adder said with a lethal glare. "I'll fucking remember this."

Walsh's look was no less heated, and in his eyes Brad saw his termination package, his brothers laughing and his parents locking him in his room.

"Okay, okay! I've got it!" Stimson said. Brad closed his eyes and took a long breath.

Walsh said, "Please, Seth, sit down. We're ready now."

Brad's sweat was cooling as a video began on the wall monitor. He was immediately dismayed. An elderly, surly-looking woman nearly filled the frame. And she was black. Oh God, thought Brad, does everything in the fucking world have to be diverse? He had just seen a black footman in a movie about Mary, Queen of Scots. If the man had been that close to the queen in real life, he'd have been eating mouse turds in the Tower of London if he wasn't hanging from a yardarm. Adder was already shaking his head. Walsh seemed to be staring through the monitor into his office down the hall.

"Dr. King began the Freedom March in Selma, Alabama, on March 7, 1965," the woman said. Adder actually rolled his eyes.

"Oh, here we go," he muttered.

"There was five or six hundred of us," the woman went on, "ordinary folks, nobody special, holding our signs and singing our songs."

Brad leaned over to Walsh and whispered, "I don't know what Stimson was thinking. This isn't the idea we talked about."

"Why is everything in the background brown?" Walsh said.

The old woman continued. "We were walking up Route 80, everybody in good spirits. We only got as far as the bridge, and there were the police, a group of them, white men, as big as football players. They had helmets and batons and everything. Well, Dr. King stopped, and the rest of us did too. We didn't know what was going to happen, nobody did." The woman was intense now, getting upset, getting angry. You could feel it coming off the screen. Authenticity was rare, Brad thought, striking when you see it. Even Adder was paying attention.

Suddenly, the woman was terrified. "The police came running at us! They were knocking people down, kicking and hitting us with their batons and shooting tear gas at us!!" The woman was trembling, shaking her head, tears spilling down her cheeks.

She's there, Brad thought, on the bridge, watching the police big as football players coming at her with batons and shields and hateful faces. "No reason to do that, no reason at all. We were just folks, just people!" She kept shaking her head, as outraged and bewildered as she must have been that day. "Well, everybody starts running and screaming. There were old people in the crowd, women and children too! But the police didn't care. They trampled right over us! How could they do that?" She stared into her memory, unable to believe that men could be so cruel and unthinking. "I got knocked down. I was hurt and bleeding and I'm trying to get up and this big policeman comes over, smacking his club in his hand. He smiles and says to me, 'Girl, you're in a world of trouble.' " The woman's face seemed to fall apart, as if everything she had ever believed about America had fallen apart too, and nothing remained but heartbreak and sorrow. Her voice got low and hollow, a sheen over her eyes. She said, "What happened next, I'll remember 'til the day I die." Freeze-frame on the woman's anguished face. The caption:

EVERYONE HAS A STORY TO TELL. WHAT'S YOURS?
BeHeard
Voice-to-text software

There was utter silence. Everyone was stunned. Adder was blank, leaning back with his arms folded. He thought a moment, his brow furrowed. "That was really good," he said, like he didn't believe it was possible. "You've got the account." He nodded at Stimson. "Keep that guy." He got up and walked out, his entourage buzzing as they trailed him.

The group stayed silent until the BeHeard crew was well away. Brad started to speak but someone shouted, "Let's hear it for Stimson!" And everyone applauded for fuck sake, clapping like they were in a goddamn romantic comedy. Even Walsh had joined in. The doofus was half smiling, confused, like he didn't know how to feel.

Walsh nudged Brad with his elbow. "Good thing Stimson stuck to his guns, and like the man said: keep that guy." He left.

Brad was in his office. His tie was on the floor. The Tums were gone. He'd been pacing for twenty minutes. Keep that guy? Good thing Stimson stuck to his guns?

Shown up again by a dimwit has-been. How humiliating, and he hadn't even gotten credit for the idea! He opened the cabinet and poured himself a shot of sixteen-year bourbon, a gift from a client. He'd been running Stimson's ads through his mind. Both the Skechers and Bayer ads involved black characters. Clearly, this was Lebron's work, but who was Lebron? They would have to spend time together to do this kind of work, but Stimson had no partner. "Who is this guy?" Brad said to the room.

It wasn't a creative exec. There were only two black execs and they had their own work to do. An outsider? Unlikely. Who would do this quality of work and then give it away to Stimson? Had the doofus paid for it? With what? He'd taken two salary cuts. Brad downed his drink and poured himself another. Maybe Lebron was somebody under the radar, he thought. Someone on staff, an assistant maybe, a prodigy like Seth Adder. Brad had a feeling the Skechers ad was created by someone relatively young; the BeHeard commercial by a person with an appreciation of history. A millennial then.

Brad remembered the black man he'd encountered in the men's room. He wasn't on staff or Brad would have known him. He was the right age and had a street background. Wasn't hard to imagine him standing at the curb, hailing a cab that drove right past him, and the man probably had relatives who had lived through the civil rights era. *You've seen him someplace before, Brad. Where?*

A vague memory was forming in the haze. Brad pictured himself standing at the elevators. Stimson was there, and he introduced his new intern. *His new black millennial intern!* This guy was Lebron, the creative genius behind those ads! Brad had Estie get him a list of the new interns. The one assigned to Stimson was named Juanell Dodson. "Well, Mr. Dodson," Brad said aloud. "You and I are going to have a little talk."

It was the morning after the BeHeard success, Dodson was still high, still wishing he'd been in the meeting to see the reaction. Stimson said they'd have to give him an assistant now. Cherise was beaming when he told her. They shared a bottle of sparkling rosé and followed it up with a two-hour love fest. He wanted her to say she was proud of him, but she didn't.

When he got to the office, Stimson wasn't in yet, probably waiting for Marge to fold his sandwich in wax paper. A call came in from HR. All interns were to convene for a special announcement. Room 8, 16th floor, ASAP. Attendance was mandatory.

Room 8 wasn't a conference room. It was a spacious office. Modern furniture, sitting area, nice view. Brad was seated on the sofa. No one else was there.

"I think I'm in the wrong place," Dodson said.

"No. You're exactly where you should be, Mr. Dodson. May I call you Juanell?"

"If you feel like it."

"Please call me Brad. Have a seat." Dodson took the chair across from him.

"Would you like water? Coffee? A soft drink, perhaps?"

"No thanks. I'm good." I'm busted, Dodson thought, but he wasn't upset. He'd be fired from a position he wasn't getting paid for. Cherise would be disappointed, but he didn't regret anything he'd done.

"I know you did those ads, and they were brilliant," Brad said.

"Stimson came up with those ads, not me." Dodson had a rule. Never cop to anything, no matter what it was. He'd had a lot of experience talking to the police.

"I understand your reluctance to come forward," Brad said. "I'd probably do the same myself."

"Ain't no need for ceremony. I'll say my

422

goodbyes and be outta here in ten minutes."

"No, that's not quite what I had in mind." Brad smiled like he had your number, like he had a surprise. Dodson hated that. "This is a special situation, Juanell. *Very* special, and if you play your cards right, you'll be set up for years to come."

Look at this chump, Dodson thought. Was he actually trying to hustle the hustler's hustler? *Watch yourself, son. You don't know who you fucking with.*

"I want you to come forward as the creator of those ads," Brad said.

"Like I said before, Stimson created those ads." Brad's running a game, Dodson thought. If he came forward, Brad would say he didn't know Stimson was using someone else's work. That meant Brad was partnered up with Dodson all along. He just didn't know it. Together they created those ads and together they were the future of the company. The board would be ecstatic.

"Come forward and two things will happen," Brad said. "Stimson will get fired, and you'll get his job. A two-year contract that can't be canceled with an option for a third. A hundred twenty-five thousand to start with full benefits. And by the way, this is your office."

Dodson was wowed but a hustler is always

cool. He didn't smile, he didn't say anything.

Brad grinned. "Well, do we have a deal?"

Dodson's impulse was to say *fuck yes,* we have a deal. Instead he replied, "I need to think on it." It was another rule. Never give in too easy. You'll be seen as weak. Like they have you, like they know your price.

"What is there to think about?" Brad said. "Let's be serious, shall we? Look, I'm a straight shooter and so are you." Dodson let that pass. "Given your background, nothing like this will ever come your way again. I'm not giving you a job, I'm giving you a career. Try to understand."

"Try to understand?" Dodson said, getting chesty. "Don't talk down to me, Brad. You better raise up your attitude, or I'll walk the fuck out."

"This is a one-time offer, Juanell," Brad said, heatedly. "Leave and it's gone forever."

"You know that's bullshit. If you want me this much today, you'll want me more tomorrow."

"Are you sure?" Brad said. "I've been playing this game a lot longer than you have."

"No, you haven't."

"If you blow the deal, won't your family be disappointed?"

"My family is my business."

It was a risk, but if he played this out, Brad might up the offer. He imagined Cherise's face when he told her her husband was no longer a bum, he was an executive in a big company making real money. "Unless you're firing me, I'll be at work in the morning," Dodson said.

"Accept the deal right now and you'll get a signing bonus," Brad said quickly. "Ten thousand dollars before you leave the building." He's desperate, Dodson thought. Playing it out was the right move. He got up and went to the door. "You have twenty-four hours," Brad said.

"No," Dodson replied as he left the room. "*You* have twenty-four hours."

CHAPTER TWENTY-SIX: MAGIC TRICK

Isaiah took a chance and drove the bike into town. The red and white paint and gleaming chrome were more than conspicuous. He used backstreets and parked in an alley. He took the three hundred dollars in emergency money out of his shoe. He went to the local motorcycle shop. He bought a Cordura motorcycle jacket with a high collar that covered your neck. He bought gloves that went over his wrists and a helmet with a smoked face shield. There was a mirror in the store. He was satisfied. The outfit hid his most identifiable feature. His blackness. He made another stop and bought a TracFone. He had to tell Grace what was happening, a call he didn't want to make.

He went back to the guest house, got his laptop, the spare key to the Mustang and a few other things. The saddlebags were handy. He drove the Electra Glide to the Mustang's hiding place. It was a rough ride.

The bike wasn't built for off-road. He drove the car to a second hiding place and walked back to the bike. He mounted up, realized something and sat there. He was afraid, of course, but the PTSD was gone and along with it, the self-loathing, bitterness and depression. No doubt it was temporary, the adrenaline and exhaustion giving him a reprieve. At the moment, he needed safety and rest. He didn't know where to go. He could think of no place in town to hide and he had no camping gear.

One of the last places cops look for you is the place you've already fled. They assume that you want to get as far away as possible. Isaiah parked the Harley in the woods behind the guest house. No one had seen him arrive, and no one had followed him. He was certain this time.

He entered the guest house and shut the door. He went into the kitchen and drank two glasses of water. He sat down at the breakfast table, put his head back against the wall and closed his eyes. He wanted to get in bed but despite his precautions, he was still afraid. This was where he was arrested and handcuffed, where he imagined himself in prison. He would nod off for a moment and awaken with a start. This happened a few times, and then he heard the front door open. He was too exhausted to run, but he had to. He got up and started for the back door. Were deputies waiting out there? He stopped.

"Isaiah?" said a tiny voice. It was Juana, the Ortegas' little girl.

"Isaiah! I'm so glad to see you," Mr. Ortega said. "Please come in." Mrs. Ortega appeared and insisted he have coffee and fresh conchas she'd made herself. Isaiah smelled cinnamon and warm bread.

"I'm on the run. The sheriff is looking for me," he said.

"Don't worry. We would be happy to have you," Mrs. Ortega said. Mr. Ortega wasn't so sure.

Juana and Alicia were tugging at Isaiah's sleeves, wanting him to play. He didn't know why, but it moved him nearly to tears. He had his coffee and conchas, Mrs. Ortega promising him a muy bueno supper. She offered him their daughters' bedroom. The girls could sleep with their mother. They giggled as they led Isaiah to their room. There was a sign on the door: FROG PARKING. VIOLATORS WILL BE TOAD. The girls swiftly removed their most prized possessions. A few stuffed animals, a bracelet made of candy, play money, a plastic bride and groom from a wedding cake and an Oscar the Grouch doll that the girls said reminded them of their grandmother Imelda.

He wanted and didn't want to call Grace. He longed to hear her voice, but there was a lot he didn't want to tell her. He called.

The first thing she said was, "Oh, Isaiah! Everybody liked my paintings! Most of them sold! I even got a review in the Ojai newspaper!" She broke down and cried. He let his own tears fall, some of them for himself.

"I'm so happy for you, Grace. I wish I was there to celebrate."

"We'll celebrate together! I'm coming up to see you, don't you remember?"

"Yes, we'll celebrate together." There was a pause. They'd been talking for twelve seconds, and she knew something was wrong.

"Are you all right?" she asked.

"Yeah, I'm fine." Isaiah knew how to lie but not with Grace. If he was a spy he'd be in Leavenworth by now.

She said in a low voice, "Don't do this to me, Isaiah. I don't need to be protected." He was about to say I'm not protecting anything but didn't. It would compound the lie and sink them both.

"I'm into something. I'll tell you about it when I see you. I'm almost done."

"That's a relief, because I'm leaving tomorrow," she said. *Tell her, Isaiah. Tell her not to come!*

"Can't wait to see you."

"Yeah, me too," she said, and the call ended. He couldn't do it. He couldn't tell her. He was too wrung out. He'd call her early, before she left.

He passed on the muy bueno supper and stayed in the bedroom. It was another addition to his long list of rocks and hard places. Cannon was looking for him, but he couldn't leave town until Crowe and Warren were locked up. He brooded on it. Juana knocked on the door. She'd brought him a bowl of carna guisado con papas. A rich beef stew with warm homemade tortillas. He finished the bowl and wished he had more.

Before you do anything else, he thought, you have to figure out what Crowe and Warren are up to. Yes, they're here to kill someone, but that's not really helpful. If you can figure out who their target is, maybe you can predict their next move. What would be their motives? he wondered. Blackmail? That made no sense. Why would you blackmail two ex-convicts who worked menial jobs? What would they have that you could possibly want? Had someone insulted them? Threatened them? Who insults and threatens serial murderers? Passion? Unlikely. Serial killers are obsessive, but they don't fall in love. The only other option was revenge. Someone from their pasts had done something so egregious they deserved to be slashed to death. But was this person from Crowe's past, his partner's, or both?

He called Billy.

"Are you okay? We were really worried about you," Billy said.

"Where are you?"

"My house. We're waiting for my mom to get home. There was nowhere else to go."

"I need Crowe's files. The last three years."

"Why do you want them?"

Isaiah's patience had left the building a long time ago. "I need them, Billy, and I need them right fucking now!"

"Sure thing! Coming right up."

Billy had uploaded the records to Dropbox so Isaiah could retrieve them there. Crowe and his partner were killing together, Isaiah thought, which meant they had a close relationship. Isaiah skimmed Crowe's parole reports, concentrating on his personal data. A clue was on the intake information form under "Known associates." A few people were listed, including Crowe's half brother, Warren Long. Isaiah called Billy again. He wanted Warren's records too.

The man Isaiah had seen with Crowe and Warren's mugshot were one and the same. Warren had a lengthy criminal history of his own. He was Crowe's only family. Warren's last charge was for sexual assault. It happened here in Coronado Springs. He was tried and convicted in the Pumas County courthouse. So who in that process deserved to die? A police report caught Isaiah's attention. An officer had stopped Warren. His vehicle matched the description of one seen in the area of the assault. Warren led the officer on a high-speed chase, nearly causing a fatal accident. The officer was finally able to execute the PIT maneuver, the suspect's vehicle going off the road and crashing. Despite numerous warnings, Warren refused to surrender and fled.

The officer chased him for approximately a quarter of a mile, catching him in a dry wash known as Alabaster Creek. Warren resisted and the officer subdued him. The report said, "The suspect sustained minor injuries." Isaiah looked at Warren's mugshot again. The man was badly beaten. His right eye closed, lips swollen and numerous bruises on his face. One shoulder was lower than the other. That didn't happen in the crash. Warren's car was a 2003 Ford Taurus. Airbags had been mandatory since 1998.

Isaiah imagined what had really happened at Alabaster Creek. After a quarter-mile chase at seven thousand feet, Warren had collapsed, barely able to breathe. He was in no condition to resist, but the officer pounded on him anyway. Isaiah had seen this kind of thing on video. The officer chases a suspect, gets him down and helpless, but beats him up anyway. Why? Most people concluded the cop was either a sadist or a racist, and in too many cases that was true. But in a number of the tapes Isaiah had seen, the cop was pissed off, furious in fact, because he'd risked his life to catch a worthless asshole. He might have left his wife a widow, his kids fatherless or a bystander lying dead on the street. The officer was frightened by the chances he'd taken and embarrassed because he'd been frightened. The officer who had pursued Warren Long was Sheriff Ronald Cannon.

Isaiah nodded as he imagined Cannon's state of mind. Warren had not only assaulted a woman that Cannon probably knew, he'd done it in Coronado Springs, the sheriff's hometown, the one he'd sworn to protect. Add in a nervous system flooded with angry adrenaline, and you could expect a little extracurricular punishment.

Cannon had testified at Warren's trial. Warren cursed him and the public defender so adamantly he had to be taken from the courtroom. Cannon. Of all the people in the world Warren could kill, he'd chosen the sheriff as his next victim. How does this happen? Isaiah thought. You work hard to unravel the case and end up with a revelation that puts you in life-threatening jeopardy. He wondered why his options so often came down to one, and it was always the equivalent of cliff diving into the kiddie pool or running with the bulls in a loincloth.

There's only one way to extricate yourself from this mess, he thought. You have to convince Cannon that there are serial killers in Coronado Springs and that he is their next victim. Do that and maybe the sheriff would see their disputes had developed from a series of misunderstandings and let you go. Maybe. The problem is you're not credible with him. How do you prove that you are? Again, there was one shitty option. He made the call.

"What do you want?" Cannon said. "Unless it's about surrendering, I don't want to hear it."

"I want a face-to-face," Isaiah said.

"Why?" Cannon sounded truly puzzled.

"I want to convince you I'm telling the truth, and the only way I can think of is to put myself at risk." Cannon didn't say anything. "I have one condition," Isaiah said. "You let me talk until I'm done before you try and arrest me."

Cannon was surprised. "Okay, fine."

"I'll be on foot."

Isaiah said he'd call at ten-thirty and provide the time and place. Cannon couldn't get over it. Not only did Isaiah want to meet in person, he said he would be on foot, not in cars facing in different directions or on opposite sides of the river. Something didn't smell right. Isaiah said "before you try and arrest me." In other words, he had a getaway plan. No chance, Cannon thought. He knew his town right down to the last stop sign. There was no way Isaiah could escape, especially on foot. But anybody they called IQ would have something up his sleeve, something sneaky and unexpected. Escaping from the sheriff's car had become a running joke in the department. *Hey, Chief, did you forget to close the door? Want a burger, Chief? I heard he stole your lunch. Were you bringing him in, Chief, or were you giving him a ride?* That wasn't going to happen again.

There were ten officers in the department. Cannon brought in four more from the Highway Patrol. They would be positioned strategically, able to cordon off an area in two minutes. Unless Isaiah had a helicopter, he wasn't going anywhere.

It occurred to Cannon that Isaiah was taking a massive risk. Was it possible he was right? Were two serial killers actually in Coronado Springs? Why would a guy like Isaiah lie? Why would he tell a story about a knife fight? But Pearce, Crowe's parole officer, said Crowe was in Sacramento. Why would he lie? The most likely explanation was mistaken identity. Isaiah thought someone else was Crowe, and let's not forget the whole mess had started with that nutcase Billy Sorensen. For now, it didn't matter. Isaiah had harbored a fugitive, escaped from police custody and, until proven otherwise, lied to a police officer.

Isaiah called as promised. The meeting place was the parking lot behind Lars Hardware Store. He said if Cannon wasn't there by 10:45 he was leaving. Cannon put O'Neal in charge. He would direct the officers during the meet. Cannon knew Lars's place. The parking lot was large, well lit, open, with two adjacent parking lots and woods at the back. Cannon snorted. Did

Isaiah really think he could escape by running into the fucking trees? There was thick brush in there. A rabbit would have a tough time getting through. A city boy would get lost if he didn't get scratched to death by the nettles, thorny brambles and branches that stuck out like pitchforks. O'Neal would have officers no more than forty yards away, all of them in good shape, including Cannon himself. There were also cars and ATVs. Isaiah would be caught in less time than it took to drive over to Lars.

Cannon arrived at the lot. As instructed, he took off his belt, radio and holster and laid them on the ground. Then he pulled his shirt out of his pants, raised it and turned in a circle. No gun, except for the .32 snub nose he had in his ankle holster.

"The gun in the ankle holster too," Isaiah called from somewhere in the trees. The smart-ass bastard, Cannon thought. He complied. The lot was empty, nothing out there but a couple of plastic bags skipping across the asphalt. The sodium lights were yellow and ominous. Cannon was confident. Even now, his officers were creating a rough circle around the lot, some held back in case Isaiah switched locations. A few were in cars or riding ATVs. Victor Lars and his son, Gunner, were on a nearby rooftop, training their Nikon 10 x 42 binoculars on anything that moved. They had police radios and knew how to use them. Isaiah would need a magic trick to get out of this.

Cannon started walking. It was quiet except for his footsteps and a vague breeze shushing through the trees. At this altitude, the nights were cold. He didn't feel it, he was focused on the trees. Isaiah would emerge from there. He was almost at the end of the lot when he came to a ditch, about two feet deep and eight feet across. The gas company was laying down a new line. There were crowd control barriers running the length of the ditch. Cannon nearly laughed. Did Isaiah really think these were obstacles? No, that was ridiculous. *Watch for the magic trick, Cannon.*

Isaiah came out of the trees and down a short slope. Only the ditch and the barriers separated the two men. Isaiah didn't seem nervous; he didn't seem anything. Weird, this guy.

"So what's this important thing you have to tell me?" Cannon said. "More bullshit about serial killers?"

"Yes, except it's not bullshit," Isaiah replied. "I'll say it again. I wouldn't be putting myself at risk unless I was telling the truth."

"What's the truth?"

"There are two serial killers in Coronado Springs. William Crowe and Warren Long."

"Warren Long? I haven't heard that name in a while." Cannon's heart was galloping in his chest. If O'Neal did his job, officers were creeping into the woods on either side of Isaiah. A flanking maneuver. "This is just more bullshit, Quintabe," Cannon said. "Warren Long is a lowlife, a drug addict and a moron, but he's not a serial killer. He's a bum."

"You said you'd let me finish."

"Then finish."

"Warren didn't come here to kill somebody at random," Isaiah said. "He's here to kill you. Crowe's along for the ride."

"That asshole wants to kill me?" Cannon scoffed. "Why?"

"I know what happened at Alabaster Creek. You beat the hell out of Warren and you already had him down." Cannon was taken aback. How did Isaiah know that?

"Only me and Long were there. Where were you?" he said.

"I saw the file," Isaiah said. "Warren's car had airbags. He didn't sustain the injuries in the crash. You ran him down and gave it to him. I don't blame you. You were angry and you had a right to be."

Cannon hesitated. How did Isaiah figure that out? "If Crowe's not here, Warren's not here," Cannon said. "I don't think you're lying, Isaiah. It's mistaken identity but you refuse to accept it."

Cannon decided the conversation was at an end, but where was the magic trick? "Stay there and turn around so I can cuff you." It came to him suddenly. Isaiah has a vehicle in the woods! He raised his hand. The GO sign. He brushed the barriers aside and jumped over the ditch. Isaiah was already up the slope and into the trees. The ATVs and two squad cars were racing across the lot. Cannon looked back and shouted, "He's got a vehicle!" Then he turned and crashed through the brush.

Isaiah sidled his way through a particular cut in the brush. It was too thick for the ATVs. They would have to go wide and find an entry point. That would take time. He had also anticipated being flanked but the woods were deep. The officers wouldn't know when or where to angle toward him. Cannon wouldn't be far behind but Isaiah had planned his route ahead of time. An immediate hard right, under a fallen tree trunk, hard left around a thicket and into another cut. Cannon could track him but only by the sound. But there was no way to be quiet when you're running for your life. Isaiah reached a small creek bed that went straight uphill. He left his cap there and kept going.

Cannon bulled his way through the tangle of undergrowth. He stopped and thought a moment. Isaiah had a destination; he wouldn't run around randomly.

"Shit," Cannon said. Macklemore Road was on the other side of the woods. That had to be where Isaiah was going. He probably had Billy or the girl waiting for him in a car. The only way for his officers to get there was to go around the woods, a twenty-minute drive. Cannon heard an officer somewhere behind him. "Get on your radio," he shouted. "Isaiah's heading for Macklemore Road. Send two units to cut him off at both ends. Tell the ATVs to go straight there."

"You got it, Chief," the officer called back. It sounded like Dickerson, O'Neal's partner. They were mean sons of bitches.

Cannon kept running and came to a creek bed. He saw something on the ground. Isaiah's cap. He yelled again. "Follow me up the creek bed!"

■ ■ ■ ■

Isaiah heard Cannon shouting about the creek bed. Good. He'd taken the bait. Isaiah was heading for a trail made by dirt bikers. You wouldn't know it was there unless you'd been there before. It ended on a logging road, a half mile away from Macklemore. He kept moving.

Cannon started up the creek bed. There was a muddy patch. He started to go around it and stopped. He didn't have his flashlight and used his phone for light. There were no footprints except his own. Isaiah hadn't come this way; the cap was a fucking decoy. "Goddammit!" Cannon shouted. He realized Isaiah couldn't keep fighting the brush. There had to be another trail somewhere. He closed his eyes and let his memory take him on a tour. He'd played in these woods as a boy, explored them with his friends, pretended they were big game hunters chasing lions and tigers. He brought his daughter here, and they rode their dirt bikes together.

"You son of a bitch," he said. That's where Isaiah was going! There was a dirt bike trail that looped through the woods and ended on a logging road. It was easy to miss. Call in the ATVs? No, they were halfway to Macklemore. Cannon could wait for Dickerson and O'Neal. They had flashlights and guns, but in the meantime, Isaiah would lengthen his lead. Cannon yelled, "Over here! This way!"

Isaiah heard Cannon shouting. He wasn't far behind. He'd figured out the hat was a ruse. Thankfully, Isaiah reached the dirt bike trail. It was steep and narrow, hemmed in by the brush and trees. He climbed the trail, tripping on the ruts and tire tracks. He was winded and cold. He was suddenly fearful it was the wrong trail. He stepped up his pace. At last, he saw the clearing and the mud-spattered Electra Glide leaning on its stand. "Hallelujah," he said.

He was going to leave the engine running but the bike needed throttle, or it died. Getting here had been hard. The Glide was for highway cruising, nothing about it was suitable for this kind of terrain. The width, the regular handlebars, the street tires, the short-travel shock absorbers and the low ground clearance. A modern dirt bike weighed around two hundred pounds. The Glide weighed six or seven.

Isaiah mounted up, stood on the pegs and

stomped the lever. The bike backfired so loud it was like shooting off a shotgun. But the damn thing didn't start. The sound had alerted Cannon. Isaiah heard him shouting, "He's over here! I've got him!" Isaiah stomped on the lever again. It sputtered and died. Another try, same results. Had he flooded it? If he did, he'd have to wait for the carburetor to clear. Cannon was close, Isaiah could hear him crashing through the brush. Another try, another nothing. Isaiah's thigh muscles were tapped out, each kick weaker than the last. Cannon was very close. *One more time, Isaiah, kick the fucking thing!* He gathered up his remaining strength, stood up on the pegs and kicked his last kick. The bike started. He looked back. Cannon had reached the trail. He was twenty yards downhill. Isaiah twisted the gas, revved the engine and released the clutch. The engine roared, but the back tire couldn't find traction. It was spinning in the dirt. Isaiah could see Cannon in the rearview mirror, his teeth clenched, fierce and coming on fast. The tire was still spinning. *Come on, come on, bite, goddammit!* Cannon was ten feet away, his eyes like search beams, sweat on his angry face.

"I GOT YOU," he screamed. "I GOT YOU, MOTHER-FUCKER!" And then, traction! Cannon lunged forward, trying to grab the seat, the fender, anything. Isaiah took off, the bike fishtailing, a shower of dirt, gravel and pine needles hitting the sheriff in the face.

The trail was full of potholes and deep ruts left by the hundreds of bikes that had used it before. There were also patches of greasy mud, erosion grooves and steep inclines. Isaiah stood up on the pegs, flexing his knees to absorb the bumps, every moving part on the old Harley squeaking and creaking and complaining. The bike felt like it was breaking apart. The headlight was weak but brightened when you revved it. At least the generator was working. Isaiah made it through a stretch of whoop-de-doos. The front tire wanted to follow the ruts, leading him off the trail and into the brush. He had to sit and wrestle with the handlebars, paddling furiously with his feet. He estimated his speed at seven to ten miles an hour. He thought he'd gone about a mile. Hiking speed was two to three. If Cannon was in pursuit, he'd never catch up. He stopped to rest, have a drink of water. He got the Cordura jacket, gloves and helmet out of the saddlebags and kept going.

He reached a hill. It wasn't that high, but

it was very steep. If you were on foot, you'd have to lean forward to make the climb. Coming the other way, the angle wasn't nearly as severe. The surface was dry dirt and loose gravel, grooved and furrowed by a thousand tire tracks and uneven rivulets where the rain had washed down. Some of them were inches deep. About midway up, there was a stretch of solid rock, then another stretch of dirt and gravel, followed by a short, sharp incline to the top.

He put the bike in second gear. Too much traction and the front tire would lift. You'd fall backward with a seven-hundred-pound bike on top of you. He revved the engine, released the clutch and accelerated hard, standing on the pegs and leaning over the gas tank to keep his weight forward. It was a struggle to stay on line, the handlebars wagging violently back and forth, the shocks bottoming out, Isaiah bouncing up and down. He had to feather the clutch to keep the revs up. If he lost momentum, he'd never get it back.

He hit the rocky patch and downshifted to first to get traction on the hard surface. There was dirt and gravel again so he shifted back to second. He made it over that too, the short, sharp incline ahead. Back to first gear, more revs, the front wheel went over the crest. "Yeah!" he shouted. But he forgot to let off the gas. The rear wheel dug in, the front end rearing like a stallion. The bike skewed sideways and threw him off.

He tumbled and rolled down the side of the hill, carried along by a conveyor belt of fast-moving dirt, gravel and debris. He was on his back, low-hanging branches slapping at him, rocks bouncing off the polycarbonate helmet. He shifted his weight onto his shoulder and took a quick glance up. The Glide was sliding down after him, going faster than he was. If they hit bottom like this he'd be crushed. He lay flat again, his head like a luge driver, watching the bottom of the incline getting closer, a pile of big rocks down there. He couldn't roll clear and he couldn't get up. He heard the bike behind him, metal scraping and screeching. He saw a thick branch hanging over his path. He didn't know if he could reach it. He leaned forward as far as he could and put both hands up high. He was going so fucking fast! *Grab hold and don't let go!* He grabbed the branch, hooked a leg over and pulled himself up, the bike sliding under him so close a side mirror whacked him on the ass.

The avalanche stopped. He let go of the branch and clambered down to the bottom.

He was sore; the rocks had pummeled him everywhere but his head. He took off his helmet and gloves and slid down to the ground, his back against a tree, breathing in gulps. He rested a few minutes, confident Cannon was still far behind. A moment later, he heard Cannon coming up the trail. He wasn't hiking, he was jogging, traveling almost as fast as the Glide. The delay had let him catch up.

Cannon slowed to a stop, probably gathering oxygen for the climb up the hill. If he reached the top, he'd see the path of the avalanche and the dust thrown up by the falling rocks. Isaiah heard the sheriff trudging up the hill.

"What do we have here? Have a little accident?" Cannon said. He'd reached the top of the hill. Isaiah wasn't in his line of sight, the trees giving cover from above. He was in a wide clearing with only the occasional shrub. The surrounding trees were too far away to reach in his condition. The moon was bright but dimmed by a thin veil of clouds, a faint deer path cutting across the weedy grass. Unless you were a weasel or a snake, there was no place to hide.

Cannon reached the bottom of the incline. Isaiah imagined him standing there, not moving, listening, while his police officer's eyes searched for a sign. He came forward and stopped. Judging by the sound, the sheriff was probably on the deer path. Isaiah was very close to him. A few yards away. He had to breathe silently, without moving his chest. His injuries throbbed. He had dirt in his nose, mouth and lungs. A layer of sweat and mud were caked on his face. He couldn't open his eyes. He had covered himself with pine needles, leaves and dirt. He had no idea what he looked like from the outside. He might be as obvious as King Tut's sarcophagus under a bedsheet. He was counting on his choice of locations; in a depression so there wouldn't be a silhouette and underneath the branches of a low bush so there wouldn't be a shadow. But the depression was very close to the deer path. Isaiah reasoned Cannon would be looking around and ahead of him, not down and a few feet in front of him.

Cannon still hadn't moved. *Come on, goddammit, I'm going to choke to death!* Isaiah was on the sheriff's left. He could hear him taking slow heel-to-toe footsteps. He drew closer. Isaiah could hear him breathing. Cannon stopped again, his shoes a foot away from his head. Isaiah was on the verge of giving up. *I can't stand it, I can't stand it!*

The sheriff was very still. He held it. And held it. He was listening for a discrepant sound. The dirt and sweat had formed a crust around Isaiah's body. He was like a fish baked in salt. It was so fucking hot. There was nothing but intense heat and claustrophobia. *I've got to move! I have to move!*

Cannon hadn't taken another step. Maybe he was looking down at the idiot covered with dirt, watching him suffocate and die. Cannon huffed. "Well, well. Look who's here." *It's over, Isaiah. It's fucking over.*

"Chief? Are you down there?" a voice said. "It's Dickerson and O'Neal." Isaiah heard them sliding down the incline. Cannon would probably be looking up at them. He had to take a chance. He had to breathe. His left hand was farthest under the bush. He lifted it and swiped the debris away from his mouth and eyes. Had Cannon seen him? There was a moment of quiet. Was Cannon pointing down at him, smiling and mouthing the words, *he's right here!*

"Took us a while to catch up to you," Dickerson said, panting. "Jesus, you're in shape. Where did he get the bike?"

"It doesn't matter," Cannon said. "He crashed and he's probably hurt. He couldn't have gotten very far."

"I radioed everybody," Dickerson said. "There are four more officers behind us. It will take them a while to get here."

"We can't wait. Fan out, be alert, draw your weapons." Isaiah was sucking air between his teeth. The sense of enclosure seemed life-threatening. He itched everywhere. *Give up, Isaiah. You're done.* He heard the officers move away, their voices growing more distant. If he got up would they see him? *I'm gonna die, I'm gonna fucking die. I'VE GOTTA GET UP!* He sat up, pawing the dirt off his face, choking and gasping for breath. He couldn't see. *TOO SOON, TOO SOON, THEY'RE STILL HERE!* He scraped the crud out of his eyes. They were gone.

He sat there a moment, scraping more crud off. Once again, he'd been inches away from total destruction. Once again, he was beat to shit, alone and without resources. Why not give up? he thought. What's the worst thing that could happen? A few years in state prison? How could it be worse than this? At least you'd get out someday. You were never getting out of this. He lurched to his feet and started walking.

He didn't know how long he'd been slogging. He heard the occasional buzz of an ATV, but it was far away. He stopped several times to rest. He kept going until he couldn't go on anymore. He was about to collapse when the hardware store's parking lot appeared. It was quiet, empty, no one thinking he'd come back here. He had change from the money he'd spent at the motorcycle shop. There was an old-fashioned wall phone in the 24-hour laundromat across the street. He'd seen it when he was doing his wash. He called Billy and told him where he was. Then he sat down against a warm dryer and fell asleep.

He had vague images of what happened next. Billy and Ava getting him into the car, arriving at a house, the porch light on. A mailbox with ABBETT stenciled on it. Brick steps and a door with beveled glass. Stairs. Billy pulling off his clothes. Climbing into a soft bed and then nothing.

CHAPTER TWENTY-SEVEN: THE SWEET LIFE

This was the day of reckoning Cherise had dreaded. She knew at some point her husband would have to make a decision. Work nine to five or come home empty-handed. But she hadn't anticipated Brad's offer. A hundred and twenty-five thousand dollars a year versus an empty checking account was a no-brainer if there ever was one. She imagined what they could do with that kind of money. The obvious things. A better this, a better that, and there would be money for Micah's education and a savings account with something in it. The health insurance at Apex was much better than her own meager plan. Security was what Cherise prized most.

When she was growing up, her family had very little. She had a younger brother with a learning disability and a little sister with asthma. Her mother, Gloria, taught fourth grade while she paid off her student loans.

Her father delivered mattresses and dining sets for Big Sam's Discount Furniture in Culver City. If the car broke down or somebody got laid off or the washing machine leaked, you did without or went into debt.

The family's fortunes were reflected in their Sunday dinners. Pot roast with mashed potatoes. Cut-up hot dogs with fried onion. Baked beans with crushed potato chips on top. A smear of peanut butter on one slice of folded Wonder Bread. The ups and downs were unpredictable, scary and shaped your view of the future. There would never be brighter days ahead. You didn't look any further than tomorrow because it might be worse than today. The ground was always shaking, nothing was ever settled, and you were always waiting for the next disappointment. "Things are okay" was the best you could do.

Cherise was a paralegal for a law firm in downtown Long Beach. She'd been promoted to supervisor and oversaw a staff of eleven. She made what some would call good money, but these days, that wasn't enough. Your income was under constant siege. You were stuck in your castle of regular paychecks while a growing army of financial demands were sharpening their swords right across the moat.

When Dodson first told her about Brad's offer, she screamed, jumped up and down and called her mother. Then she calmed herself and thought about it. Maybe Juanell would thrive, maybe he wouldn't, but that was up to him; his determination, creativity and, most of all, luck. Yes, he could up his odds with hard work, but if you were from the hood, you knew that wasn't enough. All you could do was get yourself to the finish line. Luck either pushed you over or tripped you up. Money was cover. It gave you a fighting chance, and that was all Cherise had needed her entire life. She didn't understand why she wasn't more enthusiastic. Dodson should accept the offer and launch himself on a career in advertising. That was obvious, wasn't it? It was in the family's best interests, and that was that. But another dictum of the hood was that that was never completely that. There was always some other consideration. There was always some loophole, ambush or unintended consequence, and there were a few this time too. Dammit.

It wasn't sugarplum fairies dancing in Dodson's head. It was James Brown, Chris Brown, Prince, Usher and Taiwan Williams doing the nae nae at the Night Out Club until three in the morning. At long, long last, the ex-hustler, ex-con and chronically unemployed Juanell Dodson was gettin' paid real money. And for what? Makin' shit up. That's what it amounted to. Makin' shit up. He could do that forever and not get out of bed. He could do that, eat Doritos, watch *The Godfather II,* change Micah's diaper and smoke some tree all at the same time. He couldn't wait to tell Isaiah. He couldn't wait to tell Deronda. He couldn't wait for word to spread around the neighborhood. He could walk tall and know a hundred envious eyes were following him down the street. But he'd skip all that to see the look on Gloria's face when Cherise told her the news. He couldn't wait for her to congratulate him while every corpuscle in her worn-out body shimmied with shock and humiliation. He'd walk into her living room in his T-shirt and gold chains and give her a little gift for helping him out. Maybe a snow globe with some weed in it or a bust of MLK wearing a do-rag and then say something like, "The Chairman of the Board said his all-time favorite rapper was Overdose Willy," and take her to lunch at Meaty Meat Burger and order the Triple Chili Garlic Burger with Gravy Fries and extra jalapeños. Something like that.

He went dubsteppin' into the kitchen for a Dr Pepper with a bigger smile than he'd had in his whole life. It almost didn't fit through the door. Cherise was sitting at the breakfast table.

"Hey, baby. Whas da what?" he said. "Why don't we celebrate? Pick someplace and that's where we'll go. Maybe hit the club too. You ain't seen my smooth game since we —" He stopped. Cherise had a look on her face, the one that said, *I'm about to be a big-ass fly in your ointment so you better sit yourself down.*

"Aww, come on, Cherise," he groaned. "Let me be happy for a goddamn minute."

"You can be happy all you want," she replied.

"Oh, really? Then why do I feel like my happiness is about to get hit with a sledge-hammer?"

"Far as I know you haven't made a decision yet. Are you taking the offer?" He couldn't believe she'd said that.

"Am I — hell yeah, I'm taking it. Why? What are you thinking?"

"It doesn't matter what I'm thinking, Juanell."

"Well if it don't matter, why are we even talking?" Dodson thought a moment; he screwed up his face and groaned. "Oh, no, you can't do this to me, baby. You want me to turn it down, don't you? You the one got me into this in the first damn place, and maybe you don't remember, but you didn't give me a choice. You gave me a goddamn command."

"It's true," she said in that thoughtful way she had. "I gave you no choice about getting off your behind. But a command isn't a decision. Neither of us thought things would happen so soon or that you'd be offered a career."

"Oh, come on, Cherise, you got my head spinning so fast it just left my neck, flew into the bedroom and woke up Micah. What, goddammit, do you want?"

"I want you to think about it," she said evenly. "I want you to be sure. Do you really want a career in advertising? Because if you don't, you'll resent me for the rest our lives. You'll go into that office every day thinking that bitch Cherise got me into this, and now I'm stuck. That's not good for me, you or us as a family."

"Me, you or —" Dodson sputtered. "If a hundred and twenty-five K a year ain't good for us, then neither is a patent on hip-hop or a platinum mine in our living room!"

"And one more thing."

"Oh Lord," Dodson said. "The three worst words in the English language are *one more thing.*"

"What about Stimson?"

"Fuck Stim— I mean, Stimson is not my concern," Dodson replied. "I can't help it if he's a failure. If him and Marge don't get a Winnebago, that ain't on me."

"All right, I understand. I've said all I have to say," Cherise said. She got to her feet. "Do you still want to go out?"

"How can I go out now?" Dodson said. Cherise headed for the door. "Where you going?" he said. "You leave me alone like this?"

"A man is always alone when he's making a man's decision," she said. "I love you, Juanell."

Aside from taking lessons from Gloria, this was the worst situation he could ever imagine. He went out on the balcony and stayed there all night, only going inside to get a drink of water and piss. At dawn, he went over to McClarin Park. Mo and the winos were sleeping under the eaves around the restrooms. Not even the pigeons were awake.

He sat down on a bench. He wasn't tired. The easy breeze, green grass and tall trees were comforting. It was quiet too. With

Micah in the house, he'd come to believe quiet didn't exist. He sat there quite a while but arrived at no decision. Then he realized he never would. The arguments for and against were abstract, philosophical and in your head. White people were into that, going round and round with themselves until nothing was clear and you ended up going with whatever flow didn't flow back. That shit didn't work on the street. If you stopped to have a conversation with yourself every time a dilemma presented itself, you'd either be coldcocked, locked up or taking a nap in a wooden box at Sunshine Cemetery. On the street, you decided when you had to, when you were forced to, in the moment and not before, and the choices you made determined what kind of man you were. If somebody is shooting at you and you jump behind your girlfriend, well, we all know where you stand on the manhood scale. Dodson couldn't make up his mind because he wasn't in that moment. Nothing to do now except make the moment happen.

They met in the conference room this time. Brad was seated at the head of the long white table. He looked confident, a lazy cat who'd already eaten the rat, the parakeet and three cans of tuna. There was a stainless-steel coffee pitcher and dark blue mugs on the table. Dodson sat across from him. He still didn't know what he was going to say. Let the shit happen, he thought. This is how we do it, bitch.

Brad smiled expectantly. "Well, Juanell, have you made up your mind?"

Dodson poured himself a cup of coffee and took a sip. "It's good. Fresh brewed. What is this, French roast?"

Brad soured. "My offer, Juanell?" Here it is, Dodson thought. The moment.

"No, I can't accept," he said. He sipped his coffee. "I could use a little sugar if you've got some around."

Brad was as alarmed as he was surprised. "Just like that? No, you can't accept? Why? You're not doing this for that useless blockhead Stimson, are you? You're giving up a career for him?"

"Maybe when I was hustling I could have fucked him over, but these days I ain't up to it." He took another sip of coffee. "And I can't be locked up in an office all day. Advertising is fun, but I'm already tired of it. I don't like solving problems I don't care about. If Skechers sells more or less walking shoes, who really gives a shit?"

"What about your family?" Brad demanded. "Won't they be disappointed?"

461

"About the money? Yes, they will," Dodson replied. "But they'll be more disappointed if I ruin Stimson's life and work at a job where I'm bored to shit. And then there's you. If I have to listen to your weasel-ass bullshit one more minute, I'll throw you out the window and shoot myself in the forehead."

"You're a fool!" Brad shouted, coming out of his chair.

Dodson's eyes flared. "I'm not one of your flunkies. You better sit your ass down. You disrespect me and I'll choke you to death with that fucked-up tie." Brad wilted and sat back down. "It takes people to survive in this life," Dodson said, "but you hate people and they hate you. One day, you're gonna reach out for a helping hand and won't get nothing but your hand back. No one's gonna have your back or get you out of a jam like I did with Stimson, but I'll bet you can think of all kinds of people who'd backstab you with a bayonet and have a party while you bled to death. Did I tell you the coffee was good?" Dodson got up and moved to the door. "See you on the downside, muthafucka. Adios." He glanced back at Brad. He looked beaten and empty, staring at the tabletop, a long white road that went on and on and ended in the blank screen of the monitor.

He didn't say goodbye to Stimson. He didn't want or need thank-yous. Stimson and Marge would get their Winnebago and God bless 'em. He drove home, went out on the balcony and popped open a Dr Pepper. He thought about East Long Beach and all the people he knew. This was home. He was a beat in the heartbeat here. Cherise was partially right. You can take the brutha out of the hood, but he'll bring the hood with him.

Cherise came home. She came out on the balcony, put her arms around him and rested her chin on his shoulder. "Well, I guess the advertising world can live without you."

"How did you know?" he said.

"Because I know my husband. My husband wouldn't make the best choice. My husband would make the right choice." She held him tighter and kissed his neck. "I'm proud of you, baby." She left, and he was glad, his tears falling on the roof of his car. He spent a quiet minute or two. He felt good about himself, and that hadn't happened in a while. Cherise came back and gave him the phone.

"It's Gloria. She wants to talk to you."

Next morning, Cherise went to work. Dodson was taking care of Micah and enjoying himself. He looked at the boy and felt his heart open. Hard to believe he even got to participate in making something as beautiful as his son. Look at him, he thought, stumbling around, laughing, happy, pointing at shiny things, moving things, and the love in his daddy's eyes. Dodson took him to the park. They walked down the path holding hands. Mo and the winos were waving and smiling as they came toward him. "Let us see this son of yours," Mo said.

Dodson stepped in front of his son. "You muthafuckas better stay right where you are. You think I want your nasty alcoholic breath on my boy? He might get cancer or a rash on his ass." The winos stopped, disappointed. Anything new was potentially entertaining. "I heard one of you got TB," Dodson said.

"Yeah, but I'm only coughing now," a wino replied.

"Go away."

"We ain't animals, you know," Mo grumbled. "We ordinary folks just like you." As they walked off he added, "Must be nice.

464

Staying home with a baby all day. That's a sweet life if I've ever heard of one."

Dodson left the park. Mo's remark bothered him but he didn't know why. He'd been asking himself why way too often these days. He never had to do that when he was hustling. The question was never why, it was always how. How do I con this sucker out his rent money or some variation thereof? As he neared home, he felt worse and worse. Mo's "sweet life" was another way of saying he had nothing of substance to do except babysit. He was right back where he started. Adrift, directionless and useless.

Later, he drove over to Deronda's to get his check for his help with Bobby James. "Thanks," he said, putting the check in his wallet. "Much appreciated. It'll keep me from working at one of your food trucks for a while."

"I've been thinkin' about something," Deronda said. "You know that stuff you did for me and Grace?"

"Yeah. What about it?"

"You remind me of that lawyer who worked for the president." Deronda laughed and shook her head. "I don't remember his name, but that was a shifty muthafucka right there. I'll tell you one thing, that boy knew how to work shit out."

"Uh-huh, I've gotta go."

"That dude was a fixer," Deronda said, as she followed him to the door. "That's what you are too."

"I've been called all kinds of things, but that's a new one on me."

When Dodson returned to the apartment, he opened a new box of Cocoa Puffs. He got the kitchen scissors and neatly cut off the top of the bag. He had noticed over the years that the bowl you used altered the taste. Plastic was unthinkable. There was glass, of course, but the sound the spoon made clinking against the sides was too high-pitched. Ceramic was best. Heavier than glass so it sat solid on the table and the clinking sound was midrange and pleasant. He poured in the milk, sat down at the breakfast table and began to eat. A sudden realization that made him choke and spit cereal all over the floor.

A fixer, he thought. Yeah, you can do that.

CHAPTER TWENTY-EIGHT: THE ITCH

Crowe was losing it. Warren kept ranting about EX; what he'd do, how he'd do it, and that it would take a long time. "Jesus Christ," Crowe snarled. "Shut up, will you? Keep it up and see what happens!" When Warren wasn't raving about EX, he babbled on and on about the girl who'd shoved dirt in his mouth and how he'd make her scream while he cut her into strips.

"Knock it off, Warren, I fucking mean it," Crowe said. The motel room was small and dark. You could only open the windows a few inches. The smell was like two naked men locked in a closet with spilled beer, a moldy pizza and a pile of dirty jockstraps. Crowe shut his eyes. His fantasies were filling him with a need that choked him, burned his eyes and made his dick hard. Right behind it was the anger, his blood sizzling over glowing embers; he was all hot steam and raving madness and he wanted

467

Ava right now, right fucking now. He got up and roared, "RIGHT FUCKING NOW!"

"What's wrong with you?" Warren said.

Crowe put his fists against his body and squeezed tight, trying to contain the need, the fucking need. If he couldn't, everything would turn to shit, and he'd go back to prison. Warren was still babbling and groaning. Crowe had had enough. He yanked him off the bed.

"Get up, you dumb shit!" Crowe hollered. "Do you want to go back to Quentin and get fucked in the ass by the niggers again?" Warren crinkled his forehead like he was trying to remember if that really happened. Crowe dragged him into the bathroom. He pushed his head into the sink, held it there and turned on the cold water. Crowe let Warren up, sputtering and choking. "Did you hear me, asshole?" Crowe shouted. "Do you want to go back to prison again?" He threw Warren to the floor and tossed some towels on top of him. "I don't give a fuck if you're hurt. You deserve to be hurt, letting that bitch fuck you over like that. She can rat us out, don't you understand? We have to get her now."

"No, EX first," Warren insisted. His bottom lip was stuck out like a stubborn kid's.

"For the hundredth time, that makes no

fucking sense!"

"It makes sense to me! It makes sense to me!" Warren sobbed. "You weren't there! You don't know, you don't know how bad it was. You don't know . . ."

There was no point asking him what was bad or trying to argue him out of it. He looked like what he was, a child, beaten, abused, raped and left for dead. He was hugging himself and shivering, but Crowe knew he wasn't going to crack.

"All right," Crowe said. "EX first."

Ava was taking a shower. Billy was in the kitchen making a sandwich. There was no place else to bring Isaiah but home. It was a small town, they had no resources, and Billy had no friends to take them in. Gretta came in, looking harried like she always did. She hesitated a moment before coming forward. She wanted to avoid this exact situation. Mother and son alone together.

"Billy," Gretta said, as if she were passing a coworker in the hall.

"Mom," Billy replied in the same way.

Gretta started to make coffee. She seemed to be making a lot of noise, but it was probably no more than normal. Billy's sandwich was complete, an enormous thing, made from a mishmash of incongruous ingredients. He thought about leaving, but didn't want her to think he was intimidated.

"You okay?" Gretta said.

"Yeah, I'm fine." He took a monumental bite of sandwich. He chewed, cheeks full and moving around, stuff spilling out of his mouth. She hated that. The coffee was done. Gretta poured herself a cup, brought it up to her mouth and blew on it.

"Well, I guess we have to talk about this mess."

"No, we don't."

"What are you going to do?" She took a sip, hiding half her face behind the cup. She was such a bullshitter, Billy thought, acting like she cared. She'd laid it on thick after the divorce. She felt guilty because it was her fault. He was only a kid but he remembered. She drove Dad away and kept her maiden name too. It bothered him. It was like she wasn't committed, like she cared about herself more than anything.

"I'm going to see this through," he said.

"See what through?" Gretta said. "What is this about?"

"You wouldn't get it. You never get anything."

"If you're not going back to the hospital, I'll have to call Cannon."

Billy huffed. "Better think about it. He'll

take me out of here in handcuffs. What will the town think?"

"I said that one time, and I was angry," she said. "Try and understand. I'm responsible for you. I have to do what's best for you even if you don't think so."

"You mean like committing me to a fucking insane asylum?"

"It's not an insane asylum and it kept you from doing something else ridic—" She stopped herself but it was too late. Billy sneered and wiped his mouth with his forearm. "That's not what I meant," she said. Billy was tempted to press the argument but he needed something from her.

"Will you do one thing for me?" Billy said.

"What's that?"

"Give me a little time before you call Cannon and I go to jail."

Gretta held back her first response. "How much time?"

"How much can you give me?" He could see the struggle in her eyes. She could be a hard-ass, but that would prove everything Billy thought about her.

"I'm going back to court," Gretta said. "I'll be home later. Irene and I are going camping. You have until then."

Billy was in the backyard, sitting on the

wrought-iron bench. Sparrows were drinking from the birdbath. The air was still and smelled like warm pine needles. He knew Gretta had her own problems. She never got over Dad leaving, even if it was her fault. Bitching all the time, busy all the time. Drunk drivers and bank robbers needed her attention way more than her own kids and deserved more care. Some people shouldn't be parents, Billy thought. If you're that wrapped up in yourself, fine, but don't have kids just to ignore them. He'd never have kids. Unless it was with Ava.

Eventually, Cannon would come, arrest the three of them, and he'd go back to Schizo Central. An escapee who got caught, led to his cell in shackles and shame. He'd be the object of Nathan's sneering taunts, and Dickie would feel sorry for him. *Dickie,* for God's sake. Ava would be furious. The pursuit of her sister's killer would be over.

Billy read *David Copperfield* when he was still in middle school. It made a lasting impression on him, that line: "Whether I shall turn out to be the hero of my own life, or whether that station will be held by anybody else, these pages must show." It seemed so self-evident it was stupid. Isn't that what everybody wanted? To be the hero of their own lives? Why did people do things at all if not for that reason? To overcome the odds and triumph over extreme adversity, preferably on the evening news cycle. If you didn't do it in front of an audience why do it at all? If you didn't get love from the general public, what was the point? Everything was like that now. Why get married, have a party, have a baby, play a sport, travel, get a puppy, be bipolar, commit suicide or shoot up a classroom full of kids unless you thought it was going viral? Glory and acclaim were happiness. Billy really believed that, although he conceded there were other kinds of happy.

He was with Irene, paddling a canoe across Snowshoe Lake. It was fall. Cool and sunny, bright white clouds drifting across a robin's-egg sky. The maple and aspen trees were turning red and orange, their leaves dancing, the scene pulsing with color and beauty.

Irene stopped paddling and pointed. "Look!" An eagle was swooping low over the sparkling lake, its enormous black wings spread wide and unmoving, gliding without effort, without sound, its world as valid as yours. The eagle ascended on invisible currents, rising steadily, a child of heaven beckoned home, vanishing over the green mountains as silently as it had arrived. It was an amazing moment. Revelatory and profound, yet there was no triumph, victory or applause. It was an experience and nothing more. It resonated with Billy, Irene feeling it too, neither of them talking even as they drove home. The feeling lasted until he got to his room. He sat down on the couch, pressed the remote and the TV came on, and in that split second, modern life reclaimed him and brought him back to the fold.

In all of Billy's fantasies he was the hero. The lone believer who stuck to his beliefs, suffered humiliation and injustice and saved the day. The guy who everyone said was crazy was proved to be right after all. Wouldn't it be amazing to be the hero just once?

Ava appeared next to him. They didn't talk for a while. The backyard was so big it might have been a small park. People had big lots around here, space for the sake of space, a perk of living in a rural town. The smells were a perk too, clean, cold, accented with pines and firs and woodsmoke from someone's chimney.

"I'm not the one for you, Billy," she said.

"I know." Billy shrugged. "I don't even know why I thought about it."

"It's not because of your past or that

something's wrong with you."

"Oh, really? Come on, Ava, it's okay. I know what I am."

She grabbed his arm and turned him toward her. "Listen to me, Billy. I'm not the one for anyone right now and won't be for a long time. Are you listening to me? Are you hearing me? Really hearing me? I'm a wreck, Billy. I don't even think about relationships. The idea never enters my mind."

"You don't have to make excuses. I understand."

"Damn you, Billy!" Ava shouted. She was livid. "You have got to get over yourself ! Being weird does not excuse you from being a grown-up. I know you're hurting, and there's stuff going on inside you, but that doesn't mean every fucking thing that happens or doesn't happen is about you! Jesus, you're frustrating! You have feelings for me without once considering mine or what it's like to be someone else besides you! You know what you need to do, Billy?"

"I'm afraid to ask."

"Grow the fuck up, okay? Grow the fuck up or we'll never truly be friends." Then she got up, crossed the yard and went into the house.

Isaiah's sleep was more like hibernation. When he awoke, he was wearing sweatpants and a T-shirt. There was a bottle of water and a box of Fig Newtons on the bedside table. It was sometime in the afternoon. He was still sore from his tumble off the Electra Glide. He drank the water and tried to orient himself. There was a knock, and a woman entered.

"Hello, Isaiah. I'm Gretta. Billy's mother."

"I apologize for imposing like this," he said.

"You're not imposing. You took care of Billy and I'm grateful."

"What happened last night?" he asked.

"You were in pretty tough shape. I was a medic, served on the aircraft carrier USS *America.* The experience came in handy."

"Thank you," he said.

"I did a search on you. Apparently, you're one of the good guys." Gretta pulled up a chair and sat down. "I'd like to know what's going on. You were weak, dehydrated, and you've got bruises all over your body."

"That part isn't really important right now," he said.

"Then what is?"

"Do you believe the killers are here?"

"Killers? What killers?" she said. Oh, my God, Isaiah thought. *Billy hasn't told her.*

"Two serial killers, William Crowe and Warren Long, are in Coronado Springs."

Gretta was startled and then confused. "I don't understand."

"They're here to kill someone, but we don't know who," Isaiah said. He could see it in Gretta's face, struggling to understand, too many questions to ask all at once.

"I know Warren. He's a basket full of snakes," she said. "Who's Crowe?"

Isaiah hesitated. Better now than later. "Crowe is AMSAK."

"AMSAK," Gretta repeated. She shook her head. "I'm really not following."

"I know, it's almost impossible to believe," Isaiah said. "I'm happy to tell you the story, but it's a long one. The main thing is, Crowe and Warren are here. Crowe tried to kill me with a knife. Warren attacked Billy and Ava but they got away. It's real, Gretta." She was looking at him differently, skepticism narrowing her eyes.

"Billy didn't say anything about being attacked," she said.

"I guess he didn't want to."

"You don't have any knife wounds. I examined you pretty closely."

477

"My injuries are from something else."
He was sounding less and less credible and
he knew it.

"Let's say you're right," Gretta said. "Why
would two serial killers be here?"

"When Cannon arrested Warren, he beat
him up bad. Warren wants to kill him."

"I'll have to talk to Cannon."

"He doesn't believe the killers are here."

"Why?" she said.

Isaiah was reluctant to say, but if he
didn't, Cannon would. That would be
worse. "Cannon called Crowe's probation
officer. He said Crowe was in Sacramento.
He'd seen him, talked to him."

"I'm not getting this." She was frustrated.

"I'm saying this badly, but Crowe and
Warren are here. I know they are." Gretta
stood up and turned away. She thought a
moment before turning around again.

"Was this Billy's idea?" she said sharply.

"It's not an idea. It's very real —"

"You know you're a fugitive, don't you?"
Gretta said. "Along with my son and Ava?"

"Yes, I know."

"I'll have to call Cannon and tell him
you're here." Irene came in.

"Hi, Isaiah. When are we leaving, Mom?"

"As soon as you get home from school,
assuming you're packed," Gretta said.

"Irene, do you know anything about Billy and serial killers?"

"Yeah, he told me about them," she said. She shrugged and offered a weak smile. "You know Billy." Gretta looked coldly at Isaiah.

"I should probably stay around to see the end of this mess but I'm not. I'm going camping. Billy got himself into this and he can get himself out." They left, Irene smiling over her shoulder.

"Bye, Isaiah."

Gretta didn't believe him. The alarm about Crowe and Warren had been raised in every possible way. They might be hunting down Cannon now. He couldn't do nothing. He couldn't let a man be slaughtered. Another painful task. He had to call Grace. She was on her way to a town where two serial killers lurked and he was wanted by the law.

"I was hoping you would call!" she said. There was eagerness and joy in her voice. "I have so much to tell you but I'll wait 'til I get there."

"Where are you?" he asked, hoping she was lost and heading for Mexico.

"In Bakersfield. I'm on the 5. How long does it take timewise?"

"Depends on —" He couldn't go on with

the pretense. He stopped talking. There was silence. She knew what was coming. He wished he knew the right words. "You can't come yet, Grace. I'm not . . . I can't . . . I'm not finished yet."

"And while you're finishing, I guess it's more than possible you'll be killed," she said. He didn't answer. "This happens all the time, Isaiah. I know it's your job, but you don't know how much I worry about you, how frightening it is to — don't say you'll quit, because you won't. I know that and so do you." She was crying. "I can't do this anymore. I love you, Isaiah, and I always will. I hope things turn out okay." She started to say more and ended the call.

He sat there on the bed, bloodless and struck dumb. You went all the way this time, he thought. You destroyed the best thing that ever happened to you. You crushed a bond so deep and singular you'll be lost within yourself forever. And why? Because you're inexorably drawn to the ruined cave of human perversion, where bats, red-eyed and chittering, twist and spiral around the rocks, their shit falling into filth and stench and creatures blind and glowing because they've never seen the sun. This is who you are, Isaiah. This is who you'll always be. And you will never see Grace again.

Isaiah was in the kitchen, talking with Billy and Ava. He was nearly catatonic, dazed and unfeeling, here because there was nowhere else to be. Billy and Ava were leaning against the counters on opposite sides of the island. Something was up.

"Cannon doesn't know he's in danger and he won't talk to us," Ava said. "And he'll arrest us on sight." Billy said nothing. Yeah, something was up, Isaiah thought.

"We can't let him arrest us. We have to watch him, warn him," Isaiah said.

"I'm not going," Billy announced. He shot a look at Ava and walked out.

She sighed. "I hurt his feelings."

Isaiah and Ava went to the police station and parked nearby. There were too many cops and Cannon was protected there. They went to his house and took a position a half block away. Ava's car was a Chevrolet Spark. It was very small. Sitting side by side was like sharing the same lounge chair. She was remarkably self-contained, Isaiah thought. Hard to keep yourself together while hatred churned hot in your chest and every blood cell was screaming for revenge.

Isaiah knew the feelings well.

As they sat there, Isaiah felt an itch — not on his skin but inside of him. It was scratchy and slithery, like a snake with sandpaper skin or a tapeworm with scales. What disturbed him more than the itch was that he'd felt it many times before. He'd missed something.

"Dammit," he breathed.

"What?" Ava said.

He thought about Warren. Why had he come back to Coronado Springs? Why take all those risks just to get the man that arrested you? True, Cannon had beaten him badly but surely Warren had been beaten many times before. What made this different? Criminals have a general hatred for cops, born out of fear and the threat of being locked up. But in Isaiah's experience, they didn't blame any particular cop for their misfortunes. Arrest was a cost of doing business. They blamed the witnesses who betrayed them. That was personal. But the witnesses who testified against Warren were perfunctory. A man who saw him leaving the scene. A woman who heard someone screaming.

Isaiah's mind began flipping through the pages of Warren's file. His memory wasn't photographic, but it was close. He remembered narratives, high emotions and personal stories. He found them more telling than facts. He formed character studies and linked background with behavior to understand motives. At Warren's trial, his public defender used the "excuse defense" to lessen his responsibility. His lawyer brought in witness after witness. Psychiatrists, social workers, relatives and next-door neighbors testified about Warren's early experiences. Warren vehemently objected to the tactic. At one point, he threatened his lawyer and had to be led from the room.

It must have been terrible for him, Isaiah thought. Having your life exposed would be an ordeal for anyone, but especially for a man with so many secrets, so much shame, so many things not to be remembered, not to be spoken of. To have your bed-wetting, your poverty, your inept social skills, your menial jobs, your shocking lack of impulse control, your borderline intelligence and sexual humiliation revealed to the whole world. To be described as an isolated, psychopathic deviant who lived on the fringes of normal society. To have stories told about your mother chaining you to a doghouse with a water dish and a bag of airline peanuts, and how she drove you out to Red Rim Canyon and left you there to die and how her boyfriend raped you continuously for three years. There were stories about the neighborhood kids laughing at you because you had lice in your hair and scabs on your face and paying gangsters in commissary food so they wouldn't bend you over a bunk bed and begging your half brother for money that never came, and spending eleven years of your life in prison and never having a single visitor.

It must have increased Warren's rage exponentially, Isaiah thought. He'd seen that kind of thing on the street. A kid killing someone for exposing him as a weakling, a faggot, a mama's boy or just being afraid. In the hood, self-respect was worth a prison sentence or sometimes, even death. You had to strike back, no matter what the risk or consequence. It would be even more critical for an isolated, psychopathic deviant who was already angry and hateful in the extreme, whose sense of self hung by a single strand of cobweb. The person who revealed you, who shamed you in front of the world, deserved to die, whatever the danger. A sudden recognition made Isaiah's insides clench.

"Ava?" Isaiah said. "Is Gretta short for Margaret?"

"It can be. Why do you ask?"

He remembered the name on Billy's mailbox. ABBETT. He could see the court documents as clearly as if they were right in front of him. The public defender and attorney of record for Warren Long was MARGARET ABBETT.

"Don't ask questions. Drive to Billy's right now!"

CHAPTER TWENTY-NINE: GET TO THE LIVING ROOM

When Crowe and Warren arrived at EX's house, the lights were on. Maybe the daughter was there too. Crowe grinned. "This is gonna be good." They were skulking around the house looking for an entry point when they heard a girl's voice. They peeked through a parting in the curtains and saw her, elbowing each other to get a better look. Warren inhaled through his teeth. Crowe drew in a sharp breath, his fingernails on the windowsill digging into the paint. It was her. The perfect girl. Mid-teens, slim, pale skin, medium brown hair, no makeup. She was wearing an oversize sweatshirt and jeans. She was a normal girl. A nice girl. She had a nice family too. Crowe wished he knew her name. She was taking things out of drawers and putting them into a backpack while she talked on the phone.

"We're going to Sugar Mountain," she said. "Me and my mom are going to camp."

She laughed. "No, she's not making me, I like being with her. What? No, that's not weird."

The mother came in. "Irene, aren't you ready yet? We don't want to hike in the dark." Warren was mumbling, *holy shit, holy shit, holy shit.* Crowe hardly looked at the mother. He wanted the Perfect Girl. He wanted Irene. He was having a hard time keeping it together. His hunger for horror, helplessness and screaming, open mouths had imploded. He had to fight the impulse to crash through the window and cut those bitches up now. Warren had bared his teeth. He looked like he was going to chew through the window frame.

They went around the side of the house and the sliding glass door. Crowe pulled on the handle and it opened. He nearly laughed. They went in and Crowe drew the Bowie knife. Warren had lost his in the woods. He'd gone to the sporting goods store, but the knives were too small. He spent his last money on a Gränsfors Bruks Wildlife Hatchet. It was ugly, heavy and crude. The business end was the color of a lead pencil and shaped like a medieval fighting axe. The old guy behind the counter said, "Take a whack at a two-by-four and you'll cut it in half."

Billy was in his basement room, sulking. Grow the fuck up, Ava had said. Grow the fuck up? Um, excuse me, Miss, but how did you get onto Crowe in the first place? Didn't the kid who needed to grow the fuck up break out of a hospital for you and steal government records so you'd have something to do? Fuck you, Ava, you beautiful, amazing girl. I would marry you in a heartbeat.

Billy heard footsteps. He looked up at the ceiling. Someone was in the house, a stranger, he could tell by the footsteps. The intruder was stepping too softly, going too slow. Wait, no, there were two of them. "Oh, shit," Billy said. It's the killers! Mom and Irene were in mortal danger. Billy hurried up the stairs and into the hallway. There they were. At the far end, just coming out of the living room, the two of them bigger than life, bigger than death. Startled, they froze. Crowe had his Bowie knife. Warren had a fucking axe.

"Mom! Irene!" Billy shouted. "Get out of the house!" He hoped they'd heard him. *Lead the killers away from them, Billy!* The men charged. Billy didn't run, he backed up, baiting them — and then he took off. He led them through the dining room toward the den. He remembered his hidden weapons. The killers' footsteps were close and loud. The nunchaku was in the den but he couldn't stop for it. Where were Mom and Irene? Had they left already? A hand grabbed the back of Billy's shirt.

"Got you!" Crowe snarled. Billy twisted away. The closest weapon was the Crosman air gun. It was in the living room, stuck under a couch cushion. He made a turn back into the hallway. Crowe's hand grabbed him by the shirt again and yanked him around. Billy saw a face worse than any fiend, hellion or swamp creature he'd ever seen. Crowe was so flushed, his face was a bruise, his nostrils flaring in and out, his eyes looked ulcerated, hatred oozing from them like pus. Warren was behind him, another fucking beast screaming something indecipherable.

Crowe had Billy by his T-shirt. He pulled him close with one hand and raised the knife with the other. Billy ducked, stuck out his arms and shimmied out of his shirt. *The living room, get to the living room!* He ran in, deked around the love seat and leaped over the coffee table to the couch. Fuck. He landed on the goddamn couch. He had to scramble to right himself and get his hand under the cushions. He found the air gun. It was long and heavy, the sight catching on the upholstery. Crowe came in screaming and waving the Bowie. Billy remembered. The gun had to be pumped to get air pressure! The more pressure, the more powerful the shot. Five pumps was good, ten was better. *First pump.* Crowe was halfway across the living room. *Second pump.* Crowe was at the coffee table. *Third pump.* Crowe was lunging at him. There was barely enough time to raise the barrel and pull the trigger. The pellet hit Crowe in the eye. He cried out and fell to the floor, but an instant later, there was Warren, raising that axe. No time for pumps. Billy tried to dart past him. Warren took a swing. Billy leaned sideways, the heavy blade missing him by an inch. The swing had left Warren off balance. Billy tried to go around him again, but Warren dropped the weapon, grabbed Billy and slung him across the floor. He slid like a dust mop and conked his head on the iron leg of the BarcaLounger. It felt like his skull was fractured. Warren had paused to catch his breath. Billy stumbled down the hall. Mom and Irene might appear at any moment. He had to stop Warren, not elude him. He got to the basement door. Warren came toward him. He looked like God had dropped him into a tree shredder.

"Come on, shithead," Billy said. "You let a girl kick your ass. Try me."

Warren screamed savagely and rushed him. Billy didn't move. When Warren was five feet away, he turned quickly and raced down the basement stairs. He looked up at Warren's silhouette framed in the doorway. Billy's dizziness was worse, his eyes were getting cloudy. He put a hand on a support post to keep his balance. "Come on, you stupid idiot. What are you waiting for?"

Warren bellowed and pounded down the stairs. "OH, FUCK!" he shouted. He tripped forward, falling headfirst down the stairway. Billy had paid attention to the DEER CROSSING sign and stepped over the trip wire. Warren had not. He bumped down the stairs on his belly, hit bottom, catching most of the impact in his hands. Fuck, he was strong. Warren got up looking more pissed than before. He picked up the axe. "You clumsy shit," Billy said. "What the hell is wrong with you?" He went out the other door into the dark. He couldn't keep his balance; his vision was going in and out.

Warren went after the little fuck, crossing the room and through the door. He found himself in a big space, piles of junk everywhere. Shit. The kid could be hiding anywhere. Then he heard him on the other side of the water heater.

"I'm sorry, did I lose you, asshole?" the kid shouted. "Are you tired or something?"

"I'm gonna chop the shit out of you!" Warren shouted back.

"The hell you will. You couldn't chop a carrot with that stupid thing."

Warren howled like his inner wolf. He went around the water heater and into an open aisle. At the end, he saw a single dim light bulb hanging over a staircase. The kid had an escape hatch. "I'm coming for you, fuck shit! You ain't getting no place!" He ran toward the stairs, about to take them two at a time. He slammed into something as hard as cement. There was the shock of pain. He rebounded, staggered and fell. He curled up, holding his head and screaming. He waited to get his bearings. He got up, reached out and touched the — it's a fucking wall! There weren't any stairs, it was a goddamn *painting* of stairs. This was too much. On top of everything else, he'd broken his nose and his front teeth were loose. The pain was coming from everywhere. That's it, he decided. Time to get the fuck out of here.

He heard Crowe say, "Are you down here?"

"Yeah," Warren said.

Crowe appeared. His right eyeball was red and swollen, black and green bruising around the edges. He was really excited. "The mom and the girl have left."

"All this and we fucking missed them?" Warren said.

"You don't understand. Don't you remember? The girl said they're going camping! They'll be in the woods all by themselves! Imagine what we could do!" He waited for Warren's fantasies to fill up his empty brain cavity.

Warren said, "Help me up."

CHAPTER THIRTY: WITCHES' TREE

Billy clambered out of the steamer trunk. His head was killing him. He touched the spot where he'd hit the BarcaLounger. There was blood on his fingers. Were Mom and Irene okay? He used the handrail to get up the stairs. He entered the hall, stopped and listened. Not a sound. He went down the hallway, looking into the rooms. "Mom? Irene?" he called. He saw blood on the carpet. He felt like throwing up. The pain and dizziness were overtaking him, his vision narrowing. He sat down on the floor, drew his knees up to his chest and closed his eyes.

The Spark jolted to a stop in Billy's driveway. Isaiah and Ava jumped out. The front door was locked. They raced around to the back of the house. The sliding glass door was wide open. Isaiah held his arm out to keep Ava from running in. They entered cautiously, stopping to listen. Nothing. They moved through the living room. The coffee table was tipped over. A lamp on the floor. Some kind of gun was on the sofa.

They entered the hall and saw Billy sitting on the floor. He was very still and had his head on his knees. They ran to him.

"Billy? Are you okay?" Ava said. Slowly he looked up. He had an ugly gash on his head; he seemed barely conscious. "Oh, God, I'll get some ice," she said and hurried off.

"What happened?" Isaiah said. "Where are Irene and Gretta?" Billy raised his head and put it down again.

Isaiah went from room to room. There was no one stabbed or dead on the floor. *Okay, Isaiah, think it through.* Billy had struggled with the killers, Irene and Gretta were gone. Had they been kidnapped or did they escape? He went into the kitchen. There was blood in the sink, bloody towels on the counter and bloody footprints on the tile floor. Two sets, sneakers. There were no other prints. Isaiah followed the tracks out the kitchen door and into the backyard. Judging from the distance between the prints, the killers were moving fast. The prints faded and were gone. It looked like Gretta and Irene had gotten away, but how had they missed the action in the house?

Isaiah sighed. It was obvious. The driveway came all the way into the backyard. Gretta and Irene loaded their stuff back here to save themselves a few trips. They might have been outside when everything happened or maybe they'd left already.

Okay, Isaiah thought. So Crowe and Warren break into the house to attack the women, but Billy gets in the way. There's a fight. Billy is injured and out of action. In the meantime, Gretta and Irene leave on their camping trip. Were they followed? He went back inside. Billy was groaning, his eyes were closed. Ava had an ice pack wrapped in a tea towel pressed against his head.

"I called 911. He's in really bad shape," she said.

"Billy, where did Gretta and Irene go?" Isaiah said.

Billy's head was wobbling. "Sugar Mountain."

"The paramedics will be here in a couple of minutes. Do you think you can hang on?"

"I want to . . . go with you," Billy said.

"No, you have a concussion," Ava said. "Stay put, okay?" She kissed his cheek. Isaiah ran off and she followed.

They raced out to Ava's car. Isaiah did a quick GPS. Sugar Mountain was two hours away, a straight shot south on 185, toward Tahoe. It was late afternoon. In a couple of hours, the forest would be darker than a subway tunnel, and two unarmed, unsuspecting women would be alone in the woods with a pair of unconscionable maniacs.

They got into the car, Isaiah behind the wheel. "Uh-oh," Ava said. An SUV was racing toward them, siren screaming, lights flashing blue, red, blue, red. The Spark's puny engine had less than a hundred horsepower. Cannon's vehicle had at least three times that. It was also equipped with four-wheel drive, halogen spotlights and a push bumper for executing the PIT maneuver.

"We'll never get away," Ava said.

Cannon hunched over the steering wheel. Gretta had left a message for him. Isaiah, Billy and Ava were at the house. Isaiah said something about serial killers, but she didn't believe him. Cannon knew he was driving too fast but he wanted that goddamn Isaiah, that slick son of a bitch who'd told him a bunch of bullshit and made a fool out of him. He saw Isaiah and Ava come out of the house. They saw him and hurriedly got in a tiny white car. A Spark. His niece had one.

"You're fucked," Cannon said. He was

driving a Ford Interceptor, made especially for law enforcement. No way they were outrunning him in a little buzz fart. Isaiah started backing out of the driveway, saw Cannon coming and stopped. He put it in drive and took off around the side of the house. Cannon chuckled. He was trying to get cute. Cannon approached the house, cranked the wheel, yanked on the emergency brake. The car slid sideways. He let go of the brake, punched the accelerator, bumping over the curb, following Isaiah into the narrow corridor between the house and the neighbor's fence. The Spark slipped through easily. The Interceptor was a foot and a half wider, scraping stucco off the house and knocking boards out of the fence. Cannon was trailing so close he could read the Spark's license plate.

The Spark came out of the corridor and crossed the brick patio. There's nothing back there but trees. If Isaiah crashes, that's on him. The buzz fart zipped through a space between a birdbath and a wrought-iron picnic bench. As soon as it was clear, Isaiah made a sharp U-turn, tearing up a flower bed, throwing up dirt and manure. Cannon missed the birdbath, but the right fender slammed into the picnic bench. The wooden seat broke apart, the frame mangled, stuck under the skid plate, sheets of sparks flying as it scraped across the bricks. The frame hit something and was wrenched off.

The Spark came out of the U-turn and drove into the narrow corridor on the other side of the house. Cannon made the same turn, the Interceptor fishtailing. Isaiah had improved his lead but not enough to matter. He was out of the corridor, driving over the front lawn, slowing as the car bumped over the curb and took off down the street. The Interceptor came out of the corridor seconds after the Spark and started across the lawn — Billy came staggering out of the house, waving his arms. He was right in front of the car!

"GET OUT OF THE FUCKING WAY!" Cannon screamed. He swerved so close the fender brushed Billy back, knocking him down. Cannon stomped the brakes, skidding across the lawn and into the street before the car stopped. He jumped out and rushed to Billy. "Goddamn you, Billy! What the hell were you doing?" He kneeled beside the kid. He was pale as tracing paper, semiconscious and bleeding from the head. *Oh, shit. Did you hit him, Cannon?* He got on his radio, called for an ambulance, but the dispatcher said it was nearly there. Isaiah must have called before he left. Cannon couldn't believe Billy would do something so extreme. Jump in front of a moving car just so Isaiah could escape? What was wrong with this kid? What was his story? Why did he do such crazy things? The paramedics arrived. They did a quick triage, fitted Billy with a cervical collar and put him on a spinal board. Cannon hovered over him.

"Why did you do that, Billy? *Why?*"

A paramedic said, "Step back, Sheriff, you're getting in the way."

They loaded him into the ambulance. Cannon, mystified, watched it drive away.

Billy lay on the gurney, straps holding his arms over his chest. It wasn't uncomfortable. Actually, it felt fine. The ambulance was going fast, he could tell by the tire noise. There were bright fluorescents on the ceiling and he had to look away. A lot of equipment in here. Bags, braces, things stored in overhead bins, devices he didn't recognize. The siren was muted, a paramedic seated sideways, talking on his radio. Billy closed his eyes and smiled. Isaiah and Ava had gotten away. They were going to Sugar Mountain and they would save Mom and Irene. Because of him. He had saved the day. He was, at last, a hero.

Isaiah was averaging eighty miles an hour, the fastest the Spark would go without blowing up. The tiny engine was screaming, the road noise so loud it was like the windows were open and the windshield was missing. As he fled the house, he saw Cannon's car in the rearview mirror, screeching to a stop in the middle of the street. Something had happened back there. Otherwise, Cannon would be on your tail right now. The ambulance had arrived almost immediately after that. Isaiah passed it going the other way. He made a calculation. Cannon is stuck at the scene for how long? Let's say ten minutes. What then? Cannon would try and anticipate your next move. The logical thing for Isaiah or anyone else to do in this situation was escape and speed south on 185 at eighty miles an hour. Okay, assume that Cannon is coming after you. Ten minutes at the scene, another minute to get to 185. You have approximately an eleven-minute lead, Isaiah thought. Conservative, but it was safer. The sheriff would probably hold his speed to ninety miles per hour. The highway was mostly wide turns and long straightaways; any faster would be foolhardy.

With an eleven-minute lead and a ten-mile-an-hour time differential, it would take Cannon about an hour and six minutes to catch up. Which also meant Isaiah had an hour and six minutes to catch Crowe and Warren before Cannon caught and arrested him. Before the killers slaughtered Gretta and Irene.

"Do you think we'll get there in time?" Ava said. Isaiah didn't answer.

Cannon stayed focused and alert. All he needed now was to hit a goddamn deer at ninety miles per hour. He'd been on the road for forty-five minutes and hadn't seen the Spark. Had he guessed wrong? Should he stop and go back? *No, stick it out. Your reasoning is solid.* He was worried about Billy. The accident could cost him his sheriff's badge and probably should. His temper was a goddamn menace, but never mind that. You can fix yourself later, he thought. For now, catch that damn Isaiah.

Crowe and Warren were more fucked up than they'd ever been. Warren had given Crowe a couple of Darvon, a few lines of blow and a 30-milligram slow-release Adderall for pep. Crowe's right eye had been obliterated, replaced by a big black and green leech stuck to his face. The pain had gone down but only a little. Warren was no longer human. He was something crawling out of the apocalypse, covered with dried blood, a plum-colored bump the size of an eight ball on his forehead. His nose was bulbous, broken and not in the middle of his face. A front tooth was missing, which made him look stupider than he already was. He said something about running into stairs that weren't really stairs, whatever that meant. The only thing that kept either of them going was the mother and daughter. What they'd do when they caught up with those bitches. The perfect girl, Crowe thought. At long last, the absolute perfect girl! He imagined her and Mom sitting around the campfire roasting marshmallows and telling ghost stories. Oh, they'd get a ghost story all right, except there'd be two of them armed with a fucking axe and a foot-long Bowie knife sharp enough to skin a human being.

Shareen's car didn't go very fast. It was making clanking noises. Crowe wondered about Shareen and whether the rats and coyotes had found her body and if the maggots were wiggling out of her ears. When this was over, he'd go back and take a look. Warren had dropped the same pills as

Crowe but added an extra Adderall and more lines of blow. He was rocking back and forth, shaking, nodding his head, babbling, but you couldn't make out the words.

"Jesus fuck, will you shut up?" Crowe roared. "Did you hear me? SHUT UP!" But Warren kept it up, the sound of his voice like hornets in a jam jar, sawing through Crowe's skull, the last scraps of his sanity flying out of the window. He realized he was babbling too. *Perfect girl perfect girl I'm coming for you perfect girl you're going to die perfect girl perfect girl.*

Ava was grateful to Isaiah. All he'd been through to help someone he'd met yesterday. She glanced at him. A strange man with a big heart. She felt bad about what she was going to do, but she had no choice. She thought about Crowe. The malignant shit had taken her Hannah away; Hannah, who could finish your sentences and think the same thoughts, not because of some mysterious telepathy, but because you were always together. When you went for a walk, you held hands. You slept in the same bed until you were in high school. You exchanged clothes while they were still warm. You read each other's emotions like you were turning pages in a children's book. A loved one murdered was a violation beyond death, beyond your capacity to grieve, horror on top of pain, the corruption like a bloody blindfold you could never take off. She'd decided not to kill them, but they would be punished. Neither man would ever move freely again.

Crowe pulled into the trailhead parking lot, behind the mom's car, so tight it couldn't back out. He touched his knife and gun to make sure they were there. He was giddy, nearly drooling with lust and greed. Warren was still babbling, soaked in sweat and he'd stuck out his jaw like that retard in *Sling Blade,* the sight of him so fucked up Crowe couldn't look at him.

There was a wooden sign at the beginning of the trail. Crowe held his phone up to give him light. It was a map. Trails leading to the peak, the waterfall, the canyon, the viewing sites. "Will you look at that? There's a fucking map!" He laughed. The campsite, called the Witches' Tree, was .8 miles away. That was nothing. The two men hurried to the beginning of the trail. They saw flashlight beams wavering in the dark.

"Do you see them, Crowe?" Warren said. "Do you see them?" Crowe began fast walking, Warren went ahead of him, galloping like a kid riding an imaginary horse. "Come on, Crowe. Let's go faster!"

Isaiah and Ava arrived at the trailhead. Gretta's Subaru was hemmed in by another car. "They're here," Ava said. It was almost dark and getting cold. They got out of the Spark. Ava raced around to the trunk and found the Sig.

"Have you ever shot that before?" Isaiah said, worriedly.

"No, but I know how to point it and pull the trigger." She slid the ejector up and back, sliding a round in the chamber. She put a spare magazine in her back pocket.

"Maybe I should carry it."

"I don't think so." She stuck the gun into her pants and a bottle of water into the carrier on her belt.

"I can't go very fast," Isaiah said. He was sore and limping from his tumble with the Electra Glide.

"I know," Ava replied. She found a small flashlight and said, "That's why I'm leaving you here."

"What? No!"

Ava backed away. "Thanks for everything, Isaiah, but I have to do this." She ran off. Isaiah watched her flashlight beam disappear into the dark. He was deeply afraid.

Crowe and Warren weren't smart in the conventional sense, but they were cunning and ruthless. The gun would be heavy in Ava's hand. It was hard to aim under the best of circumstances, but harder still if you're cold and trembling and full of hate. She wouldn't be expecting the kick. She might drop the gun or shoot Irene or Gretta. Whatever happened, Isaiah thought, it would be terrible. He searched around in the car for another bottle of water but there was none. He found a three-inch folding knife in the side bin and stuck it in his pocket. Then he dry swallowed his last three Tylenol, laced his shoes up tighter and started walking.

The campfire created an amber dome, textured darkness all around.

"I'm sorry I made us late," Irene said. "Not very smart."

"It's okay. Everything turned out fine," Gretta said. The tent was the pop-up type and easy to set up. They'd built a nice fire. They heated cans of soup in the embers and ate fresh bread from Eve's Bakery and watched the orange sparks jump and vanish into the night and smelled charcoal mixed with the great outdoors. They looked at each other through the flames, the heat wiggling the air.

"Isn't this the best?" Irene said.

"Yes," Gretta replied. "It sure is."

Warren and Crowe couldn't see the bitches anymore. For a while, they thought they heard laughing but not anymore. The trail was steep, their legs like cement pillars, their breathing scorching their throats. It was a stupid thing to do, Crowe thought. Two ex-cons whose workouts consisted of rolling joints and sharpening knives shouldn't be climbing a goddamn mountain in the middle of the fucking night. *The altitude.* Crowe hadn't thought of that, and he hadn't thought to bring flashlights, water or jackets. Warren was in complete agony, whimpering and wheezing and moaning.

"My heart's going too fast, Crowe! I think it's going to blow up."

The dark had no depth and no end. They were thirsty and hungry. They were in their shirtsleeves and it was getting cold, a breeze stirring up dust that stung their eyes and crusted their lungs. Crowe couldn't tell how long they'd been hiking. Maybe they were close to the campground, or maybe they were forty yards from the parking lot. The darkness made the whole thing seem futile and idiotic, like they were on a treadmill in a coal mine or on a conveyer belt that emptied into a garbage dump.

Crowe had discovered the human body doesn't give a shit about your agenda. The need for food, water and rest were its main concerns. Lust was somewhere between watching sports and washing your hair. Warren stopped and sat down on the ground.

"I'm dying, Crowe," he sobbed. "I'm not kidding. I'm dying. We have to go back! Please, can we go back?"

"We can't," Crowe said. "The parking lot might be farther away than the campground, and those cunts have food and water." It was too dark to see Warren, but Crowe could feel him there, like a dead horse in a room with the lights off.

"I can't do it, Crowe, I can't," Warren said in snotty heaves. His voice trailed off. "I'm gonna die, I'm gonna fucking die."

Crowe wanted to sit down too, but that would be the end. The forest rangers would find them, two fossilized assholes lying on the trail hugging each other. The same rats and coyotes that ate Shareen would eat them too. Warren began hitting a rock with his hatchet. Somehow that seemed like the right thing to do. Suddenly, Crowe lifted his face into the breeze and went still. Ten seconds, twenty seconds.

Warren said, "Crowe? You're not dead, are you?"

"I smell smoke. A campfire."

"I don't care. I want to go back."

"You won't say that when we get there," Crowe said. "Can't you see them? Their skin, their hair. I bet they smell good." Warren stopped hitting the rock. Crowe went on. "I want to cut the girl's clothes off. It freaks them out, you know? When the buttons fall off? Who do you think screams the loudest? The mom or the daughter?" There was no response. Crowe could feel Warren's liquid brain percolating on high heat.

Warren said, "The mom."

CHAPTER THIRTY-ONE: GO FASTER, ISAIAH

Ava jogged every morning, lifted weights, swam laps at the Y and took power yoga. Twice a week, she climbed up and down the 147 steps on Lindy Avenue with the fitness nuts and the off-duty firefighters. She'd always felt an obligation to be in shape and so had Hannah. For health, yes, but that wasn't the main thing. They each had the vague sense that one day they would need their physicality to protect each other. Ava was disappointed she'd tired so fast. She was breathing heavily, she was cold, her thighs were burning, and the gun was like carrying an anvil. Her adrenaline had surpassed her rational mind. A steady gait would have been faster, but she had no intention of stopping. *Keep going. For Hannah.*

Cannon made a hard turn into the parking area, throwing up gravel on the wooden

511

sign. Three cars were there. The Subaru belonged to Gretta. A car he hadn't seen before was parked so close they were touching bumpers. The third car was the Spark. What was Gretta doing here? Probably camping. There was nothing else to do. The second car worried him. Someone had deliberately parked it so Gretta couldn't get out. Why would someone want to trap her here? Cannon wondered. "Oh, shit," he said. It was Isaiah's serial killers. It wasn't mistaken identity. IQ was right.

Maybe he'd be in time to rescue Gretta and Irene, but more likely not. Isaiah was banged up from the fall with the Harley. Cannon tried to radio Dickerson, but he was out of range and there were no signal repeaters out here. He unsnapped his holster. He put on his field jacket. He got the riot gun and a bottle of water out of the trunk. Then he turned on his flashlight and started running.

Isaiah had slowed from his already slow pace, his steps the same size as his feet. The cold air was dry. He'd read somewhere that putting a pebble on your tongue helped keep moisture in your mouth. A ridiculous idea. Now his mouth was dry and tasted like a pebble. He was walking with his hands folded over his chest and his head down. He couldn't make out his shoes. *This is what you do, Isaiah. This is who you are, and you will never see Grace again.*

The trail was like a ledge winding around the mountain. Isaiah saw someone behind him with a powerful flashlight moving fast. It had to be Cannon. If he arrests you now, Gretta and Irene will be murdered. You can't outrun him, and you can't take him on. *Figure this out, Isaiah. Hurry!*

He felt naked and vulnerable standing behind a tree. It was an absurd way to hide, but there wasn't much room on either side of the trail. He heard Cannon's footsteps, so steady it was like he was marching. He peeked. Cannon was an intimidating man under normal circumstances, but more so in the dark with his uniform, badge, riot gun, the flashlight up-lighting his square, grim face. Frankenstein in a khaki uniform. He was very near, his pace never faltering. Isaiah tensed, readying himself to move, his pains more intense as he stood there getting colder and stiffer. He could smell Cannon's deodorant. Cannon was fifteen feet away, ten, five, he was parallel . . . and Isaiah let him pass.

He waited until Cannon was well up the

trail before he came out of hiding. There was a moment's relief. Cannon was going to catch Ava before he did and get to Irene and Gretta much sooner. Cannon had a riot gun. For who? Isaiah wondered. Carry that thing all the way for you? Couldn't be. Was Cannon finally a believer? Isaiah searched around in the dark and found a stout branch. He used it as a hiking stick and walked on.

Ava had stopped to rest. She looked back and saw a flashlight, a bright one, and whoever it belonged to was keeping up an incredible pace. Couldn't be Isaiah. It was Cannon, she thought. He doesn't believe in the serial killers. If he arrests you, Irene and Gretta are finished. *Go, Ava. Go fast! You'll never have a chance at Crowe again.*

The campsite was set on an extended ledge that jutted out over the canyon. A rock wall on one side, a sheer cliff on the other. The Witches' Tree was at the end, opposite the trail; tall and leafless, its twisted branches reaching into the sky.

Just as Crowe had predicted, mother and daughter were sitting around a campfire, talking and laughing and drinking something hot out of tin mugs, their tent and camping gear scattered around. They had no idea monsters were watching them, monsters that would eat them like s'mores, hot and sticky and sweet. Crowe and Warren had been hiding outside the perimeter of the light for a good fifteen minutes, resting and waiting for their breathing to slow. They'd taken more Adderall, their pain and discomfort overwhelmed by their driving needs and surging adrenaline.

"We don't want them to see us until the last second," Crowe whispered. "We'll have to move fast."

Warren was nodding, staring at the bitches, grinning and jumpy. "Yeah, yeah, right." The bumps on his head were like budding antlers, his nose like a walrus's snout. His injuries took up his whole face. He made slushing sounds, breathing through the gap where his front tooth used to be.

"They'll take off, but I'll fire in the air and they'll stop," Crowe said.

"Yeah, women are pussies," Warren said, chuckling at his own joke.

"You ready?"

"I'm ready as hell."

Irene was about to pour water on the fire and stopped. Two men burst out of the

515

darkness, greased with sweat, screaming, with their mouths wide open, their faces horribly injured. They looked like cannibals, high on something that makes you dance and fuck all night. The big one had a huge knife; the smaller had an axe. They were running hard, but not very fast. Irene's first thought was confusion. She couldn't connect the two men with anything. *Wait a second, are these Billy's serial killers?* "Mom?" she said.

Gretta was on her feet, staring. "That's Warren Long."

Irene grabbed her hand. "Run!" There was only one way to go. Across the campsite, past the Witches' Tree and into the darkness. Two shots, BLAM! BLAM! The flashes lighting the night and echoing down the canyon, bullets ricocheting off the rocks.

They kept running, frenzied shouting behind them. They reached a steep slope. It was pitch-dark, but Irene knew what was down there. Riprap and boulders, some round and smooth, others like prehistoric cutting tools. There were a thousand crevices to get stuck in, fall and smash a kneecap. Irene looked back. The killers were very close. BLAM! BLAM! Bullets punched holes in the air.

"Come on, Mom!"

They started to descend. You wouldn't do this in the daytime, Irene thought. She climbed down slowly, between, around and over the riprap, using her hands, sticking her boot out to touch the next foothold. "Careful, Mom! Keep going!" They had no advantage here. The killers would be directly above them, and there was no cover until they reached the bottom where the forest began.

Irene heard the killers coming. Any second, she expected bright beams and more gunshots, but there were none. Had the killers gassed out? "We're almost there, Mom!" She reached the bottom and stumbled into the safety of the trees. "We made it!" She turned around. No one was there. She looked up. Gretta was at the top of the slope, held in a flashlight beam and shading her eyes. She'd waited for the killers so her daughter could get away.

"Mom, no!" Irene screamed. "Come down, please come down!"

"Go, Irene," Gretta said. Her normal voice seemed louder than shouting. "Go, my darling. If you love me, please go." The beams were getting brighter. Irene could hear the killers laughing. "Mom, please come down!"

"You would do the same for me," Gretta insisted. "Go now, sweetheart." She looked down the incline. She couldn't see her daughter and yet their eyes met. She smiled lovingly. "I'll see you on the other side." She stood straight, raised her chin and looked squarely into the beams. They might take her life but never her dignity. It broke Irene's heart. The smaller man went face-to-face with Gretta, snarling like a rabid dog and waving that fucking axe.

"I got you! I fucking got you!" he screamed.

The big man was pissed. "Goddammit, where's the girl? I don't want this old bag! Where is she?" He cupped his hands over his mouth and screamed, "WHERE ARE YOU YOU GODDAMN CUNT?" He fired blindly. BLAM! BLAM! BLAM!

"GO NOW, IRENE!" Gretta screamed. "GET OUT OF HERE! GO!"

"I'm okay, Mom, I'm safe!" Irene yelled, but they'd taken her away. "YOU COW-ARDS! I'LL KILL YOU. I'LL FUCKING KILL YOU!"

She turned and walked farther into the trees, sobbing and enraged. She didn't feel like herself anymore, like a junior in high school who played softball, had lots of friends and got good grades. She felt feral and vicious, with only an instinctive need to

rip flesh, taste blood and watch those motherfuckers die.

Big Man yanked Gretta along by her arm.
Something in her knee had popped; the pain
was excruciating. She could see the fire. She
knew once they got there, it was the end.
She started to scream but held it back. She
wouldn't let Irene listen to her mother die.
She couldn't believe it. Billy's serial killers
were real. The big man must be — what was
his name? Crowe. That's right, Crowe. As
they reached the campsite, she thought he
was going to throw her into the fire. Instead,
he shoved her to the ground. "Try something, okay? I want you to." He turned to
Warren. "Go get some more firewood."

"Why do I have to do it?" Warren whined.

"Just do it, Warren, for fuck's sake! It's
getting dark."

Warren left, muttering. The wind came
up, Gretta's fear growing with the fluttering
flames. Crowe was behind her. She could
see his gargantuan shadow. He bound her
hands with a strap from a backpack. She
could hear his breathing, feel his need to
violate and plunder. He started to hum,
walking around her, occasionally touching
her with the knife.

"Warren will be back in a minute," he

said, grinning. "And then we'll begin." This was actually the end, Gretta thought. She didn't fear death. She feared dying. She held back another scream.

Warren returned and threw wood on the fire. "There, okay? Satisfied?"

The flames billowed, glowing brighter, crackling louder, sending swarms of sparks hopping into the air. Warren began dancing around, hooting and laughing and jabbering, the poster boy for lunacy. Gretta closed her eyes and thought of Irene. How she was getting away. How she'd never see her again.

The fire's radiance writhed and flickered on Crowe's face, one eye dull, the other like a bomb crater, the knife gleaming in his hand. He didn't look like Satan, he *was* Satan, and she was on his cutting board, about to be carved into slices like a country ham. He stood over her, his looming figure blotting out the heavens. He laughed and started to kneel. In the same instant, Warren was beside her on his knees, cackling and raising his axe. Crowe caught his wrist and twisted the axe away from him.

"I go first. I always go first," Crowe said.

Warren got to his feet and reached for the hatchet. "Gimme, it's mine!" he shouted. Crowe was a head taller than Warren. He held the weapon up high, Warren on his tiptoes like a bully was holding his glasses out of reach. "Gimme it, Crowe! Gimme it!" He screamed in Crowe's face, "GIMME IT, YOU FUCKER!" Warren stopped. The Bowie knife was under his chin.

"I always go first," Crowe said. He took Warren's axe and hurled it into the darkness.

"Fuck you, Crowe! Fuck you!" Warren yelled. Then he picked up a flashlight and stormed off after it.

Gretta was alone with Crowe and somehow that seemed worse than the two of them, like the torture would be more personal, more intimate. He kneeled beside her and grabbed a bunch of her hair. He twisted it until she yelled and cut it off, tossing it into the fire, each hair a sizzling fuse before it disappeared.

"Are you ready?" he said. "I think you're gonna like this." He looked off into the dark. "We'll wait for that stupid prick. If we don't, he'll be a bigger pain in the ass than he is already. He put the point of the knife against her shirt and cut off a button. "It won't be long," he said. He smiled. His teeth were yellow. "It won't be long at all."

He wants to completely dominate your body and your mind, Gretta thought. Nothing you can do about your body but you're not going to give him your mind. Your very self. *Defy this motherfucker with your last breath.* She smirked at him, her eyes amused and contemptuous.

"If I could spit on you, I'd do it now." Crowe reared back in surprise. She screamed the only thing she knew would hurt him. "IRENE GOT AWAY! THE ONE YOU REALLY WANTED GOT AWAY! YOU'LL NEVER GET HER! YOU'LL NEVER GET MY DAUGHTER!" Crowe roared like no beast that ever roamed the earth and raised the knife with two hands. As he started to bring it down, a rock came whistling out of the darkness at a speed only the All State catcher from Palomino High who threw out more base stealers than J. T. Realmuto, who led the major leagues, could throw. She missed the strike zone but hit Crowe in the elbow, apparently his crazy bone. He shrieked like he'd been shocked with a cattle prod. He got to his feet, holding his elbow, turning around and around, kicking up dust, grunting and moaning with pain. Furious, he went for his gun, but a high and outside slider clipped his ear, and he bawled even louder, clamping his hand to the side of his head while it bled like a bloody nose.

"HIT 'IM, IRENE!" Gretta screamed.

"KILL HIM! KILL HIM!"

Irene came out of the dark with a rock as big as a grapefruit. She rushed over to Crowe, holding the rock overhead, about to finish him off. Warren barreled into her so hard she was lifted off her feet and slammed into the ground. Warren couldn't stop his momentum. He tripped over her and stumbled forward, windmilling his arms, sliding face-first into the campfire like cleats into second base. A volcano of sparks erupted around his head. Warren scrambled to his feet, screaming, face blackened, embers burning his clothes. He slapped at them wildly, ripping off his T-shirt and yanking down his pants. He lunged for a bottle of water, tripped over his cuffs and fell over a campstool. He lay there in the dirt, sobbing into his arm.

Gretta was stupefied. It was like a slapstick movie shot in a burning insane asylum. Irene was lying still. "Oh, no," Gretta said. She called out to her. "Are you all right? Irene. Are you all right?"

Crowe was bent at the waist and muttering, "Jesus Christ, Jesus fucking Christ." His ear was torn, blood all over him, one arm dangling like a hung prisoner. Warren got up, his face a gooey mixture of snot, tears and soot. There were charred holes in his clothes, an eyebrow had burned off, skin peeling off the walrus snout, his forelocks brown and frizzy. The killers looked like dazed idiots who'd been tortured by a tribe of sadistic primitives. They could hardly stand, exhausted and bewildered. They looked at each other in disbelief as if to say, how could this be happening? We only wanted to murder people. Crowe straightened up, his hands on his hips. He was panting, saying, "I think we're okay, I think we're okay."

"Are you sure?" Warren gasped.

"Yeah, yeah, I'm sure, everything's okay."

"Stay right there or you're fucking dead!" a voice shouted. It was Ava. She was holding a gun with two hands. Crowe and Warren froze. She stepped closer; her hands were shaking. Warren held up his palms.

"You already fucked me up once. Wasn't that enough?"

"Not even close. Lie down on the fucking ground." Warren bent his knees, but didn't lie down. "Did you hear me, you fucking asshole?" she shouted.

"Don't kill me, please," Warren said. "I did wrong, I know that, but I won't do it no more." He's stalling, Crowe thought, waiting for her to make a mistake. Smart boy. Crowe took a sideways step away from him.

"Stay there!" Ava said. The gun was heavy; she struggled to keep it aimed. Instinctively, Warren took a step sideways, widening the gap between himself and Crowe. Ava moved the barrel back and forth between them. She didn't know what to do with two targets. She was crying, her face pleading, begging them to go along. "Get down on the fucking ground!" she screamed. She lifted her aim and fired two shots into the trees. BLAM! BLAM! The gun bucked and jerked her hands over her head. Crowe took off left and Warren went right. The girl brought the gun down, swiveling clumsily toward Warren, and fired. BLAM! BLAM! BLAM! But he was already gone. She swiveled the other way and fired at Crowe. BLAM! BLAM! BLAM! But he was out of sight, behind a tree.

The girl screamed in frustration and fired two more in Crowe's direction. BLAM! BLAM! *Click.* She was out of ammo. She pulled a spare magazine from her back pocket. She tried to insert it, but she hadn't released the one that was already there.

Crowe came out of hiding, smiling, walking toward her, not hurrying, rubbing his fist like he was polishing his knuckles. Ava was breathing through her teeth, fumbling with the spare, eyes darting at him, frantic now. He reached out to grab her. She tried to hit him with the gun. He caught it, twisted it out of her hands and tossed it away. He collared her with one hand and hit her with the other. She was knocked backward and fell to the ground. She lay there bleeding and unconscious. Crowe stared, seemingly incredulous. How did this puny little bitch make it all the way here? A bewildered, tearful Warren staggered back into the campsite.

"Them shots went right past my head!" he yodeled.

Gretta was lying on the ground, her hands bound behind her. Irene was lying still. She hadn't moved since Warren barreled into her. "Irene?" Gretta said. "Irene, sweetheart, are you all right?" She tried to stand up, but the pain in her knee was crippling. She lay on her side and inchwormed her way toward her. She struggled for breath, her throat clogged with dust. She glanced at the killers.

Warren was seemingly in despair. He was sobbing, beseeching. "What's going on, Crowe? I don't know what's going on!" Equally confounded, Crowe cupped his hands over his mouth and shouted into the night:

"ANYBODY ELSE GONNA FUCK WITH US? BOY SCOUTS, LITTLE OL' LADIES, THE GODDAMN MARINES?"

Gretta reached Irene and glanced back. Crowe had stopped shouting. He was looking at her, Warren too. *They remembered why they were here.* Warren picked up his axe. Crowe drew his knife. They lumbered toward her, a cyclops and an incinerated scarecrow, grinning, going faster. Gretta tried to cover Irene with her body.

"NO! NO! STAY AWAY!" she screamed. "TAKE ME! TAKE ME! I'LL DO WHATEVER YOU WANT!" She lay back and kicked at them. "GO AWAY! LEAVE US ALONE!"

"Kick all you want, bitch, but you're done." Warren laughed. He tipped his head back and howled at the moon.

"Over there," Crowe said, suddenly grim. A flashlight beam was on the trail, bobbing up and down in the darkness, really bright and coming fast. "Whoever that is, he's really humping it."

"Something else? It can't be," Warren moaned.

"Shut up. We've got to get ready." Crowe looked at Ava sprawled on the ground. "She's out of it. Put the other two in the tent."

527

Cannon heard gunshots and someone yelling. He saw the light of the campfire. He picked up the pace. He was heaving and sweaty as he reached the edge of the light. The fire was low, ghostly shadows on the rock wall. Cannon smelled charred wood, gun smoke and pine. Ava was nearest him. She was on the ground, semiconscious and moaning. Beyond her, close to the fire, a man was lying on his side, curled slightly, his back to Cannon. He was motionless but alive. There wasn't the melted stillness of death. It wasn't Isaiah. The area was surrounded by darkness. There was no way to secure the scene.

"Mr. Crowe? Mr. Long?" Cannon said in his cop's voice. "This is Sheriff Cannon of the Coronado Springs Police Department. There's only one way out of here and my officers will be arriving any minute now. If you shoot me, they will beat you into shit puddles and bum hole you with their flashlights just before they pour gasoline over your heads and set you on fire. Just sayin'."

Ava was hurt, no way to tell how badly. He put the shotgun down and drew his pistol. He hunched low and ran into the clearing. He grabbed Ava by her arm and dragged her back to safety. An ugly, swollen bruise on her face but no gunshot wounds. He checked her breathing. She was okay, but that didn't mean she was okay. She opened her eyes, and they flashed with alarm.

"It's Sheriff Cannon. Stay still and be quiet." A strangled voice came from the tent.

"Sheriff, it's Gretta Abbett. I'm hurt, my daughter is bleeding. Please help!"

The tent was on the other side of the campfire, a long way to be out in the open. The flap was down. Maybe it was a setup, Cannon thought, but he'd be hard to hit. The campfire was almost out, and he was wearing a Kevlar vest. Hitting a fast-moving target in low light was hard to do for anyone but a trained marksman. Cannon holstered his sidearm and picked up the riot gun. If he fired into the dark, he wanted to hit something. The man lying on his side worried him. He might be a decoy. The shotgun would favor him.

Cannon breathed in deeply, got low and took off, scuffling around the campfire as fast as he could go. He reached the tent and hunched down. "I'm here. Everything's going to be okay."

Gretta shouted: "Watch out!" BLAM!

BLAM! BLAM! Bullets came through the tent flap, aimed low, below the vest, one of them catching Cannon in the thigh. It was a mule kick. He dropped the shotgun and collapsed. He reached for his sidearm, but it was underneath him, the pain overwhelming. *You're fucked, Cannon. And so is everybody else.*

Crowe crawled out of the tent, a gun in his hand. He'd put the barrel to Irene's head and told Gretta to yell for help. She'd pay for that last part. Warren got up from the ground. Pointlessly, he brushed himself off. He'd complained about being the decoy, but Crowe threatened to shoot him. Warren tossed Cannon's shotgun aside but kept his pistol. The sheriff was on the ground, holding his bleeding leg.

Warren kicked him. "Remember me, you pig? Yeah, not so badass now, are you, motherfucker!"

Isaiah was in darkness at the perimeter of the campsite. He knelt next to Ava. She wanted to sit up, but he held her down. "No. Not until we know you're okay."

"Sorry about leaving you."

"Doesn't matter. You have water, don't you?" She turned slightly, and he slid the water bottle out of the carrier. He opened it. She drank and he did too.

Cannon was on the ground, curled into a ball, losing blood, helpless. Warren was pacing back and forth, taunting him, waving the axe and kicking him. Crowe was yanking Irene out of the tent, Gretta screaming at him. All Isaiah had was the folding knife he'd taken from the car. The killers had guns. One of them would have to be taken down and disarmed. There was only open ground between Isaiah and the killers. Rushing them was suicide.

Isaiah was on one end of the campsite, hidden in the trees. At the other end was the Witches' Tree, the tent and campfire in the middle. To Isaiah's left, a sheer rock wall. To the right a cliff. Step over the edge and you'd fall into a canyon so deep you couldn't see the end of it. He thought a moment and didn't like his prospects. He had to get over the edge, find footholds, his hands on level ground. Then he'd have to sidle along until he got even with the tent. He'd be behind it and out of view. Until he got there, his head would be in the open. The killers were yelling louder, the intensity and volume rising, Gretta pleading for her daughter's life.

Isaiah stayed in the trees and moved right,

to the cliff. He swung one leg over and got a tenuous foothold. He swung the other leg over and found another foothold, keeping both hands on the ledge. Only his toes, fingers and the balls of his feet were keeping him upright. He didn't have to look to know what was waiting for him. A long fall and certain death. He started moving, carefully extending his lead foot, finding an extruding rock, a divot or a ledge of dirt, testing it before putting his full weight on it, bringing the other foot to the same spot, keeping his hands in synch.

He sidled along slowly, too slowly. Crowe and Warren were getting louder and wilder, ready to feast, but if he hurried, he might fall. *Go faster, Isaiah.* The wind picked up, the canyon a wind tunnel, the force of it nearly blowing him off balance, grit flying in his face. He stopped to rest, both feet inserted into a narrow crevice — *it gave way*! He nearly cried out. Lunging forward, he got his elbows over the cliff edge, legs bicycling, trying to find traction, dirt and gravel falling into the canyon. He was holding himself up with his forearms, trying to dig into the rocky cliffside with his toes, his lungs burning black. For a moment, he knew he was going to fall. He almost gave up, but the impulse terrified him. With a final burst of energy, he threw a leg up and over onto flat ground. He wrestled his body after it and lay there, breathing in gasps. Amazing what you can do when you think you're going to die.

He was just inside the circle of light, clearly visible; all the killers had to do was turn and look. Irene and Gretta had been dragged near the fire. They were sitting next to each other, their arms folded in on themselves, heads bowed like they were waiting for the firing squad. Cannon was curled up, holding his leg with both hands and trying to stanch the bleeding. His pant leg was soaked, blood all over the ground. Warren was standing over him, muttering and drooling, an axe in his hand. Crowe was waving the Bowie knife around, circling the women, jeering and laughing at them. He stopped. "The fucking fire is almost out again!" he bellowed. "Get some more fire-wood, Warren."

"You go get it," Warren said, belligerent. "I did it the last time."

"Warren, I said go get some more wood."

"No, goddammit. I did it the last time." Crowe moved in close. Warren stood his ground, the two psychotics a foot apart.

"Look, you fucking imbecile. I'm not telling you again," Crowe said. "Go get goddamn firewood!"

"Tell me all you want, but it's your fucking turn!" Warren's grip tightened on the axe.

"War-renn . . ."

"Fuck you, Crowe. It's your goddamn turn. Let it get dark for all I care." Crowe jammed a gun under Warren's chin and fired. BLAM!! Warren's head snapped back and he collapsed like he'd bled out all at once. Isaiah was shocked a moment, got his senses back and crawled for the tent.

Crowe stood over Warren's body. "I told you, didn't I?" he screamed. "You stupid shit! Didn't I fucking tell you?" He kicked Warren viciously, again and again. There was no remorse, only rage. He stopped, exhausted, reeling, wheezing and gulping air. He found a flashlight and hunted around for more firewood.

Isaiah continued crawling until he reached the back of the tent. He cut open the fabric with the folding knife. He slipped inside. He heard Crowe dumping wood on the fire, the flames rising, crackling and spitting, Crowe's silhouette enormous against the tent flap. His back was turned. Isaiah hunched down, got his weight beneath him, holding the knife low. He took a deep breath and launched himself through the flap.

He hit Crowe like a linebacker, swinging the knife up to gut him. Crowe was propelled forward, but Isaiah's timing was off. The knife hit nothing. He lost his balance and nearly fell, extending his knife hand to catch himself. He dropped the knife, his palm landing in the embers. He cried out and snatched his hand back. He stepped away a few paces, holding his wrist, his palm burned to shit.

Crowe had dropped the gun but kept his balance. They were on opposite sides of the fire, looking at each other through the blaze, the air shimmering with heat, sparks teeming like fireflies, the flames reflected in their sweat, flickering gold, shadow and amber. Crowe stood tall and drew the Bowie knife. Isaiah readied himself. He looked for a weapon, but there was none. Crowe charged through the fire. He was massive, his eyes like the flames themselves, clouds of sparks fleeing his clomping footsteps. Isaiah sidestepped him but barely. Crowe whirled around to face him. Isaiah was too worn-out to run.

Crowe grinned. "I'm going to cut you off at the knees, boy." He came forward, Isaiah backing away, passing the tent, the cliff behind him. He started to go right, but Crowe mirrored him. He feinted left and went right again, but Crowe stayed with him. Isaiah was too slow to get around him. His hand hurt bad. The cliff was getting closer. It was like the gulley all over again. The wind picked up, the trees hissing their terror. Isaiah kept retreating. All he could do was attack. He'd get slashed but maybe not killed. Maybe go in high, try and duck under the blade and hit him in the knees. Crowe was holding the knife in front of him, waist high, waving it back and forth. It didn't matter if Isaiah went in high or low or backward. He'd be stabbed, gutted and thrown on the fire.

"Didn't I tell you this would happen?" Crowe said, coming closer. "What goes around comes around." He had to talk loud over the wind. "I'm either gonna kill you or you're gonna jump. Jumping is probably better, but you might not die right away. You'd be lying there watching the critters eat your guts." He twirled the knife in his hand. "Death would be a fucking holiday." He's right, Isaiah thought. *Don't let him get you.* Crowe stopped. Isaiah stopped. In his periphery, he could see he was on the very edge of the cliff. He could feel the emptiness behind him.

"Well?" Crowe said, grinning. "What's it gonna be?"

Isaiah turned his back to Crowe. He looked down into the abyss, the wind roaring, leaves and pine needles pelting his face. *Jump, Isaiah. You'll never see Grace again.* He closed his eyes, bent his knees, his legs tensed — BOOM! BOOM! The concussion nearly knocked him over. He spun around. Ava was there, her swollen face contorted beyond torment, beyond horror. She was holding Cannon's riot gun, wisps of smoke from the barrel whipped away by the wind. Crowe had been thrown forward, his head at Isaiah's feet. There was only the faint light from the campfire. Isaiah squinted down at him. Crowe looked strangely intact.

"Look what you did to me, look what you did," the killer groaned. He tried to move but was rigid from the waist down. Isaiah looked closer. Crowe's pants were in shreds, his legs a bloody mess. Ava had kneecapped him. She dropped the gun and it clattered to the ground.

"That's for Hannah," she said. Isaiah put his arm around her and led her away. When they were near the fire, she fell to her knees. She put her face in her hands and wept, saying over and over again, "I want my sister. I want Hannah."

The police and paramedics arrived. There

was nowhere to land a helicopter. Isaiah, Ava, Irene, Gretta, Cannon and Crowe were rushed down the mountain on stretchers. Warren followed in a body bag.

Billy had suffered a concussion and his shoulder was dislocated. He lay in the hospital bed, groggy from the painkillers, a swath of gauze covering his head and supporting his chin, his arm in a sling. He'd seen Gretta briefly. She was on a gurney, and they touched hands for a moment.

"Things will be better," his mom said, and she shut her eyes.

He felt terrible. He'd tried to save the day and screwed everything up. It was all his fault. He wondered if it had been worth it. Two serial killers were out of commission. That was something, wasn't it? But the price. Mom, Irene, Ava, Cannon and Isaiah were all badly injured. How Isaiah had managed to do what he'd done was a miracle. If there was ever somebody who never had to apologize for who he was, it was Isaiah, hands down. Ava had been right. He always thought about himself first, but now he had a reason not to. He had to help heal his family.

Ava came in. She was wearing a bathrobe that was too big for her. The side of her face was badly swollen. Her eyes seemed recessed, in shadow. She looked beautiful. She sat down on the bed and put her hand on his.

"It was my fault, Billy. All of it. I got you into it." He started to speak, but she cut him off. "Don't be a martyr. If you're blaming yourself it's because you want to." He said nothing. "I'm leaving tomorrow, I've got to get home. They're sneaking me out early. There's press all over the place. They think you're a hero, Billy." She leaned over and kissed his cheek. "And so do I." She walked to the door, turned, and looked at him in a way he'd never forget. "I'll call you," she said. And she was gone.

Billy didn't move for a long time. Ava wasn't a daydream anymore or a damsel in distress and not the key to his happiness. She was an ordinary person in great pain and sorrow. Maybe she would call him, maybe not. He'd accept it either way. He wasn't a hero, no matter what anybody said. But he'd been courageous. He'd faced danger and hadn't backed down. He thought a moment and smiled. What the hell, Billy boy. Maybe you're a hero after all.

Isaiah awoke. His hand was bandaged, the

pain was dulled by the meds. His belongings were in a white plastic bag hung on a chair. He remembered the Ortegas visiting him. Mrs. Ortega brought him food. Mr. Ortega brought him a TracFone. He called Deronda and left a message. Please ask Grace to call him.

The doctor came in. She said the others were here in the hospital and resting. They were all badly injured but none of them critically so. Everyone would recover eventually. The doctor said she was keeping him for forty-eight hours. He had an IV for hydration, pain meds as needed and antibiotics for possible infections. Mostly, he had to rest. The doctor left. Isaiah wanted to get out of there as soon as possible. He didn't want to see the others. He didn't want their gratitude and well-wishes. They would never be friends or even stay in touch. The only thing they had in common was blood and death.

Despite what the doctor said, Isaiah knew none of them would really recover. They'd forever be haunted by nightmares, flashbacks and an ever-present sense of danger. Ava would see the riot gun blowing Crowe's legs to pieces and wake up screaming. The consequences of violence were crippling even when you're righteous. And they lasted until your heart stopped beating and the pain left you forever.

There would be no more sheriffs hunting for you or knife fights with serial killers or suffocating with dirt on your face or escaping from a motorcycle gang or hanging on to cliffs by your fingernails. He'd rather have PTSD. He'd rather be sick and depressed than wallow in shit with the infectious offal of humanity, where no one should linger, let alone have a career. He wished he was someone else. He wished Marcus had never died, and he'd gone to college. He wished he'd become a scientist or a cook or a garbageman or anything but what he was. A man alone who sought justice for those who couldn't seek it for themselves, who was driven to follow the dark path wherever it led, however deep and horrific.

Something dawned on him. The PTSD symptoms had vanished. The fear, the physical pain, the intense concentration and the constant machinations of his mind had overcome them. Work had overcome them. Was that his choice? he wondered. Work or be sick? Work or be nothing? Be sick, he thought. Be nothing. Step out of the cesspool and don't look back. Sit on the banks of Rush Creek and watch the sunlight shimmering off the reeded pools and birds darting through the trees. Sit there forever and not see another soul. Who cared about anything if Grace was gone? She wouldn't call back. He'd lost her forever. He dozed. The phone buzzed. He was instantly awake.

"Grace?"

"It's me," Deronda said. "Are you okay?"

"Yeah. I'm fine." There was a pause. She wanted to say something but didn't know how.

"What?"

"Grace has gone missing."

"Missing? What do you mean?"

"I mean she's missing and nobody knows where she's at," Deronda said. "Last time I talked to her was a few days ago. I called and texted her a bunch of times, but she don't answer. I was hoping she was with you."

The room was suddenly cold. "No, she's not," Isaiah said. He got out of bed. "Did you call the police?"

"They said to wait seventy-two hours and it's seventy-two hours now. I'll call them again, but —"

Isaiah interrupted. "Did Grace leave things behind? Car keys, phone, that kind of thing?"

"No, they was gone, her car too. The police said she might have gone on a long weekend somewhere, but she always told me before." Isaiah was putting on his clothes. The nurse came in.

"Sir? You're not supposed to leave yet."

"Go away," he said sharply, and she did. "Keep calling her, Deronda, and keep asking around. Do you know Carter Samuels?"

"The cop? Yeah, I know him."

"Tell him what you told me and call Dodson too."

"Dodson's already on it. So is Cherise, Gloria, TK, Mo and the winos, Michael Stokeley and his crew. Your ex-clients too. Everybody in the damn hood is looking for her."

Isaiah pulled on his shoes. "I'm on my way."

"One more thing?" Deronda said. "I found something. I didn't think nothin' of it, but I showed it to Dodson and he flipped out. He tried to explain but it sounded crazy to me."

Isaiah stopped. "What? I don't understand."

"It could have been anybody's," she went on. "I didn't attach no importance to it. You seen one you seen 'em all."

"What are you talking about?"

"You can go to the store and pick out any one you want, got 'em in colors, rhinestones, you name it —"

"Deronda, *what are you talking about*?"

"A dog collar. I found it in the driveway."

ACKNOWLEDGMENTS

My thanks to Rick Smith and Peter Klein, whose knowledge of the ad world was indispensable, and to Ed Bartel, for his seminar on Harley Davidsons for Dummies. As always, my everlasting gratitude to the crew at Little, Brown and Mulholland, and to my agents, Esther Newberg and Zoe Sandler. Most of all to my wife, Diane, the sweetest person in the world.

ABOUT THE AUTHOR

Joe Ide is of Japanese American descent. He grew up in South Central Los Angeles, where his favorite books were the Arthur Conan Doyle Sherlock Holmes stories. The idea that a person could face the world and vanquish his enemies with just his intelligence fascinated him. Ide went on to earn a graduate degree and had several careers before writing his debut novel, *IQ,* inspired by his early experiences and his love of Sherlock Holmes. Ide lives in Santa Monica, California.

The employees of Thorndike Press hope you have enjoyed this Large Print book. All our Thorndike, Wheeler, and Kennebec Large Print titles are designed for easy reading, and all our books are made to last. Other Thorndike Press Large Print books are available at your library, through selected bookstores, or directly from us.

For information about titles, please call:
   (800) 223-1244

or visit our website at:
   gale.com/thorndike

To share your comments, please write:
Publisher
Thorndike Press
10 Water St., Suite 310
Waterville, ME 04901